THE
DRAGON
IN
THE
FOREST

THE
DRAGON
IN
THE
FOREST

BY RICHARD PLANT

DOUBLEDAY & COMPANY, INC.
GARDEN CITY, NEW YORK, 1948

With the exception of the historical persons and
the actual places playing a part in this novel,
all characters, places, and incidents are entirely
the product of the author's imagination and
bear no relation to any person, or event in real
life.

Printed in the United States at
The Country Life Press, Garden City, N. Y.

First Edition

TO W. D. B.

THE
DRAGON
IN
THE
FOREST

1. THE LINE IN FRONT OF H. KREMBSLER'S fish store grew longer and longer. Willy couldn't see its end: it disappeared in the cold morning fog that covered the desolate streets of Frankfurt-on-the-Main in this fall of 1917. The boy found himself squeezed between two fat women with stolid faces who obviously disliked having a seven-year-old boy waiting in the same line, conversed in loud voices over his head, and seemed to ignore him deliberately. The boy was weary. He had been up since six o'clock because everything depended on whethei one was able to grab a place at the beginning of the line. Mother had given him a cup of "Kornfrank Coffee, the Chickory Brew That's Good for You," which tasted like five-day-old mutton soup, and both of them had said very little. The kitchen had been warm, at least, and Willy hadn't wanted to leave the tiny peat fire in the small "Coal-Saver Stove" which stood on top of the big kitchen range. The Coal-Saver Stove had been put into the kitchen a year ago, in the winter of 1916. It was the invention of a Prussian professor and highly recommended as a patriotic thrift measure by the authorities of the former Free City of Frankfurt. The Coal-Saver Stove, also called "War Ersatz Stove," digested contentedly peat, wood, or bricks made of wet, compressed newspapers. Mrs. Halder always said she was only waiting for the day when she could throw it out for good. It would be like Christmas, she told Willy, to light the friendly big range which filled half of the kitchen and which Willy had christened "Big Anna" because it was as big and comforting as Anna, the cook and maid, who had been with Dr. and Mrs. Halder ever since he could remember. . . .

The woman behind Willy nudged him sharply, and the boy stumbled forward. He had almost forgotten where he was. A cold wind began to rise, gushing out from the narrow passageway of the Hoch Strasse, sweeping over the large Opern Platz, almost deserted at eight in the morning, and tumbling pieces of newspapers along the waiting line. The fog lifted slowly; across the street the houses displayed their tired morning faces. Willy became conscious of the insistent odor of fish that came from Krembsler's—a sharp

1

and foul smell that reminded him of the frogs he had seen last year by the lake near Cronberg, and of the garbage Anna threw out in the evening. The city was filled with the smell of dried Norwegian fish, and repeatedly Willy had been told to be grateful that it had arrived at all. For quite some time most of the people of Frankfurt had lived mainly on a diet of turnips.

Willy buttoned his old winter coat and tried to muster up some gratitude for the Norwegian fish. He couldn't. He couldn't feel anything; he was cold and he concentrated on closing his mind to the aggressive fish smell which grew stronger now that he moved farther up in the line.

"Two pounds of the dried stuff and one of fresh fish is all you can get, Mrs. Dengler," called the fat woman ahead of him to the fat woman behind him.

"Anyway, Mrs. Gruber, it's better than turnips," shrilled Mrs. Dengler in Willy's ears. "My husband says he can't stand it any longer. Turnip marmalade, turnip vegetable stew, turnip soup, turnip everything."

Mrs. Gruber laughed heartily, and some other people in the line, glad for the diversion, chimed in. Mrs. Dengler stepped aside as if she wanted to see how far the line had progressed, walked to Mrs. Gruber and whispered something in her ear. Before the boy realized it, she was in front of him, shoving him back without turning. Willy tried to block her, but Mrs. Dengler's broad rump had already settled solidly next to her friend. At this moment the line moved up again. Mrs. Dengler gave Willy a second push so that he fell back, stepping on the toes of the woman who had been behind her.

"I'm sorry," he stuttered. He felt angry and helpless. He knew he was small for a boy of seven, and now, as often before, he wished fervently he were as big as his uncle Julius and could beat her fat face with both his fists.

"Never mind," said the woman behind him; "never mind, my boy. There's always one who cheats. How old are you?"

"I'm seven and a half, but I'm not very tall," said Willy, who had heard too often that he was small for his age and wanted to say it first. He turned to the woman. She was tiny and seemed very old, with a face made all of wrinkles.

"Step along, my boy," said the old woman. "Thank God, they are getting ahead there a little faster."

Mrs. Dengler laughed again, and Willy began to think she was making fun of him. There was a new wave of the dried fish, and for a moment Willy felt weak in the knees. His stomach was empty, and the hunger, together with the smell from the store, made him a little dizzy. The old lady was talking to him again.

2

"Aren't you Dr. Halder's son?" she asked. "You don't have his blue eyes but otherwise you are his spittin' image. Don't you live on Reuter Weg?"

"Yes, I do," Willy said while the line gained some ground. The wind lashed his face, and little icy gushes crept up his sleeves and ran down his back and his legs. "My father is Dr. Halder," he said loudly in order to make conversation and to show Mrs. Dengler that he ignored her. "We live at sixty-six Reuter Weg. How did you know?"

For a moment the old lady stared into space. Behind her were two soldiers who looked at Willy and gave him big, unshaven grins. Finally the old lady's face broke into a thousand more wrinkles; she put a thin hand on his shoulder and said: "Tell your father you met Mrs. Winkler. Mrs. Ella Winkler. Yes, he'll remember. In 1903 he treated me for the first time, and then in 1914 he operated on me. Just before this dreadful war began . . ." Mrs. Winkler stopped as if she had said something wrong. She looked around, with little birdlike movements, but the two soldiers were talking to each other. Only Mrs. Dengler had turned, and Willy stared at her. Both she and Mrs. Gruber glared back. Suddenly the two soldiers stepped out of the line and called to him. The one with the shoulder insignia of a corporal said: "Halder you say, kid? Do you have a relative, a big fellow, name of Julius? He has your coal-black eyes."

Willy felt elated. Perhaps the two soldiers would help him to get his place back. Perhaps they would beat up Mrs. Dengler, and, if possible, he decided, Mrs. Gruber too.

"That must be Uncle Julius," he said. "He is ill at the Ginnheim hospital. He is very big."

The two soldiers were now standing next to Willy, outside of the line. Both shook his hand heartily, and the corporal said: "I'm Georg Elmer and this is Private Kasimir Korn. He comes from Bockenheim, I'm from Frankfurt myself, Rebstock Strasse. We are sure glad to meet you, Will. Julius is our best friend." They began to laugh, and rubbed their stubbly chins.

"Our wives ordered us to get fish at eight in the morning, so we stayed up all night. Now we have a hangover as big as the Opera House. Say, you look kind of green yourself. Are you all right?"

Willy nodded. He noticed that there were some murmurs of protest from several people in the line because it looked as if the soldiers were trying to repeat Mrs. Dengler's maneuver.

"All right, all right," Georg said in a loud voice. "We just want to talk to this young gentleman here. We are not trying to cheat, not us. We leave the cheating to other people. Isn't that so, Willy?" Then they stepped back behind Mrs. Winkler.

3

Willy nodded again. Surely Mrs. Dengler had heard what Georg said. It was impossible not to hear it. Even people far up the line turned their heads and glanced in his direction. Come to think of it, Mrs. Dengler was the only one who didn't turn around. In fascination, Willy studied her neck. It was a thick, round neck arranged in three rolls of fat, and it was growing redder and redder, roll by roll. Willy turned away. He didn't want his place back now. It made him uncomfortable to have people watch him.

At this moment Mr. Krembsler, the owner of the fish store, stepped out of his shop. Over his unpressed pants he wore a white apron soiled with blood and dirt. He hung up a big sign, saying: "Only One Pound of Fish to a Customer."

"We are lucky if we get the pound," whispered Mrs. Winkler, pushing Willy gently. "Go on, Will. Now that they can get only one pound, it will go much faster."

The boy didn't answer her, and he didn't move. He stared at Mr. Krembsler's apron. It looked bloodstained. But since when did fish have blood? With the opening of the door, the smell of dead fish had become more penetrating than ever. Willy couldn't close his mind to it, no matter how he tried. It was in the air, nauseous and hateful, and it attacked him. Suddenly, out of somewhere, rose the vision of the dead frogs he had seen last year by the lake near Cronberg. He hadn't recognized them so he had gone nearer, and there they were, their greenish-gray bellies puffed and glittering in the hot summer sun. It seemed to him as if Mr. Krembsler's apron was swollen, like the belly of one of the frogs. Or was it Mrs. Dengler's face that became bigger? Now it began to grow; it came closer; the stench of garbage was there, very near; somebody threw garbage at him, refuse and fish. They started whirling around, fish and refuse and frogs, until everything around him was one oversized, spinning, hostile wheel.

He fell down, his shopping bag slipping into the gutter.

"For heaven's sake, help the poor child," cried Mrs. Winkler. "My God, what shall we do?"

"We'll take him home, Kasi and I," said the soldier Georg, pushing away the people who crowded around Willy. He turned to Mrs. Winkler. "Sixty-six Reuter Weg, wasn't it? Will you take our share of the fish to Dr. Halder?" Then, almost tenderly, he lifted the boy and took him in his arms. "You see, madam, we can't come home to the wife without the fish. Get going, Kasi. Good lord! The kid doesn't weigh more than a chicken."

It could be the ocean or the waterfall near the lake in Cronberg. There was a persistent, friendly roar, growing louder and perhaps coming from the sun which shone down on him, red and warm. No,

4

it couldn't be the sun. It was warm and friendly, but it smelled different. With an effort Willy opened his eyes and raised his head. He was lying in the kitchen on a green sofa, looking straight into the peat fire in the little stove. A gray, indefinite light fell through the window. There was Mother, her back turned toward him, busy with the stove, and there were two men in field-gray uniforms. The boy blinked and tried to remember. He felt strangely weightless and unaccountably happy. Now he recalled it all: these two were the soldiers who had talked to him while he stood in line in front of the store. For a moment he saw Mr. Krembsler, but the picture disappeared immediately. Willy didn't have a real conception of what "fainting" meant but he had heard about it, and he almost felt proud that it had happened to him. By now everything was quite clear: the white kitchen walls, the sink, the dishtowels over it, looking like some battered flags in his history book, the big black range with the Coal-Saver Stove on top, and the shelves with the familiar jars, SUGAR, SALT, PEPPER, FLOUR. On Father's and Big Anna's chairs sat the two soldiers, their heavy hands folded in their laps, their eyes closed. And the whole kitchen was filled with an exciting, energetic fragrance that made him feel good. Willy remembered one of the fairy tales in the book by J. J. Stoll (*Fairy Tales and Sagas, Collected and Adapted for German Boys by J. J. Stoll, Schoolmaster, Appointed to His Highness, The Grandduke of Baden*), in which the prince had brought home the most precious black bottle of essences, enchanting the entire court of the King with the Black Beard. But the essence was brewing in the white chipped enamel pot in which Mother usually boiled the Kornfrank.

"What is it, Ma?" the boy asked in a voice whose clearness came as a surprise to him.

"Willy!" said Mrs. Halder, and sat down next to him. She held him to her for a moment, without pressing him hard. She felt soft and warm. The boy buried his face in her lap. It wasn't often that Mother embraced him or that he embraced her. He couldn't remember when it had happened last.

He leaned back a little and repeated: "Ma, what smells so good? Is it a new Kornfrank? And where is Anna, and Pa? Did I bring home any dried fish at all?"

Mrs. Halder put his head down on the cushion and stood up. The boy again noticed the white strands which ran through her soft brown hair like the mountain glaciers in the Alps on the map in his room. There was even some white in the bun which Mrs. Halder wore low on the nape of her delicate neck. He also saw that her eyes were moist but decided to ignore it.

Mrs. Halder removed the enamel pot from the stove. "You're

5

asking too many questions at once, as usual. Father is in his hospital, Anna went out shopping, and you didn't bring home any fish. Now this, Willy, is real coffee. No chicory, no acorn, no ersatz. How does it smell to you?"

The boy sniffed the air. His body still seemed very light, and, for some reason, everything had an unreal look. Even the kitchen wore a new expression. Perhaps, he thought, it was because of the green sofa which belonged in the parlor and had no business being in the kitchen. He also remembered that Mother had told him often not to put his feet on the sofa. Now his feet were on it, both of them.

"How do you like it?" repeated Mrs. Halder, taking four cups and saucers out of the cupboard and spreading a fresh tablecloth over the kitchen table. It was Willy's favorite—the blue damask one with the faded flowers.

"It's wonderful," Willy said. "Why can't I always have this instead of Kornfrank or milk?"

"Because we don't have enough real coffee. Real coffee comes from far away, from South America. During the war the ships don't get through. They are being torpedoed and nothing reaches us."

"I know," Willy said. "It's called the Blockade, and it's the English who want to starve us so they can occupy Hamburg and Bremen and Berlin and Frankfurt and . . ."

"Who told you so?" interrupted Mrs. Halder.

"Dr. Krausel, our geography teacher," the boy replied. Dr. Krausel had never mentioned Frankfurt as one of the aims of the English occupation but Willy liked to enumerate cities and was simply carried away.

"Did he say anything about coffee?" continued Mrs. Halder.

This time Willy remembered very clearly. "Dr. Krausel said we could get along very well without coffee. He said that coffee was a foreign drink and that Napoleon had introduced it and that it made your heart ache."

"Do you believe him?" asked Mrs. Halder.

"I don't know." Willy hesitated. "It smells too good," he finally concluded. "Perhaps Dr. Krausel has a bad heart. I want to try real coffee. After all, I've never had it. May I, Mother?"

Mrs. Halder had walked over to Georg. "Wake up, Corporal," she said, and shook his shoulder. "Wake up. Coffee's ready."

Georg opened his eyes, stretched his legs, suddenly recalled where he was, and sprang to attention. "I beg your pardon," he said. He gave Kasimir a resounding slap on the back. "Hey, wake up, Kasi. You can't sleep here. You're not at home, you lug."

6

Kasimir, too, sprang to attention, apologized, and then all three sat down at the table.

"You stay where you are, Willy," said Mrs. Halder. "You're much too weak to get up." She poured the brown, steaming coffee into the cups, came over, and gave one to Willy. "Don't drop it," she added.

Georg looked for a long time into his cup. "Real coffee, Mrs. Halder! You shouldn't have done it. We know how tough it is to get even an eighth of a pound. I haven't had real coffee since—I don't know when."

"It's nothing like Kornfrank, and I don't think it will make my heart ache," declared Willy after having gulped half a cup. "My teacher, Dr. Krausel, thinks we shouldn't drink coffee because it's an un-Germanic drink, and because it makes your heart ache," he explained so Georg and Kasi would understand. But Kasimir only looked at him with dull eyes while Georg, sipping slowly and trying to make it last as long as possible, repeated: "You shouldn't have done it, Mrs. Halder. Now if Sergeant Julius comes visiting, he'll get no coffee, and it'll be our fault."

"Don't you worry about my brother, Corporal," answered Mrs. Halder. "I always tell him how lucky he is to have Dr. Halder give him his special treatment right here. That doctor in the barracks seems to be impossible. Julius gets all the medicine he needs from my husband. You know how concerned he is about his health. I sometimes think his health is the only thing in the world he's really interested in."

Georg put his cup down so fast that the saucer rattled, and said: "Yes, that's right." Then he walked over to Willy and inquired, a bit abruptly, "How are you feeling, kid?"

It cost Willy some effort to remain calm. Obviously, Corporal Georg was worried about Mother's remark concerning Uncle Julius's health. Therefore, in some way, Georg must know about Uncle Julius's secret visits to Father's laboratory, about the bottles Julius sneaked out and took to the Ginnheim barracks. Probably Georg also knew that he, Willy, had helped Uncle Julius, by delivering the bottles several times. That was the reason Georg and Kasi had been so friendly to him, Willy concluded, and brought him home. Corporal Georg was afraid Mother had been told about the whole thing. . . .

The boy tried to think fast. He couldn't tell Georg anything while Mother was around. If he could only find a way of talking to Georg alone, he could explain why there was no reason for worry. Suddenly Willy had an idea.

"Mother, couldn't I lie down in my room? I feel so tired." This,

7

Willy realized, was almost untrue. But it might give him the chance to be alone with Georg. The corporal seemed to grasp the plan immediately.

"Let me carry the boy to his room," he said, "and then Kasi and I can take the sofa back into the parlor. All right?"

Mrs. Halder, who had started clearing the table, looked at Willy. The boy couldn't make out whether there was a very slight smile in her dark eyes or not. Her voice seemed perfectly calm as she said: "All right, Georg. Willy will show you his room. Please put the bedspread over the armchair. Will you help me dry the dishes, Kasimir?"

Willy threw off the cover and got to his feet. He was much weaker than he expected. Without Georg, he realized, he would never make it to his room. So he didn't lie, after all. He really was tired out and needed help.

Georg put his arm around the boy's waist, Willy leaned against him, and together they slowly crossed the hallway into Willy's room. Georg deposited the boy in the big armchair, took off the bedspread, folded it neatly so that it formed an exact square, lifted him off the chair, and put him to bed.

"Mother doesn't know about the bottles, and if she knows she won't tell," the boy whispered. "Don't worry."

"Let me think a minute," the corporal said, "just one minute."

Willy fell back onto his pillow. The sheets greeted him with a cool touch. His eyes followed the familiar outlines of the rivers of South Italy on the enormous map over his bed. Slowly he began to spell the names of the cities next to him: Palermo . . . Bizerte . . . Tunis . . . Alexandria.

Georg went to the window and beat a tattoo on the glass. Of course the boy didn't realize what a dangerous game Sergeant Julius and the soldiers of the second Ginnheim barracks were playing. To the kid it was just some fun with "bottles." To Georg and his friends it was a question of survival.

Dr. Halder, a specialist in digestive diseases, made the urine analyses for his patients himself, since the pharmacy was too busy. If the urine contained sugar, he marked the patient's bottle with one cross; if it contained albumen, the bottle showed two crosses. Sergeant Julius Pallavant had been sick in the Ginnheim hospital for many months. He didn't trust the army physician whose main aim was to process all patients for the front as fast as possible, and had asked his brother-in-law to make an analysis. His urine contained albumen, Dr. Halder had explained to him. As long as he had albumen, something was seriously wrong with him, and he couldn't be sent to the front. Sergeant Julius didn't want to go to the front. In 1917 he didn't believe in a German victory. He and

8

his company had started fighting in German East Africa in 1914, and they had more than enough. Many had caught malaria, some beriberi, and others certain diseases which the Ginnheim doctors couldn't identify.

Some weeks ago Dr. Halder had told his brother-in-law that his urine was now almost normal. The army physician had congratulated him on his chance to serve His Majesty on the front very soon. One night, while Sergeant Julius was visiting with his family, Dr. Halder was called away. Julius managed to sneak into the laboratory. By the uncertain light of some war matches he discovered a bottle that was marked with two crosses, poured half of its contents into a flask he had brought with him, and refilled the bottle with warm water. He slipped out, the flask hidden in his hip pocket. Nobody had noticed him. Back in the latrine of the Ginnheim barracks he concocted what he supposed was a credible mixture of his own and the borrowed liquid, and awaited, somewhat anxiously, the medical verdict. Soon he was told that he had had a kind of relapse, which the doctor attributed to his stay in the tropics, and that he could not serve the Kaiser on the front for some time.

After having sworn Georg and some other friends to strictest secrecy, Julius had told them the source of his albumen and shared with them whatever he managed to carry out of Dr. Halder's laboratory. None of them was sent to the front.

Soon it had become difficult to slip into the laboratory. Since Willy worked there regularly, cleaning or drying bottles, and could enter and leave easily, Julius asked the boy to help him. Willy had managed to smuggle out the contents of several bottles and took them out to Ginnheim. Georg realized they would be court-martialed if they were caught. He also didn't want the boy to guess what risks they were taking.

He turned back from the window. "Sorry, Will," he began, but stopped when he saw that the boy had fallen asleep. Georg decided not to wake him but to tell Julius the whole story and have him find out whether his sister really knew anything. Georg was almost sure she did.

Mrs. Halder looked up from the stove when he came back into the kitchen. "Will is sound asleep," he announced. "Come on, Kasi, let's take back the sofa and get along home. We must be at the barracks by three."

Kasimir folded the paper whose headline proclaimed a decisive German victory in France. "Right," he said. They carried the sofa into the parlor.

When they returned, Mrs. Halder gave each of them a package, wrapped in at least five layers of newspaper. "Here is your fish,"

9

she said. "Let me thank you again. Mrs. Winkler surely couldn't have brought Willy home. Come again."

The two soldiers left after having thanked Mrs. Halder once more for the coffee treat. On the stairway they met Anna, carrying a bundle in each arm and giving them a disapproving glance.

"Good morning, miss," said Georg. When Anna didn't answer he shrugged his shoulders and walked down, the package with the fish pressed under his left arm. He could hear Mrs. Halder's subdued voice as Anna opened the kitchen door.

2. MRS. HALDER FOLDED THE *FRANKFUR-ter Zeitung* she held in her lap and put it on the mahogany sewing table next to her. From the dining-room window she could look out into the garden where the snow lay soft and comforting over the flower beds in the diffuse light of the Frankfurt November. She had almost an hour before going on her weekly hoarding trip to Cronberg in the Taunus Mountains and Melanie Halder very much wanted these moments to herself. For she must get used to the idea that finally, in this winter of 1918, the war had come to an end.

Mrs. Halder, descendant of a family of wealthy merchants who had settled down in the Free City of Frankfurt in the sixteenth century, had begun to loathe this war much earlier than Theodor, her husband, or most of her friends. Why, she herself didn't quite know. It was not that she had more insight into the strategical situation of Imperial Germany than Dr. Halder or the four big Frankfurt newspapers. It was her innate horror of conquest, misery, and bloodshed, her aversion against everything blatant and overbearing, which made her acutely uncomfortable any time she had to witness an army parade. Perhaps, she reflected, it was her heritage from her father's side—the Pallavants, one of Frankfurt's oldest families, never liked the Prussians and refused to accept the magic syllable "Von" when Bismarck offered to knight them. To them, the world had come to an end when the Free City of Frankfurt was annexed by the Prussians in 1866. They called themselves "Must-Prussians," disapproved of Chancellor Bismarck with his schemes of conquest, and could never muster the necessary enthusiasm for the war against the "arch enemy," the French, neither in 1870 nor in 1914.

Whenever Melanie Halder conjured up her childhood in the age-old, dark patrician house on the Main Quai, overlooking the broad, ever-flowing Main River, she saw Uncle Eugen Pallavant pacing up and down the enormous dining room and heard his angry voice:

"They're parvenus, these Prussians, that's what they are. They

11

have come to power too fast. They must show the world they're better than anyone else. They won in 1870 but that won't satisfy them. They've always been war-drunk, these Prussians, and they'll get drunker and drunker. Don't you ever marry a Prussian, Melanie."

Mrs. Halder, taking in the white, silent garden from her window, couldn't help smiling. She remembered it all so well. Somehow, the scene appeared to her now like an old-fashioned steel engraving. Uncle Eugen's wrathful pose had become petrified; her mother, the dining room, and—this was the remarkable thing—she herself as a little girl, were there, tiny figures in overprecise blacks and whites.

Melanie again took up the *Frankfurter Zeitung*. Yes, there it was, the "final armistice" after the drawn-out, anxious weeks. Of course Uncle Eugen's cherished hope—that Frankfurt become a Free City again—would not come true. But here was another alarming story: the returning soldiers and sailors had formed committees, similar to those of the Russians, and were ready to drive out not only their officers but the kings, grand dukes, and dukes who had reigned over Germany's kingdoms, grand duchies, and duchies for so many centuries. Mrs. Halder found herself rather pleased by the prospect. The war had taught her to lose what respect she had left for the military higher-ups who seemed nothing but super-Prussians to her.

With the exception of the Grand Duke Max of Baden, most of the German nobility impressed her as rather foolish. "A wine merchant from Frankfurt," Uncle Eugen used to say, "or a senator from Luebeck or Hamburg, is a hundred times more the real aristocrat than any shabby duke or grand duke who'd never have survived without a loan from our banks." This, Melanie believed, was carrying the proverbial Frankfurt pride too far, but she agreed with Uncle Eugen: the aristocracy, including the Kaiser and his strutting sons, had done very badly in this war which they had started. For some reason, Melanie had taken a particular dislike to the Imperial Family and, especially, to the Kaiser's sons. The *Frankfurter Zeitung* hinted that the Kaiser might abdicate and that the people of Munich had proclaimed the "Republic of Bavaria." . . .

Somehow, Melanie couldn't believe it. How would all her friends behave, most of whom had displayed an ardent patriotism during the war, a fervent belief in the ceaseless German victories even after it had become apparent to the Pallavants that, as Uncle Eugen had said, the "Prussians" were licked even if they didn't know it?

When Dr. Halder had come home a year ago, a thrice-wounded

12

medical officer, decorated with many gleaming medals for bravery, skill and other qualities Melanie couldn't remember, she had given a home-coming party. She recalled the night very distinctly. In the middle of the evening several of their guests had left, burning with indignation. For Dr. Halder had the temerity to declare that the Generals Ludendorff and Hindenburg had lost their bearings completely, and that defeat was inevitable. What about the grand strategy of His Majesty, the Kaiser, what about the U-boat war which Admiral Tirpitz was waging so relentlessly, asked Professor Raeber, his black beard pointing militantly at Dr. Halder. Without raising his voice, Dr. Halder repeated that the war was lost. Then he added something which Melanie herself had often thought during the long evenings when she sat alone in the unheated apartment: that it might be a very good thing if the war was lost. Perhaps a better world, a better Germany would emerge out of blood and chaos. This was too much for Professor Raeber and most of the guests who departed in a huff without thanking their hostess for the potato pie and the cups of Kornfrank, served by Melanie in her best gold-rimmed, monogrammed china. From then on Melanie felt even closer to her husband. He needed her more than ever because he was ostracized by almost everybody.

After three years of medical work in front hospitals Theodor was what people called in hushed tones a pacifist and even a socialist. His own father, old Judge Halder, and his sister Helen were shocked.

Melanie looked at her hands. She had always been proud of them—they were long, with strong, straight fingers and tapered fingertips. They also used to be white and smooth. Now they were scaly, several scratches on the back simply wouldn't heal, and she had to fight the temptation to wear her one pair of gloves oftener than necessary.

The door opened and Dr. Halder came in. He kissed her lightly on the forehead and stretched out on the sofa.

"Forty-five minutes if I'm lucky," he said. "The patients will start ringing the bell at two-thirty, as usual. Of course, if the streetcar conductors go on strike, I'll have a more peaceful afternoon."

He closed his eyes. Melanie fought back an impulse to go over and stroke his hair, which was white, very strong, and curly. She knew he wanted to be left alone. His face, deep-lined and almost square, seemed old for a man of forty-five. It was a typical doctor's face—that of an unhurried and forebearing man.

"I'll leave you alone in a minute, Theo," said Melanie lightly. "But how's that about the strike? What did you hear?"

"The whole hospital is talking about nothing else," answered Dr. Halder without opening his eyes. "They stopped almost all traffic

13

in the suburbs, Ginnheim, Roedelheim, and Bockenheim. The workers' and soldiers' committees are going to march to City Hall and demand a new city council in which they'll be represented. Of course, if they stop the streetcars altogether, there'll be trouble. You'd better cancel your trip to Cronberg."

"Cancel!" cried Melanie. "Now that Mrs. Petersen promised me potatoes, green vegetables, and real butter! And Willy enjoys hoarding trips more than anything else. You know, Theo, since Julius and his friends left Ginnheim hospital, Willy has grown away from us. He seems lost and quotes his Greek sagas more than ever. I know more about Orestes, Achilles, Patroclus, Clytemnestra and her brood than I ever want to know. It seems to me he doesn't like school and escapes into mythology as soon as it's over."

Dr. Halder opened his eyes. They were of an unusually intense blue, and even though he was smiling, they looked infinitely weary.

"Melanie, you shouldn't have encouraged Julius' scheme. Do you realize that with Willy's knowing and my unknowing help Julius managed to keep himself and several of his buddies from serving as cannon fodder for His Majesty? If Helen ever found out . . ." Dr. Halder chuckled.

"I'm glad the war is over, if only for Willy's sake, silly as it sounds," said Mrs. Halder. "He was in such a turmoil because he actually shared a secret with several grown-up soldiers and played a part in their plans that he hardly ate any more. And when the soldiers went away last week and gave him that hoop with their names inscribed in it—you know he insisted on showing it to everybody? Well, it's all over now. The least I can do is take him along to Cronberg. What's the name of the Petersen boy whom you treated and who's never in when we call?"

"The boy's name is Harold," mumbled Dr. Halder. "I'll try to be at the station at six thirty-five, but take a taxi if the streetcars are on strike, and be careful."

"Yes," said Melanie, "sleep well and don't worry." She touched his hair lightly and went out.

In the foyer sat Willy, fully dressed in his winter coat, a knitted wool cap on his head. His clumsy shoes, with their thick, inflexible wooden soles, made his feet seem unnaturally large.

"Why, Will——" Mrs. Halder began, but the boy interrupted her. "Our train leaves at two forty-five, Mother. We'd better hurry."

His eyes were shining, and Melanie knew that for him another afternoon of glorious adventure was beginning, as full of unforeseen happenings as his sagas of Ulysses or Achilles.

"Wait a second, Will," she said, "I must get my disguise."

14

3. THE TRIP IN THE CHILLY THIRD-CLASS

railroad compartment from Frankfurt to Cronberg was uneventful, and Mrs. Halder felt a little foolish. She wore an old and slightly theatrical cape, designed for pregnant women, and from time to time she let her neighbors catch a good glimpse of her. This was part of the "disguise." It was completed by a special kind of pocket, fashioned from odd pieces of corset, which she wore under her dark dress and which made her appear pregnant.

At the moment the pocket was filled with old newspapers. On the return trip she expected to have it full of food supplies. The disguise protected her from being searched by the gendarmes who policed all trains. It was strictly forbidden to buy food in the country. Since there was very little of it available, even if one used all his ration points, everybody tried to buy directly from the farmers.

Suburban trains were watched with particular care: the police figured—correctly—that only a few people would spend money for a long trip in order to buy some tidbits, while it was much more profitable to try to get the food from the farmers in the neighboring Taunus Mountains. Also, quite a number of Frankfurt families had relatives among the farmers; many themselves came from little villages of the Main-Rhine region and turned first to their own people.

The Petersens were old patients of Dr. Halder. Farmer Petersen, a taciturn, gnarled man with red hair, ill at ease in his stiff Sunday best, and his younger, more loquacious wife, had brought the limping Harold when he was six years old. Soon the farmer left, saying he had to look after his cattle and quoting the Bible at length. Mrs. Petersen, almost relieved, then told how the old women in Cronberg considered Harold accursed, what with his limp, his red hair, and his freckles.

While Dr. Halder examined the boy, Melanie entertained Mrs. Petersen in the kitchen. Mrs. Petersen, a retiring little woman, in turn invited Mrs. Halder out to her big farm in Cronberg. When

15

Dr. Halder assured her an operation of the kneecap would cure her son, and that in about five to six weeks Harold would be able to walk like other children, Mrs. Petersen kissed Mrs. Halder's hand and said if the Halders ever needed anything from the farm it was theirs.

The operation was a success, leaving Harold with a kneecap only slightly deformed but functioning well. After four weeks he galloped around with the village boys like one of them.

During the war Mrs. Petersen lived up to her promise. Since her husband and Heinrich, the old farmhand, were beyond draft age, the farm continued to prosper. In 1916 Mrs. Petersen took to reserving some potatoes, some beans, or a pint of milk for the "saviors of my son" as she called the Halder family. In her opinion, Mrs. Halder and, possibly, Willy were as much responsible for Harold's recovery as Dr. Halder. And without the Petersens' milk and vegetables Melanie was sure Willy might have succumbed to the rickets, as did so many other children in Frankfurt. . . .

Mrs. Halder turned to Willy and said over the rattle of the train: "Perhaps you'll meet Harold today. Mrs. Petersen said he didn't have to work outside and would be there to play with you."

"She said that last time when we came out," Willy answered without much enthusiasm. "And please, Mother, don't ask Mrs. Petersen to tell Harold to play with me."

"All right, Will," said Melanie, drawing her cape around her. Willy, remembering his part, helped her settle back in the hard seat and, on her request, fished the smelling salts out of her bag. The people in the compartment watched them, and an old woman remarked, so that even the two gendarmes standing outside could hear it, how nice it was to have a child who showed concern for his mother while she was in an—interesting condition. Willy looked at his mother, and Melanie nodded with her eyes. The gendarmes surely must have seen them and noticed her "condition." Since there were only a few trains running, they stood a good chance of having the same gendarmes on the return trip and not being searched.

Willy was so excited he kept on talking after they arrived in Cronberg, all the way up the steep hill, until the orchards and houses of the Petersen farm, contentedly lying under a cold and brilliant winter sun, rose slowly into view.

After having reached the farm, Melanie settled down in the stiffly furnished farmhouse parlor—Mrs. Petersen wouldn't let her sit in the kitchen though Melanie found it much more comfortable there than in the parlor, which reminded her of a funeral home. Willy was told to go to the stables and "play with Harold, who is expecting you."

16

Reluctantly the boy walked through the garden and the huge orchard. It was no good, he knew from experience, to try to stay with Mother and Mrs. Petersen. They were busy talking about women's things: clothes, food, and what was good for what if one were sick.

Today, for the first time, Hal was there. Previously, he had always been working somewhere on the farm. Willy didn't know him and shrank from meeting him now.

Ever since he had entered elementary school, Willy had discovered that he liked very few of the boys and that very few liked him. Although the school, selected by Dr. Halder, was "progressive," it admitted no girls, the teachers taught as they had for twenty years, the discipline was strict. In vain Willy had looked for a Patroclus or an Achilles—in his beloved Greek sagas the hero always had a devoted companion with whom he shared perils and joys. He met only enemies.

After a while Willy found the two cliques of the class, the rich one and the loud one, aligned against himself, his pencils gone, his seat smeared with ink, his schoolbooks dirtied. Several times the loud gang—led by a boy whom Willy called Ajax the Terrible— attacked him on his way home, took away his schoolbag and turned it upside down so that Willy had to fish his books out of the gutter. This delighted Ajax the Terrible who, watching from the next corner, made loud comments which no passerby could fail to hear. One morning Willy arrived very early and covered Ajax's seat with a transparent sticky glue. The plan succeeded, Ajax tore a hole in his pants, but his gang beat Willy up during recess. This again called for revenge.

Ajax, a big, slow-witted farmboy whose real name was Fritz Backes, spoke the nasal dialect of the countryside around Frankfurt. This very morning Willy, following an impulse, had taken a new kind of revenge. While he appeared to answer several of the teacher's questions quite correctly, he imitated Ajax's poor, ungrammatical speech. The class had tittered. The teacher didn't understand why several heads turned to Backes, who sat there in a helpless rage. After school the Ajax gang had laid a trap, but Willy, taking a complicated detour, had eluded them, if only temporarily. It was humiliating; he tried not to think about it now. Probably Harold wasn't much better than Ajax. . . .

Willy had reached the stables; he could hear the lowing of the cattle, and the strong smell of the animals came out to him.

Somewhat doubtfully he opened the door. The big cows gave him a soft brown look, and innumerable chickens began to cackle indignantly. On a wooden stool sat a tall, redheaded boy, a carving knife in his hand. He got up and came toward him.

17

"Better close the door. The cold's coming in," he said gruffly. "Are you Will Halder?"

Willy nodded. "You are Hal Petersen, aren't you?" When Hal didn't answer, he added, though he knew it was wrong while he said it: "Mother wanted me to come over and play games." Again the other boy didn't reply. He sat down again and kept on carving.

"You don't have to play if you don't want to," Willy said finally. He walked toward the enclosure where the cows stood, and stroked their soft backs. If Hal wanted to cut him, all right. The stable was full of things Willy had never seen, and he could explore it by himself. He turned toward the horses at the other end of the stables.

"Watch out!" Harold ran after him and grabbed his arms. "Petri is a mean horse and hates strangers. He kicks even me when he's in a foul mood."

Willy stopped. "Thanks," he said. Hal, seen face to face, didn't look so gruff after all. His carrotty hair was unkempt, and freckles ran over his nose, over the high cheekbones up to the gray-green eyes. In one hand he held the piece of wood he had been carving. It wasn't finished, Willy noticed, but it resembled a big brown cow, with a friendly head and enormous udders.

While he walked away from the horses with Harold he said: "Say, that's good. I wish I could do such things. Which cow is it? The one next to the entrance?"

The redheaded boy looked at him with surprise. "Yes, it's Hertha. How did you guess?"

Willy pondered awhile. "I don't know. It's the way she holds her head. The angle, I mean."

Hal drew a second stool, got a second carving knife and a piece of wood out of a drawer, and handed them to Willy. "Here. Why don't you have a try?" he said.

For quite some time they worked in silence, Hal intent on his carving, Willy trying to achieve something remotely like a cow. He failed miserably. The more he carved and chipped, the less it looked like a cow. Yet, sitting there in the warm stable next to Hal, whose breathing he could hear, he suddenly felt secure and at peace. It didn't matter that he was less skilled than Hal. He just wanted to sit there, with him, and watch the cow emerge from the wood, looking more and more like Hertha.

"Her eyes are bigger," he said once, and Hal made the eyes larger, carefully chipping off tiny bits. When it was finished, Hal held the carving up for inspection.

"Like it, Will?" he asked, his eyes gleaming.

"Looks just like her," said Willy. "Look what a mess I made!"

"Not so bad for a beginner," remarked Harold. Willy took the

18

wooden Hertha and admired her. "Have you other carvings?" he asked.

Hal hesitated and Willy didn't repeat his question. Although he ached to gain Hal's confidence, to see all the wooden figures he had made, to share his pride, he knew he mustn't hurry the boy who was slow, like all country people, and whom he wanted as a friend.

"Stand up, Will," Hal said all of a sudden. When Willy obeyed, a little bewildered, Hal put his hands on his shoulders and said: "Promise never to tell this to anyone?"

Willy nodded, overcome.

"Shake on it," Hal ordered. Solemnly they shook hands, and then Hal led Willy to a remote corner, pushed some worn-out blankets aside, revealing a tool box with an iron lock. Carefully Hal opened it with a rusty key from his pocket and spread the contents on the floor, piece by piece. There were horses, cows, goats, a house which Willy recognized as a copy of the Petersen farm, and some human heads. Willy knelt down to have a better look.

"They're wonderful," he whispered after a while, looking up to Hal, who smiled, almost embarrassed.

"Why, that's Father," Willy cried, pointing. "When did you do this?"

"After your father operated on me here," Hal answered, indicating to Willy a deformed kneecap with a deep scar on it. "I have never shown them to anyone. Father and Mother don't like my doing them. They won't even let me draw figures on paper."

"That's funny," Willy said. "When I doodle at home, Pa says he hopes I'll do better next year at the Goethe School when we have drawing lessons."

"Drawing lessons?" Hal repeated, unbelieving. "You mean they teach you that at school?"

"Sure, drawing and painting and everything," Willy said. All at once, unexpected and miraculous, an idea had come to him. "Look Hal. Why don't you come to Goethe School with me next year? Then you'll have to do drawings and all that, because the professors tell you to, and your parents couldn't stop you."

"Pa and Ma won't let me go to that school. They say it's too expensive, and the city boys would only make fun of me." Harold sounded uncertain but Willy knew he wanted to be urged and persuaded.

"If my mother talks to your mother long enough, your father will have nothing to say," Willy declared. "Mothers always win."

Hal didn't answer, and the two boys stood silent, facing each other in the dim light of the wintry afternoon. Underneath the silence a thousand indefinite noises filled the stable—the chickens scratching for food, the restless moving of the livestock. There was a wave of affection and joy rising within Willy, something new and overwhelming—the way he sometimes felt for Mother when she bathed him and everything was close and warm. Only this time it was a stronger current that took him away from Mother, out of the circle of the family, and carried him toward somebody his own age; it transported him to an unexpected sudden height, making him happy and apprehensive all in one. Willy couldn't account for this feeling that filled him to overflowing. He simply felt strong enough to tackle all kinds of dangers, even Ajax the Terrible.

"Look, Hal," he began, but the other interrupted him. Willy realized that Harold was as confused as he.

"Would you ask your mother to talk to my mother or your father to talk to Dad—I mean." Harold bent down to put the carvings back into the box, locked it, and kicked back the blankets.

"I'll ask her today," Willy said in a matter-of-fact tone which didn't come too easily. "Mother is very efficient. Don't worry about the boys at Goethe School making fun of you. I'll take care of them any time."

For a moment Hal stared at him; then he broke out laughing.

"I bet I can lick 'em all," he said, walking Willy toward the door. "Let's go get some cookies."

The sharp winter air brought tears to Willy's eyes. A flat red sun seemed pasted on the horizon as the boys walked toward the house where one window was lighted. Hal was almost a head taller, and his hand on Willy's shoulder was unusually large. It occurred to Willy that if Ajax the Terrible should enter Goethe School, he might not find it so easy to play rough. Because, for the first time, Willy would have a friend. Who was Achilles, who Patroclus? Who would give his life for the other and swear devotion to the bitter end? At this moment, walking with Hal toward the house where Mother was waiting, Willy didn't remember which of the two Greek heroes gave his life for the other, and couldn't decide whether he himself was Achilles or Patroclus. But he was ready to give his life for Hal, right now if necessary, and forever.

4. ON THE RETURN TRIP THE GENDARMES were particularly nasty. Unfortunately the train crept along even slower than usual, giving the policemen ample time to search every compartment and every person. Melanie Halder, the "pocket" under her dress nicely filled with potatoes, green vegetables, and butter, had never seen them so persistent. They rummaged through every woman's bag, peered into the pocketbooks of the few men, and ordered one of them, who seemed unusually corpulent in the Germany of 1918, to come with them to be stripped and searched. Mrs. Halder and Willy exchanged anxious glances. After a long time the gendarmes, muttering angrily, tossed their victim back into the compartment: they hadn't found any food hidden in his clothes. He was genuinely fat. The passengers in the compartment duly pitied him, and began to exchange their views on policemen who, an emaciated housewife whispered to Mrs. Halder, could be bribed with food and, if one was young and pretty, with other favors. Melanie shushed her with a nod toward Willy, but the boy was standing at the window oblivious to what went on around him. Melanie knew that something had happened to him, and she guessed that it concerned the Petersen boy. Watching the two walk toward her, she had easily deciphered the expression of ecstatic bewilderment on Willy's face—he hadn't learned to hide his emotions, and Melanie doubted that he ever would. On the other hand, if he decided to keep something from her, as in the case of her brother's laboratory operations a year ago, he held out pretty well. What troubled Melanie was that he easily made up glib, almost convincing stories if he was cornered. Melanie decided not to ask any questions about Harold Petersen. In his present state he'd give her a highly colored account interspersed with allusions to his beloved Greek heroes.

Suddenly the train stopped with a jolt, nearly throwing the passengers from their seats.

"Look, Mother," Willy cried, pointing out of the window. "Look. The bonfire. Come here fast."

Melanie, forgetting that she was supposed to move cautiously, rushed to the window. The train had come to an unscheduled stop shortly before the tiny station of Bockenheim, a shabby Frankfurt suburb. The station was flooded with people. Obviously a demonstration was in progress; hundreds of somberly dressed men and women marched in close formation over the tracks, carrying huge placards saying: "Down with Reaction. Long Live the People's Republic," or "Workers, Awaken. Our Time Has Come." Other signs, painted with crude red letters, read: "We Want a Democratic Government. Down with the Kaiser and His Gang," or "The Kaiser Fled, Our Rulers Fled, Long Live a Free Germany." Outside the station two overturned streetcars were burning, and the bright flames threw a brilliant and sinister light over the faces of the marchers and their placards. A policeman, trying to disperse the yelling crowd around the streetcar, was jostled back, stripped of his uniform, and beaten over the head.

"The revolution!" hissed the fat man, squeezing himself between Willy and Melanie. "The Kaiser has forsaken us. This is the end!"

Willy bounced with excitement. "It's beautiful," he cried. "Look, Mother, the fire, it's eating up the whole streetcar."

By now everyone in the compartment was standing up, straining to get a glimpse of the revolution. To Melanie's ears came the crackling of the burning cars, the shrilling of the children dancing around the flames, and the clatter of hundreds of heavy wooden war shoes on the march. Perhaps this was the revolution; perhaps now that the Kaiser and the numerous German princes and dukes had fled, a new world was on its way. For a moment Melanie was caught by the excitement. This, at last, might be the beginning of the new Germany for which Dr. Halder cherished such high hopes. Why shouldn't these people get their chance? They couldn't do much worse than those in charge before, who lost a war that had ruined the country. . . . The burning of the streetcars, Melanie admitted to herself, didn't make much sense, though, and suddenly she began to worry about getting herself and Willy home safely. The people behind crowded her against the window sill, and Melanie remembered just in time that no woman in her supposedly delicate condition would tolerate this.

Resolutely she pushed the people back. "Willy," she called, "come away from the window. You might get injured. Excuse me, I don't feel so well," she added to the woman behind, who immediately stepped aside. The others followed and went back to their seats. Mrs. Halder got out the smelling salts and held them to her nose.

"You must not excite yourself, dear," one of the women said. "Keep quiet under all circumstances."

Melanie nodded gratefully, putting her hand on the pocket

under her dress. She was afraid the butter might have started to melt.

Willy was still at the window. "They're putting up a sign on our locomotive," he exclaimed. "It says, 'Long Live the Republic.' Listen, Mother."

Everyone listened. A roaring cheer went up, the demonstrators began marching again, their heavy shoes clanking against the metal of the rails. They were making room for the train, and after some time it began to inch along accompanied by three piercing whistles from the engine.

The conductor entered the compartment. "Keep your seats," he announced in the tone of a schoolteacher fed up with the pranks of his pupils. "The train will be at least thirty minutes late because of this." He made a disdainful gesture toward the window. "In case we cannot bring the six thirty-five into the station, we'll stop at the Rebstock freight depot. From there you'll have to walk. There are no conveyances whatsoever. May I point out that the railroad company is not responsible for events beyond its control. No refunds will be given."

The conductor left, and after a few seconds, Melanie heard him repeat the same speech in the next compartment.

Why Willy chose this moment to blurt out his plan of persuading Mr. and Mrs. Petersen to let Hal enter Goethe School with him, Melanie couldn't fathom. She tried to listen patiently, wondering how they'd reach home, and whether there was a chance to let Theodor know that they were all right. In his eagerness, Willy told the story not very coherently, yet Melanie was touched. She realized that Will needed a friend when he entered that unknown territory, the Goethe School, as much as Harold Petersen needed drawing lessons.

"And if you talk to Mrs. Petersen so that she can talk to Mr. Petersen, they must let Hal come with me, Ma," Willy concluded. "Will you talk to Mrs. Petersen real soon?"

"Yes, Willy, I shall. But you'd better discuss it with Father and me when it's more—peaceful."

"Oh, yes, Mother," said Willy, suddenly sobered because he encountered no resistance.

"Rebstock freight depot," shouted the conductor; "everybody out." But the passengers refused to leave. There were shouts of "Get the train to Frankfurt," and nobody listened to the conductor's pleas that the signals were all against them, and where were the gendarmes? The gendarmes seemed to have disappeared completely. Finally a group of people, led by a giant young sailor wearing a red paper rose behind his ear, went up to the engineer and persuaded him to take the train into Frankfurt. They re-

23

mained there, and made the whistle shrill wildly into the falling dusk, while the train rattled on.

Melanie, looking out, discovered with a shock that the whole area around the main station was totally deserted. Usually the vast maze of tracks, signal towers, and bridges that spread around Frankfurt's main station was full of puffing, noisy trains, with clouds of white steam overhead. Now, there wasn't a single train, not a single steam cloud. The tracks lay empty and glittering under the yellow electric arc lights which went on, as usual, at seven o'clock wartime. The only train, moving against frantically flashing signals, was the short, shabby six thirty-five from Cronberg, stopping at Platform 10, in the middle of the station, with a placard saying "Long Live the Republic" on its chimney stack. Mrs. Halder, her cape billowing around her, waited and let the others get out first. The arc lights, rocking in the November wind, gave an almost ghostlike illumination as Melanie and Willy stepped from the train.

They were the last passengers, far behind the crowd, walking toward the eight-foot-high iron entrance gates. The railroad administration had a good reason for making them so high. If one wanted to meet a train, or accompany someone to his compartment, one was forced to purchase a platform ticket for ten pfennig which then was collected by two uniformed railroad employees guarding the gates. This constituted a considerable income for the German railways, and there was a high penalty for entering the platform without the so-called "perron ticket." Many people considered this an unwarranted expense and preferred to wait outside the gates. Dr. Halder, however, had always waited for Melanie on the platform, and now, when she couldn't find him, she began to be apprehensive. They had almost reached the huge iron gates of Platform 10 when Melanie stopped and pulled Willy back. "Listen, Will," she said. "Listen."

It sounded first like the soft roar of faraway thunder. Then it came nearer, grew louder, filled the huge reverberating hall. There was now the sound of hundreds and hundreds of marching feet. The few people near the gates stood stiff, frozen by the sound. Melanie gripped Willy's hand. She could distinguish voices; they were singing a marching song but it was not one of the many patriotic anthems the soldiers used to sing while marching off to war, three or four years ago. Melanie hoped she wouldn't have to run, because that would mean throwing away all the food in her "pocket."

The rhythmically marching feet had reached the main gate. The song, echoing in the empty hall, was deafening.

"All the wheels are standing still, when our strong arm has its

24

will," they sang, raising the placards which pleaded for a Free Germany and a True People's Republic. There were many soldiers and even more sailors in the procession, and they walked in stiff military fashion as if they were passing in review before an invisible superior.

Willy jumped up and down with excitement but didn't say a word. His damp hand clutched Mrs. Halder's. Fascinated, Melanie watched the scene unfolding before them. The demonstrators stopped, almost directly in front of track ten. In the sudden overwhelming silence that followed three men broke from the crowd and marched toward window eight, next to track ten, where a sign said, in slightly-damaged gilt letters, "Imperial Railroad Administration." The window was the last of a long row along the tracks, interrupted by the iron gates to the platforms. The youngest of the three, a private, carried a huge sign that demanded: "Self-Administration. A People's Government." The second was a typical trade-union leader, with nickel spectacles; the third was an enormous longshoreman with tattooed hands and a turtle-neck sweater.

The trade-union leader knocked at the window. No answer. He banged again. The two guards on track ten turned, protecting the gates. Then the longshoreman hammered at the window till it echoed through the entire hall. Finally, with a crash, he smashed it. A wave of excitement went through the crowd which stood rigid, watching.

A head appeared at the window, the head of an old man with white whiskers and blazing blue eyes.

"What do you want? What's the idea of smashing this window? I'll have to pay for it. Go home, all of you."

"Open the gates," demanded the union leader. "We are going to occupy the station."

"I can't open the gates," shouted the man. He disappeared, then suddenly emerged from a little door which Melanie had never noticed before. He stood very tall and erect in the blue uniform of the Prussian railroad employee. He wore several war decorations on his chest.

"I can't let you in," he shouted. "We're expecting several troop trains. The whole system is in confusion. I have to obey orders."

"Open all the gates," demanded the union leader. The crowd moved nearer. Melanie, sensing the threat, prepared to run away, if necessary, out into the empty freight yard.

"We don't want the troop trains here. They may have orders to shoot at the workers," said the trade-union man firmly. "If you

25

want to avoid bloodshed, open the gates. We'll occupy the platforms, man the signal towers, and redeploy the trains."

"Man the signal towers?" The old employee's voice was scornful. "Do you know how to operate them? Do you want to cause accidents? These troops are returning soldiers, your brothers, your sons and friends. They have no orders to shoot. Do you want to kill our home-coming heroes?"

"To hell with 'em," said the stevedore. "Let us in, do you hear?" He grabbed the employee and pushed him back. The union leader pulled him away from the old man. "We'll occupy the station in an orderly fashion," he declared, and there came an assenting murmur from the crowd. "We want no bloodshed. The tracks must be occupied by us, the people."

The soldier carrying the placard nodded. Since the sign was very large, he had to twist his head at an unnatural angle which made it impossible for him to say anything.

"You cannot enter the platforms," the old employee bawled. "You know that you need perron tickets, ten pfennig each." He made a sweeping gesture toward the other windows. "You can purchase them here. How many are you?"

The three men didn't answer. Then the trade-union leader turned toward the crowd and said, somewhat sheepishly: "How many are we?"

The crowd stirred. People began to chatter, the tenseness broke, and all of a sudden they seemed to split into small groups. They didn't appear like demonstrators any more. They almost resembled a club setting out for an annual convention. Nobody answered the leader's questions. Obviously the demonstrators didn't know how many they were. The old employee, quickly seizing his advantage, turned again to the trade-union man, who had begun to sweat. "Go home, brother. You haven't enough money to buy the platform tickets. It would amount to sixty marks at least. Ask them whether they want to spend sixty marks on perron tickets."

The longshoreman scratched his head; the young soldier wanted to say something but, feeling he might look ridiculous with his head twisted around the placard, remained silent. The union leader stepped back and raised his hand.

"It'll cost sixty marks to purchase the perron tickets," he announced.

"I haven't seen that much dough in years," a joking voice shouted, and some people in the crowd laughed. But there was no response, no reaction to the announcement that they would have to buy tickets in order to seize the station.

The railroad employee, almost sure of victory, stepped forward.

26

He looked remarkably like a popular portrait of the Emperor Franz Joseph of Austria, and he managed a paternal smile.

"It's dinnertime," he shouted. "Leave the railroad station to us old-timers and go home. Soup's getting cold."

The crowd moved, undecided. Then at the rear end it began to break up; some older women turned away from the line and moved toward the exit. Others followed, the soldiers and sailors putting their arms around the girls. The sign bearers, relieved, lowered the placards, and within a few minutes the demonstrators had disbanded. The employee, erect in his blue uniform, watched them go away. Melanie, behind the iron gates, only a few feet away, could see the triumphant expression on his face. She watched him disappear into the hut and lift the telephone receiver.

"There's Pa," cried Willy suddenly, pointing toward a side entrance. They passed the big iron gate, which the two guards relinquished, and hurried toward Dr. Halder, who was waiting next to an ambulance car with the inscription CENTER HOSPITAL.

"What's the ambulance for?" cried Melanie, taking his hand. "Can't we take a cab?"

"The drivers are all out demonstrating," declared Dr. Halder. "This was the only vehicle available. Have you heard that the revolution has come, that a new democratic government has been formed? Did you see them take over the railroad station? Those reactionaries in Berlin won't send troop trains against us, the new Frankfurt government."

Melanie pushed Willy into the car and, clinging to her food pocket under her dress, slammed the door.

"You should have seen the revolution," she said while Dr. Halder drove quickly through the darkened streets. She was half-laughing and half-sobbing. "They didn't storm the railroad station, Theodor, because they were told they needed ten pfennig tickets to enter the platforms. An old man told them to go home, and they went. He looked just like Emperor Franz Joseph. I'll never forget it. They wanted an officially approved revolution."

"You must give them time," said Dr. Halder. "The Germans don't know how to manage a real revolution. They've never succeeded in one."

5. THE GOETHE SCHOOL, WILLY'S PLACE

of higher learning for the next nine years, lay near the peaceful Goethe Park, not far from the fashionable Frankfurt West End but also not far from the industrial Rebstock neighborhood whose ugly houses began uncomfortably near the end of the park. The school (comprising what would be high school and the first two college years in America) called itself a "Progressive School."

Although the Goethe School was more modern than similar institutions in North and East Germany, the school authorities endeavored to keep as many of the old traditions as possible and introduced only those new methods, ordered by the social-democratic Ministry of Education, which they couldn't avoid. The names of its classes set the pupils apart from other boys. Willy and Harold entered the first class, the so-called Sexta in 1920. The school insisted on keeping the Latin names: Sexta, Quinta, Quarta, Lower Tertia, Upper Tertia, Lower Secunda, Upper Secunda, Lower Prima, Upper Prima. Many of the parents didn't understand Latin and were therefore forever uncertain in which grade their boys really were at the moment.

What Director Bruhn considered the most modern feature of his institution, what made it a "Progressive School," was the fact that the boys started French in Sexta, Latin in Lower Tertia, and not vice versa, as in the more backward Lessing Gymnasium. This, Director Bruhn assured Dr. Halder when he registered Willy and Harold, made study easier for the ten-year-olds, whose brains were not mature enough for the beautiful logic of Latin grammar but well enough developed to cope with such an easy, light-hearted language as French. Professor Noll, the French teacher, he added, spoke the language like a native and had an inexhaustible treasure of suitable French literature at his disposal.

This, Willy discovered after half a year, was more than exaggeration on Director Bruhn's part. Dr. Noll didn't speak French like a native. He had a heavy German accent which Willy unconsciously imitated only too well. Mrs. Halder, hearing Willy

28

for the first time, was shocked. Like most children of the old Frankfurt families, she had been tutored by a French governess from the time she was six, and spoke French perfectly. She read aloud from the French Primer to Willy, who listened attentively. He read back to her, and after the third try Melanie was satisfied that he sounded almost like her.

Some days later Dr. Noll asked for volunteers to read aloud an anecdote about Voltaire's stay in Potsdam, which he had not read previously to the class. Although Harold, who sat next to Willy, tried to stop him, Willy volunteered. Without much effort he read the anecdote, making it sound liquid and fluent and quite different from anything the professor had ever recited. A murmur rose in the classroom when he had finished, and Harold whispered proudly: "Very good, Will." Professor Noll, fidgeting at his desk, took Willy to task for reading too quickly but commended the reading as a whole.

"You read almost as well as a Frenchman," he said, polishing his pince-nez viciously. For the rest of the period he bombarded the class with complicated grammatical questions and trapped not only Willy but Hal, Goldschmidt, Pueschel, Von Rainer, and Duester, giving each of them a bad mark in his famous little black book.

When school was out, at one-fifteen, the Sexta gathered in the Goethe Park. Gerhard Pueschel, a white-blond athlete and the strongest in the class, told Willy in no uncertain terms that he was responsible for the bad marks.

"Stop showing off your French or I'll beat you till you're black and blue," he said, shaking his thick curls. Two of his gang held Willy and tried to twist his arms. Hal pushed them away and planted himself next to Willy.

"Lay off, Pueschel," he said calmly. "Noll is a mean bastard and he was out to get us anyhow. Remember last Friday? First he was all sugar, and then suddenly he sprang that written examination on us."

Pueschel relaxed and gazed at the flower beds of the Goethe Park.

"That's right," he said after a while, stepping back. "Noll is a mean bastard. I flunked that exam, and my old man gave me a beating. But Halder shouldn't make him mad by showing off. He was mad today, wasn't he?"

"Yes," agreed Hal. He had fought several times with Pueschel and though Pueschel was stronger, the result had been undecided. They didn't call each other by their first names—only very good friends did that in German schools—but they respected each other. Hal turned around.

29

"See here, Will," he began, but stopped. Willy had taken the prize pupil Richter's glasses, holding them like a pince-nez on his nose. Pulling down his mouth and narrowing his eyes, he began to recite the Voltaire anecdote in Dr. Noll's rasping voice. He sounded exactly like Professor Noll.

He looks like him, too, Harold thought, while the others broke into loud laughter. Pueschel couldn't get enough now, and Willy repeated his act.

Finally Harold managed to get him away. "My train leaves at one fifty-five," he said. "Are you coming?"

The Main Station, only fifteen minutes from the Goethe School, was by no means on Willy's way home, but almost every day he walked Hal over and waited with him for the train. Usually they had about fifteen minutes to themselves. They sat on one of the hard wooden benches, facing the platforms and the maze of glittering, twisting tracks running out into the Unknown. They listened to the roar of the trains which came from faraway cities and held for them an almost seductive power—a never-failing invitation to escape and adventure. They savored the station's million noises, the hooting of the engines, the puffing of the white steam that clouded the main hall whenever an overland express pulled in. The iron carts heaped with luggage clattered over the stone floors, people shouted for porters, hurried toward the gates, into the restaurants, their shoes making an irregular rhythmic pattern that never ceased. All this united into a sound blanket that enveloped the two boys. They heard it and they didn't hear it; they had invented their own game and lost themselves in it, station-drunk.

Today they had very little time, but when the Transcontinental Express steamed in, and the stationmaster called: "Train from Constantinople, Bucharest, Budapest, Vienna, Salzburg, Stuttgart, going to Berlin, Hamburg, London," Willy couldn't resist.

"We would take very little luggage," he said, looking up to Hal who, even sitting, was much taller. "We would have our initials on it and go to London by sleeper. Where do we go from there?"

"What about a hunting trip to Scotland?" asked Hal, who had read Sir Walter Scott. "Scotland has beautiful swamps and waterfalls and people go hunting all the time. From there, we might take the boat to . . ."

"Norway," Willy continued. "Big forests there, you could do a lot of carving. What's the capital of Norway? We would stay there for a while."

"Hammerfest is the northernmost city of Europe," Hal went on, not quite logically. "The northern lights must be something to see. We would take a cruise to the North Pole." He put his arm around

30

Willy's shoulders which were thin and angular. They always made Hal feel guilty. His own shoulders were about three inches broader —they had measured them—and one couldn't feel any bones.

"The North Pole is too cold," Willy said dreamily. "Remember the ship in Nansen's *Through Night and Ice?* No, I know where we'll go from Norway. We'll travel to China on the Siberian Express and visit Tibet. Did you read Maximilian Kern's *The Eye of Lo-Fo?* It will take us a year to explore Tibet and China."

"I don't care," Hal said. "I want to get away from home. Every morning I wish I were somewhere else."

Willy nodded. He shared Hal's passion for unknown places, for remote countries, rich with promise, that called to them from the geography book. He had invented the traveling game, and with his passion for names he knew more European towns than Hal, probably because Hal didn't have a map over his bed. Yet he didn't share Harold's desperate desire to get away—despite everything, he loved 66 Reuter Weg, and sometimes he was afraid Hal might leave Cronberg and start out all by himself for Berlin or Hamburg or Paris, and leave him to finish eight years of Goethe School.

"We'll go away, that's certain," he said; "perhaps when we're in Tertia or Secunda." A whistle shrilled; a dilapidated little train limped in on Track 8.

"The Bebra train," Hal said, taking his arm off Willy's shoulder. "We must go." The game was over, the spell broken—irretrievably. "By the way," Hal added, "Pueschel, that big brute, was right. You did show off your French. Learn it from Mother?"

They walked toward Track 10, where the one fifty-five for Cronberg stood, looking somewhat ill-tempered.

"Yes, I learned it from Mother," Willy admitted. It made no sense to make up stories for Hal. He saw right through them.

"It sounds good," Hal admitted. "But why must you always stick your neck out? Noll hates you for it. It's no sense fighting a teacher."

"I didn't——" Willy began, but Hal, pausing before the gate, interrupted. "You're my best friend, Will, but you're always up to something. Either you ape the teachers, or you know too much, or you show off and get the others in trouble. Know what I do? Nothing. Exactly nothing. If you do only what you have to, they leave you alone. I don't volunteer for that pig, Noll, and I don't get into trouble. You always do."

When he saw Willy's crestfallen face he added: "It's for your own good. You know what? Next time Noll calls you, make some mistakes. Read as bad as me, and make him feel good. You can manage that. It's common sense."

31

The "common sense" was borrowed from their *Reader for Sexta,* where a long anecdote with no particular point bore that name, and Willy knew it. Hal's idea, however, intrigued him.

"You mean for me to play stupid. That's wonderful, Hal. Perhaps he'll give me a better mark for reading bad."

Hal pulled out his season pass ("Reduced Rate for Pupils of Institutions of Higher Learning").

"By, by, Will," he said. "Don't overdo it. If I know you, you'll read worse than Duester, and there'll be trouble again. Medium-bad, that's it." He squeezed Willy's left arm, as he always did, and went through the gates. Willy turned away quickly. He didn't want to see the train leave. It gave him a twinge. Silly, he knew, yet it happened every day at one fifty-five. It seemed to him that Hal was going not to Cronberg, but much farther.

There was no one else like Hal, Willy decided again, while he waited for trolley Number 19 to take him to Reuter Weg. No one else understood him. Today, fortunately, he could bury himself in the second volume of Maximilian Kern's *The Eye of Lo-Fo.* The hero, Dr. Feuchter, and his companion, strong, honest Hans, were imprisoned in the head of the man-eating goddess Lo-Fo.

While Number 19 rattled through the Mainzer Landstrasse Willy tried to figure out what Hal and he would have done in a similar situation. Well, there were about three hundred more pages, so Maximilian Kern must have found a way out. As for the French lesson, Willy decided not to tell Mother anything, but to rehearse the anecdote called "Voltaire à Potsdam," pronouncing all *j*s, *che*s, and *g*s as hard as possible, and making all French nasals sound like Pueschel's. It was a new part, and Willy enjoyed playing all kinds of parts. Not only was it useful for getting out of tough spots, he had discovered, but it was fun pretending to be somebody else. After a time of pretending it became difficult to decide which Willy was real and which wasn't.

"Je me rends à ma maison," he said aloud to the startled conductor when he got off on the corner of Reuter Weg and Grueneburg Strasse. It sounded like "She me rands a ma maissson," and it made him chuckle. He rushed up the stairs and rang the bell where a polished nameplate announced: Dr. Theodor Halder, Gastroenterologist. Visiting Hours: 12–1; 3–5.

"Late," called Big Anna, "always late. Soup's on the table."

"I must consult Dr. Halder immediately." Willy made a wild grimace. "I'm afraid my appendix is full of albumen. It hurts. Oh! oh! *Je me sens malade, ma chère déesse Lo-Fo.*"

"Go wash your hands," said Big Anna, shaking her head.

32

6. THE YEAR 1921 PROVED ONE OF POLITI-
cal unrest for Germany. There were revolts and
epidemics just as in 1920. One day in August Dr. Halder came
home deeply perturbed. Members of one of the so-called "Free
Corps"—Theodor called them "Black Gangsters"—had killed
Secretary of State Matthias Erzberger. Dr. Halder, who had become a member of the City Council and secretary-general of
the city's Theater and Fine Arts Commission, tried to explain
to Willy what the assassination of the well-meaning Catholic
statesman meant, but in his preoccupation failed to notice that
his son didn't listen to him at all. Willy was worrying about his
mathematics homework and Professor Eberhard Lattau.

During the first three months of his third year in the Goethe
School, life had been as usual. He and Hal, who was quite disappointed by Dr. Reichmann's drawing lessons—copying of water
pitchers and soiled Greek statues—kept pretty much to themselves. Sometimes they invited their classmates, Robert Goldschmidt and Oscar von Rainer, to Cronberg to eat apples and play
games on the Petersen farm.

Professor Lattau, the new mathematics teacher, looked fat and
deceptively jolly, was as redheaded as Hal, came from Stolp in
Pomerania, and enjoyed the reputation—transmitted by grape-
vine from the Upper Tertia—of being a "strict disciplinarian." A
former officer, twice gassed during the Battle of the Ardennes,
he showed no signs of emotion while making life hell for the
Quarta. Mathematics, he declared during the first lesson, was the
basis of everything: strategy, business, and philosophy.

"The fact that Goethe School and the whole city of Frankfurt
are dedicated to progressiveness," he said, his yellow eyes fixed on
the wall, "does not relieve you of the necessity of doing your
mathematical homework with utmost exactitude. I shall not tolerate
slothfulness. You'll get only the marks you deserve. My motto:
Strict but just."

After some months the Quarta found itself slowly approaching
a state of hysteria. Professor Lattau didn't slap faces in anger like

33

Dr. Hahn, who was sorry a minute later, but delighted in surprising the pupils with unexpected examinations, particularly during the last period on Thursday when the boys were weary. He distributed low marks profusely and introduced a new system to punish "those who seem to think mathematics a joke." Though the School never had afternoon classes, he made the "loafers" return in the afternoon and seated them far away from one another in the amphitheatrical physics laboratory where they had to work out complicated mathematical puzzles. The few who solved the problems correctly were permitted to go home. The others had to stay on, until six o'clock, if necessary.

Whether it was fear which stupefied Willy, or whether he simply had no gift for mathematics, his marks grew steadily worse. In the half-yearly report which the school sent to parents, Director Bruhn noted that "Wilhelm must endeavor to improve his record in mathematics." Pueschel, Pleimes, Duester, and André, the fat boy, received similar warnings. None of them, however, Hal noticed, was so benumbed in Lattau's presence as Willy, or if they were they didn't show it. Lattau was the only teacher Willy couldn't imitate. The moment he entered the classroom Willy tightened up; he had taken to biting his nails, and this, in turn, gave the teacher a chance to roar at him; when he was called to the blackboard to solve a problem, he stuttered, faltered, and failed each time. The only equally inept pupil was Franz Duester who was two years older than Willy and had flunked two previous classes. He was commonly called a "leftover." He was equally bad in French, German, Latin, and singing. He and Willy always got the worst from Lattau, who called them "the calamity twins."

In October the coal shortage became so acute that the trains from Cronberg stopped running on schedule. On several mornings Hal didn't show up. Most of the time the classroom remained icy cold. The Quarta did its lessons wrapped in winter coats and mufflers. They felt even more helpless against Professor Lattau's bullying. Strangely enough, the boys of the Quarta didn't turn against their tormentor but against the three who consistently received good marks: Goldschmidt, Von Rainer, and Richter. Goldschmidt, a dark-haired, soft-eyed Jewish boy with a limp, couldn't fight, and therefore was left alone; Von Rainer, blond, slender, and prematurely cynical, conceded readily that Lattau probably favored him because of his nobility, disarming Pueschel and his strong-arm gang by this admission; this left Richter, a bespectacled, aloof, thinnish boy, who excelled not only in mathematics but in all other subjects. His memory was famous throughout the school. Not once had he been trapped by Lattau.

It was on a Thursday in October, when the Quarta was expecting a particularly nasty written mathematics examination, that the rumor of the cholera epidemic reached the class. Hal was absent —the trains from Cronberg being what they were—and Willy had heard it first from Schmidt of Upper Tertia. Rushing back, he gathered his classmates and told them the dreadful, the exquisite news.

"No examination today!" exclaimed Goldschmidt. "It's too good to be true."

"Three or four days off is worth any epidemic," declared Von Rainer. The others agreed. Cholera was better than Lattau. Only Richter dissented.

"Cholera is a dangerous disease," he said. "Do you know that in India millions of people are killed yearly by cholera? I hope it's only a rumor."

A storm of protest drowned his words. Someone gave Richter a push that sent him tumbling over a bench, and Pueschel grabbed him and said, "I'll show you. Just you wait, you lousy teacher's pet!"

Their first teacher, Professor Hahn, told them an epidemic was threatening Frankfurt and they were to go home immediately. There would be no school Friday or Saturday. He asked Halder to notify Petersen, and advised the class to call the school office Saturday morning to find out about Monday's schedule.

Willy let the others leave first. An epidemic meant Father would be busier than ever and he would have to open the door for patients all day long. The idea didn't please him and, mulling it over, he went to the window. The sky over Frankfurt, as it happened sometimes in the fall, spread out in an almost defiant blue, and a reddish-blond sun made the trees look unnaturally purple. On such days the musty-sweet smell of cider came out of every restaurant, particularly in the Old Town section, and the old people said: "Here's our Free City summer again. The Prussians couldn't take that to Berlin!"

Taking in the blue sky, Willy wondered what to do. Should he go to the station? No, not without Hal. He picked up his satchel and sauntered downstairs. Outside, he found Franz Duester waiting for him. Any time Harold wasn't around, Duester waited for him. Since they both were Lattau's favorite victims, Duester considered himself Willy's pal although Willy didn't like him particularly.

"Do you know where the others are?" Duester said in his hoarse, changing voice. "Near the tool shed in the park. Pueschel and the whole gang. They took Richter. Come along."

Willy hesitated. He didn't want to go home and he didn't want to go with Duester. But he couldn't shake him off, he knew from experience, so he gave in. It was the right day for a walk, after all.

Silently they crossed the Goethe Park toward the tool shed. The gravel paths were covered all over with flaming maple leaves. The shed, hidden by several high shrubs, couldn't be seen from any point in the park.

On the lawn around the shed sat the pupils of the Quarta, watching the fight. Mehling, Pueschel's sidekick, held Richter's glasses. Richter lay in the mud, kicking and struggling, while Pueschel held Richter's head down and ordered: "Say: 'I'm a stinking, lousy teacher's pet.' Say it."

Richter, his face streaked with dirt, clamped his lips together. The Quarta waited. A new excitement held them—Willy began to feel it too. It was almost like a trial, held by the Visigoths or some other Germanic tribe, as Felix Dahn described in *The Battle for Rome*. A day of judgment for Richter, the traitor, who knew too much and never had any trouble with Lattau.

"Give in, Richter," Willy said, coming a little closer. "You know you're licked."

Mehling pulled Willy back. "You keep out of this, Halder. We aren't through with him. Pueschel has plans."

Pueschel suddenly let Richter go. He got to his feet, his blond hair over his eyes.

"Tie him to the tree," he said to Mehling, who produced several leather straps from his satchel. Three of Pueschel's gang dragged Richter from the ground and held him to the plane tree.

"Turn him around," Pueschel ordered, and they pushed the boy's face against the tree so that his nose began to bleed. Then, very carefully, Pueschel wound the leather straps around Richter's waist, around both legs and arms, and tied him to the trunk. Mehling ripped off his shirt, and Pueschel unbuttoned his trousers, which fell crumpling around his legs. Then he tore off Richter's shorts.

"Form a circle," he ordered, "so nobody can see us." The boys obeyed, surrounding Richter, who had twisted his head so his nose didn't touch the hard bark. His eyes were closed but he didn't cry.

Duester, standing next to Willy, began to breathe faster, and Willy saw in the eyes of his classmates something he had never seen before, a savage joy, a malign relish in doing something forbidden and hurtful. The nude boy was their prey, and they would make him do whatever they wanted. He was their slave.

"Ten lashes each," commanded Pueschel, "and I'll go first, to give you the idea. Hey, Richter. Once more. Say: 'I'm a lousy, stinking teacher's pet,' and you can put on your pants and go home."

Richter didn't move. No sound came from his lips.

36

Then the sharp swish of the leather strap cut the air. Willy, crowded in by Duester and Pleimes, watched the blows fall on the boy's tiny white buttocks. They all envied Pueschel, and Willy, too, itched to hit Richter, to show him what it meant to be hurt, hurt by Lattau, by bad marks, by the daily humiliation of being the worst in mathematics. There was a new excitement mounting in Willy, somehow tied to all the forbidden things which adults hid from him and all boys, and to which he had not yet found the key.

"Who's next?" asked Pueschel. Mehling broke from the crowd. He hit Richter's back so hard that a long red stripe leapt out below his shoulder blades.

"What's the matter, Willy?" said Duester, when Willy suddenly elbowed his way through the crowd. "Are you crazy?"

But Willy had stepped up to Mehling, ripped the leather strap out of his hand before Mehling realized what was happening, and turned to Pueschel.

"You're killing him," he said in a shrill voice. "Leave him alone. He's bleeding. Don't you see? He's bleeding."

Pueschel hit Willy on the chin. He stumbled back, but Duester caught him just in time.

"Want some too?" asked Pueschel, punching Willy again. "You can have it right now. Your backside is no better than Richter's."

Willy fought back, his face burning, but Duester dragged him away, half-pushing, half-leading him, and then they both ran very fast, until the older boy made him sit down on a bench at the other end of Goethe Park.

"You're bleeding," Duester said, offering a dirty handkerchief. Willy, trying to fight back the tears, took his own and pressed it to his chin.

"All against one," he said painfully. "They're real cowards and they're rotten. We are all rotten. Let's call somebody, a policeman . . ."

"No sense stopping them," said Duester in the tone Hal used when Willy proposed some impossible scheme. "If you squeal you'll have the whole gang against you for the rest of the year. Let's get out of here. They'll come after you for sure, once they're through with Richter."

"I can't go home now," said Willy, blowing his nose.

"We can go to my house," said Duester. "Nobody in the Old Town gives a hoot how you look." He hesitated. "I live on Wasser Strasse. Have you ever been there?"

Willy shook his head. He felt exhausted. The splash of sunlight on the bench, the timid breeze, the whole October-summer forenoon, began to appear unreal. He hadn't been free on a weekday morning for so long, he had almost forgotten there could be a

37

forenoon without school. Now he was ready to follow Duester, to let him make all the decisions. Willy yielded to an urge to surrender his own will. It was so pleasant to do exactly what somebody else wanted.

The Old Town began right behind Frankfurt's main square. It seemed to Willy that he had never really seen it before. The narrow-gabled houses, crowding one another, seemed bent with age. Wood beams ran all along their fronts, and their third floors protruded so much they almost touched the gable across the street. Duester led the way, through twisting dark alleys, through uphill lanes. The cathedral towered over the Old Town, protective, and at the same time with a superior air, as if disapproving of the humans below.

"This is Antonio Platz," Duester announced, when they had reached a small plaza with an old stone fountain in the middle, surrounded by narrow houses with peaceful faces.

"Did you ever take a good look at the man on the old fountain?" Duester asked, smirking. "Go and tell me what you see." Willy stared at the nude stone figure of a satyr who spouted a huge jet of water into the air in an almost perfect arc. He was very muscular and he looked like Pueschel.

"I've seen him," Willy lied, "let's go."

"You're stupid, Will," Duester said, "but I'll tell you later."

He led Willy through another dark lane which the light-blue sky overhead made appear doubly dark and threatening. Clotheslines stretched across, and some dirty children played hopscotch on the cobblestones. There was a musty fragrance in the air.

"Cider," Duester announced, "from real Frankfurt apples. They're brewing it right here at the Golden Pheasant. Good, isn't it? Let's have a glass."

Willy protested, but then realized that Duester was ashamed to have him see the house he and his family lived in, and followed. They walked up three steps to a house over whose entrance hung a big golden pheasant. Willy let Duester go in first. Before he entered the house, which seemed peculiarly gloomy to him, Will turned around. His face was still burning and something ached in his throat. Perhaps he shouldn't go in. While he hesitated, his glance fell across the street and he saw a Madonna standing in a niche. The brass plate underneath had caught some of the sunlight and threw it up over the slight wooden figure.

"I'll be right in," Willy said, and hurried over to the statue. "Unknown Master," he read. "Around 1438. Called the Madonna of the Forgiven Sinner." Willy looked up at the neat wooden folds of her gown, and the Madonna smiled at him, forebearing, sweet, and a little empty. The gold of her crown was chipped. There were

38

only three graceful fingers on her right hand, holding the child against her.

She shouldn't stand here, Willy thought. She is too beautiful. He realized that she was quite different from anything Hal had ever done, and he decided to show her to Hal. Perhaps one day Harold could make something as wonderful. . . .

"Where the heck are you, Will?" Duester called. "Come in."

The room was so badly lit that Willy could hardly find his way. Duester led him to a corner, pushed him onto a chair, and gave him a thick glass filled to the brim.

"To a long epidemic," Duester said. Willy drank fast. It tasted different from the cider Mother had given him last year.

"But that's—another cider," he said, and Duester broke out laughing.

"You bet," he said. "That's hard cider, real wine. The other is kid stuff." He motioned to a man behind the counter. Without asking, the man put two more glasses in front of the boys. Willy had never seen a man with a more ratlike face. He even had two protruding yellow teeth at each corner of his mouth.

"This is my school friend, Wilhelm Halder," Duester introduced him, "and this is Heinrich. Heinrich knows everything that happens in the Old Town, even in the morning."

Willy's head was swimming and he didn't want the second glass.

"Anything going on upstairs?" Duester asked with a meaningful grin.

"What's upstairs?" Willy inquired, trying to sound casual.

"Something you don't know and should," Duester answered. "Wait." He walked over to Heinrich, who gesticulated, pointing upstairs. It seemed to Willy that Duester handed the waiter some money and received a key. Duester motioned him to come over.

"Promise to keep your mouth shut about this to everyone, including Petersen," Duester said. "I'll show you something terrific. Do you have one mark?"

Something in Willy told him he shouldn't give Duester the money, that the thing to do was to get away fast. Yet, thicker than before, there was an air of unreality that took this forenoon out of everyday life and gave it to another Willy, a second Willy who couldn't be held responsible for anything. He handed Duester a one-mark bill, picked up his satchel, and followed him up three half-lit flights into a tiny, murky bedroom.

"Keep quiet," Duester whispered, "and no light." Noiselessly he opened a closet, knelt down, and motioned Willy to follow. The hard floor hurt Willy's knees but he was too absorbed to care. He knelt there, inhaling the stale air, close to Duester, who began to push aside a board. It moved easily. Through the crack they peered into the next room, lit by two lamps with pink silk shades. Willy recognized the uniform of a sailor on the floor, and a woman's dress, and some other things on the chair.

At first Willy couldn't make out what was happening on the one bed but then he saw, pitilessly clear, the two entangled bodies, a huge man and a woman who looked white and placid and wore stockings. The man's face was red; he held the woman down on the squeaking bed. For one second Willy thought the sailor wanted to kill or torture her. Then, all at once, the boy understood that the sailor had pushed himself into the woman, that he now possessed her, as the books said, and that this was the secret he had guessed at a thousand times, the supreme and frightening thing forever hidden from him by the grownups. It was incredible that people did such things, as terrible as Richter's torture. The sailor's thighs were covered with a dark fuzz and the woman's flesh looked loose and pasty in the glow of the pink lampshades. Willy's throat burned; something almost like fear gripped his heart. If this was The Enigma, the one secret boys were not allowed to know, if this was why men and women wanted to be together, if this was the meaning of all the whispered jokes he had heard, of all the words he had seen scrawled on walls, scratched into trees—he wanted no part of it, ever.

Half-stumbling, he got up and out of the closet.

"Quiet!" whispered Duester. "You sissy. I should've known you couldn't take it." He was still kneeling, and in the murky light Willy saw that he was fumbling with himself, on his face an expression not unlike the sailor's.

Willy threw his satchel over his shoulder, rushed down the half-lit stairway, falling twice, stumbling, getting up again. He met no one. He missed the last step of the entrance to the Golden Pheasant, ashamed and terribly sober. As he scrambled to his feet, he saw the Madonna. For a moment her smile, sweet and remote, held him, then he turned away and began to run. The maze of irregular lanes bewildered him; the wooden gable fronts, the cobblestone pavements looked all alike, yet he sped on. After a while he began searching for street signs. He must get to Antonio Platz with the fountain; from there on he was safe. But the dark alleys confused and misled him. Everywhere his nostrils caught the musty smell of cider rising from hundreds and hundreds of winecellars in the Old Town. His heart beat fast and he felt a sting in his left side. Yet the sooner he escaped the faster he could forget the picture, the unspeakable scene. Suddenly he found himself on Antonio Platz, its narrow houses looking peaceful under the blue autumn sky.

Willy stopped, staring at the satyr on the fountain. Now he understood why Duester asked him to take a good look. The figure was naked, absolutely naked, and he exhibited, defiantly and without shame, his desire. The stonecutter had made it for all to see whose eyes had been opened. Duester knew, and now Willy knew, and he wondered, as he began to run again, whether it could really have been there when they had crossed the square before.

It was only when he had reached 66 Reuter Weg that Willy stopped running. He pressed his hand to his aching left side, and he became aware for the first time that all the time he had carried along his schoolbag. Across the street the clock in the grocery store showed one o'clock. Time for lunch. Yet he wasn't hungry. He couldn't sit down opposite Mother at a table with a clean tablecloth and tell her what had happened in school. Everything was different now; he knew the secret of the grownups, but they didn't know that he knew it.

Reluctantly he walked upstairs and knocked at the kitchen door. Big Anna opened it. She looked at him without saying a word, and Willy rushed to her and began to cry. Big Anna patted his back and let him cry himself out. She didn't scold him, she didn't ask questions. She took a fresh kitchen towel, dipped it into water, and began cleaning his face. There was still some blood on his chin. The boy was shaking, and Anna couldn't stop him. It was not only the shock; it was not that he had found sordidness and brutality and wasn't prepared for it. The morning in the Old Town had taken away something irretrievable. The years of innocence were gone. One of the doors of childhood had closed on Willy for good.

After a while the boy began to quiet down. He couldn't tell Anna about Richter because in his mind this was connected with the Golden Pheasant and Duester.

"Better get to bed," said Big Anna. "Silly boy. Crying like a baby. If you go now, nobody will see you, and I'll tell your ma after lunch you aren't feeling so good. There's an epidemic in town and the doctor and Mrs. Halder will be very busy."

Willy nodded. The tension had left him. He was limp, and if he could sleep he wouldn't have to think.

On the dresser of his room he found a note from his father saying Hal had called and expected him in Cronberg tomorrow, if a morning train was running. Tomorrow, if he had the courage, he'd tell Hal everything, and perhaps Hal would understand. Hal always did. Willy unmade his bed mechanically and put the note on his pillow. He undressed, looking at the familiar outlines of South Italy on the map over his bed. The names of the Sicilian cities that had seemed wonderful and like music to him last week didn't interest him. They were just places on a map. The bell rang. He listened to Anna opening the door and leading a patient into the waiting room. An irresistible sleepiness began to creep over him. He wouldn't have to go to school for some time, and he wouldn't have to see Lattau and Duester because the epidemic had fallen upon Frankfurt and given him some days of grace. He didn't deserve them, Willy knew, he didn't deserve them at all; and then he gave himself willingly to strong, dark sleep that took charge of him and led him away.

7. MOTHER AGREED IT WAS A GOOD IDEA

for Willy to take the two-fifteen to Cronberg.

"Did the cholera keep Father very busy?" he asked his mother when they sat down to a slight lunch. "The potatoes are very good," he added. If his mother was surprised she didn't show it. Willy always praised her food only when he was uneasy—sweets alone brought an immediate response, and he hadn't had any for a long time. Today he looked gray and his hands fidgeted. Obviously he was trying to be nice to her and ate everything on his plate. Also, he wanted to tell her something and couldn't. Melanie didn't ask him. She promised to call Mrs. Petersen, and hurried him on his way to Cronberg.

"He looks peaked," Anna stated reproachfully, clearing the table. "The air in Cronberg will do him good. I hope he'll bring back some of them Golden Fruit apples. We could bake a pie for Sunday."

"If I have enough money to buy shortening and flour," Melanie said, checking through her household book. "Everything has gone up again. Mueller wanted thirty-nine marks for a pound of flour yesterday. I told him he was crazy."

She went to the phone to notify Mrs. Petersen.

"Hal has been waiting for Will all morning," reported Mrs. Petersen in her high voice. "Do you know what it was they did to the Richter boy?"

Melanie didn't, and Mrs. Petersen told her the version Hal had given her, who in turn had it from Rainer who, unfortunately, had left the scene shortly after Willy and Duester. Melanie didn't like the story at all and she began to wonder why Willy hadn't mentioned it.

Hal, on his side, was annoyed that Willy couldn't supply more information. When Willy's report had reached the point where Mehling hit Richter, emphasizing how Richter wouldn't budge and never cried out once, he paused. Now, surely Hal would ask him where he had gone with Duester.

But Hal was only concerned with the affairs of the Quarta.

43

"I bet Bruhn and Lattau are going to give Pueschel and Mehling hell. Want an apple?"

They were walking through the Petersen orchard, picking apples and putting them into baskets. It was cold and clear. Not far away some children had started a fire of potato vines and its blue smoke drifted away in a lazy circle toward the Taunus Mountains. Willy threw Hal's apple quickly into his basket. He couldn't eat apples now. They tasted too much like cider.

"I don't care what they do to Pueschel or to anyone," he said abruptly. He looked at Hal, who was busy plucking the exuberant-looking apples and dropping them in his basket. Why couldn't Hal give him an opening?

"Look, Hal," he started, taking a deep breath, "Duester and I . . ."

Hal turned. The grin on his face showed he was in an exceptionally good mood.

"Never mind Duester. I can't stand him. He smells. Didn't you ever notice? But he got you out of it, thank God. Lattau and Bruhn haven't got a thing on you." Hal spit some apple seed in a wide arc against a tree. "Mrs. Richter called Bruhn and there'll be a teachers' meeting," he went on, "and Mrs. Richter has called the Parent's Council too. Perhaps they'll kick Pueschel and Mehling out, with something like a dishonorable discharge. Then no other high school in Frankfurt will take them. Serves them right.

"Don't let it get you, Will. Don't worry. Let's take a climb up the Little Feldberg. You aren't sick or anything?"

Willy shook his head. All of a sudden, while he looked at the drifting smoke of the fire, it came to him that he could never tell Hal about the Golden Pheasant. Why this was so, he was unable to figure out. Hal was in such a good mood, so happily intent on collecting apples, on assuring him there was nothing to worry about, Willy couldn't spoil his vacation with hideous revelations. More than ever Willy wanted to share everything with Hal, but since yesterday the world had changed. It hurt to hide anything from Hal—it was like betrayal. Yet Willy realized there had been other times when his friend hadn't understood him. He couldn't make Hal see why it was impossible to solve the problems Lattau wrote on the blackboard. How fear attacked him, numbing his knees, parching his throat. Hal had never grasped it, perhaps because Hal was never frightened. He belonged to the day side of things, and the Golden Pheasant and everything that went with it— the fear, the forbidden, shocking thrill, belonged to the night side. Perhaps it was only right that Hal be left out of such things. Willy breathed deeply of the light, crisp air. For a second he felt older than Hal, immeasurably older, and this, too, he must hide from him.

44

"I'm all for the Little Feldberg," he said. "How long will it take us?"

"You don't feel like it at all," Hal answered. "You can't fool me. But we'll go just the same, and I'll explain to you, once more, the principles of equation. Next time you must prove to Lattau that you are not a complete moron."

How simple they looked, those words on the blackboard. Willy stared at them while Professor Lattau wrote word after word in his elegant, flowery handwriting. Willy read the text but it made no sense. In his knees the familiar trembling set in. It was the last period on a Thursday, the second week after the cholera epidemic.

"Simple, this one," Hal whispered to Willy.

"Quiet," said Professor Lattau, swinging around. "If I catch one of you gabbing I'll make him come to the amphitheater every afternoon this week." The Quarta froze. For a second he took in the silence, relishing it.

Once more Willy fastened his eyes on the blackboard. "In a certain class of forty-five pupils the boys outnumber the girls by seven. How many boys are in the class?"

Simple, Hal had said. Yes, it must be. The main question was: what was X? Willy tried to remember everything Hal had explained during their trip to the Little Feldberg. Once you have found X, you can begin to manipulate. The number of boys must be X. Yet Hal had pointed out that one must be suspicious. What at first glance looked like X was often a derivative of X; the real X was hidden somewhere else. Where could it be concealed? Was X, by chance, the number of girls?

"You have five minutes for this ridiculously easy problem," declared Professor Lattau. "Write it clearly. I want no corrections. Schupp, you will collect the papers."

Schupp rose like a shot. "Yes, Professor," he said, and plumped down again. The seat next to him, Richter's place, was still empty.

Five minutes is much too short, Willy thought. He wrote down, "Let X be the number of girls." This was the less obvious X, therefore it probably was the right one. These two sentences were full of traps, of deceptive devices. Perhaps one could simply guess. Just write down something like: the number of boys is 32.

Hal threw him a sidelong glance—he wanted to see how Willy was tackling it. Seeing Hal's face helped. Willy remembered the sample problem they had scribbled on the back of an envelope while sitting on top of the Little Feldberg. Hal had set down two columns, rehearsing him patiently. So:

Let X be the number of girls.

Then X plus seven is the number of boys.

45

This was it. How wonderful. Perhaps he would really solve it this time. Altogether, there were 45 pupils in the imaginary class. The Quarta had only 21 and now, without Richter, there were 20. Of course Richter would come back. Then the Quarta would have how many boys? No! No! No! X plus 7 was the number of boys. Altogether, 45. Why was his throat so dry? Willy wanted a glass of water, but there was no way of getting it now. What had Hal said? Add the different Xs and put down how much they make together. The girl Xs and the boy Xs together. Tomorrow Duester would make a dirty joke about the many girl Xs and boy Xs getting together. Only four or five of his classmates would understand it, and Duester would look for another victim to enlighten. He usually took them to the bicycle shed after everybody had left. Fortunately, Hal had refused to go there. . . .

$$X + X + \text{seven} = 45$$

Correct. Or was it? Hal's pen was scratching. That meant he had turned the trick, found the key to the puzzle. Why did people invent such problems? Who wrote these books? Furiously Will wrote:

$$2X + \text{seven} = 45$$

No, this looked wrong. It didn't conform to the pattern Hal had been drilling into him. His heart began to beat. Willy could hear it distinctly.

"Two minutes to go!" announced Professor Lattau.

It seemed to Willy as if the teacher was giving him a sly look, probably to check whether his paper was empty. He must write down something, just to fool him.

$$2X = 45 - 7$$

Heavens, this sounded correct. It made no difference whether it was boys or girls, cows and steers, or cats and dogs, Hal had said. Look at the problem. How much was 45 minus 7? Well, this was ridiculous—kid stuff. It was 38. Willy began to scribble feverishly. Beads of sweat stood on his upper lip as he put down: 2X equals 38. He looked up, straight into Lattau's eyes. There was triumph in them, the exaltation of the hunter who has cornered his prey.

"Two minutes are up," the professor thundered. "Schupp, collect!"

Hal turned, and seeing Willy's face, shook his head. The school bell rang with the brutal suddenness of a trumpet sounding reveille in the barracks.

"Just one more moment, gentlemen," said Professor Lattau,

46

shuffling the papers. "I expect to see some of you again this afternoon. For an extra performance at the amphitheater. André, Duester, Halder, Pleimes, Pueschel. At three-thirty on the dot. Class dismissed."

One part of Harold's prediction came true: Professor Lattau had nothing on Willy as far as the Richter case was concerned. Director Bruhn's "Special Committee," after nine weeks of investigation, named Pueschel and Mehling as the main offenders, letting the others off. Pueschel and Mehling received a severe reprimand for "having acted in a most unbecoming manner toward a comrade and thus having excited disapprobation of the Goethe School." Any further offense on their part, they were warned, would result in expulsion.

After about three weeks Richter reappeared, keeping more aloof than ever. The second part of Hal's prophecy, that Bruhn and Lattau would give the two main culprits hell, did not come true at all. Director Bruhn read the committee's findings aloud to the Quarta while Richter blushed. Willy couldn't help thinking the report made Richter sound guilty.

"The poor fellow," Melanie remarked, when Willy told her how Richter had reacted to the public reading.

"Richter went away all by himself after school, not looking at anyone. And those two"—he stopped because Mother disapproved of curse words and the Quarta had recently taken to using the dirtiest expressions whenever possible—"those two pigs called him a sissy and said they'd get him again. You know, Mother, Lattau is extra friendly to Pueschel now instead of to Richter."

"Don't bite your nails, Will," said Melanie. "Look at your fingertips. They look as if mice had been nibbling them."

"Do you think they were fair to Richter?" Willy asked, hiding his hands. "Shouldn't they have kicked those two out? That's what Hal said." His voice rose, and he didn't notice that it broke on the top note.

"Hal's right," said Melanie, rising. "Perhaps we should have mobilized the Parents' Committee. But it's over now. Try to forget it. Bruhn isn't fair, the school isn't fair. Willy, sometimes I'm afraid nobody in power is fair."

Willy looked up in surprise. Mother sounded bitter, and this was something new. The old dining-room clock announced three o'clock. Mechanically he gathered his notebook and mathematics book and put them in his satchel. He was due at the amphitheater. He managed to smile at Mother while there rose in his throat the familiar sensation which gripped him whenever he had to face "The Beast."

47

"Lattau again?" Melanie asked, writing in her black budget book.

"Yes, Mother, but this time I think I'll be out early," Willy reassured her, a false note of confidence in his voice. He left hurriedly, his heavy shoes clattering down the stairs. His back looked so frail and forlorn that Melanie was tempted to rush after him and stop him. Instead, she went into the kitchen to check with Anna whether she could afford to buy bread. A loaf cost one hundred and eighty marks.

One Sunday in January 1923 Herbert Lange, Theodor's brother-in-law, paid the Halders a visit. His electrical supply business was going better than expected, he said, and he had acquired the exclusive distribution rights to this new invention, the radio, for southwest Germany. He hadn't come to talk about his business, however, he declared, waving his cigar. He had come to warn Theodor and Melanie: the mark was going down, the dollar going up. One had to be on guard; the country's whole economic order was being undermined. Dr. Mattern-Alvarez, the Argentine banker on Beethoven Strasse, who had his "finger on the world's pulse," predicted a complete revolution of the monetary system, and, Mr. Lange added, the only thing was to acquire some foreign currency. The French occupation of the Rhineland was paralyzing Germany's biggest industrial area, and while the French didn't get any of its coal, steel, or machines, thanks to the stanch patriotic resistance of the people, it still crippled the whole of German business.

Melanie, seeing the anger in Theodor's eyes, asked whether Herbert didn't want a cup of coffee—yes, a grateful patient, a coffee wholesale dealer, had paid his bill in coffee instead of marks—and thanked him for his warning. She inquired about Helene, his wife, and why didn't their Hans ever come and play with Willy?

Dr. Halder, however, was not to be sidetracked. He refused to purchase foreign currency. It was unfair and anti-social, he pointed out: the very buying of foreign moneys undermined the mark.

After some more virulent arguments Herbert left rather abruptly. Melanie saw him to the door. When they were alone, he startled her by taking her hand and saying:

"If you ever need American dollars, Melanie, come to me. If I still have 'em, I'll give you some. Theodor is an idealist—even though he is a socialist—and doesn't know the world. I'm only afraid he'll be hit harder than we ordinary businessmen."

During the coming weeks Melanie often remembered Herbert's visit. Last year the dollar had been around five hundred marks—that was high enough, but at least it had stayed there for a while and she was able to charge Theodor's patients accordingly. In

48

February the tide began to rise. On a Saturday the dollar was rated 1,200 marks, rose to 4,000 on Monday, climbed steadily and pitilessly to 12,000 the next Saturday, and while Melanie was helplessly counting the latest reichsmark bills which assured her they were worth 10,000 marks in gold, the dollar hit 17,000. Mr. Mueller, the grocer, had entered the race. His prices jumped from hour to hour. He was chasing the dollar, but he never caught it. The price tags on his merchandise, the price tags on everybody's merchandise, were scribbled lightly in pencil so that they could be erased as soon as the new stock-market reports appeared in the papers. Soon the price tags for clothing, furniture, for anything of more lasting value, showed so many zeros that Melanie couldn't decipher them. Was this coffee table in Gerson's Department Store 2,000,000, 20,000,000 or 200,000,000? Who could afford to buy a table now? Who could afford to buy anything? Who could afford simply to exist?

Melanie had lived through the anguish and loneliness of the war years; she had somehow managed to muddle through the first postwar years, when there were only beets and fish. She had finally overcome the chafing disappointment when, after the collapse of the Kaiser's armies, there came, half against its own will, the new republic, and she had realized that it was far from being the new, progressive state she and Theodor had lived and hoped for. Now, she had the feeling of fighting a gigantic octopus whose tentacles grew stronger day by day, and who was drawing everything into an abyss from which there was no way back. It spread over the country; she could almost see it squatting on the map in Willy's room, moving its multiple arms, destroying Germany, city by city, state by state. Could she fight the specter? Could anyone fight a monster that was invisible, intangible, yet ever present? Was it born of the war, had the state fathered it, or was it Satan's changeling?

One Friday Melanie woke up in the dead of night. She moved with infinite care, for Theodor slept lightly, expecting to be called on a case any moment. She was glad he could sleep at all. Since the new, the third, grippe epidemic was threatening Frankfurt, he had drowned himself in activity, working twelve to thirteen hours a day. She went to the kitchen and opened her black budget book. The figures glared at her: two eggs, 8,500 marks; two cans of canned milk, 3,400 marks; one pound of corned beef (American), 15,000 marks; half a pound of margarine, 7,000; shoes for Willy? No, there were no shoes for Willy, because the cheapest pair she could find cost 170,000 marks.

Yes, she owned government bonds. "I Gave Gold for Iron," they proclaimed. Four efficient-looking eagles adorned the corners. There had been many drives for the five issues. Each time the

49

speeches had been more fervent, the music more stirring, and victory was just around the next corner. The government bonds were not only an absolutely safe investment, they were guaranteed, with holy pledges by the almighty state, to pay dividends. If one acquired enough, one could retire, after ten or twenty years, into a little house all one's own. Melanie, too, had given gold for iron. Now she and millions of other housewives found that the government bonds were worth nothing, or, perhaps one should say, they were worth exactly their face value. Twenty-five, fifty, or a hundred marks, with interest. How little was 100 marks? Melanie couldn't compute it, nor could anyone else. One of her neighbors, Mrs. Sigbert, had actually wallpapered one of her rooms with them, and that was about all they were good for.

Every morning around six long queues began to form in front of the meat and grocery stores on Reuter Weg and, for that matter, all over the country. Every woman carried a large shopping bag, filled with five-hundred-, thousand-, and ten-thousand-mark bills. At noon the new stock-exchange rates would be published and then everything would go up again. One must shop as early as possible, and, as Melanie soon discovered, it was best to buy staples: canned sardines, rice, sausages (with questionable filling), flour, grits, or barley. Nineteen seventeen had come back, Melanie thought as she stood in line hoping that Mr. Mueller, who had always liked her, would play favorites and give her more than the other women.

In February Melanie asked Theodor's patients either to pay cash before leaving his office or to bring her food and commodities instead. Several patients arrived with gilded vases and china figurines, others brought huge family oil portraits, and some carried cartons with old clothing. Such things were called "commodities" and businessmen were always speaking of the "flight into commodities." The dealer who bought Melanie's commodities was Erwin Duester, a brother of Willy's schoolmate Franz, a man with "connections." He was a heavy-set, dark-faced fellow with sad eyes and lush lips much too red under a tiny mustache. Melanie knew that people called him a speculator and profiteer, but she had no choice. The others were no better.

Mr. Duester usually rang the bell in the morning after Dr. Halder had left, and though Melanie had told her husband about him, she always felt as if in some way she were betraying Theodor. Then began a strange and unreal bartering in the parlor where she stored the commodities which represented her income. They had agreed to evaluate the commodities in terms of the pre-inflation mark with the provision that Mr. Duester would multiply the pre-inflation price of the food by ten. A small table, for instance, was worth eight pre-inflation marks; a dozen eggs had been eighty pfennig in 1918. This meant that a dozen eggs was now worth eight marks—exactly the value of the table. At first Melanie and Mr. Duester exchanged no social amenities, but one day he startled her by saying: "Would you like to buy the house you live in?"

"How could I?" answered Melanie. "With what? How many billions is it?"

Erwin Duester pointed to the corner where Melanie had stored her treasures. "You can buy the first and the second mortgage for two pair of shoes, a man's suit, and a couple of good antique chairs like the ones you have here."

"Those are real Empire," Melanie said. "My father bought them in Paris in 1875. They were part of Empress Eugénie's boudoir."

Erwin Duester shrugged his shoulders. "As you wish, Mrs. Halder. I thought I was doing you a favor."

After he left in his glittering black limousine, Melanie began to feel foolish. Perhaps she should have sold the chairs. What did real Empire chairs mean today? They had graced Eugénie's dressing room, and that was where they belonged. They were survivors of a long-lost period, secure and gracious. That period was extinct. In the Frankfurt of 1923 Empress Eugénie's three-legged, gilded chairs were utterly out of place.

Some days later Mr. Duester arrived with canned salmon, two pounds of unexpectedly white flour, and a pair of shoes for Willy, size seven and a half. Melanie was nonplused—she had once mentioned that Willy needed shoes, size seven and a half, and that she couldn't buy them. Mr. Duester asked for so little in exchange that Melanie's suspicions arose. Mr. Duester seemed to sense it and stated his real business very soon.

"I won't be able to visit you any more, Mrs. Halder," he said. "I'm organizing my own big office, Goethe Strasse 20, from where I shall conduct my transactions. My business demands that I be near the phone most of the time. Yesterday I sold two carloads of American army beans to the city of Stuttgart. If I hadn't been there, I would have lost a good deal of money—solid money."

"I don't think my husband would like me to carry men's suits and old tables to Goethe Strasse," said Melanie.

"I wouldn't ask a real lady like you to do that," declared Mr. Duester. "My trucks will call for your things any time you wish. You can notify me what food you want in exchange. Did you know we expect the dollar to go up to 200,000 the first of June?"

"It seems to make you happy," said Melanie with more anger than she liked to show. She had long ago made up her mind that she must not get incensed over the morals of a profiteer.

51

"It doesn't make me happy, but I must look out for my own skin. Mrs. Halder, since this is the last time I'll be at your house, let me tell you it's been a pleasure to deal with you. May I make you an offer?"

Now it comes, Melanie said to herself. The real price for the flour and Willy's shoes.

Erwin Duester opened his wallet, displaying a thick bundle of American dollars, French francs, and Dutch gulden.

"I have a customer, a Mr. Bombach, who is willing to pay the highest price for your Empire chairs. As a matter of fact, he is willing to buy the entire parlor—green rug, Venetian chandelier, brocade curtains, painting, and all."

"He can't have the portrait," interrupted Melanie. "It's Grandmother, painted by Marie Vigée-Lebrun. It belongs in the family."

"All right, forget about—er, the painting. Mr. Bombach has recently come into the possession of a great fortune. He wants to furnish his new villa in Westend Strasse with only the best, and he is willing to pay in dollars, francs, or gulden. I think I can get you a good price, something like"—Mr. Duester paused—"one hundred dollars, which I would pay in installments. Of course I'm entitled to the customary percentage."

Melanie had never learned to bargain—her generation wasn't brought up to sell furniture—but she knew that her parlor was worth much more. It seemed sinful to give away the parlor, the only room in her apartment which was something of a luxury. It contained all the polished, graceful pieces from her father's house, and most of them had been in the Pallavant family for several generations. But if she could manage to get hold of foreign currency . . . Mrs. Sigbert's family lived on one American dollar a week, sent by a relative in Cincinnati.

"It's worth two hundred dollars and more," she said, "and if you have any knowledge of antiques you must realize it."

"Accepted, on one condition," said Duester. "Mr. Bombach wants to meet you, privately, at a restaurant, to talk things over, and he wants you to help him make the parlor in his villa exactly like yours."

Melanie didn't say yes or no then. She needed time to think it over. Theodor would be against it because he knew how much she loved the old pieces. But Theodor was unaware that they couldn't exist on what his patients brought in, and Melanie didn't want him to know. Herbert Lange, her brother-in-law, first pointed out how dangerous it was to deal with a notorious parvenu like Bombach. He also told her how Bombach had made his fortune. He had supplied the Austrian Army with rotten marmalade, made of foul apples and beets, sweetened with saccharine, and had bought

52

tons of American corned beef, abandoned by the American occupation army as unfit for consumption, selling it to the food administration of Saxonia. It fed the poor of Leipzig for a while, until too many of them got sick. Melanie wasn't quite sure whether Herbert, while condemning such transactions, wasn't secretly admiring Mr. Bombach's astuteness.

It was Willy who finally helped her to a decision. He reported that Franz Duester, his classmate, had offered him some wonderful Dutch chocolate after they had left the physics room where Lattau had kept them as usual. He always felt hungry at five-thirty. Was it all right for him to accept chocolate from Duester, and what could he offer in exchange?

Melanie promised him some sweets soon. She telephoned Erwin Duester, implored him to include two bars of chocolate in his next delivery, and agreed to a meeting with Bombach the next evening for late supper at the Hotel Imperial. She hadn't been to a place like the Imperial for a long time, and she defiantly decided to wear an old-fashioned, long evening gown, although all women this year were wearing short dresses which exposed their bony knees.

From the moment she entered the musty hall of the Imperial Melanie had the feeling that all this was not real. Someone else was sitting here under the badly dusted potted palms, eating an impertinently rich supper and carrying on a conversation with Erwin Duester and Mr. Bombach. Mr. Bombach didn't look like the popular caricatures of the newly rich, but he came close to it. He was corpulent, given to hearty laughter, yet he wore only one diamond ring on his left hand. But his face was shrewd and well kept and his pebble-like, darting eyes, Melanie noted, missed nothing. In his factories, he said, attacking his Peach Melba, people were working again, and this was good. Unemployment was decreasing, thanks to the inflation which enabled industry to resume export. He was also thinking of buying some chemical factories in Hoechst, near Frankfurt, and perhaps this hotel here. After all, he had paid all his debts—in marks, Erwin interpolated humorously—and it was his duty to expand and expand and give employment to more and more people.

"Would you like a liqueur?" he asked Melanie.

"Curaçao," said Melanie.

It worked. Mr. Bombach wasn't quite sure what Curaçao was and she caught an expression of approving admiration on Duester's face. In a strange way, Erwin, who gave the impression of a sensuous rodent in his uncomfortable dinner jacket, was her ally tonight.

53

In the meantime F. Fassbender's All-Mandolin Band was filling the dining room with noise, twenty-one mandolins erupting rhythmically in newly imported American dance harmonies. Sometimes one mandolin whined alone, then, for no apparent reason, all instruments united in cheery discords. The musicians seemed to pluck the strings viciously, as if shaking off something particularly unpleasant. No matter how loud they played, it always sounded to Melanie like quarreling bluejays, only magnified. American jazz had invaded Germany, and F. Fassbender's band, originally designed for more sentimental moods, twittered through such syncopated pieces as "I'm Forever Blowing Bubbles" or "Yes, We Have No Bananas" with great eagerness and aplomb. Melanie stared at the dancing couples, the men in padded jackets, tight pants which stopped short several inches above pointed shoes to exhibit violet socks; the women in glittering rayon dresses cut low to expose their flat breasts and scrawny shoulder blades.

Though Mr. Bombach was occasionally forced to shout over the vigorous chatter of the mandolins, Melanie grasped clearly the details of the proposed transaction. He wanted the parlor, Empire chairs, rug, chandelier, table, chest, and all the porcelain figurines. She could keep the portrait—until later, he added, smiling. Two hundred dollars' cash would be paid to her by Erwin in installments. No receipt, no record, of course. In turn Melanie was to assist Mrs. Bombach in embellishing the room with a good oil painting and more furniture.

"According to what Erwin told me, you have much too little in your parlor, Mrs. Halder," Mr. Bombach added, a shade reproachfully.

"I shall be glad to help Mrs. Bombach with the arrangement," said Melanie, "but I must insist on a receipt for my furniture. Also, I can't let you carry the pieces away all at once. I must replace them, piece by piece, so people won't notice."

She didn't tell them that Theodor knew nothing about her selling the parlor, and although he would eventually notice it, she wanted to delay the moment as long as possible. There ensued a spirited bickering between Mr. Bombach and Duester, with Erwin taking her part and, surprisingly, winning. Mr. Bombach slipped her twenty dollars under the table. This was the down payment, worth two chairs at least. Tomorrow his office would draw up an agreement which would serve as a receipt, without, however, committing Mr. Bombach legally. Melanie felt disgusted and desperately weary. For a moment she forgot the two men at her table. It seemed to her as if the mandolins were forever twanging their exasperating melodies while the dancers went on and on, turning in a dance of death, the death of money, the death of a world.

54

In all the cities of Germany the orchestras were blasting, the couples spinning, celebrating rack and ruin, the doom of all values, with mandolins, trumpets, and saxophones.

There was nothing left but to celebrate; you got nothing for your work, you got nothing for your money if you saved it. Spend it fast before the house falls down, first mortgage, second mortgage, and all. The money was dancing, too, the bills whirled from the presses, thousands, hundreds of thousands, billions, falling from the sky like locusts, leaving nothing but waste.

And the commodities, too, the inanimate objects changing hands so fast, joined the merry-go-round, chairs and tables, clothing, shoes. In the Middle Ages they had feasted and danced the plague: suddenly Melanie saw before her the chiseled etchings, The Skeleton Dances, hanging in the sedate gallery in Frankfurt—Death beating his drum, the cavaliers and their ladies in precious brocades, swinging their legs, and their backs putrefied and eaten by the disease. Here was the new plague, and this time Death was not beating his drum; Death led a jazz band in "You're the Cream in My Coffee." The cavaliers and their ladies were dancing again, the one-step of gold turned to ashes, the foxtrot of war bonds turned to wallpaper. Why didn't the skies open and rain fire on this Sodom?

The music stopped on a dissonant twitter and the silence jolted Melanie back to reality and the Hotel Imperial.

She looked up. Erwin and Mr. Bombach were scribbling figures on the back of the menu. They seemed to have forgotten her existence.

"If you don't mind, I'll go home," Melanie said. "Mr. Duester, you can send your men for the first two chairs tomorrow morning. Please don't forget the two chocolate bars you promised for my son."

She insisted on going home alone. The night was mild and quiet. On the Opera Platz Melanie bought the morning edition of the *Frankfurter Zeitung*. The old woman in the stand, one of Theodor's first patients, looked at her for a moment, then said: "Good evening, Mrs. Halder. That's nine thousand marks, please. The dollar is up to 180,000."

For a second Melanie was tempted to give her the twenty dollars she had in her purse. The moment passed. She handed the old woman a ten-thousand-mark bill and walked slowly toward Reuter Weg. There were green buds on the trees in Opera Park and the wind from the south smelled of spring. The stars were out, compact, small, and glittering like golden dollar pieces.

8. ONLY AFTER THERE WAS NOTHING left of the old parlor but the green rug and the portrait did Dr. Halder become aware of it. He had always been blind to any change Melanie effected in the apartment, and since she had replaced almost every antique piece of furniture with a cheap but respectable-looking substitute, Theodor took a long time noticing it. By that time—it was June—the dollar had climbed to 310,000 marks.

Dr. Halder had become so depressed by the ruin the inflation had brought to the country that he took his wife's arrangements with Duester and Mr. Bombach with comparative calm. Melanie had almost hoped he would insist on her ceasing any traffic with Erwin. As it turned out, he left it all up to her. Often he spoke to her with a sort of desperate indifference which frightened Melanie. In the evening, when he came home from party or council meetings, he would tell her only that they had discussed where the new water works was to be located and whether the two Frankfurt theaters should become city property or not.

Of course everyone in the Social-Democratic party was frightened by the devaluation of the mark but saw no way out. As Marx had proven, some of the party theorists pointed out, the laws of economics were irrefutable, and soon after the crisis a new prosperity was bound to come. The paradox was this: The German Government at that time was by no means dominated by Social-Democrats and liberals. It was a government of manufacturers, shipping owners, and bankers. Yet the liberal and left-wing parties were blamed for every evil wrought by the inflation. Most citizens of Frankfurt, where the Social-Democrats, the Catholic Center, and the Democrats held the majority, were convinced that their local representatives could stop the dizzy rise of the dollar and that "the revolution of 1918 was the real root of the disaster." Theodor's and his friends' attempts to mobilize the party leaders, call an emergency meeting, and map out a campaign had been thoroughly frustrated.

"You at least have achieved something," he told Melanie one

56

night, having returned from another wearisome meeting. He drew up a chair next to Melanie, who sat in her favorite place, near the window, mending Willy's worn socks. "You have sold our chairs and received food in exchange. I'm sorry we can't exist on what I earn."

"Don't be ridiculous, Theo," said Melanie. "Before the deluge we lived on what you earned. Do you know on how much the Sigberts next door manage? On one dollar a week, sent by Mrs. Sigbert's brother in Cincinnati. Mrs. Goldschmidt, the mother of Willy's schoolmate, Robbie, has been selling the silver spoons made by her great-great-grandfather. And Judge von Rainer's official salary, which is still coming every week, is just enough to buy one breakfast roll, I heard."

Theodor shook his head. After a while he drew a letter from his pocket and handed it to Melanie. "Here's another shock. Read this. What shall we do?"

Director Bruhn was sorry to inform Dr. and Mrs. T. Halder that Willy's grades had reached a new low. Not only in mathematics but in other subjects as well. In many complicated phrases the director advised Dr. Halder to reprimand his son severely. If Willy didn't make a determined effort, he would have to repeat the class.

"I talked to Willy," Dr. Halder said. "He's going through a difficult period. If Lattau would stop making him work three afternoons a week, perhaps he'd pull out of it."

Melanie agreed. Something had to be done. She felt apprehensive. In her efforts to keep the house going, she had neglected Willy.

The next evening, shortly after supper, Willy suddenly got up from the table, rushed to the bathroom, and vomited violently. When Melanie knocked at the door, asking him whether she could do anything for him, she heard him sobbing. The sobbing, in turn, made him retch once more. Melanie reproached herself bitterly. She couldn't let things go on like this.

When he came out of the bathroom, his face cardboard gray, with brown shadows under his eyes, she asked him what was wrong. Willy stubbornly avoided the issue. He was sulky and un-co-operative. Yes, he had been at the amphitheater almost three times a week for the last months. He implored Melanie not to approach the professor.

"Ever since Mrs. Richter complained, most of the teachers have been treating Richter like a dog," he explained. "I don't want them to do that to me."

Melanie sent him to bed early and decided to go ahead, nevertheless.

57

The next morning she telephoned Director Bruhn, inquiring whether Professor Lattau wasn't, perhaps, treating Will a trifle severely. The director was politeness itself, and barricaded himself so cleverly behind decrees, writs, and statutes that Melanie could only say, "Thank you," and hang up, feeling completely frustrated.

Her next step was to rally the Parents' Committee. This was another innovation, deplored by Director Bruhn and introduced by the Weimar Republic, which enabled parents to take a more active part in school life.

Melanie went to its chairman, Mrs. Wenger, an energetic member of the People's party, and told her what the afternoon sessions had done to Willy. Couldn't the Parents' Committee launch a protest?

Mrs. Wenger shook her head. The Lower Tertia parents had to get together and present their case to the Parents' Committee as a whole. Then, if at least half of the Lower Tertia parents approved of Melanie's proposal, they could go into action.

"I'm all with you, Mrs. Halder," Mrs. Wenger concluded. "Until now the Parents' Committee has concerned itself only with small matters, such as whether the boys should be allowed to go to school on roller skates. What you propose goes much further. Would you like the addresses of all Lower Tertia parents?"

"Thank you, but I can't visit them all personally, can I?" Melanie said.

"Of course not. Write a note to them on our stationery and visit those whose sons are Willy's co-sufferers and then the parents of the two pupils' representatives. Incidentally, what do you think of this idea?"

Melanie didn't quite know what to answer. She knew that in the Goethe School, as in all other high schools, each class elected two pupils to register complaints, make suggestions—in short, to represent them. It was a step away from the authoritarian system of old, designed to give the boys a sense of not being merely passive objects, but of having a word to say about their own school. According to Willy, the two "representatives" in his class never did anything but collect money for some school charity.

"Well, I say boys of thirteen or fourteen are not mature enough," declared Mrs. Wenger when Melanie hesitated. "I'd start the system in Lower Prima."

After some more talk about the rising prices Melanie put the official Parents' Committee stationery in her bag and left. It took her all afternoon to type twenty-one letters on Theodor's old machine. The meeting of the Lower Tertia was to be held next Friday, at Dr. Halder's house. Melanie set aside Tuesday and Wednesday

58

afternoons for the people she was going to visit: the "Pupils' Representatives," the Von Rainers, and the Schupps; the Andrés, the Pueschels, and the Pleimes, whose sons were in the same boat as Willy. She would leave out the Duesters—she couldn't picture herself asking help from Erwin Duester's mother.

Before she set out, she called Harold in Cronberg, asking him not to tell Willy about her crusade. Without realizing it, she treated Harold as a grownup and an ally in anything concerning Willy.

"Did you know what made Willy so sick?" Harold asked her, and when she said she didn't, he continued: "I got it from Erich André, the fat boy. While the boys are sweating over Lattau's darned problems, he conducts chemical experiments. Some of them make an awful stink, because he fools around with chlorine gas. André got sick, too, that day."

"Thanks, Hal," Melanie said, and hung up. She was so incensed she could scarcely think. And in this mood she set out on her campaign, a righteous wrath burning within her. This time the almighty professor had made a mistake and played into her hands. Every mother would see that at once.

Melanie looked over her addresses. They indicated precisely the social status of the residents. In Frankfurt, a street address was, to the experienced, as good as a biography. Mrs. von Rainer and Mrs. André lived in the residential West End, Mrs. von Rainer in a villa on Beethoven Strasse, Mrs. André in a huge mansion on Bockenheimer Allee. Melanie had put them first on her list because they probably would make a social occasion of her visit and take much more of her time. However, she hadn't expected to meet Mr. André, one of Frankfurt's most prominent bankers, who, it turned out, had gone to school with Uncle Eugene Pallavant.

Mrs. André, a tiny voluble woman, served tea in a parlor whose antiques obviously had not been replaced by imitations. As the maid entered with a second helping of tiny sandwiches, Melanie, for a moment, had the distinct impression that the Andrés had successfully managed to ignore everything that had happened since 1910. After Melanie had explained the purpose of her visit, Mrs. André hesitated. "We'd love to come to your house next Friday, but . . ."

Mr. André interrupted her. "That's not the point, my dear. The point is whether we should induce the Parents' Committee to take action against Professor Lattau. Frankly, I don't think so. Teachers must have absolute authority to do what they deem necessary. If they decide my son Erich has to work three afternoons a week in order to learn the essentials of math, back to work he goes. He must learn how to handle figures if he wants to enter the banking business. We would undermine the school authority if we took action."

"Professor Lattau has overstepped his authority," Melanie said coldly. "His chemical experiments make the boys sick."

"My son didn't get sick," Mr. André asserted. "Boys must learn to work under tough conditions. Why, when I went to school, the teachers used to beat us. Did me a lot of good."

Melanie was tempted to remark that she doubted it, but instead thanked them and left, the butler softly closing the door behind her. Defeat No. 1. Looking at the close-shaven green lawn she wondered how anyone could manage to live so comfortably through war, defeat, and inflation.

Melanie hurried toward Beethoven Strasse. At least she didn't share Mr. André's authority worship. He'd rather see his son Erich killed than interfere with the divine right of teachers.

Melanie stopped and looked at her list. This must be the Von Rainer house. The plane trees partly hid the two-story stucco villa which had once been white. The small garden seemed to be drowning in wild roses, and the grass to the right of the house was much too long.

No gardener, Melanie told herself, and for some reason this seemed to be a good omen. There was no maid or butler, either, and Mrs. von Rainer's dress was as threadbare as Melanie's. Melanie had met her once but didn't remember her as looking so frayed and defenseless.

"My son told me about that professor," she said, when they had settled down in a dark drawing room almost depleted of furniture.

"I'm with you, my dear. I shall come next Friday—on one condition." Mrs. von Rainer glanced around and lowered her voice. "My husband, the judge, mustn't know. He's so upset these days, he talks about the end of the world and the end of all justice and decency. I don't want him to know about this teacher Lattau. My son and I are trying to keep everything unpleasant from him. Do you suppose, my dear, we mothers could stop that man?"

"I'm positive," said Melanie. "If we approach the principal together, he'll give in and force Lattau's hand."

"Approach the principal?" repeated the old woman, as if Melanie had suggested something almost indecent. Then with a tiny, almost girlish laugh, she added: "You're probably right, my dear."

There was a pause while Mrs. von Rainer stared at the wall where a lighter square on the rose wallpaper indicated a picture had once hung. Then she said abruptly: "Sold. Everything is sold and there still isn't enough. My husband is judge in the highest court in Frankfurt, Mrs. Halder. Oh yes, they raised his salary last

60

week, but when it arrived it was worth exactly one pound of margarine." Her mouth began to quiver and an expression of fear came into her eyes. "How do you manage? How do you pay them? The butcher? And the grocer?"

"I manage very badly," answered Melanie. She felt an urge to confess that she had sold her family pieces to a profiteer, that it was wrong to do so, and that it was the only way for her to survive, but she suppressed the urge and went on: "Haven't you any friends in the country? Some people with a farm?"

Mrs. von Rainer's pale eyes searched hers, then wandered away and fastened again on the light square on the wall. "People in the country? I don't think so."

"I'll ask Mrs. Petersen to let you have some vegetables. Her Harold is your Oscar's friend, you know."

"Oh yes. Oscar went out to Cronberg several times. How nice of you to suggest this, Mrs. Halder. But I couldn't really ask Mrs. Petersen, could I?"

"Of course you could," said Melanie gently. She had never seen anyone look so broken. Mrs. von Rainer would never go out to Cronberg. She hadn't been introduced to Mrs. Petersen. Mrs. von Rainer would stay in the gray villa, selling her furniture and her jewelry piece by piece, wondering what would become of her and the judge. She would sit here, in the drawing room, all by herself, staring at the empty square on the wall.

"Would you like some of my wild roses?" asked Mrs. von Rainer when Melanie was leaving. "I have so many and you've been so nice to me."

"Thank you—no," said Melanie. Mrs. Rainer remained at the door, and when Melanie once more turned to wave to her it seemed as if the roses had suddenly grown over the door and Mrs. von Rainer had faded into their rosy thickness.

It was late afternoon when she arrived at the suburban district of Bockenheim where Mrs. Pleimes lived. Walter Pleimes, so Willy had once told her, was almost as stupid as he. Lattau loathed him, and Melanie decided to make the best of this. She had trouble finding the address: one house looked exactly like the next, neat and gloomy, with the same ridiculously small garden in front and a stone dwarf or deer guarding the entrance.

Mr. Pleimes, a supervisor in the city's taxation bureau, turned out to be an elderly man with vague features. He excused his wife, who was preparing dinner—throughout the entire conversation Melanie tried to identify the smell but came to no conclusion—and listened to her story.

Mr. Pleimes, it soon became apparent, didn't grasp the aims of

61

the Parents' Committee. Repeatedly he inquired: "You mean it is legal for us parents to petition the school officials?"

Melanie, slightly taken aback, assured him it was quite legal. Still Mr. Pleimes insisted on more detail.

"The meeting at your house, Mrs. Halder, is a preliminary one to put a motion to the larger body which thereupon will take action. Is that it?"

Melanie, who knew a legalistic mind when she met one, answered: "Correct. At least one half of us Lower Tertia parents must agree on what to present at the next session."

Mr. Pleimes pondered this for a while. Apparently he was afraid of becoming involved in something likely to offend the higher-ups, and in his mind the school authorities were in constant, though invisible, communion with his superiors at the city tax bureau. Of course he wouldn't admit this but entrenched himself behind formal reservations.

"In Civil Service one learns to examine every step thoroughly," he assured Melanie, "before one approaches one's superiors."

He was, Melanie thought, like a photographic negative of Mr. André. Mr. André wouldn't interfere because he worshiped authority and represented it; Mr. Pleimes refused to act because he was afraid of it.

"I'll look into the matter again," he promised, and Melanie knew that her efforts had been wasted.

The next day she received several telephone inquiries from the parents to whom she had written, among them one from Mrs. Petersen who didn't mind making an extra trip for the meeting on Friday. Left on her visiting list were the Pueschels and the Schupps: Kurt Schupp was one of the two pupils' representatives. Old man Schupp, an engine driver and trade-union representative, was one of the oldest Social-Democrat leaders and, according to Dr. Halder, an upright man who had fought all his life for the railroad workers' rights. Although he and Theodor had sat together on many city boards over a period of years, Melanie had never met Mrs. Schupp. Old man Schupp, like most trade-union people, instinctively shrank from any close contact with Dr. Halder who, no matter how much he did for the common cause, belonged to another caste, a man with a doctor's degree and not familiar, as the saying went, with "the stark realities of proletarian life." Melanie would have to exert considerable tact with the Schupp family, therefore she first called on the Pueschels.

The Pueschel Paper and Candy Store hid in a murky lane not far from the Roemer, Frankfurt's illustrious old building where once emperors had been crowned. It was the most disorderly shop

Melanie had ever seen. Souvenirs, candy bars, post cards, carved animals, and stationery crowded the shelves up to the ceiling. Any time the door opened or closed, chimes rang out the first bars of the "Lorelei."

Mrs. Pueschel, blond and hefty, like an enormous opera diva cast as Marguerite in *Faust,* left the store in charge of her husband and led Melanie into the back rooms which served as living quarters. There were three dark cubbyholes for Mr. and Mrs. Pueschel and their two sons, all filled with supplies for the store. Melanie picked her way past some cartons of chocolate to a rickety chair. Mrs. Pueschel, she discovered after a while, had never been informed where young Gerhard spent his afternoons. She assumed he was at his athletic club where he put in most of his time, training for his ultimate aim, the Reich's Sport Badge. Mrs. Pueschel also had never before heard of the Parents' Committee. She immediately disapproved of it.

"Gerhard is having enough trouble in school," she said, not without a certain pride. "He's so strong and has such good brains that the others are jealous. We have to do without a lot of things to send him to that school; we're small people. Besides, I don't think Lattau will like what you are doing, madam." Mrs. Pueschel's hard blue eyes seemed to pierce Melanie.

"Your Gerhard could spend more time on his exercises if he didn't have to waste three afternoons a week with Professor Lattau."

"Gerhard tells me Lattau has been nicer to him lately," Mrs. Pueschel said. "In any case, I must consult my husband, who is very busy. Working himself to the bone, he is." Mrs. Pueschel rose and pointed to a house across the street. "That's why we're working ourselves sick," she called out loudly, as if addressing a large gathering. "Do you know whose house that is?" Melanie didn't. "The Rothschild house," Mrs. Pueschel informed her furiously. "That's where they were born. Now they own Grueneburg Park, live in two castles, and eat strawberries in wintertime. They have made the inflation, they and the other Jews. Like Gerson and his department stores. First they sell everything so cheap that we can't compete and then they ruin the reichsmark."

"I'm sorry to have bothered you, Mrs. Pueschel," said Melanie, rushing past boxes of carved animals toward the shop exit. Mrs. Pueschel followed her.

"It's the money we must pay the Enemy," she recited. "We are in the bonds of Interest Slavery, my husband says. But we'll break 'em. Here"—she picked up a brochure and handed it to Melanie—"I won't charge you because you came all the way down here to visit us. It's written by Count Reventlow. He knows."

63

The chimes rang the beginning of the "Lorelie," the door shut, and Melanie found herself in the dark lane holding a brochure: *Germany in the Bonds of Interest Slavery.* By Count L. von Reventlow. Published by the Racist Party of Germany.

Melanie, hurrying along, was tempted to laugh. Wouldn't it be just her tough luck to come across one of those fanatic women who were forever preaching the Racist gospel and whom nobody took seriously? It was a blessing, she decided, turning toward the Liebfrauen Markt where the Schupps lived, that Mrs. Pueschel wasn't interested in the committee. She would have ruined any meeting.

Melanie remembered just in time to put away Count Reventlow's brochure before ringing the Schupps' bell on the third floor of a narrow, gabled house. Both old man Schupp, a white-haired giant with enormous hands, and his wife, a quiet woman whose face recalled a Duerer woodcut, received her. The apartment reminded Melanie of the Pleimes'; but the starched curtains were as spotlessly white as Mrs. Schupp's apron and the whole place exuded that particular cleanliness which Melanie had often found in the houses of people who had worked hard all their lives with never a moment's relaxation. Melanie was led into the living room, lined with bookshelves.

"Marx, Engels, Bebel, Lasalle. All complete," explained Mr. Schupp, lighting his old-fashioned pipe. "Also every book ever written on railroads. How is the doctor?"

Melanie said Theodor was very busy, and told her story, which by this time seemed almost unreal because she had repeated it so often. Mr. Schupp seemed to be disappointed. Melanie's purpose was not political, he said, and he was concerned only with political or trade-union issues. When Melanie pointed out, appealingly, that the parents must take concerted action, he said with a trace of bitterness:

"Do you think the other parents, like the Von Rainers or the Andrés, would like to sit with me on any committee?"

"This has nothing to do with the case," Melanie said. She must overcome the eternal suspicion of the lower class against the outsiders. Turning to Mrs. Schupp, she suddenly began to tell her about the selling of her chairs, of the Venetian chandelier, of the entire parlor, and how she had neglected Willy, who looked miserable and was losing weight. . . .

"We are no better off than you, Mrs. Halder," said Mr. Schupp, when she had finished. "Or perhaps one could say you are no better off than we." He looked at Melanie as if he were seeing her for the first time. "Never thought of it," he said, "but we're all paupers now, doctors and engine drivers and everyone. It's

64

all in Marx, of course," he added, pointing to the shelves. "That man predicted everything."

"All right, Father," said Mrs. Schupp in the tone of a reverend's wife who has listened to her husband's quoting the Bible once too often. "What are you going to do? I think we should attend the meeting."

Old man Schupp wouldn't commit himself. Perhaps, he pondered, he should first discuss it with some party leaders. But Mrs. Schupp, defiantly, promised to come. Melanie thanked them and went home.

When she drew up the balance it didn't seem too good. Two out of five were with her: old Mrs. von Rainer and Mrs. Schupp. According to Big Anna there had been more telephone calls from the other parents. She'd better start clearing the parlor of the assorted rubbish which Theodor's patients had brought. Once the stuff was out, the parlor seemed alarmingly like Mrs. von Rainer's gloomy place. It wasn't really a drawing room any more; the new rug was too small; the chairs looked plump and unhappy. Only Grandmother Pallavant was unchanged, gazing aloof and elegant out of her gilded eighteenth-century frame.

The meeting of the Lower Tertia parents was a pathetic failure. Less than half of them showed up. Mrs. von Rainer, Mrs. Schupp, and Mrs. Petersen appeared dutifully. Around ten o'clock Melanie served lemonade, made of real lemons, which was generally appreciated, but shortly afterward the meeting broke up in a mood of defeat.

After they had gone, Dr. Halder said: "You know, if Director Bruhn had summoned the parents to form an association, they'd have come. All of them. But to act on their own, without orders from above . . ." He shrugged his shoulders.

"I know all that," said Melanie, "and so do you. In the last elections the majority voted Liberal-Democratic, Center, and Social-Democratic. That means they believe in the Republic, doesn't it? It should also mean they have a certain amount of faith in themselves and their own power. But they're afraid of those in command. And Parents' Committee action probably looks like rebellion to them. It doesn't make sense. Or does it?"

"Those who voted for the Center and Social-Democrats were working people," answered Theodor, "or those few who were sick of the war and fed up with the military and caste system. Let Anna wash those lemonade glasses, Mel, and go to bed."

"You know what old man Schupp's objection was?" Melanie said, rinsing the glasses. "He wasn't interested because it isn't a political or a trade-union issue. Then he wanted to consult the

65

higher-ups in his party. That man is just as narrow-minded as the others. Sorry, Theo, but he sounded like any conservative businessman."

"Old man Schupp is the typical old party fighter," answered Dr. Halder. "I admit he's ponderous and anything outside his railroaders or the party routine probably baffles him. But when it comes to the essentials, you can rely on him. You mustn't be unjust and ask too much."

"I'm not unjust," Melanie said, putting the last glass into the cupboard. Lately she had begun questioning many of the things to which she and Theodor had clung so stubbornly for years and which so few people shared with them. Her beliefs, which had lain anchored within her, had broken loose and drifted away, leaving a void. She couldn't share her husband's faith in the big organizations of German workers, their spirit, and their efficiency. Yet she must not let him see how insecure she had become. Theodor depended on his principles much more than she did.

She went into the bedroom. Theodor, the *Frankfurter Zeitung* in hand, followed her.

"Perhaps old man Schupp didn't like my looks," she declared, and her husband answered, as she hoped he would, that she was simply fishing for compliments and easy ones at that.

"The dollar is quoted at 330,000 tonight," Theodor said. "Have you any money for tomorrow? Do you have to get up early to buy food?"

"I'll let Anna do the shopping tomorrow," Melanie said, brushing her hair. There was far too much gray in it—it seemed to have doubled during the last few months. "I'm going to talk to Lattau as soon as possible."

The next morning Melanie held another telephone council with Hal, who assured her the professor was still carrying out his experiments. The janitor of the physics building had let Harold in, and one could smell the gases two floors below the amphitheater. Harold promised to keep Willy away from the reception rooms where Melanie was to see the professor on Monday between 11 and 12 A.M.

The moment she saw him, Melanie immediately identified Lattau as the typical Prussian officer to whom the school was but another version of the barracks. His eyes, almost slits above the rosy cheeks, held no expression whatsoever.

Melanie chose a cautious approach, telling him that recently Willy had come home feeling ill, and that her husband, Dr. Halder, after a careful examination, had diagnosed general exhaustion and nervous stomach disorder.

66

"Times are not easy for us parents, Professor Lattau. We can't always give the children enough food, and I'm afraid there is danger of overtaxing the boys' strength."

"We teachers must uphold the standards of higher learning," answered the professor, with scarcely concealed irritation. "Those who can't keep step with us will, in due time, fall back and be eliminated from the institutions of higher learning."

"Until recently, Willy's marks were excellent," Melanie said. "He's passing through puberty, which is a trying period for any boy, and I'm afraid he's very much like me—he has no talent for mathematics." She smiled at the professor, whose expression, it seemed, rejected her smile.

"You are a woman, Mrs. Halder; you don't need mathematics. Boys do. It's the basis of all knowledge, of engineering, physics, ballistics, and the science of war. The most efficient training for the brain. If we coddle our youngsters, they'll never amount to anything. We need good brains to rebuild Germany. The younger generation is getting soft."

"Do you imagine you are hardening the younger generation by keeping the boys away from home three afternoons a week?"

"I'm not keeping them for my personal enjoyment. These boys are lazy. They simply will not learn the small amount prescribed by the curriculum." He was almost shouting, and his left eye began twitching in an uncontrollable tic.

"I'm sure my son does his best," she answered calmly. "What you call the extra training, Professor Lattau, has just the opposite effect. Particularly since you started your experiments with gases, which are having a disastrous effect on the boys' health."

This, Melanie told herself, was her trump card. The experiments put him in the wrong, and he must know it. But she had underestimated the enemy. Professor Lattau, his eye twitching, simply began to yell.

"The experiments have nothing to do with it. If the boys aren't tough enough to stand a little smoke, how do you expect them to stand the real hazards of life and war? Germany needs tough youngsters, not coddled milksops."

Melanie, stunned by this outbreak, could only stare at him. Why, the man was trying to bully her as if she were a private in the infantry and he could have her court-martialed for insubordination. She should have shouted back at him but it was too late now. She gathered her gloves and turned toward the door.

"I'm sorry if I shouted," said the professor in a tone which to Melanie indicated clearly he wasn't sorry at all. "I have been gassed twice in the war and can't always control the volume of my voice."

Melanie, seeing through his maneuver to cover himself if she

67

should report the incident to the principal, paid no attention and walked out.

What was to be done? She stepped through the long, dark hallways of the school, past the playgrounds which with their skimpy trees looked like prison courts in the sharp light of the June sun. She felt beaten, completely and utterly beaten.

That afternoon Willy came home almost two hours earlier. He had solved the problems this time, he reported. He was obviously relieved, and Melanie managed to make him eat at least three quarters of his supper.

Several times after that he appeared early. Melanie began to hope that perhaps he had really started losing his fear of Lattau and the mathematics and taken the first decisive hurdle. Then one Wednesday afternoon, when she was watching for Will, Harold appeared instead, telling her Willy would probably be late again and furnishing the explanation for the recent change.

The boys had evolved the following scheme: Willy, taking a seat near the window, wrote the problems on a small piece of paper and rolled it into a ball. While Lattau was busy with his apparatus, he threw the ball out of the window into the yard. Harold, hidden by the bicycle sheds, picked it up and wrote the solution on another small piece. Karl, the janitor of the physics building, a man from Cronberg who resented the experiments because they increased his cleaning duties, kept the washroom unlocked so that Harold could slip the paper into the roll of tissue paper in the first cubicle. When one of Lattau's victims had received permission to go to the lavatory—given only once during the afternoon—he locked himself in, studied Hal's paper carefully, and put it back for his successor. The last one flushed it down the toilet. This scheme had been successful until this Monday, when Pleimes, who was the last one, got sick, vomited, and forgot to destroy it, Now the boys were afraid Lattau might find out. He had become suspicious and taken to searching the building. While he did this he locked the boys in the amphitheater after he had called in a young substitute teacher of botany, Dr. Ray.

"He hasn't caught me yet," Hal finished, "but I'm scared. Not for myself," he added, "but think what the Beast would do to Will and the other kids. You know what could be done? That is, if you'll help."

"I'll help you, Harold," said Melanie. It struck her that Harold's boyish and slightly unethical plan had been more successful than all her straightforward efforts.

"Let's take Lattau by surprise," Harold said. "Dr. Ray doesn't know anything about the experiments and how to stop them. Last

68

time André and Pleimes had to throw up again. Because of the fumes. That's where Lattau made his biggest mistake."

"I don't see it," said Melanie.

"I think it's like this. So far Lattau could always say the fumes were harmless and Will and the others were only using them as an excuse for their stupidity. We had no witnesses. Now there's Dr. Ray and the janitor who's with us because he comes from Cronberg and can't stand Lattau. I'm sure one or two of the boys are going to be sick today because Lattau has to repeat the same experiment. I fixed it with André so they'll all complain about feeling bad and ask for permission to leave the room. If I know the Beast, he'll get suspicious and call Ray so he can prowl around the building. When he's on the top floor, Karl will unlock the door. If we're lucky one of the boys will——"

"I understand, Hal," Melanie interrupted. "But it sounds too fantastic."

"Let's go right now, Mrs. Halder," urged Harold.

Melanie, feeling slightly foolish, called a taxi. When they arrived, Harold took over. He led Melanie through a back lane into the physics building where the janitor was waiting. Karl, an old man with a martial mustache, reported that Lattau already had asked in Dr. Ray. Karl and Harold, it was agreed, would call Melanie when Lattau was on the top floor, and it would be her job to rush up and "make a big scene," as Hal put it.

The two crept upstairs. The building was very quiet. After a while she became aware of the acrid stench of chlorine gas oozing from above. Then there were heavy steps walking down the stairs, stopping, starting up again, and finally disappearing upstairs. Probably Lattau, patroling the building. To Melanie there was something humiliating in her waiting there in the janitor's dark basement. A righteous anger overcame her, filling her so completely that her fingertips began to tingle.

"Mrs. Halder!" This was Hal's voice. Melanie dashed up two flights—she never knew how fast—and suddenly found herself in the amphitheater, Harold and Karl at her side. The green fumes were so thick that at first she couldn't distinguish anything. She heard the boys coughing, and then out of the fumes there emerged the figure of a young man with spectacles—Dr. Ray—vainly trying to stop the smoke which billowed out of a contraption on the desk. Then she saw the boys, sitting far apart from each other. There was Will, doubled over, near the window. Next to her, near the entrance, a fat boy—probably André—had his face turned to the wall, retching miserably.

"What is this, madam?" said Dr. Ray, but Melanie had rushed

to Willy and thrown open the window next to his seat. Karl and Hal followed her, jerking open all the windows. Melanie took Willy's hand and he followed her toward the door, stumbling and coughing. When he saw André, he stopped, his face turned ashen. He tried to fight it, but his body began to heave and forced him to vomit.

"I'll help him," said Hal, who suddenly appeared at her side. She let Willy go and turned to Dr. Ray, who had been talking to her without her even noticing it.

"You have no right to come in here, madam. I'm awfully sorry about this, but I must insist. Professor Lattau will be very upset."

Melanie walked past him without bothering to answer. There, in the door, stood Lattau, gripping Hal and preventing him from taking Will away. Before she really knew what she was doing, she had wrenched Lattau's hand off the boy's arm and pushed Hal toward the washroom. The smoke had gone by then, although the choking smell still hung in the room.

"Leave this room at once," Lattau began, his eye twitching in a hysterical wink, but Melanie didn't let him finish.

"You'll pay for this, Professor," she shouted, and she didn't care how loud her voice sounded or how shrill. She didn't need to "make a big scene"; she was full of holy wrath and nobody was going to stop her.

"Don't think you'll get away with this. Director Bruhn will hear of it today and so will all the teachers in the school. You could have killed the boys."

"You had no right to come here," Lattau shouted back at her, but Melanie simply laughed in his face, and he began retreating toward the dais.

"No right? That's priceless. But you had a right to poison your pupils. That's what the school pays you for, no doubt. A fine teacher you are."

Lattau opened his mouth but no sound came. Melanie knew that this time she was the stronger. The bully was beginning to cringe. Her head was clear now; the first flush of anger had gone and she measured her words carefully. The boys were staring at her. She recognized André, the fat boy, and the blond one must be Pueschel, looking ridiculously like his Wagnerian mother.

"Let's get this straight. I can have you barred from every school in the country. You went too far and you know it. Just try to deny it. We have three witnesses: me, the janitor, and Harold."

"So it was Petersen who hid in the building," Lattau said. "I'll see to it that he gets properly punished."

"If you start anything I shall sue you. Director Bruhn wouldn't relish having this trial in every paper in Frankfurt. Your career

70

will be finished. One false move and I'll send a report to Director Bruhn tonight, registered mail."

The boys had gathered around her, Hal holding Will, who stood in the doorway, an expression of unconditional admiration on his face.

"Go home, children," said Melanie. The boys obeyed silently, bowing to her before they left and not looking at the professor.

Melanie and Hal, with Willy between them, followed. Professor Lattau had covered his twitching face with his hands while Dr. Ray busied himself with the apparatus.

Hal managed to grab a cab in no time. The driver raced through Bockenheimer Strasse whose plane trees, laden with healthy green leaves, swaggered in the breeze. Willy took a deep breath. He looked first at Melanie, then at Hal, on his other side, and said: "I'm hungry. Can Hal have a bite with me, Ma?"

Melanie's eyes met Hal's for an instant. She saw in them a maturity far beyond his years, a complete understanding and an acceptance of the fact that he was just as responsible for Willy as she, and always would be. It was as if for a fleeting moment Hal and she were united, with Hal her equal and as near to her as anyone could be.

She covered her eyes. Her arms and legs were tired, as if she had been swimming for hours in a heavy surf.

"Of course Hal can have something to eat with us," she said, hoping the boys wouldn't notice her shaky voice. "How about some apple pie?"

"Apple pie would be swell," Willy said.

9. THE LAST TWO WEEKS UP UNTIL SUM-
mer vacation—the month of July—Professor
Lattau treated the Lower Tertia with remarkable indulgence. Not
once did he shout; not once did he threaten. In the written examination Willy received a "sufficient-to-good"—an unprecedented
event. One afternoon Lattau's former victims—the "Amphi-
Brothers" as they called themselves—André, Duester, Pueschel,
and Pleimes, invited Willy and Hal to celebrate their liberation at
André's house. The whole meeting abounded in noisy good fellowship, heightened by the enormous amount of hot chocolate and
cake served by Mrs. André. Willy successfully pretended to share
their spirit. He wanted to forget the months of humiliation as fast
as possible.

The party ended with the "Amphi-Brothers" composing a letter
of thanks to Mrs. Halder which even Willy had to sign. The letter
and the raucous behavior of his mates who cheered the event as if
their football team had scored a big game made Willy quite uneasy.

On the first vacation day he discussed it with Hal during one of
the endless walks of which they had grown very fond. They
reached the conclusion that the others had been just as much
frightened by Lattau as Willy, but that they had never realized how
scared they were.

"You took it all too hard," Hal explained further while they
were walking toward the Nidda River for a swim, "just as you take
everything too seriously. Your skin isn't thick enough."

Willy turned this over in his mind during the following weeks
which he spent at the Petersen farm. Usually the Halders had gone
away in July to some mountain resort, but this year they couldn't
afford it. In a way, Willy was sorry, but during the long vacation
weeks that followed he forgot about it because he began to enjoy
life again.

When he awoke in Mrs. Petersen's enormous old-fashioned
guest bed he sometimes felt like a train coming out of a narrow,
dark tunnel into the light. He remembered a colored picture in his
geography book, showing a long train emerging from the Gotthard
tunnel into the overwhelmingly fancy Italian landscape, all blue

72

sky and super-green trees. This, somehow, summed it up. The days had lost their threat. Monday, Wednesday, Thursday—the amphitheater days—were ordinary days now, at his disposal, to be used for swimming, hiking, reading—whatever he pleased.

Often the two boys got up early. Willy never failed to notice how different this was from getting up early for school. The alarm clock rang at the same time; there was a short instant when Willy, still half asleep, felt the familiar dread in the pit of his stomach; then came the blissful moment when, fully awake, he became aware that this was Cronberg, summer, vacation. He was getting up now because he wanted to, because he and Hal had planned some trip, not because he was forced to. Those two "seven o'clocks" should have different names. Time, he pondered while washing, had many faces. Today, it was like a friend bringing a present. Yet, even so, it was baffling. It belonged to the many problems Willy recently had come to consider urgent without finding a solution.

Mrs. Petersen was calling from downstairs: breakfast was ready. Hal wanted to know why, in heaven's name, he was dawdling when they were going swimming near Koenigstein.

Later on Willy had to postpone his speculations on the riddle of time because it was quite a steep climb up to the old fortress, Koenigstein. Willy, who recently had developed a craze for castles and ruins, started exploring the fortress thoroughly. Hal took out his pad and began sketching. The fortress was easy to get on paper. Yet Hal didn't want it to look too forbidding, as most fortresses looked in sketches.

The trees sprouting out of the stone masses, the even curve of the surrounding hills, the greenery growing on the rocks, gave it an almost contented air, as if in the long run of centuries the ruins had become reconciled to their fate. They fitted into the Taunus landscape with its round-shouldered mountains, merging into each other gradually. There were no sharp lines in the flat land either, where orchards alternated with wheat fields. Every inch was put to use. It was an old landscape, without harshness or violence.

Hal, without being conscious of it, was now trying to get some of this feeling on paper. After a while he noticed two people watching him. Two boys, an older and a younger one, in short corduroy pants and open shirts, were looking over his shoulder.

"We didn't mean to disturb you," said the older one, "but it's wonderful to see the fortress come out on your pad. My name is Gerhard Roden, this is Harry, one of our 'Cubs,' We are the Hamburg section of the *Wandervogel* and we're on our 'big hike.' Say, where can we find a good hayloft?"

Hal had seen the Wandervogel, the "Hiking Birds," before. With

73

guitars and pitch pipes they used to march through Cronberg every summer, wearing short pants and open shirts. They had always stirred his old desire to go to remote places and countries.

When Willy returned from his exploration, Hal introduced him to the Wandervogel. The troop gathered around Hal and Willy, and Hal led them to his favorite swimming hole, on a peninsula in the Nidda River. Gerhard Roden, the oldest one, was responsible for the whole troop, though each of the bands and packs had its own sub-leader. Altogether there were twenty-five of them, all healthy-looking, and all bathing without trunks. It was one of their principles, Gerhard explained, as he stretched out next to Hal and Willy, to let the whole body soak in the healing rays of the sun.

Hal began asking questions about where the troop had been, and after a while Willy recognized in his face the rapturous expression he had worn whenever they played their imaginary traveling game at the station. Yet Willy couldn't share Hal's enthusiasm, and the afternoon was somehow spoiled. He didn't say much when Hal led the troop back to Cronberg and installed them in a neighbor's barn.

In the evening Hal begged Gerhard to tell him more about the movement. While listening to Gerhard's persuasive, slightly reedy voice, Willy realized that Gerhard was out to make them join and that Hal was already won over.

He left the two sitting in the orchard and went to bed early. Before he fell asleep he recognized he was jealous, and that he was afraid Gerhard and his troop might steal Hal. He made up his mind to join the Wandervogel if Hal wanted him to. He would pretend to be as enthusiastic as necessary and always keep from Hal the wish that Gerhard and his horde had never appeared.

During the remaining vacation weeks Hal talked a great deal about the Wandervogel. He began organizing longer trips to the more remote parts of the Taunus so that they often stayed away from Cronberg overnight. While Hal sketched the decrepit castles in which the region abounded, Willy wandered around, talking to the farmers, trying to get a hayloft for the night. He learned to imitate the backwoods dialect, full of obsolete expressions.

Willy tried hard to enjoy these trips as much as possible because there weren't many days left. One part of him enjoyed them. The other part, the other Willy, was waiting for Hal to bring up the question of their joining the Wandervogel.

Hal didn't broach the subject until the last day, an unusually hot and humid afternoon when they had gone swimming to a remote spot in the woods. Hal took off his bathing trunks—he had started this only recently—and remarked: "Feels much better without them. Healthy too." Willy, recognizing echoes of Gerhard Roden, hesitated, not only because of his opposition to the Hiking Birds, but because he had recently grown some dark wisps of hair on the lower parts of his body while Hal's was still smooth, with only some faint reddish down. Hal went into the water and after a while Willy took off his trunks, closed his eyes, and let the sun burn his back.

"Now," said Hal, returning and showering a rain of cool drops over Willy, "let's face it. Why don't you want to join the Wandervogel? You have something against them. I know you have, you can't fool me."

"I have nothing against them," Willy lied, "but they seem so stuck up." This Hal denied vehemently, and they argued over it all afternoon. Finally they reached a compromise. Since the summer was almost over and there was little hiking done in winter, they would delay everything until next spring.

"Of course they have their 'nest evenings' in the winter," Hal said, "when they learn songs and play the guitar and such things. But I won't go there now if you promise to think it over till spring."

Willy agreed. He gazed off into the landscape simmering quietly under the heat. The high poplar trees lining the river looked like exclamation points. And while his eyes followed the stream which ran in "S" curves toward the horizon, he was suddenly seized by an overwhelming melancholy. This was summer's end, the end of the long vacation; next Monday school would start, five hours a morning, six days a week.

"Perhaps Lattau won't even be back," Hal said, putting a wet arm over Willy's neck. "Relax, Willy. You're tense as a bowstring."

When Willy didn't answer, but lay very still, he began massaging Willy's taut neck muscles. "It was a wonderful summer, Will, wasn't it?"

"A wonderful summer, Hal," Willy repeated, and the tears started to well up in him.

Professor Lattau, according to an official bulletin on the school blackboard, had resigned "due to ill health." Instead there appeared Richard Hagen, a twenty-nine-year-old substitute teacher, slim, dark-haired, and quick of movement, who won the Lower Tertia's approval with his first lesson. He was a graduate of the Berlin Central Institute of Education and Instruction, the center of Germany's progressive education movement, the "Resolute School Reformers," and decried as "radical" by Director Bruhn and every nationalistic teacher.

The Resolute School Reformers, among other things, advocated a new policy toward the pupils. If a pupil was deficient in one field but made up for it by accomplishments in another, he, or she, should be treated with understanding. This the young teacher tried to explain to his new charges.

75

"A curriculum should not be a straitjacket," he said. "If someone is very bad in drawing, perhaps he is good in physics. Let me tell you something which I'm sure you didn't expect a teacher to admit. There are some people with almost no talent for math. They are math-blind. The same with music. I knew fellows who couldn't tell the difference between Beethoven's Fifth and 'Yes, We Have No Bananas.' "

The Lower Tertia laughed, and Hal nudged Willy under the bench.

"I'll try to make everything as simple as possible," Hagen went on. "If I find someone with very little talent for math, he must simply do the best he can. He can make up for it in other subjects. This doesn't mean you can loaf here. Don't get that idea. You need math for everything. Does one of you know today's dollar quotation?"

Oscar von Rainer knew it. "Ninety-eight million marks," he said.

Mr. Hagen said it was 98,850,000, and began to tell them some details of the inflationary process, interspersing it with mathematical problems as they occurred in every household. To Willy, he was a revelation. He didn't act like a teacher but like a friend of the family. Still, Willy often stumbled over questions which Hal and most of the others answered without the slightest delay.

One day in September Hagen told Willy to wait for him afterward. When the Lower Tertia had filed out he asked Willy whether the lessons were too complicated for him. Willy, his voice breaking several times, answered that everything mathematical was tough but that geometry, which they had just started, was a bit easier because "one could see things." The young teacher then told him that the main thing was to have no fear.

"Once you're afraid of it you have what we call a block," he told Willy. "I think you are one of the real cases; that is, you have very little talent for math. Any time you get stuck, come to me. Together we'll lick it."

When Willy told Hal, who had waited outside, Hal said, "I've heard two things about Hagen. Number one, he was one of the first Wandervogel in Frankfurt. Kurt Renner told me. He's leader of the troop. That's why Hagen is such a swell guy. And second, he sometimes has to go for days without a meal."

Willy couldn't believe it.

"I know it from Kurt Renner. Since Hagen is a substitute teacher, his salary comes late. By the time he gets it, it isn't worth a thing. He could use some of André's fat."

During dinner that night Willy mentioned Hagen's situation, but Melanie signaled him with her eyes and he began talking quickly about something else. Without ever having been told, he knew that

76

Father mustn't be bothered with anything unpleasant during dinner. The dinner was skimpy, but Father wasn't paying any attention to it anyhow. Father also had failed to notice that Mother didn't wear her sapphire ring any more. Willy knew it had gone to Erwin Duester, like so many of their possessions.

Countless small incidents had begun to open his eyes to the gruesome battle Melanie and so many other people were fighting. He remembered Mother's whispered morning conversations with Erwin, and the Duester trucks carrying away so many things. He remembered how he and Anna had taken a full bag of thousand-mark bills to the grocer to get sardines and a loaf of gray bread.

Since Melanie avoided talking about it, Willy had pumped Big Anna, who saw no reason to hide anything. She hated Erwin. Listening to her, it seemed to Willy as if school and everything to do with it sank away, descending slowly through a trapdoor just as the witch had disappeared in the afternoon performance of *Hänsel und Gretel*. Anna was right: something was wrong in a world in which Mother had to sell the things she loved and Richard Hagen went hungry.

Willy was discovering what he called "the enormous world," the realm outside, which had been obscured by the school up to now. He was happy that Hal understood the difference between the "enormous world" and their own. Only Hal didn't worry about it, while Willy came back to it again and again.

Since there was no amphitheater any more, he often went shopping with Melanie. He enjoyed it. He saw her sometimes as a new person, almost a stranger; yet, at the same time, he felt closer to her. He watched her save and scrape and fight—the money for the parlor was gone and Melanie was living on the gulden Mr. Bombach had paid for Grandmother Pallavant's portrait, whose surrender, in the end, she couldn't avoid.

One late afternoon in September, as Willy was opening the door for Dr. Halder's patients because Melanie and Big Anna were out shopping, the mailman appeared with a registered letter from the Frankfurt Creditbank. The mailman let him sign for it.

"Seems to be for you, anyhow, Master Halder," he remarked. The envelope was addressed to Mrs. Melanie Halder and underneath in thin type was written: re account W. Halder.

Willy was curious. Father and Mother usually did business with the National Bank. Why now a letter from the Creditbank on his behalf? To his annoyance, the patients kept him running all afternoon. Only long after dinner, when Theodor had left to lecture a women's club on one of his pet subjects, "Uncooked Food and Its Nutritional Value," did Willy have a chance to approach Melanie about the letter.

77

He saw at once that she was trying to dodge the subject. She busied herself in the kitchen cleaning shelves while making conversation about Shakespeare.

"I think we'll take you to one of the plays," she said. "You're old enough."

"All right, Mother," Willy said, not to be diverted. "What about the Creditbank letter?"

"Just a bank statement," said Melanie.

"Come on, Mother. I'm not a baby any more. One day you'll have to tell me anyhow, so why not now?"

Melanie went into the living room. It was almost dark outside; the garden below sent a chill through the open window. The air smelled of autumn. Melanie settled down in her armchair and took the letter out of her sewing bag. This—Willy had gathered long ago—was her hiding place. Everything Father wasn't supposed to see she hid among the socks and the balls of colored wool.

"All right, Will," Melanie said. "I guess you're old enough to be told about our finances."

"But I do know," he interrupted eagerly. "I know about the chairs and Grandma's picture and how it all went to Bombach."

"This concerns you," Melanie said in such a low voice that the boy could hardly understand her. "You and your future. Your grandfather George Pallavant left a trust fund for you. He wanted you to study in Paris and London as he did. The money would be yours the moment you finished school. I was to tell you then, not before. He made me what they call executor of the trust. He left you fifty thousand marks—enough to finish your studies. Nobody can touch a trust fund, or so Grandfather George thought, and I believed it too. Here." She handed Willy the letter, taking up a bit of sewing so he couldn't see her face.

"We sincerely regret to inform you," the Creditbank began, "that due to circumstances beyond our control we no longer can carry the trust fund for Wilhelm Halder set up by Mr. George Pallavant. The expenses attendant to administering a fund of 50,000 marks are much too high in proportion to the present value of the capital. We are herewith forwarding to you one million marks, since we have no banknotes of smaller denomination." A million-mark bill was enclosed. Willy glanced at the envelope: the canceled stamp was worth four million marks!

Melanie took the letter back. She had been crying. It must mean a great deal to her, much more than to him. He had lost a fund of which he had known nothing, and since he was used to millions and billions, fifty thousand seemed very little. He wasn't going to worry, and Mother mustn't, either. He lit the small lamp on her sewing table and said:

78

"You'll spoil your eyes, Mother, sewing in this light."

Since Melanie didn't answer but kept on with her stitches, he put his arm around her shoulder and went on: "I'll go to Paris and London anyhow, Mother. We'll find a way. That trust fund—it doesn't hurt me. I would've had it when I got out of school. That's four and a half years off. I can't even imagine how things will be in two years, when I'm in Lower Secunda."

Melanie had stopped sewing. Her shoulders relaxed under his hand. Standing near her, he felt stronger, for once, more sure of himself than he ever had during a talk with Mother. There was an urge rising in him to protect her, to fight for her. It filled him with confidence and pride. It seemed as if the difference in their ages didn't count any more. The moment held a special importance which he felt strongly but could not quite express. Mother sitting there, the white strands in her hair catching the light, her face bent over her sewing: he knew he would remember this for years to come because he was conscious, terribly, and stunningly conscious of himself, of the ridiculous fact that this was he, Willy, and this was Mother, who looked too weary for any more fighting.

"Don't frown, Will," said Melanie. "You look like a grownup if you do that. Although, for that matter, you almost are."

She put the letter away in the sewing table and without discussing it they both knew that Theodor was not to be told about it.

In November the miracle happened. The Rentenmark was born, one billion marks equaling one rentenmark. Neither Melanie nor any of her friends understood why, all of a sudden, money had regained its value. Of course this "stabilization" left the Halders with no capital or savings. Millions of other German families, formerly comparatively well off, found themselves in the same situation, but they were all willing to accept the new green bills. Since the country as a whole believed in the new rentenmark, so the experts explained afterward, the stabilization worked.

There was a desperate struggle back to normalcy. Most people praised Dr. Hjalmar Schacht as the savior, the wizard who, with a stroke of his wand, had dammed the waters and restored solid ground. To Willy and Hal, Dr. Schacht made a quite incongruous figure as a savior because he always wore an old-fashioned stiff collar and his features had no more warmth than a cash register. Hal made a caricature of Schacht shortly before Christmas. Willy showed it to his father one night during dinner and to his amazement Dr. Halder was delighted with it.

"It's too bad," Theodor said, "that fox Schacht is getting all the credit. Of course after that business in Munich anything can happen."

"I haven't read the *Frankfurter Zeitung* for four weeks," Melanie apologized. "I was too busy figuring out how many zeros in a trillion. What's going on in Munich?"

"Gerhard Pueschel says great things have happened in Bavaria," said Willy. Pueschel's tales had sounded like the adventure yarns by the prolific Karl May whose books he devoured, though he knew they were trash.

As Theodor unfolded the story, Willy didn't quite understand all of it. He was unfamiliar with the different parties, the split groups, the official and not-official Reichswehr troops, et cetera.

First, there were the governments: the official one in Berlin, led by Dr. Gustav Stresemann who, Theodor said, was basically a good man but up against overwhelming odds. His Reichswehr Minister, Von Seekt, had trouble with government number two, the Bavarian one in Munich, led by the ultra-conservative Chancellor von Kahr and the head of the Bavarian branch of the Reichswehr, General von Lossow. These two had declared themselves independent of the Berlin Government.

"We are the real executors of the German people's will," they simply said.

It was pure mutiny, of course, but they had powerful support. The Bavarian Reichswehr, Dr. Halder explained, like many other Reichswehr groups, contained special "black" regiments, fanatical young gangsters not officially recognized as Reichswehr soldiers, but paid by the Reichswehr, nevertheless. They all belonged to the Racist party or some similar split group.

"Never mind party labels," Dr. Halder said. "They change them every week."

The Bavarian Reichswehr, incited by the "black" cadres, had plans. First they would march in and overthrow the two neighboring states, Saxony and Thuringia, in which the liberal and left-wing parties held the majority. Then they would march to Berlin. In a desperate move, the Berlin authorities forced the two left-wing governments to resign—they had no choice, thought Dr. Halder— and thus removed any pretext for the Bavarians to march in. This upset the radicals greatly. The Berlin Racist leaders rushed to Bavaria to discuss a general uprising with the two Munich leaders: old General von Ludendorff, the brains of the German General Staff during World War I, and a Bohemian named Adolf Hitler, founder of another split movement called, at the moment, the National Socialist Workers' party.

Now came the feud within the ultra-rightist camps—quite a disgusting episode. The raffish elements, led by Hitler and his deputies, Goering, Frick, Roehm, and the inevitable Hess, tried a regular putsch. During a meeting, called by Kahr and Lossow

80

in the popular Buergerbraeu Keller, Hitler and some of his troopers occupied the hall and blackmailed Kahr and Lossow into forming a new Bavarian government including Hitler. Both Kahr and Lossow swore a solemn oath of allegiance to this new regime. The moment they were free and out of danger they double-crossed the National Socialists, who, the next day, staged a big parade. Lossow's Reichswehr troops fired on the marchers. Some people were killed; Hitler hid himself, the others fled, and the revolution was off. The Buergerbraeu putsch was laughable, Theodor concluded, but the strength of these well-armed black Reichswehr and Racist troopers was nothing to laugh at.

"Where did Hitler hide and what happened to Kahr and the Bavarian general?" Willy wanted to know.

Dr. Halder shrugged his shoulders. "It's not clear. They arrested Hitler, Hess, Ludendorff, and the others later on. They didn't do anything to Kahr and Lossow, probably because the Reichswehr bigwigs said they had, after all, 'saved Bavaria.' I think old General von Ludendorff will be acquitted."

"He's a madman," Melanie said resolutely. "Mrs. Sigbert showed me a magazine he and his wife publish in which he says one should abolish the Christian religion and start a kind of Wotan cult. I think he belongs in an insane asylum."

"So do the Hitler people, the Racists, and all the others," Theodor said heatedly. "But who's going to put them there? Just picture our party making such a proposal. The brave and honored Marshal Ludendorff! The great leader of the world war, the friend of good old Hindenburg! We could never put it through."

"Phew! That's even tougher than math," Willy said, getting up. "But I'll show Pueschel what I think of his Munich heroes."

After Christmas the Lower Tertia had started Latin. A new teacher, Dr. Preiser, drilled them in the various declensions and conjugations. He was an old man of astonishing vigor. He blew up easily, scolded, thundered, drove them mercilessly during the twelve sessions per week. Professor Preiser did not belong to the Resolute School Reformers, like young Hagen, and at first Willy found him choleric and gruff. Every day he introduced new difficulties, calling the class blockheads, fools, morons, if they didn't catch on at once. He treated those who, like Willy, showed a special talent for Latin, particularly rough.

"Whoever fails in the Easter examinations must repeat the Lower Tertia," he warned them when they stumbled over some new rule such as the use of the "absolute ablative."

To this he added one day: "Do you realize that repeating a class means you have to study all that old stuff again?"

81

Willy, slightly surprised at this new note, looked up. The professor's green eyes twinkled for a second, and in a flash of recognition Willy realized that the choleric manner, the scolding, the invective were an act, put on to make them work. Hal agreed: Preiser was a good egg.

When the feared Easter examinations arrived, the written problems in Latin, prepared not by Professor Preiser but by Director Bruhn, seemed surprisingly easy. Almost the whole Lower Tertia—with the exception of Duester and Pueschel—succeeded in doing competent work. Willy received an "Excellent" in Latin which more than balanced his low mark in mathematics—young Hagen graciously called it "Barely Passing." Professor Preiser, so the principal told them in an end-of-term speech before the Easter vacation, was going to be their main teacher during Upper Tertia next year. He would take over Latin, history, and German.

During this winter of Latin frenzy Willy and Hal had never discussed their agreement concerning the Wandervogel. Willy knew that Hal had been approached by their local leader, Kurt Renner, a medicine student at Frankfurt University. On the other hand, Hal had been busier than ever drawing and caricaturing. Whenever Willy went out to Cronberg he found him sketching. Hal also tried out different woods for different sorts of carvings, and his collection of animals, heads, and statues had steadily grown. Hal, it appeared, was too preoccupied to remember the Wandervogel. As it turned out, Willy was completely mistaken.

82

10. THE DAY AFTER EASTER HAL INVITED Kurt Renner out to Cronberg and together they persuaded Willy to come along on a "tryout hike" with the troop. Willy and Hal had to prove their worthiness: one couldn't join the Wandervogel the way one joined a bowling club. Because of the uncertain Easter weather they would undertake only a short ten-day hike. Kurt Renner, a skinny nineteen-year-old, with the features of a fanatic child and a crew haircut, told them they needn't buy any clothing.

"We don't care for uniforms," Kurt Renner said. "We are a unit, spiritually and emotionally. Uniforms smack of regimentation. The Wandervogel was born out of rebellion against regimentation." He sounded sincere, Willy thought, but a little flowery and conceited.

Melanie would have liked Willy to stay home but she raised no objections and even went shopping with them. In a secondhand store they bought two knapsacks, two cooking pots, and other camp utensils. On her own, she added a first-aid kit from Theodor's cabinet and needles and thread, although, she remarked, she couldn't picture any boy sewing on a button properly.

Since from the start of the trip all the boys accepted Willy and Hal as equals without displaying any signs of considering themselves superior, they soon felt thoroughly at home. When the train reached the drowsy village of Schwalbach, Willy had almost forgotten that he hadn't wanted to come along. But not completely.

During the whole trip he experienced a strange feeling of cleavage within him, a sensation of being two people at once. The first time this had happened was in the Golden Pheasant when he and Duester had sneaked up the stairs to watch the sailor and the woman: then, one part of him was acting while the other denied it, insisting it was not really happening.

This time, while Willy wandered along dusty roads and through endless forests, Number One, as he was tempted to call him, was enjoying himself thoroughly, while Number Two was observing everything, including the actions of Number One, with a critical eye, analyzing and frequently disapproving. Often, particularly when Willy was tired, Number Two faded. On other occasions Willy found himself carried away by a view: a valley, unveiling itself abruptly to display a flexible, silvery ribbon of water, flanked by blue mountains and running toward the spires of a half-ruined castle, unearthly and magical and beckoning from the distance. Then, too, Number Two kept silent as if not to spoil the moment.

Hal was happily sketching the scenery whenever there was a moment of rest. He also turned out to be an experienced outdoor cook. The troop's admiration seemed to flatter Hal, who was equally efficient in the preparation of complicated meat stews or simple pancakes.

Willy made no attempt to cook, and the members of his pack didn't insist. He was convinced they gave him a bad mark, but they never said a word and were quite pleased when Willy, after the third day, had learned the words of their songs. The Wandervogel did a great deal of singing, usually in the evening while sitting around the fire wrapped in blankets and huddled together for warmth. Willy was pleased to discover that he had a very good memory for both melodies and lyrics. Although his voice was still rough in spots, he managed to handle it by singing harmonizing higher or lower notes when he couldn't reach the proper ones. His pack leader, a dark-haired, taciturn youth called Ferdinand Rohn—Ferdy for short—was the musical leader and conductor. However, both he and Kurt made it a point to emphasize that nobody, not even the leader, had any "post" in the Wandervogel: everything was done by consent and the free will of the group.

One night when they had reached the Rhine near Ruedesheim, Kurt made a speech. He looked more ascetic than ever, with the shadows and lights dancing over his face.

This fire ceremony, he began, was a time of heart searching, of communion with nature and one's self. The movement was not afraid of emotions. On the contrary! It was born out of emotions, of rebellion against the stifling society in which Germany's youth was forced to live. It was born out of mutiny against the spirit of money-making, of industrialism and materialism. Let us flee, the first Wandervogel said, from offices and schoolrooms and Sunday-afternoon promenades on dreary main streets. Youth must discover itself, live its own life.

He paused for a moment. Willy, recalling some of his own Sunday afternoons, found himself listening almost against his will. Kurt was speaking especially for his and Hal's benefit, so much was clear; but why did he use such a heavy ceremonial tone? One of the boys threw new twigs on the fire, and Kurt went on.

What the grownups couldn't understand, was that the Wander-

84

vogel had no written program, that they didn't go wandering through the land to learn woodsmanship or the names of flowers and animals. They rediscovered the old songs, long forgotten because of the cheap music-hall ditties so popular with the common herd. Yes, the Wandervogel were an élite, the best of the land.

Resenting the mechanization of modern times, they turned to the ancient Germany, its castles, its treasures. They felt akin to the mercenaries, the soldiers of the past, who had roamed the country, sleeping in the woods, fighting, living off the land. Soon their songs were on the lips of wandering groups everywhere, songs about the Thirty-Year War, songs about the peasants and the simple pleasures of life, songs about comradeship and death on the battlefield.

Kurt gave Ferdy a sign and Ferdy, accompanying himself on his guitar, began a long ballad about a group of valiant soldiers who, some hundred years ago, had got lost in the Bohemian forests. Whenever Ferdy finished one verse, the whole troop joined in the chorus, which went something like this:

> They call us freebooters and we are hell-bent.
> We need no house. The trees are our tent.
> Grass our pillow, the earth our bed,
> Hey, farmer! The fire on your roof burns red!

After the third stanza Willy was able to sing second voice, sometimes rising above the others, sometimes diving below. Ferdy gave him an approving nod. The ballad consisted of more than ten verses—the soldiers committed feats of the most extraordinary daring—and when they had finished there followed a long silence.

Kurt then took a deep breath and started reciting a poem by Joseph von Eichendorff. Willy was struck by the verses—it was the first time a poem had said anything to him—yet he also noticed that Kurt inserted pauses where they didn't belong, and he made up his mind to study it next day to see whether he couldn't do better. Also, the longer he looked into the flames, the more drowsy he became. He struggled to keep his eyes open but several times his head fell against Ferdy's shoulder. Kurt had reached his climax, but Willy listened only with half an ear.

Away from the raffish world of commerce, free from the discipline of home and school, the Wandervogel had developed their own laws, the "inner laws of youth." Also the relationship between group and leader was something radically new. The group didn't elect its leader, he somehow grew out of it, giving and receiving complete devotion.

Kurt then launched into a hymn on "self-determination." He repeated the word over and over so that Willy, despite his drowsiness, couldn't help remembering it. The Wandervogel had proven that youth was capable of molding its own fate. The old people, the bureaucrats and moneymakers, bigshots and lawyers, had nothing to offer to Germany's youth, nothing! He ended by emphasizing the virtues which the movement had come to appreciate in boys and girls: one must be unaffected, straightforward, and responsive.

The fire had almost burned down. Willy was so tired he didn't even argue when Hal began teasing him about his falling asleep during "the ritual." When they finally went into the barn, Willy drew his blankets tightly around him, and the only thing that reached his consciousness was the clean smell of the freshly mown hay which surrounded him like an ocean.

Willy was grateful to Ferdy Rohn for taking him under his wing during the following days. Kurt seemed slightly annoyed, probably because Willy had shown no pronounced enthusiasm for the fire speech. Ferdy taught him more songs and in addition some canons and fugues by Mozart, Bach, Brahms, and "Unknown."

"You know, 'Unknown' is the greatest German composer," Ferdy joked one day as they sat at the foot of an enormous castle overlooking the Rhine. "I imagine these songs came first from the lips of some simple craftsman or soldier. Then a monk or a church musician wrote 'em down, and from some of them he made rounds. I don't believe an untrained man could compose a fugue. Do you?"

Willy agreed: only a professional man could set down a fugue. He felt tired and content. They were leaning against a stone, gazing at the Rhine below whose broad back seemed to carry the many tiny boats somewhat reluctantly. The troop had walked for miles and miles that day, having gotten up at four in the morning. This hike had been particularly tough, so Kurt explained later, to find out whether the two guests "could take it." Willy had made it by sheer force of energy, and Kurt had congratulated him on his endurance. "Real Wandervogel material," he called him. Hal seemed to be able to walk forever without getting tired. Right now he was sitting on Willy's other side, his pad on his knees.

It had dawned on Willy during these days that Hal was already one with the group. He had fulfilled his dream—the old game they had played so often in Frankfurt's Main Station. True enough, he wasn't traveling to London or Hammerfest, and they weren't riding the Orient Express. Yet each time they reached another village, Hal's enthusiasm rose anew. During the day Willy kept close to Ferdy, and in the evenings he was so tired that not once had he "mulled things over" with Hal.

As he now turned toward him, away from Ferdy, Hal, as if struck by the same impulse, got up and said: "Come on, Will. Let's go to the other side of the castle and see if we can get a glimpse of France. See you later, Ferdy."

When they had settled down away from the others, Hal put down his pad. "All right, Will, tell me. Do you like the Wander-vogel or don't you? They like you, that much I know. To tell the truth, I'm having a wonderful time. I like seeing places, sleeping in haylofts, and everything. Most of the kids are nice too. What about you?"

Will tried to be honest, but he was confused. Contrary to his expectations, he had enjoyed the trip. He loved the early mornings in the woods, the quiet of the forests, the smell of the hay in the lofts, the lush vineyards stretched over the hills along the Rhine. At times he was one of them, and it was wonderful to lose oneself in their unity. At other times, the "other one," Number Two, was watching and disapproving. Number Two disliked Kurt's oratory. It was always something ancient about which Kurt raved, ancient songs, ancient heroes, ancient history. Kurt loathed industry with a personal fervor. The only people he seemed to value were sol-diers, explorers, and artists. To Willy, this was somewhat absurd.

All this he tried to take into account. Yet, since it was much too complex, he said, knowing he wasn't saying what he meant, "I like the trip, Hal, much more than I expected to. I don't like Kurt's speeches. He—well, he hates so many things and he's so grand about it."

"Never mind Kurt's speeches. Half of the time I don't even know what he's talking about. I wonder sometimes if he does. He's just giving us the old 'Wandervogel routine.' "

"What do you know about the routine?" Willy asked. It was just like Hal to ignore what he didn't like, forget it, and enjoy the rest.

"Ferdy's told me a lot about the old days," Hal said. "Don't forget, the movement is over twenty years old. Just watch the meaty farewell speech Kurt gives us tonight or tomorrow night. Don't forget there are only three days left."

"When did you talk to Ferdy? I never saw you two together."

"After you hit the hay, my friend. You know you fall asleep like a shot. Bang and out. I'm not half so tired and Ferdy's an old hand at the game. So we gab. Did Ferdy speak to you about Kurt?"

"Never. Why?"

"He did to me. The funny thing is, he doesn't like him, either. Even less than you do. And Kurt is leader!"

"Funny," Will said. Then they walked back to join the others.

After another long hike they spent the rest of the day in a village near Assmanshausen on the Rhine. It was decided they stay over-night in a youth hostel close by which was especially designed for wandering groups, and which Kurt seemed to distrust.

"Nothing like this in the old days," he remarked when they arrived. Then he added, "Still, we are responsible for all this. We started it all."

The hostel, constructed like a lighthouse, on top of a hill, had been built a year ago. It was ultra-modern, with straight white walls, a flat roof, enormous windows. The dining room was decorated with murals, depicting scenes from the Rhenish Peasants' War. Ferdy, having discovered a tinny piano, began to indulge in complicated harmonies. Soon they were singing again, sitting in the music room, the windows open, before their eyes the broad Rhine Valley over which the shadows soon started to fall rapidly.

Kurt didn't want to say much, he declared, when they had finished singing. He wanted them to remember the sunset and the Rhine Valley as it lay there before them. Twilight was the most bewitching time of the day. One of the early Wandervogel had once written to a friend: You ask me what we want? Escape from the plodding day into moor and twilight. One couldn't say it better, Kurt thought.

This hostel was new, so new it frightened him. It was too comfortable, too clean, too "at your service." Comfort was dangerous. The first Wandervogel had refused every comfort.

These days were past and, in a way, Kurt declared, this was a pity. For out of the self-immolation had been born that close-knit unity, the Wandervogel troop. The glory of Germany's past had been a fruit of sacrifice, too, and Kurt began to delve into ancient history. In spring the best young men of a Germanic tribe were elected to be killed as a tribute to some pagan god, and those chosen considered themselves honored.

Willy, listening carefully, for this was the promised "meaty" farewell speech, felt uncomfortable, and so, obviously, did Ferdy. Kurt went on praising chivalry and self-denial. It seemed to Willy that he got an almost physical thrill out of describing self-sacrifices. Why, Willy couldn't help wondering, why couldn't one go hiking without all this? Without the worship of ancient history, medieval knights, and immolation?

When Kurt paused for a moment to catch his breath, Ferdy dashed to the piano and began to play one of the troop's favorite Mozart songs. Kurt, taken by surprise, didn't attempt to continue his speech, and the boys, after a second, took up the melody. Only Kurt remained silent.

Soon they decided to turn in. For once, Willy was wide awake. Since nobody in his pack exerted any pressure about going to bed, he easily slipped out of the dormitory.

Outside the night was clear. From the surrounding forests a breeze carried the pure scent of woods. Mingled with it was the sweet smell of lilac bushes whose white candelabra shone through the darkness all down the hill. Far off, at the foot of the slope, the Rhine seemed only a glow, reflecting the timid light of the villages and the hard sparkle of the stars in a ceaseless, nervous glitter. Nearby, someone struck a chord on the guitar.

"Hallo, Will," Ferdy said. "Where's Hal?"

"Asleep," Will answered. "It's wonderful up here."

Ferdy began playing some intricate harmonies.

"Look, Ferdy," Willy said, with a determined effort, "why must Kurt spoil everything? Why the hell doesn't he stop making these speeches? Most of them go over the kids' heads anyhow. I liked the trip. Honest. I thought I wouldn't, but I did. If only Kurt would stop his rantings about sacrifices and the early days."

"The trouble is," Ferdy interrupted, "the early days were quite different. Believe me. I've been a Wandervogel since I was nine. My older brother, Heinz, was one, too, under Richard Hagen. No speeches of this kind for them, no, sir."

"Why? What happened? If Kurt is making them for our bene-fit——"

"He doesn't make them for your benefit, even though he wants Hal and you to join. No, his ideas are new, I guess. You see, the old Wandervogel split into many groups after the war. We belong to the New Wandervogel. The old troops really had no program but hiking and being by themselves. They wouldn't accept girls, either. Today, every group's trying to get up a platform. Look, Will, are you going to come along on the next week-end hike? Are you going to join us? Incidentally, congratulations."

"On what, Ferdy?"

"You see, you forgot. It's five past midnight. Tomorrow—or today—is your birthday. Hal told me."

Willy looked at him, almost nonplused. Ferdy was right. It was his birthday and he had forgotten it completely, for the first time. At home, Mother always had awakened him with a kiss and there were presents spread out on his night table. It had been a festive day, created for him. Now, away from home, it was a day just like all the others.

"How old are you?" Ferdy asked. "And what are you going to do?"

"I'm fourteen," Willy answered, inhaling the air deeply. He recalled the long Sunday afternoons, the drudgery of school, of irregular Latin verbs, of math, the stupidity of his mates, Duester's eternal foul jokes . . .

"I think I'll come along, Ferdy," he said.

"Good." Ferdy's hand squeezed his hard. "Stick to me. I'll teach you some wonderful Bach fugues. To hell with Kurt's sermons. We'll simply ignore them."

Life these days, Willy often mused during the next months, resembled one of those modern subway stations where trains came in and left on three different levels.

First, there was Upper Tertia, very much like Lower Tertia, with twelve Latin sessions a week and plenty of history and German literature, all taught by Dr. Preiser. Willy secretly looked forward to Preiser's lesson, particularly those devoted to the drama. Whenever the teacher discussed a new play, he let the boys read and act it out as dramatically as they could. Soon Willy was established as the leading speaker and actor in Upper Tertia. Oscar von Rainer ran a close second, specializing in youthful heroes while Robbi Goldschmidt good-naturedly simpered through the female roles which nobody wanted. Often Willy memorized long stretches of classical plays so that the next day he could act without consulting the text.

Professor Preiser once slapped his back and growled: "You're a conceited ass, Halder, and don't fancy yourself as something special. But your reading is a shade less stupid than that of your dear colleagues. Stick to it."

Willy would have liked to stick to it, but the second level of his existence, his life with the Wandervogel, took all his spare time. On Saturday afternoons, weather permitting, Hal and he set out for their week-end trips, Hal with a cooking pot over his knapsack, Willy carrying his pitch pipe which by now he had learned to play rather well. Kurt had put Hal and Willy in different packs, taking Hal in his own and putting Willy into Ferdy's group. Although Willy mistrusted Kurt's motives, it turned out to be a beneficial arrangement during the next stormy months in the Wandervogel.

The third level was home. He sat down to dinner with Father and Mother, helped Melanie with her shopping, and typed the bills which Theodor was reluctant to send to his patients. At 66 Reuter Weg, everything was so much a part of him that he hardly noticed it any more—the way Big Anna sang in the kitchen, Father's stories about politics, and Mother's replies intended to put him in a better mood. Often Willy felt guilty for spending so little time at home, particularly since neither Theodor nor Melanie reproached him. Melanie had even been extremely friendly to Kurt Renner when he came calling on her one day.

On this occasion Kurt, the orator, had been rather tongue-tied, and it had dawned on Willy that Melanie didn't fit into Kurt's picture of "mothers" in general. Apparently in Kurt's mind they were all housewives, forever busy with washing and fussing about diet and such piffle. Mothers were timid hens, worrying about their brood, without any conception of the higher, the truer, the more exalted aims of the movement. Since Melanie did not once implore Kurt to see that "Willy doesn't catch cold," asked none of the meaningless "mother questions" for which Kurt had prepared such soothing answers, this seemed to leave him demoralized. As Willy saw him to the door, Kurt said:

"Your mother is remarkable. Really, you're a lucky guy. In one way." He stared at Willy. "It's dangerous too," he added, "dangerous for you, Will. Good-by. See you Saturday, four-fifteen." He slammed the door.

Dangerous? Mother? It took Willy some time to figure out why. Then, putting himself in Kurt's place, trying to think in his twisted manner, he understood. Kurt needed friction, something against which to chafe; the movement had been born out of opposition—and Melanie offered him none. There was something unhealthy about this, something over-relentless, and it made Willy uneasy.

He mentioned it to Hal before they went to sleep during a trip in June. Hal simply waved it aside.

"Your mother just made him feel bad because his own nags at him all the time. She hates the movement and Kurt must listen to her rantings each time he comes home."

"Hm. Perhaps that's it," Willy answered, unconvinced. By now he should have learned that Hal was blind as far as Kurt's ideas were concerned. Hal didn't deny Kurt's shortcomings; yet he never bothered about Kurt's or anybody else's speeches. It hurt Willy that Hal had deserted him, leaving him alone to grope his way through what Kurt proudly called the "Wandervogel religion."

Ferdy shook his head when Willy told him about Kurt's remark.

"Remember, Will, what I said on your birthday when you decided to join us? I said we'd pay no attention to Kurt's sermons. I'm afraid I must take that back. I think Kurt is preparing something big."

"What do you mean?"

"Don't know yet. But something's in the air."

In July, during the summer vacation, the troop went on a four-week trip, the highly praised Big Hike. Kurt had prepared an ambitious program: they were to take the train south to the Alps, meet a troop from Karlsruhe at Kanderthal, a tiny village at the foot of the mountains, and then set out together on several climbing expeditions. The Karlsruhe group would consist of a boys' troop and a girls' troop, and they might do some folk dancing.

Willy was overwhelmed by the Alps. When he stepped out of the youth hostel in Kanderthal, he just stood there motionless, unable to take his eyes off them.

The mountaintops, covered with a cold white, seemed to touch the sun, and a gleaming, long glacier, like some prehistoric creature, ran down alongside the threatening mass of stone and ice. They had been there long before life existed on earth. Cold and monstrous, their hulks towered over the puny human settlements which they seemed to despise. How could the villagers endure to live forever in their shadow? It almost bordered on insolence to think of climbing the Kanderhorn, the Weatherpeak, or the Paradise Rock—Willy half-imagined the mountains would shake off any intruder.

They attempted the Kanderhorn first. After several hours of slow, wearisome climbing, the troop made a stop at a large alpine hut in the middle of a green pasture like a balcony. They were extremely tired, and the thin air made them feel slightly drunk. They stayed overnight in the comfortable lodge.

The next day the Karlsruhe group joined them on the plateau, twelve boys and seven girls. Their leader, a silver-blond, athletic nineteen-year-old named Otto Fels, introduced Willy to his group. Willy had never met any Wandervogel girls and he wondered whether they would be like the girls he knew at home, always giggling and forever busy with their faces and dresses. The Karlsruhe girls, like all those in the movement, wore no make-up, obviously paid no attention to their dress—shapeless linen tunics with wooden buttons—and acted very intense. Their leader, Trudi, a large girl with a jutting chin and blond braids wound around her head, impressed Willy as a severe disciplinarian, much stricter than either Otto Fels or Kurt. The other girls were all rather plump, forever cooking or singing. In the afternoon the girls started Part One of the "meeting ceremony."

They performed what they called "ancient Swabian folk dances," accompanied on the guitar by one of the Karlsruhe boys who, Willy discovered immediately, wasn't half so good as Ferdy and didn't have the rhythmical strength to keep the girls in line. The old Swabian dances entailed a lot of swinging around, stamping, and clapping of hands. The girls perspired visibly, often lost the beat, and after a while Willy found himself fighting an urge to laugh. Most of the girls wore numerous long chains of wooden beads which got in their way when they had to manage a fast turn. Perhaps it was the background of the motionless, inscrutable mountains which made the dancers look so incongruous. When some of the boys joined in a number announced as particularly gay, Willy caught Ferdy's eye and saw that he was equally flabbergasted. Hal had sneaked around to Willy and, for a second, opened his sketchbook. He had caricatured the dancers, giving them elephantine legs and feet.

92

Otto invited Willy to participate in a "sunrise workout," and since Willy wasn't quite sure what it was, he got up at five and went along to a place hidden from the hut by a cluster of fir trees. In no time Otto had taken off all his clothes. Completely nude, he stretched his arms toward the sun which, rising behind the peaks, turned the snow fields into a blinding and reddish glitter. While Willy hesitated, Otto began jumping up and down on his toes. His tanned body was covered with heavy muscles which moved like snakes, his shoulders jutted out like wooden planks, and he had shaved his chest.

Mechanically, Willy undressed and, led by Otto who barked short commands, joined in the exercises. The other boys seemed to find it quite natural that soon Trudi and three of her girls appeared, equally nude, and started on their sunrise workout, more lyrical in character than that of the boys.

Willy pretended not to be embarrassed at all. He couldn't help giving the girls some quick glances. Trudi, although built on large lines, had small, firm breasts and seemed to be much stronger than the other girls, who were rather loosely put together and, Willy concluded, shouldn't jump without bras. Surprisingly, their nude bodies held no particular excitement for him. He figured this was because everybody was naked and he simply couldn't think of sex while doing strenuous push-ups and knee-bends, with the stony mountains staring down on them.

Afterward Otto asked Willy to sit down for a "get-acquainted-talk." Willy plumped on the ground, covered with sweat. Otto's body seemed perfectly dry. He said:

"Don't you do this every morning?" Willy answered no, he didn't, whereupon Otto began explaining his reasons for carrying out the exercises with military promptness, praising the human body as "the most perfect instrument in the world."

"Truthful, natural relations between men and women are much easier if the two sexes get used to meeting one another in the nude," he said. "If everybody devoted himself to muscle development and body culture, Germany would be better off."

"Why?" Willy asked. He noticed that Otto had taken stock of him and next to Otto's his body looked puny. He was also conscious of several ugly red pimples on his back.

"Because the next generation, produced by better developed male and female bodies, would be healthier and more beauteous. Perhaps we would develop into a truly Nordic race."

"What does the Nordic race look like?" Willy inquired.

"Well—tall, muscular, and mostly—er—blond. This doesn't mean that dark-haired people like you can't be Nordic, Will. Don't misunderstand me."

93

Willy made a quick estimate. "About three quarters of the boys in our troop have black or brown hair. Same with your boys and girls."

Otto laughed. "Quite an intelligent kid, aren't you?"

He rose, stretching his arms toward the sky. "I wish we still worshiped the sun like those old primitive tribes," he said.

As he stood there, his eyes closed, his arms raised in a conjuring gesture toward the brilliant sun, his figure reminded Willy of something he had seen before.

"Say, Otto, have you ever been on the cover of——"

"Right you are. The last one on the April issue of *Health and Beauty*. You see, I'm an athletics instructor. Pays very little. So Trudi and I have done a lot of posing for the sports magazines. They pay handsomely. You should develop your muscles, Willy. Daily exercise for every part of the body, and you will become a perfect sample of the . . ."

"Sure, sure," Willy answered. It struck him as strange that Otto displayed such pride in having so often been photographed naked —or almost naked. The nudist magazines, Willy recalled, had flooded the newsstands during the last few years. They all pretended to teach muscle development, healthier living, or body hygiene. Their nude males and females, sitting at the dinner table or listening to music when not busy exercising, behaved as if it were the most natural thing to be nude in all situations. Some of the boys in his class bought them quite regularly, though not for daily exercises or healthier living.

"Let's go back and have breakfast," Willy said. "I'm hungry."

As they walked toward the hut, Trudi took Willy's arm. "You're not bad-looking Will, in a—well, dark way. But you're too skinny." She played with his arm muscles and for a second ran her hand down his body. "Otto is going to speak on 'You and Your Body' one of these days. You could profit by it. Of course he's a lousy speaker."

She left Willy, hurrying along with big strides. Willy wondered. What did she want? Or did he know what she meant?

The permanent camp in the Kanderthal Valley, into which they moved soon, consisted of three hay barns—one for the Frankfurt troop, one for the Karlsruhe boys, one for the girls. A clear, ice-cold brook plashed through the pastures. From the farmhouses near by they bought milk, eggs, and home-baked bread.

Whenever Willy had a chance, he sneaked away to be alone. As usual, he had struck up a friendship with a native, this time an old gnarled farmer's woman who always sat in front of her house waiting for her family to come back from the fields. She liked Willy, gave him as much milk as he wanted, although she bore no sympathy for the Wandervogel as a whole.

"Being together in the nude," she once said in her strange mountain dialect. "Boys and girls. It's a sin!"

Willy listened attentively while Grandmother Zacharias talked to him about her life. She told him almost the identical story each time, but Willy, trying to catch the particular color of her speech, never tired of listening. He also met her grandson, Seppel, a thick-set farmboy whom he taught—not too successfully—to play the pitch pipe, while Seppel told him the incredible curse words in which the Bavarian dialect abounded.

Soon the troops developed a craze for body culture, for sunrise workouts, and athletics even after dark, which disrupted the normal functioning of the camp. The Frankfurt boys began to talk constantly about their bodies, measured each other's chests, and ran around without clothes whenever possible. Many of them went for long walks with one or another of the Karlsruhe girls. In the evenings the couples held hands or the boys rested their heads in the girls' laps. Willy thought none of the Karlsruhe girls attractive. To hold hands, to put arms around each other publicly, seemed silly to him. Otto and Trudi never held hands—a fact which puzzled the Frankfurt group.

Ferdy and Willy had long since found out why: Otto loathed Trudi because she had more brains than he, and Trudi tried to incite his troop against him. It was she who suggested to Kurt that Otto give a talk on body culture. Kurt, who didn't cherish Otto's present popularity, finally persuaded him to speak to them.

It was such a clumsy gibberish that even the most ardent admirers of the body beautiful could hardly hide their snickers. Groping for words, Otto tried to tell them about the new, extravagantly beautiful Nordic race to be achieved by regular, devoted exercises. In the middle of his ramblings Trudi left the fire, accompanied by three of the older boys.

"This silly stuff about the Nordic race," Ferdy whispered to Willy, and Hal added: "Do you think I'm Nordic? After all, I'm red, not blond."

The next morning was chilly. The mountains wrapped themselves in dark clouds, and the three boys decided to skip the sunrise workout. They were alone in the camp, trying to make the wet twigs catch fire so they could prepare the morning cocoa. The water had just become lukewarm over the timid flames when, all of a sudden, there was a commotion behind the cluster of trees where the others were doing their exercises. They heard shouting and yelling, intermingled with high shrills. Willy jumped up, the others following instantly.

Before Willy's eyes there unfolded a spectacle he would never forget. The nude boys and girls, howling and shrieking, were fleeing in a disorderly scramble toward the camp, pursued by a posse of sturdy young farmers, armed with pitchforks and buckets. The farmers yelled at the retreating nudes, calling them the filthiest names they knew. They had gotten hold of a few of their clothes, holding them over their heads like banners. Some of the fleeing Wandervogel boys, protecting the screaming girls, had stumbled, and the farmers emptied their buckets over them, buckets of fresh brown manure whose pungent, evil stench soon filled the air. Although the farmhands roared and threatened, telling them to get the hell out of the valley, Willy at once realized they weren't really dangerous because whenever they got hold of a victim they just gave him some good whacks on the buttocks, dowsed him with manure, and let him go. As they came nearer, Willy saw that they were holding Otto, who was howling, and putting up a surprisingly weak fight.

Willy was seized by an irresistible fit of laughter. While the others were darting toward the barns, the farmhands stopped, held Otto in place with four pitchforks, and emptied the last and biggest manure bucket over his head. Willy, Ferdy, and Hal gripped their big pot of hot water and rushed toward them to rescue Otto. They succeeded in splashing two of the farmhands, who left Otto in his stew and turned against the three, who would have been badly battered if it hadn't been for their leader, Seppel Zacharias, Willy's pitch-pipe pupil.

Holding back his men, Seppel yelled: "Stop. These kids are all right." He turned to Willy: "Get the hell out of Kanderthal. We don't want no naked people in our village. Tell your rotten sergeant to call it quits. If you aren't out by tomorrow, we'll break up your camp and every bone in your dirty naked bodies."

He pushed Otto toward them. "Take this bundle of sh— along and this too." He threw the conquered shorts, the shoes, and the girls' underwear at them, and, mechanically, the three boys caught them. Then Seppel gathered his posse and, swinging their empty buckets and pitchforks, they sauntered leisurely away, obviously satisfied with the result of their sunrise workout.

With his big handkerchief Willy began cleaning Otto's face. When Otto opened his eyes, still sticky with the drying manure, Willy turned away, embarrassed. Otto, the crusader for the Nordic race, the owner of the perfect body beautiful, was crying.

The next day they broke up camp. Fortunately the weather had turned worse, a cold wind sweeping down from the mountains. Thus Otto and Kurt could keep up the pretense they were returning earlier because of the unreasonably cold weather. After

96

they had boarded the train the next night, Kurt, who had escaped the manure bath, told his group that, confidentially, Otto had failed as a leader.

Around midnight the Karlsruhe group left the train. Otto and his boys hardly bothered to say good-by while the girls were ostentatiously friendly. Trudi kissed Hal and several others rather ardently—more to infuriate Otto, Willy suspected, than out of passion.

The trainride to Frankfurt took all night. Most of the boys dozed on the hard wooden benches of the third-class compartments. Willy, unable to sleep, went to the open window and watched the darkened landscape rush by, forests and streams and forgotten-looking villages faintly visible under a hazy moon. The night wind stung his face but he did not care. It had been a bad summer. Perhaps he would have had a better vacation staying at home, reading the plays in Father's library, Shakespeare, Goethe, Schiller, Molière.

He began walking through the train, searching for Hal. Before he had gone far, the door of one compartment opened and Hal came out.

"A rotten Big Hike. You know, you and Ferdy and I saved Otto from being beaten up. Of course we're getting no credit for it. Trudi says we humiliated young Siegfried."

"Young Siegfried was running away. He deserved his mud pack. He probably even suspects me of having known in advance about it because of Seppel Zacharias."

"He does," Hal shouted over the rattle of the train. "Trudi said so. Aw, let 'em go hang. You know what? Last summer was much nicer. Just you and me, no trouble, no morning exercises. Trudi thinks . . ."

"What's this Trudi business, Hal? Since when?"

"Oh, I got to know her quite well." Hal grinned. "She even gave me a good-by present."

He thrust a photo into Willy's hand. Despite the dim light, Willy could distinguish the two people on it: Otto and Trudi, naked against a mountain meadow, in a position which could be an athletic exercise, a part of a dance, or an embrace. Across it was written "To Hal. In remembrance of sunny days."

"You escaped only because you're so skinny," Hal said, putting the picture into his wallet.

Willy stared at him. "Escaped what?"

"Oh, Trudi tried to make every boy up there," Hal said, while the train thundered over several crossings. "I thought you knew. She didn't like the thin kids, though."

Willy was still baffled. How could Hal be so casual about this?

97

So unconcerned? He remembered the Golden Pheasant, how shocked he was, how it was still haunting him.

"No reason to get upset," Hal said. "I know what you want to know."

When Willy didn't answer, he continued, "Yes, she did. I was one of them. First time for me but not for her. The inscription is wrong, though. It wasn't a sunny day but a cold night. If you ask me, the whole thing is greatly overrated."

"Are you going on another picnic over the week end?" Melanie asked Willy one night in September. The fall, as often in Frankfurt, was mild and sunny—a real Free City Summer, as the old people called it.

"Not a picnic, a hike, Mother," Willy corrected. "Why?"

"Father has been made a member of the Theater Committee. We'll be getting tickets regularly. We have one for Saturday night, *The Tempest.* But we can't go. Mrs. Suter-Kottlar has asked us over."

"Who's she?"

"The dramatic soprano of the opera, if that means anything to you. Well, make up your mind."

Willy decided to defy the Wandervogel. He called Hal, who declared he wouldn't go, either.

Some weeks before, Melanie had bought Willy his first suit with long pants. Saturday evening Willy put it on slowly, enjoying the knowledge that he would look quite grown-up in the blue suit, white shirt, and one of Theodor's red-and-blue neckties. When he kissed Melanie good-by, she said, smoothing his hair: "I like you much better this way than in your dirty corduroy pants. Have a nice time. And don't think I didn't notice Father's tie."

Bismarck Place, where the City Playhouse had been built around 1880, was near Reuter Weg and Willy arrived much too early. The old woman who showed him to the first seat in Loge Number 17 smiled and said:

"Here's your program, young Mr. Halder. Take a good look around. We have been repainted for Shakespeare."

Willy took a good look. The Frankfurt playhouse was all red and gold. Red plush seats, red moldings over the entrances, thick red carpets, and a gigantic red stage curtain. The walls were gilded, as were the columns holding the three balconies, the ceiling, the elaborately ornamented wall lamps, and the metal parts of the enormous, glistering Venetian chandelier—a giant version of the one Melanie once had in her green parlor. Willy—though he had almost forgotten—had been to the theater once before, *Hänsel und Gretel,* and it had made no impression on him whatsoever.

Now, from the moment he sat down he felt an inexplicable,

devouring elation. Something big was going to happen. This moment held a significance which eluded him but which, nonetheless, filled him, strong and demanding. Again and again he gazed down into the orchestra where people strolled in, quite at ease—they probably went every day. The women wore low-cut gowns, some of them held fans, and when they turned their heads, their jewels threw facets of light in Willy's eyes like signals from a lighthouse. The humming of voices grew louder; the theater was filling up. At the last moment a girl came in, out of breath.

"You're late, Miss Reger," Willy heard the old usher say.

He gave the girl a quick glance. She seemed small, with a very white skin and brown hair, cut short like a boy's. There were no other people in the loge.

He hurried through his program. What strange names! Prospero, the rightful Duke of Milan; Antonio, his brother, the "usurping Duke of Milan." What exactly was usurping? Miranda, Antonio, Gonzalo, the "honest old Counsellor," Ariel, an "airy spirit"—he wasn't sure whether a spirit was a ghost—and Caliban, a "savage and deformed slave."

Suddenly a hush descended over the theater. Slowly the lights grew dimmer while the glow from the footlights shone on the bottom of the curtain. For a moment the theater held its breath. Willy felt anything could happen now. Then a soft music set in. Majestically, the curtain rose. The music stopped. And then everything did happen. When the act was over, Willy turned to the girl beside him. He simply had to talk to someone.

"It's—beyond everything," he said, feeling a bit foolish and wiping beads of sweat off his upper lip.

The girl looked at him. "Every minute is wonderful," she said. "Could I have a look at your program?"

Will gave it to her. She asked several questions; obviously she wasn't quite certain about Prospero's and Sebastian's relation. Willy told her as well as he could.

During the last act he was conscious of her. Once or twice they whispered together. They agreed that Prospero shouldn't have let Antonio and Sebastian off so easily. What, Willy wondered, would become of Ariel now that he was released from service?

Before he knew it, the last act was over. He joined in the applause until his palms hurt.

"Do you often come to the theater?" he asked the girl. "By the way, I'm Will Halder."

"I'm Maria Reger," she said. "I know who you are. My mother is on the Theater Committee just like your father. I've been here often; it's our box. I never saw you here before, though."

"I'll be here as often as I can," he said. "Shall I take you home?"

"Thanks, but Mother is waiting for me downstairs," Maria said. "See you next week, then."

He walked home through the Eschenheimer Promenade with its every bench occupied by a couple. He had completely calmed down now—as a matter of fact he was as exhausted as after a long week-end hike. He should have a bad conscience for skipping a trip. But he hadn't. Thinking back, a surge of joy took possession of him. He would try to work in the theater; wasn't he the best reader in Upper Tertia? Could he tell Hal? Yes, Hal would understand and so would Ferdy. But Kurt? And the others in the Wandervogel? So what? He didn't care. He must see as many plays as possible, classic, modern, everything. He'd study them, line by line. Mother would give him more tickets. It would be nice, too, to see Maria again.

The following Saturday Willy gave a spirited reading of the jealous Colonel Buttler in *Wallenstein,* the echo of Shakespeare's verses still in his mind. Afterward, Dr. Preiser asked Willy to wait for him. He took Willy to his study on the second floor. It smelled of dust and bitter tobacco. The professor took out a pipe and began sending blue clouds into the room.

"Halder," he said, "I watched you just now. Let me ask you a question. Have you ever thought of a stage career?"

"Since last week," Willy answered, slightly awed by the teacher's unfamiliar mildness, "when I saw *The Tempest.*"

"Hmm. Figured something had happened. Mind you, this is between you and me. Teachers, you know, are not the boneheads you kids like to think. Don't contradict me!" He was his old blustering self again and Willy felt much more at home. "I'll tell you: the theater is a disease, and it's the toughest profession of all. At fifteen, every other kid dreams of himself as a 'dramatic actor.' You can do one thing, though. Start early. Get busy, study as many plays as you can digest. When you're through here, try to get into the Municipal Acting School. That is, if your parents'll let you. Can Petersen work with you? You know, you need some-one to work with."

"Hal lives in Cronberg."

"Right, I forgot. I'm getting feeble-minded. Ask Rainer or Gold-schmidt after you've talked to your father. Now, don't think you're going to get better marks. You'll have to work even harder since you've got more brains than these super-robots in Upper Tertia."

When Willy reported this to Melanie she said: "You're much too young to think about a profession, Will. Of course Father hopes you'll help him with his practice one day. Aren't you in-terested in medicine?"

100

"Sorry, Mother, no. I'd be as bad at it as I am at math."

"I'll talk it over with Theo," Melanie said, "but I wish you'd change your mind."

After conferring with Theodor for several weeks, Melanie told Will he was old enough to know what he was doing, and if he was set on studying plays, to go ahead. Only, she added, he was undertaking too much: homework, Wandervogel, and now this. How would he cram it all in?

As it turned out, the Wandervogel had to cancel their fall trips because the weather suddenly turned cold. Hal had informed Kurt Renner about Willy's studies and at the few "nest evenings" to which Willy went he read poetry to the group. Kurt always selected poems glorifying famous campaigns and their leaders—to Willy a rather monotonous diet. Yet he didn't argue. It gave him a chance to see Ferdy, who was studying music and working his way through the university by playing the piano in a night club. This way Willy could keep in touch with his group; also it might be good exercise to recite poems one did not like.

Oscar von Rainer simply had no time to read plays with Willy. His father planned to take him out of school after Lower Secunda and send him to Hannsberg, in Middle Germany, where Oscar's uncle had a shoe factory. Oscar didn't care for business but, he declared, they were so poor he had no choice.

"Imagine me studying Gabelsberger shorthand and bookkeeping," he said in his offhand manner. Even in his shabby blue serge suit he gave the impression of a well-groomed young man, and there was something provocatively superior about him which sometimes made Willy squirm.

However, Robbi Goldschmidt agreed to study with Willy once or twice a week after dinner or on week ends when Willy wasn't on a hike. Because of Robbi's limp, Willy took to visiting his place on Hoch Strasse, near Opern Platz.

The Goldschmidt residence was one of the oldest inhabitable houses in Frankfurt. Engraved in stone over its front entrance was the Goldschmidt family crest, two hands working the filigree of a crown. The house won Willy's heart the first day he entered: its high-ceilinged rooms, many panelled with a red-brown wood which centuries had given a soft patina; its heavy, wide staircase, mounting from the entrance hall in a sweeping arc; its small square garden around which the whole building was centered, with a stone cistern and statues. The garden gave the impression of having been transplanted from a more southern country—perhaps, Willy pondered, Prospero's Milano?—and it remained mild there, even on chilly days, though the boys never found out why.

For more than four centuries the Goldschmidts had been

101

jewelers and metal craftsmen. They belonged to Frankfurt's Jewish aristocracy. With unconcealed pride Mr. Goldschmidt showed Willy his collection of rare papers, among them a yellowed parchment, dated 1490, which first mentioned the family name. His prize possession, however, was a letter of thanks from the United States: Mr. Goldschmidt's father, together with some Frankfurt banking houses, had helped finance Abraham Lincoln's war of liberation.

Soon the Goldschmidts regarded Willy as one of the family. In some ways, Mrs. Goldschmidt resembled Melanie, with her dark hair turning white, her oval, finely cut face. She was, Willy concluded, after he came to know her better, like Melanie when she was distressed—Mrs. Goldschmidt always looked as if she were trying to hide a secret grief which she could tell no one.

Was she concerned about Robert? Willy couldn't tell. Robbi seemed to have accepted the fact that he was a cripple as a perfect matter of course, never complained about being excluded from so much of life. Once he began questioning Willy about the Wandervogel with such eagerness that Willy forgot Robbi could never participate. He explained how it was, seeing new places, awaking in the woods in the early morning, sitting around the fire and singing. Carried away, he gave a much happier picture of the Wandervogel than he had planned.

When he had finished, his eyes met Mrs. Goldschmidt's. Although they smiled at him he read in them a deep-rooted melancholy, a lifelong pity for her son which she took pains to hide from him. The next second her face was blank, and Willy wondered whether he had imagined it.

With Robbi's father things were quite different. Arthur Goldschmidt, a large, easy-going man with a booming voice like Preiser's, spoke the most typical Frankfurt dialect Willy had ever heard. He amused Mr. Goldschmidt by imitating him—on request.

If anything, Robbi was more eager than Willy to get to work. He got furious when his father showed Willy the collection of goblets, tankards, snuffboxes, and other ornate items, made in the Goldschmidt family shops during the past four hundred years. Willy especially loved the gold and silver dessert spoons in whose bowls an eighteenth-century engraver had etched pictures of Frankfurt's old towers or heads of monsters taken from local sagas. The spoon collection contained more than ninety pieces. In the inflation Mrs. Goldschmidt had sold many of the best, yet, even so, it took Willy quite a while to investigate them.

Early in the spring of 1925 Willy fell ill. It was a new, insidious variety of the grippe against which, Dr. Halder complained, medical science had no weapons. It took Willy several weeks to recover and

102

then he was constantly so tired that his father ordered him to stop all extra activity. He allowed Willy one more evening with Robert because Willy insisted he had to "break it personally" to Robbi.

The Goldschmidts celebrated his recuperation. Mrs. Goldschmidt had prepared hot chocolate and some delicious weightless biscuits, made, she said, of eggs, sugar, and sweet air.

The boys took the chocolate and the biscuits to Robbi's room.

"Look, Will," Robbi said as Willy began browsing through the bookcase. "Look what I've got."

Willy was slightly taken aback. Robert had bought nearly every play in *Reclam's Universal Library,* a popular paper-bound edition which republished the better-known pieces of world literature, for from ten to twenty-five pfennig. All volumes were dyed a peculiar dirty pink, with the trade name "Philip Reclam, Jr.," and the title printed in old-fashioned Gothic letters.

"You shouldn't have done this," Willy managed to blurt out. "It's crazy. You know, I've got to stop."

The words failed him—something unusual for Willy. He plumped into a chair.

Robert began limping around the room. "You mean you won't come here any more. Is that it?"

"Yes," Willy said. "Father won't let me after this stupid grippe." Although this was true, he felt he sounded like a liar.

"Tell me something," said Robert. "But be honest." He paused, obviously trying to overcome an obstacle. "Is it because we are Jews?"

Willy was nonplused. "Why, Robbi. That doesn't make any sense. If I—I mean, if that was it, I wouldn't have come in the first place. I knew you were Jewish."

Robbi looked at him, and for a second he reminded Willy of Mrs. Goldschmidt. Then, for the first time, he began speaking about himself, about the fear which never left him: that he would always lose his friends because he was a Jew. He also told Willy a strange story. In Sexta he had wanted to be friendly with Pueschel, but Pueschel would have nothing to do with him.

"Why Pueschel, of all people?" Willy couldn't help asking. "He's such a stupid brute."

Robbi attempted a meager smile. "Maybe that's why. Then I saw what good friends you and Petersen were, and got envious. When you and the others were in trouble with Lattau, I wished I were worse in math so I could be with you five 'amphi-brothers.' At least then I'd belong somewhere."

Of course, there was always the family. His cousins, the wealthy Goldschmidt-Rothschilds, invited him frequently to their house, and with his other cousins, the Bonwitts—less rich, thank heavens —he spent his summer vacation in Norderney, on the North Sea. But he was doubly an outcast: because of his limp and because of his religion. He stopped, then added:

"Never mind me, Will. Father always says I'm oversensitive."

"What does your mother say?"

"We don't talk about it, but I know what Mother is afraid of. She says even in our good old Frankfurt, where we have been for so long, people do talk against the Jews. Another crazy thing: I think Mother is almost glad I have this crippled foot. Because it keeps me at home and protects me from many things. But sooner or later——"

Willy was strangely moved. He wasn't sure whether because of his weakness from the grippe or because of Robert's sudden candor. The Goldschmidts belonged here as much as this house. They had been in Frankfurt before most of the so-called old families. It occurred to Willy that he had been too busy with himself, with his craze for the theater and before that, with the Wandervogel, and going further back, with his own fears of Lattau. . . . Robert was much worse off than he, and through no fault of his own.

"Hal and I like you," Willy said, a little hoarse. "You've been swell helping me with the plays and all. I owe you a lot. No, don't interrupt me. I do. I'll make up for it, somehow. God, I wish I could take you with me and Hal on a trip with the Wandervogel."

"The Wandervogel? Never. I couldn't, you know, and they wouldn't take me. It's twice impossible."

11. IN APRIL HAL BECAME A VICTIM OF the grippe which seemed to have settled down in the Frankfurt neighborhood for good. For a change, Melanie almost urged Willy to join the short Easter excursion of the Wandervogel—particularly since they were going to the Bergstrasse, one of the warmest regions in Germany, famous for the early flowering of its fruit trees. Kurt had assured her there would be no long hikes; they planned to stay in one spot because it was to be a meeting of several southern groups. Ferdy took six days off and Willy, glad to be out of the sneezing city, went along.

The rail trip to the valley lasted only a few hours. The cherry and apple trees, showing off their pink and white blossoms, filled the air with sweetness. The Bergstrasse always celebrated June in April, and the landscape reminded Willy of the drawings in one of his fairy-tale books, in which the trees had indulged in a merry dance whenever no mortal was watching. He explored the whole valley at both ends, discovered several prosperous farms, each with a large hay barn.

The Karlsruhe group had arrived before them. Otto greeted Willy and Ferdy as if they were long-lost pals. He looked even more muscular and Siegfried-like—if possible—and nobody was tactless enough to mention the battle of Kanderthal.

"Too bad Hal couldn't come," Otto said. "He'll miss out on Hellmuth Handler." Neither Willy nor Ferdy had ever heard of Hellmuth Handler and apparently didn't react properly, because Otto continued reproachfully:

"Oh, don't you know him? Founder of the entire movement in South Germany. Former world war officer, twice wounded, twice decorated. Unique personality. You'll meet him tonight." He slapped the boys on the back and stalked toward the Karlsruhe tents, his head high, parading his chest.

"Always posing," Ferdy said. "What the devil are you doing, Willy? Counting?"

"Hm. Who else is going to stay here besides the all-too-familiar Karlsruhe gang?"

"One troop from Mainz and one from Mannheim, I guess. Why?"

"How many altogether, would you say?"

"For heaven's sakes—about fifty more."

"Are you sure? There are six barns full of the most wonderful hay—I happened to peek in today. All ready to be occupied, with room for about three hundred people. Why do we have to put up tents like Karlsruhe? And why did Kurt tell me the barns were 'not safe' when there are signs on the wall saying 'Formation A,' 'Formation B,' plus some typed instructions signed H. H.?"

"We have no 'formations' in the movement," Ferdy said. "Perhaps the signs are leftovers from last year."

"The signs are brand-new," Willy answered. "Something's up, Ferdy."

The events of the next days followed each other so swiftly that later on Willy could recount them only with difficulty. The first night Kurt introduced Hellmuth Handler, who was to be in complete charge of the camp. Hellmuth was the only "old Wandervogel" Willy had ever met. At first sight he looked ridiculous: a cadaverous man of about forty-five, with long, thin legs resembling those of Melanie's Empire chairs. Hellmuth was nearly bald, with only a few hairs creeping over his pate like anemic blond worms.

As he addressed the boys and girls, his harsh voice almost castigating them, he ceased being ridiculous. He became dangerous. A ruthless logic pervaded his sentences, and it seemed to Willy that his voice was pulling the listeners toward a definite goal —what it was, Willy wasn't yet sure.

Hellmuth told them about his life as an officer on the Russian and French fronts. The war had been terrible, he granted, but it had also been glorious. The real core of a man revealed itself in battle: his courage, his leadership, his faculty for sacrifice.

To Ferdy and Willy this intoxication with sacrifice was a familiar rigmarole—Kurt had harped on it often enough. But Hellmuth went much farther.

War was a crucible. The baser human metals were ejected, the pure ones remained. The cowards experienced only the fear, the numbing shock, but the real men, the elect, were ennobled in battle. This, of course, was something uniquely German, this experience of the "baptism of war." Out of it grew new, steel-hardened shock troops.

And the war—this Hellmuth drove home—was not over. It wasn't over because life on this planet was an eternal war; because Germany was being slowly strangled to death by the shameful Peace of Versailles—unless she rose and threw off the shackles.

106

For this moment everybody must prepare. Be ready! must be the watchword. Who held Germany's destiny? The young! But youth must unite. Today there were too many factions, sectors, split groups.

"I'm an old Wandervogel myself," Hellmuth cried, "but I see the signs of the times. The romantic days are gone, the days of exaltation with deep forests and old castles. Escape from the plodding day into moor and twilight? Posh! Dated! The age of self-determination, of half-hearted rebellion is over."

According to Hellmuth, all these things—precisely the few Willy liked—must be abolished. Instead, all young groups must unite in a new, ascetic order, obeying the leaders, living in a monkish, or, better, soldierly spirit. Yes, part of the previous freedom had to be surrendered. Only subordination under those in command could bring about the changes toward which they were to strive. . . .

Willy caught Ferdy's eyes and knew that Ferdy was as shocked as he.

Hellmuth went on. For a long time the Wandervogel had been isolated. Now was the moment to unite, to found one gloriously big army of young people. The government should have done this, the Weimar Republic.

Hellmuth laughed scornfully and, Willy noted, theatrically. The republic didn't give a damn about its young people. It didn't give a damn about the veteran, back from the war without a job, a place, a family; only, perhaps, with a body shot to pieces. The Weimar Republic, produced by whining pacifists and foreign racketeers, was built on profit, on money. So, what happened? They made an inflation, these Socialists and Jews. Money, the very foundation of the republic, lost its meaning. It was a huge, ghastly joke, put over on the veterans and the coming generation.

By now Hellmuth was shouting. When his lips formed the word "money," it sounded as if he were spitting out a poisonous seed. Youth had to unite—now. Here into this valley—he had invited many friends so that they could meet and know one another. At the end of their stay in the valley he would present them with a new program and their leaders would take a vote on it—he didn't believe in everybody voting.

Hellmuth grabbed a huge burning log, held it over his head and waved it. Within a few minutes small torches at the far end of the valley flared up as if in answer, then came nearer, bigger and bigger, while the air resounded with the singing of hundreds of voices, the stamping of many feet. Three solemn processions of boys and girls approached the fire, holding torches and standards over their heads. Willy, like the others, had jumped up.

107

"The 'Young Stahlhelm,' the 'Free Germans,' the 'Falcons and Eagles,'" Hellmuth called out triumphantly. "They bid you welcome!"

The processions stopped short of the fire, raised the banners three times, and turned away toward the barns singing a song Willy had never heard.

"You shall meet them tomorrow," Hellmuth announced.

Willy and Ferdy went into their tent. The cool night air drifted in, carrying a fragrance of apple and cherry blossoms. Willy couldn't sleep. His head ached as if someone had punched him. Was Ferdy, on his right, really asleep?

"Thank God you're awake, Will," Ferdy whispered. "Lord, you were right about those signs in the barns. Hellmuth had it all arranged."

"Sure," Willy said. "All staged like a play. They must have been waiting for the torch signal. Tell me, Ferdy, what are we going to do?"

"Let's wait and see. Perhaps there are some more like us who don't want to join Hellmuth's new group. Perhaps we have a chance to stay as we are."

Willy lay awake all night, listening to the thousand noises from the meadows and woods, forcing himself to "mull things over." Baptism of war, soldierly orders, subordination—what ill-tasting rubbish. Willy didn't understand the inflation—but he knew it wasn't made by the Social-Democrats or the Jews. All Hellmuth could think of was war; it was his element; he wallowed in it. Slowly, out of the past, there rose in Willy the remembrance of the war years when he had been small: the cold and the hunger and the wounded. Hadn't he once fainted waiting in a line to get dried fish? Hadn't Melanie often said he would never have survived the last war year, the turnip winter of 1917, without Mrs. Petersen's greens and milk and eggs? Willy harbored a deep and consuming hatred, perhaps instilled by Melanie, against everything connected with war, against violence and destruction. No, he would not join an "All-German Youth" under Hellmuth—never. He would talk to Kurt, "stick out his neck," as Hal called it.

Willy was prepared to be fed a lot of heroic-sounding arguments. But neither he nor Ferdy was prepared for the swiftness with which Hellmuth carried out his attack.

"Due to extraordinary political happenings," read a message put up on the camp's bulletin board the next day, "we shall hold a fire ceremony tonight at eight o'clock sharp. Each troop is expected to contribute to the program."

Willy refused to recite a poem Kurt had brought along—proof

that Kurt had been informed of Hellmuth's plans, because the poem fitted the occasion too neatly—and the Frankfurt group contributed only several songs. Thanks to Ferdy's previous efforts, they came off splendidly.

The extraordinary event was the election as *Reichspräsident* of the former general, Field Marshal Paul von Hindenburg (age: seventy-eight), always referred to as the "Venerable Marshal." To Hellmuth and his friends of the "Young Stahlhelm," the "Free Germans," and the "Falcons and Eagles" this meant the nationalist forces, after many setbacks, were gaining ground. "A symbol of the upright, lifelong soldier," he called the new president, and amid roaring applause he proposed that the vote on the merger be held now. Neither Willy, Ferdy, nor anyone else had a chance to protest. The moment Hellmuth had finished each troop leader arose—Kurt and Otto among them—took a slip of paper from a hat held ready by an assistant, scribbled something on it, and threw the slip back into the hat. Trudi was called to count the ballots.

"Unanimous in favor of the merger," she shouted, and there followed another round of applause.

"We shall formulate a new program," Hellmuth declared quickly —Willy was convinced he had it already typed—"and I have a surprise for the boys. All boys will meet at six-fifteen tomorrow morning in the Stahlhelm barn."

For once Willy agreed with Hellmuth. He really had a surprise. The barn had been equipped with a kind of platform, and around seven o'clock there appeared three young men of military bearing, tall, smooth-shaven, and tough: lieutenants of the Reichswehr, Germany's official army, here strictly incognito. One of them mounted the platform and told them the Reichswehr was genuinely interested in the youth movements.

Because of the Peace of Versailles the Reichswehr had been limited in number, was forbidden to train air pilots, and to own heavy guns of any kind. Yet, why couldn't talented young men be instructed in things military on a strictly private basis? The officer gave his audience a conspiratorial wink. Most of the things he was ready to show them, he asserted, were just fun: map reading, construction and use of small firearms, the regulation rifle, and the small machine gun. In the beginning it would be similar to the things the Boy Scouts did, only, of course, the Boy Scouts, in typical Anglo-Saxon style, had no "mission." They were happy to be trustworthy, loyal, helpful, friendly, courteous, kind, obedient, cheerful, thrifty, brave, clean, and reverent. The officer grimaced and the boys laughed, as expected.

Those determined to acquire a useful skill would be taken to the

109

Roehn Mountains during the next summer vacation—all expenses paid, of course—and trained in the art of flying glider planes. If they proved efficient, they could study for a regular pilot's license.

"The *Luft Hansa* is always looking for mechanically gifted youngsters to fly transport planes. The experience you get flying gliders is an entrance ticket to the Hansa, and there're plenty of jobs in South America. You're really safeguarding your future, boys."

Nearly all the boys enlisted for the glider training. The second officer, Lieutenant von Arnim, a dark-haired, almost scholarly type with a soothing voice, unrolled an enormous map reproducing the Bergstrasse Valley on a huge scale. The map was quite different from the one over Willy's bed and served a quite different purpose. For more than three hours Lieutenant von Arnim explained the numerous symbols. Then he called one boy after the other and quizzed him. Willy and Ferdy were getting weary and hungry. They couldn't get out. Hellmuth had locked the barn and put the big key in his pocket.

"Tonight you'll be sent on a special map drill," Von Arnim concluded. He put a bundle of small maps on the table, then distributed them among the boys. There was only one map left over.

"You'll be put into trucks and deposited in the woods near by. You'll be equipped with a compass, a flashlight, regular army rations, and this map. Your objective: to return to camp in the shortest possible time. Whoever arrives first is the winner."

At two the barn doors were unlocked. The boys streamed back to their stations. Willy persuaded Ferdy to participate in the night drill.

"I must find out what else they have in store," he said grimly. As always, Willy wanted to see the whole play. From a purely theatrical point of view, he admitted to himself, Hellmuth's show was well staged.

Ferdy was incensed. "I'll punch in Kurt's rotten face and beat it home," he said.

But he came along on the night drill. Although each boy was supposed to shift for himself, Willy and Ferdy managed to meet shortly after the truck had deposited them in a dark forest around midnight.

It took them half an hour to discover that the map, though reproducing faithfully the outlines of paths, brooks, and hills, labeled everything purposely wrong. A tiny village named Odenberg, for instance, was listed as Eschwege. It was a test, a fraud to mislead them. Nevertheless, they groped their way back, Willy arriving at five o'clock, Ferdy, not to be too conspicuous, ten minutes later. They weren't the first, however.

110

The next day they learned to operate the regulation rifle and the small machine gun on a range hidden in the Odenwald Mountains. They took a machine gun apart, then put it together with great care, which prompted Hellmuth to observe: "Isn't it astounding? To me a machine gun is more beautiful than any cathedral."

Lieutenant von Arnim taught the boys how to draw a map for themselves, how to gauge the terrain, calculate the measurements, the right scale. On two evenings he gave a short course in "History of Strategy." Often, Willy noticed, Von Arnim addressed him when speaking to the boys in general. This encouraged Willy—prompted by Ferdy—to ask the last day, after the others had left, "Pardon me, Lieutenant, are you also instructing groups in other parts of the country? I mean, after they've been united? Or is it a secret?"

"Anything concerning us is a secret," Lieutenant von Arnim replied. "However, as Hellmuth must have told you, an attempt is being made to unite all groups everywhere. You see, since America forced its Dawes Plan on Germany to bleed us white, and since those last elections when the national parties lost, we must work from the bottom. It wouldn't be worth our while to start on South German formations alone, would it? Why didn't you register for the glider plane training?"

The question was shot at Willy like a bullet from one of the machine guns whose construction delighted Hellmuth. Willy was baffled. So Von Arnim had checked up on him.

"Sorry, but I already took a job for the summer," he answered, playing innocent. "I have to help my parents. We lost all we had in the inflation."

Von Arnim appeared satisfied. "Too bad," he said. "You seem to be a smart kid. We need fellows like you."

"Thank you, sir," Willy said.

This meant Von Arnim admitted a surprise strategy. Apparently it was part of a larger plot to incorporate the Wandervogel into the nationalistic groups.

Ferdy agreed it made no sense to protest. There was only one thing to do. The moment they returned from the range, the two packed their things, pitch pipe, guitar, and all, and went into Kurt's tent. Kurt was alone.

"Good-by, Kurt," Willy said. "We've leaving. For good. We're taking the next train home. You knew what was coming and didn't tell a soul. I think that stinks."

Kurt's face changed to a deep red. "You're crazy. Hellmuth arranged it all."

Ferdy put his guitar on the floor. "You're a liar and a coward, Kurt Renner," he said. "Of course you knew. You even had a fitting poem for Willy to recite."

111

"And what if I did?" Kurt said, retreating a little though the narrow tent didn't offer much leeway. "As your leader I have the right to decide. We must have a united German . . ."

"Leader, my foot," Willy said, full of a cold rage. He advanced toward Kurt but Ferdy was faster. He lunged out and punched Kurt on the jaw so hard that he reeled against the canvas wall, nearly bringing the tent down. Ferdy threw himself at Kurt in a boundless fury, but Willy finally managed to stop him, dragged him away, pushed knapsack and guitar into his hands, and pulled him out of the tent.

Willy had never seen anyone so blind with anger. Ferdy was breathing heavily, refused to budge, and glared at Willy as if ready to hit him too.

"For heaven's sakes, stop it, Ferdy," Willy said in the tone of Prospero reprimanding Caliban. "You'll have the whole camp after us. I want to catch the next train."

He walked away, and shortly Ferdy stumbled after him. "God, to think it should end like this," he said. "But I'm through with the Wandervogel for good."

"There are no Wandervogel any more," Willy said. "Only a United German Youth Movement. Being drilled with rifles and machine guns for the next glorious baptism of war."

As they hurried toward the station, a strong wind began to blow. It fell upon the fruit trees, shaking hundreds of blossoms onto the ground and spreading a pink-and-white dotted shroud over the peaceful valley.

Willy slept until late next afternoon. His room had been thoroughly spring-cleaned and smelled friendly and hygienic. He hadn't seen anyone when he got home, just left a note for Mother. Now he was hungry and wanted to tell her everything. Melanie would understand. He only wished he had talked more about the Wandervogel before. He needed someone to tell him he had done the right thing.

His blue suit hung over a chair, neatly folded, and pinned to it he found a note: "Having party. Come in. Love. Mother."

For a moment Willy felt a pang of disappointment. Just now, when he was ready to open his heart to Mother, she was having her monthly women's gathering. He washed and dressed carefully, cursing the visiting ladies. Every month they got together, one month in one house, one month in another, drinking coffee by the gallon and consuming an astonishing amount of sweets.

Helen Lange, Father's sister, was one of them. She was always trying to get him to visit and "play with Hans," his cousin. Hans, two years younger, seemed perfectly colorless to Willy. Hans,

112

however, had taken Willy as model and even followed him into the Goethe School, although the Lessing School was much nearer the Lange house.

At least there'd be sweets, perhaps cherry pie or those round plum tarts, Big Anna's specialty. He walked into the parlor.

Melanie put down her coffee cup and kissed him. She was hostess now, and Willy behaved as was expected of him: the modest young son. Politely he greeted the ladies, even allotting a friendly nod to Aunt Helen, and answered their foolish questions while taking his place at the big table. Why were the ladies conversing so loud, with such forced nonchalance? What was wrong? He looked around for the sweets.

There were none. Instead, Melanie had set up a huge cold buffet, consisting entirely of raw food: grated carrots, grated apples, sliced pears, sliced cucumbers, chopped celery, spinach, beets, and dishes of salad seasoned starkly with lemon juice. For years Father had lectured on raw foods and their nutritional values, and this time Mother had followed his advice and treated the visiting ladies to a health-food *Kaffeeklatsch*.

They appeared outraged. Their plates were still loaded with the raw food. They filled and refilled their coffee cups, chatting with great animation, and refusing to become enriched by nutritional values.

Willy felt cheated, but Melanie wasn't embarrassed at all. She seemed secretly amused, and Willy guessed she had arranged the raw-food treat to shock the ladies a little—Mother liked to do that once in a while, and she certainly had succeeded this time. Though he would have preferred sweets, he decided to support her. Glancing at Aunt Helen, he cried: "Oh, what wonderful stuff, Mother! Let me have a lot of everything—carrots, spinach, celery —and what's this?"

"Chopped nuts with raisins," Melanie explained sweetly. "So glad you like it, Will."

He munched the carrots and the other cold vegetables. Ah, sweet remembrance of cherry pie and plum-tart days. . . .

"Very good, Mother," he gloated. "Could I have some more?"

He gulped his food down and his mother refilled his plate. Although the vegetables, chopped, sliced, or grated, tasted drab, he simulated profound satisfaction. The ladies were watching.

"Probably very good for growing boys," Helen Lange burst out. "Of course we eat enough salads on hot summer evenings."

The other ladies nodded consent. Encouraged, Mrs. Lange continued: "You must be starved after this Easter trip with the Wandervogel. Oh, Willy, do you know about Hans?"

"No, Aunt Helen I don't. Never see him."

113

"Well, it's not his fault," Helen Lange snapped. "We ask you often enough."

"Would you like some more chopped nuts or grated carrots?" his mother inquired.

"Anyhow," Helen Lange was not to be distracted, "we talked to your leader, a nice young man called Kurt—something. Hans has been accepted by the movement. I guess you'll see a lot of him this summer."

Just like Hans to follow him, the way he had followed him into school! He would fit in fine too. Hans would think Kurt simply swell and swallow Hellmuth's tirades whole.

A wave of weariness washed over Willy. He wanted to figure things out alone. Yet, he mustn't spoil Mother's party. He'd play his part. Strangely enough, amid this abrupt dropping of his spirits it struck him that the ladies looked like a funny bunch of angry, flustered pigeons, with Aunt Helen the leader. What was she prattling about?

"I asked, aren't you home early? Your leader, this Mr.—whosis —told me you'd be back day after tomorrow."

"I left for good," Willy said lightly. "The Wandervogel has joined several other groups. I didn't like them, so I left."

"Why, after all these years!" Mrs. Lange sounded scandalized, as if he had abandoned a good job. "Now you can't look after Hans."

"I'm afraid not." Willy got up and bowed to the ladies. "Hans'll find his way around. He's a clever fellow."

Aunt Helen wasn't certain how to react. Was Willy serious? Therefore, she simply smiled.

"You must visit us soon and tell Hans everything," she called after him. Willy could still hear her voice as he asked the long-distance operator to connect him with Hal, Cronberg 2–456.

It took more than one visit to Cronberg to satisfy Hal's curiosity. Again and again Willy repeated what had happened, but the more he went into details, the more Hal demanded to hear, and it slowly became obvious that he was in a dilemma.

Even after Ferdy had come to Willy's support, giving Hal a minute account, Hal hesitated and procrastinated. By pressing Ferdy for details he found out that Ferdy had not seen the signs in the barn which aroused Willy's suspicions, and on several occasions he attempted to defend Kurt. Hal hated to leave the movement, that much was clear. On the other hand, he had to concede there was no Wandervogel any more, and the new United Youth followed a direction which Willy and Ferdy would not accept. Also, the grippe had left Hal so weak that Dr. Halder would

114

not let him go on week-end hikes, and in some way Hal seemed to hold this against Willy.

He grew more morose than Willy had ever known him. He took to running off after school with some mumbled excuse, avoiding Willy's company. The whole Upper Tertia would have teased both of them mercilessly—after all, they'd been inseparable—if Oscar von Rainer hadn't spread a story, implausible to Willy but just the right shade of romantic untruth to keep the Upper Tertia in check.

Hal, Oscar confided one day when Willy wasn't around, was having an affair with a married woman. He had to pretend to be mad at Halder because he didn't want Willy to be involved. . . .

Franz Duester, seizing the occasion, declared Petersen had nagged him for details about how one went about "it," and what was the best way to avoid making babies.

This unlikely alliance of Duester, the undisputed expert on things smutty, and Oscar, the leader of the upper stratum, protected Willy and Hal. Unfortunately, it also helped Hal retreat even more into his sullen isolation.

Both Robbi Goldschmidt—whom Willy had told the whole story—and Ferdy insisted Kurt Renner was working on Hal to come along on the next Big Hike to Poland, Czechoslovakia, and Romania, planned for the coming summer. Once Willy tried to talk to Hal when he visited Theodor for his weekly checkup. But Hal cut him short, in his eyes such a hurt look that Willy knew he couldn't speak to him now. Probably Hal suspected Willy had made up half of the happenings, the way he used to fabricate fantastic stories at the station . . . Didn't Hal know that when it really mattered Willy didn't lie?

Hal went on the trip. Melanie had it from Mrs. Petersen who was completely nonplused when informed that Willy had left the troop. Hal hadn't said a word to anyone. The last day of school he rushed away as usual, without saying good-by. Franz Duester invited Willy to come down for a visit, alluding to their adventure at the inn long ago. He'd be at Mosler's, he said, the new bath house on the Main River, as often as possible. Mosler's, in contrast to the other conservative baths, featured a family section where men and women could swim together.

"They say from one spot you can peek into the women's cabins," Duester added. "I'll show you when I see you."

Never before had a summer vacation started so badly. Everything, it seemed to Willy, conspired against him. Hal had gone; Ferdy took a job with a small orchestra in Nauheim, a famous spa nearby where, Melanie insisted, all the guests were over seventy;

115

Robbi joined his Bonwitt cousins in Norderney on the North Sea; the Von Rainers went to an inexpensive country place which, according to Oscar's description, left one no choice but to lead a clean, dull life; Frankfurt's opera and playhouse had closed for the season, and Willy didn't dare call Maria Reger—after all, he didn't know her well enough.

Theodor was invited to speak at the annual Convention for Internal Medicine in Hildesheim on another of his favorite topics: "Health Insurance for the Lower Income Brackets." He was overjoyed to get a chance to expound his progressive theories to that august but unprogressive body, the annual specialists' convention. In addition, they would pay Melanie's fare if she chose to accompany him.

"I guess you'll be left alone with Big Anna," Melanie said to Willy on his first vacation day. "She'll take good care of you. If anything happens, look up Uncle Herbert Lange."

"Sure, Mother. And write me. Let me know about Father's speech."

Big Anna took better care of him than ever before. Food had become more plentiful in the middle twenties. For the first time since the war Big Anna could buy almost anything she pleased, and she made it her goal to fatten Willy who, she was fond of saying, still looked like "the turnip winter of 1917."

During the initial vacation weeks Willy plunged into plays. By concentrating on Shakespeare's historical dramas and involved German five-act tragedies, he hoped to overcome the increasing despondency which had taken possession of him ever since the last hike.

He would settle down to a hearty, prolonged breakfast while Big Anna regaled him with reports about the grocer, the neighbors, or her opinion of the Dawes Plan which, she had heard, forced the Germans to pay America billions, simply billions, up to 1988. Yet Willy couldn't muster up any vacation feeling. Nothing could shake off the heavy weight that seemed to have settled in the center of his being. Soon all plays appeared drab. He couldn't concentrate. The only books able to hold him were the detective stories on the lowest shelf of Theodor's book case. For hours he buried himself in Sherlock Holmes's adventures.

In the heat of the day he left the unnaturally quiet apartment, taking along his bathing trunks and a volume of Conan Doyle and went to the modern Mosler baths.

He would stretch out on one of the hard wooden bunks in the men's section deep in Sherlock Holmes adventures, while the loudspeaker bleated the latest jazz numbers. He could see into the family section, decorated with unhappy-looking potted plants and

116

shrubs. It was seething with noisy, yelling kids, whining babies, while the restaurant spread the vulgar odor of frying fat over the river. It mingled with the typical smell of Mosler's, a blend of damp wood, tar, and sweating bodies which, to Willy, was to be forever connected with this frenzied and lonesome summer at Mosler's.

As Willy picked his way past the tightly packed people in the family section he was aware of the couples, stretched out on the planks, their arms around each other, eyes closed, a blank expression on their faces. Sometimes they just held hands; more often, in the Germany of the twenties, they went as far as Mr. Mosler's relaxed code and the situation would permit. To Willy the couples became a source of heinous attraction. He watched them, spied them out, often squatting down behind one of the potted-tree arrangements which hid the couples from everyone but him. It thrilled and angered, frustrated and attracted him.

One day he ran into Franz Duester. For a week Willy had been alone except for Big Anna, and he was grateful even for Duester. Strangely enough, Franz still sought his company although during the last three years Willy had evaded his clumsy attempts at being friendly. Franz seemed to bear no grudge against Willy, didn't inquire once about Hal, and behaved as if they were the best of pals.

Noticing the thick curly hair on Franz's chest, Willy asked: "Honest, Franz, how old are you? No kidding this time."

Franz Duester laughed. "I don't look like a baby any more, eh? Well, between you and me, I'm seventeen and a half. I flunked twice."

Willy believed him. This explained his hairy chest, his solid body. Recently Willy had begun worrying about himself—would he grow up in time? He wasn't tall. Hal always said he still looked thirteen. However, Father's big book, Dr. Morell's *The Sex Problem,* which Willy read avidly every night after Anna had gone to her attic room, emphasized in the chapter "Puberty: Male," that different types matured differently and that the Germanic races were slower than the Latin ones. All to the good, in the professor's opinion.

During these days of watching the couples behind the shrubs, of staring at the girls, Willy had nourished a growing anxiety. If he only knew definitely whether by now he was "ready." Willy didn't discuss it with Duester that day nor the following ones, but the question burned within him.

One day Franz took Willy to the famous peephole. Franz swam to the end of the big pool in the family section, then dived as far under the bathhouse as he could. Half of his face was under water, and every two seconds he hoisted himself up to gasp for breath. Willy followed him. They clung to one of the wooden

117

planks which supported the structure—they smelled foul and moldy —and through a crack they could glimpse a tiny square of the women's section. While Willy was gazing at a fat woman sunning herself, he suddenly felt an acute humiliation. What was he doing here, his nose pressed against the rotting plank, only to get a peek at some tired, naked flesh?

"It isn't worth the trouble," Franz agreed when they settled down on the men's sun roof. Here one could indulge in the ritual of sun-bathing without trunks. To Willy the sun roof was peaceful. They couldn't watch any girls from there and the quiet made him drowsy. Franz, however, carried on—tales about what he'd do if he would get "a piece," or reports on his brother Erwin's marriages, all of which had turned out badly. Franz, chuckling, said he knew why. In a short time Willy was wide awake again, his mind full of vague, tickling, torturing visions which he began telling Franz, partly to get rid of them, partly because he liked storytelling.

Franz would listen, enraptured. He was the ideal audience. Though Willy knew it was a cheap triumph, he enjoyed tantalizing Duester with elaborate descriptions of orgies, stopping at the last moment because, he insisted, he couldn't remember the end. While Willy talked, he noticed how engrossed he became in his own stories, so that his mind, like Duester's, was running along one single avenue. They spent day after day this way, speculating on "the thing," watching the girls, discussing whether they could be had, and how, and wondering whether other boys were luckier, and why.

In the middle of July Willy met Duester's friend Hugo Lammer, an athlete of about thirty-five, blond, simple, and, as Willy discovered to his amazement, unable to discuss anything but sex and airplanes. He was very experienced, he said, had been twice married, twice divorced, and was now carrying on with several women. By profession he was a pilot in the Luft Hansa. Planes and women were his life, he sighed, and it reminded Willy of the way people in old-fashioned novels talked about horses and dogs.

One late afternoon, after Franz had left, Willy found Hugo on the sun roof which, because of a cloudy sky, was almost empty.

"Beautiful big woman over there," Hugo said, his hands describing the contours as he always did whether he talked of planes or of girls. "Have to wait a while before I can take off my trunks."

He grinned at Willy, who instinctively looked away. He knew what Hugo meant.

"Never mind, kid," Hugo said after a while, settling down. "I guess I'm as good as any guy up here. That's my secret with the girls."

Despite the six hundred pages of Dr. Morell, despite all the afternoons he and Franz had devoted to "the thing," Willy didn't entirely grasp Hugo's allusion. When Hugo explained in elementary terms, Willy was shocked. So girls paid as much attention to men as men to girls. Did they talk about everything too?

"I want to ask you something"—Willy gathered his courage—"but don't tell Franz, please."

"Shoot, kid," Hugo said. "I won't talk."

"Well, I've been wondering all these weeks about myself. If I'm really grown up. You know, if I should meet a girl and everything went all right, whether I would . . ."

Hugo looked up. Clouds were rushing across a gray sky and a hot wind kicked paper scraps around the roof.

"I know what you mean. It's easy. I can tell you when we leave. Better get going now, it looks like a thunderstorm."

What then followed was for Willy in the years to come a bundle of half-blurred, half-painful, violent impressions—an agonizing scene which imprinted the summer smell of wet wood and sweat forever on his mind. He would remember forever the narrow, sticky cabin in which they dressed, how Hugo grinned, urging him to go ahead and try it, try hard and try again; how his heart throbbed as if ready to burst out of his body, and the tumult in his head and through his body; how he suddenly weakened, nearly fell, how Hugo helped him, held him, and how suddenly, after he had despaired, stuttering an apology, the paroxysm had come, a merciful outburst, while his head whirled, the sweat trickling down his face into his mouth with a salty taste. Never would he forget the brownish walls of the cabin, the ladybug slowly crawling across it, and the instant and new sensation of relaxed lightness which overtook him. . . .

Then had come Hugo Lammer's callous laugh and his "You can make plenty of 'em happy," and the walk home, while the rain rushed down, drowning the world. At the door of his house he hesitated, drenched to the skin, trembling but completely sober, all frenzy faded. And now these summer weeks seemed like an illness passed, already far away. He would carry this day with him for a long time. Watching the torrents of July engulf Reuter Weg, he also knew that the fever, gone now, would come back, and that he would have to fight it again.

Three days before school, in the middle of the night, Willy was awakened by the house bell. He was alone: Melanie and Theodor hadn't returned yet; Big Anna slept upstairs. He put on his pajama trousers, pressed the buzzer. Probably a patient who didn't know Father was away. It had happened before. He glanced downstairs.

"Why—Hal." Before him stood a tanned and tired Hal, with

119

tousled hair, a heavy, dusty knapsack on his back, his corduroy pants torn. He looked as if he hadn't slept for days.

Hal threw the knapsack down. "Could I stay here? No train to Cronberg at this hour. It took me three days and two nights to get here from Poland. Give me a glass of water, Will. That is— if you'll let me stay."

They looked at each other. Now, Willy told himself, was his chance to tell Hal how badly he had behaved, how childish. . . . Yet he couldn't. He was too glad to have Hal home. Hal looked as if he might crumple any minute.

"Of course you'll sleep here. On the couch in the living room. Now wash up and come into the kitchen. I'll get you something to eat."

As if he were used to obeying Willy, Hal did what he was told. While getting out bread, butter, cheese, and milk, it occurred to Willy that he was doing exactly the things Mother did when he came home, hungry and tired, and that Hal was taking over his, Willy's, part. Thoughtfully he set the table. Tonight he wouldn't say anything. Very likely he didn't have to mention a thing: he knew Hal was on his side again, and that was enough. Willy began to hum an old tune Ferdy had taught him. He wasn't aware of it because of the happiness rising within him, which threatened to overflow, and which Hal must not notice. Through Willy's mind flashed the story of the prodigal son, although it seemed absurd that he should be the father—or the mother—and Hal the son.

Between yawns Hal devoured sandwiches and drank all the available milk. His appetite proved so contagious that Willy also ate a big Swiss cheese sandwich. Then he left the kitchen, pulled the sheets out, and prepared a bed on the sofa.

"Tomorrow," Hal murmured while he crawled in. "Tomorrow I'll tell you everything."

Willy put the kitchen in order and went to his room, to bed. Just when his mind was wandering off, a noise startled him. In the half-darkened room stood Hal, drunk with weariness, his hair falling over his face.

"I can't sleep," he whispered, and sat on Willy's bed. "I must get it off my chest. I was a goddam idiot. You should've seen what they made us do on this trip. Harvesting for the German farmers in Poland and big speeches about how they must remain German and such nonsense. All the time I kept thinking about you and Ferdy and what you'd said. I don't know what got into me, Will. I didn't want to give it up, I guess, and so I kidded myself into believing you'd painted things worse than they were. All my fault, Will. If you want to throw me out, go ahead."

Never before had Willy seen Hal so upset. His speech sounded

120

a little thick, probably because he was so tired, and it wasn't like Hal to talk this much anyhow.

"Here"—Hal held his head near to Willy—"punch me on the jaw. So we're even. You must be mad at me. Go ahead."

He stopped. In the dim light Willy saw tears in his eyes. Hal never cried. Willy couldn't remember a single instance.

"Go back to bed," Willy said. "I'm not mad. Not any more. It's all forgotten. You're exhausted, that's all. Tomorrow you tell me the whole story."

Hal started to make a move but couldn't. His head hanging, he began to tremble. Willy got up, took him by the arm, and walked him into the living room. Like a child Hal let himself be put to bed. When Willy had tucked him in, he stopped shaking. In no time he was asleep.

Willy went back to his room. His own summer—he called it the frenzied summer whenever he thought about it—had been bad enough, but Hal must have suffered more. Why all this? Why couldn't life be reasonable and easy without the torments of loneliness, broken friendship, and sex? No answer, he decided. No one had an answer because there was none and, besides, according to Dr. Morell, he and Hal were simply passing through "puberty, a period characterized by unhappiness and unfulfilled longings." Tonight, though, he didn't feel unhappy. Dr. Morell was wrong there. And Hal would be all right tomorrow, puberty or no puberty.

"I'm busy, Robbi," Willy had to say often during the next months. "I'll be over as soon as I can."

By now Robbi Goldschmidt should have given up, but he wouldn't. "You must go on with the plays, Will. Why, you don't remember a single thing any more and Preiser . . ."

"Never mind Preiser. There are more decisive issues in life than plays. Besides, my marks have been so lousy I must get back to work or I'll flunk."

The "decisive issues" were certain books he had discovered and the discussions he frequently had with Father and Ferdy Rohn. A new view opened for Willy. Compared to it everything else appeared puny and insignificant.

It had all started with Bellamy's *Looking Backward*. Willy had devoured it one evening—at first a nice adventure story, like *The Eye of Lo-Fo* years ago. Yet, when he had finished it, it struck him that here was a much better world than the one he lived in— an ordered, friendly community with no hungry children, no rivalries between nations, no wars. In a way Mr. Bellamy had gotten rid of all the things Hellmuth worshiped, and this held an immediate appeal for Willy.

The more he pondered all this, the more he realized how much was wrong with the present. Since he had lost his place in the Wandervogel, he felt drained, and even Hal's return didn't make up for the new aimlessness. Studying Bellamy, everything Hellmuth stood for became more wicked. Up to now Willy had kept the Bergstrasse happenings from Father; now, one night in September, he began telling him about it.

Theodor was busy that night, as usual. Yet, as Willy grew angrier and louder, he snapped the microscope shut and gave all his attention to his son. When Willy tried to put into words what Bellamy had done for him, he got bogged down.

Dr. Halder let Willy exhaust himself. Then he said: "I know all of Hellmuth's slogans, son. It's the old nationalistic tune. I've been exposed to it in the City Council for many years. Believe me, I'm sicker of it than you. But since when are you interested in Bellamy and a better world? I thought you were studying plays with Robert Goldschmidt?"

"Not any more, Father. Bellamy and all this is much more essential. I must read all the books on the subject."

"I doubt whether anyone could," said Dr. Halder. "There are far too many. And besides, why must you? I don't think you should get involved in all this."

"In what?"

"In politics, if you're thorough. Don't think because I've been in the Social-Democratic party for years, I want you to get tied up too. On the contrary. Don't repeat my errors."

"Tell me which books to read first," Willy said stubbornly, and finally Theodor gave in.

Wading through the heavy volumes of *Our Economic System,* numerous theories of *Scientific Marxism,* and such popular brochures as *A Handy Guide to Capital, Labor, and a New Society,* Willy discovered that strange, large edifice called historical materialism, or Marxism. It served as a basis for the Kommunist party (K. P.) and, with many alterations, for the Social-Democratic party (S. P.), both of which claimed to be the only church of true doctrines.

Willy was glad he could discuss the "Scientific System" with Ferdy Rohn. Ferdy had joined the "Socialist Youth," where his talents as choirmaster and conductor found a rich field. He now spoke of his years in the Wandervogel as if they had been symptoms of an interesting though dangerous disease and called them a "youthful and bourgeois aberration."

Like hundreds of young people in the middle twenties, Willy and Ferdy became deeply engrossed in economic theories, lost themselves in philosophical quarrels concerning the true nature of

122

the "Scientific System," and got passionately involved in the clashes between its two representatives, the S. P. and the K. P.

The question for Willy and Ferdy, as for those not caught by the nationalistic groups, was: which party to join. The more violent-minded rebels who throve on tension joined the K. P., which seemed to offer permanent excitement. The more cautious ones who, like Willy, distrusted fanaticism of any kind and instinctively shied away from boisterousness and frenzy, turned to the S. P.

Ferdy had been converted to the new beliefs, which he passed on to Willy, by his energetic girl friend, Helen Rudert, the outstanding personality of the Socialist Youth, Frankfurt district. Night after night he expounded the "Scientific System" while they promenaded along the Main River, impervious to the September chill.

Sometimes it seemed to Willy as if a long succession of pre-viously locked doors were opening and some of life's riddles, which he thought couldn't be answered, turned out not to be riddles after all. Karl Marx, Ferdy said happily, had found a key to history and nature.

"One can predict history," Ferdy liked to conclude his short course. "Isn't it perfect?"

Soon Willy joined the Socialist Youth, for short called S. Y., an annex to the Social-Democratic party. He regularly went to meetings and debates, typed circulars, addressed letters, or counted contributions. This left him less time for his study of the Scientific System which, he sometimes thought, tended to simplify every-thing in an almost sullen manner.

After a few months, however, Willy had to admit that no matter how earnestly he worked with his comrades, he was looked upon as an outsider. True, he was the son of Dr. Halder, who "had long been with the party," and who represented it on many committees where the trade-union secretaries didn't feel at home: the Music Committee, the Theater Committee, et cetera. Yet Willy was no worker and no worker's son.

Though Ferdy denied it during their first quarrel, according to the Scientific System, workers were, in some hidden way, superior people. History, so it went, had chosen them to liberate mankind; their opinions alone were untainted by selfish interests. Therefore they possessed by birth, so to speak, qualities denied to someone like Willy, and this made him somewhat less valuable. His new comrades, earnest, industrious youths who struggled stubbornly through evening courses on economics and trade-union history, never said so openly—Ferdy was right in this respect. But in a thousand ways Willy was treated with a politeness which kept him forever in an honorable but pronounced isolation.

Around Christmas there began such a turbulent period that both

123

Willy and his comrades forgot he was one of them only by adoption. The expropriation of the former princes put Germany, and especially the left-wing parties, in an uproar.

Most of the reigning nobility had fled, panic-stricken, before the 1918 revolution, leaving their huge estates and holdings behind. Now they considered the time ripe to sue the German people for return of their large properties. Some of them even demanded more than they had owned before, as a kind of compensation for their prolonged absence.

"Have you heard the latest?" asked Helen, the intellectual wizard of the group, at a special meeting. Her dark eyes gleamed and she shook her hair out of her face with a violent gesture.

"The Duke of Coburg has sued the government for 300,000 gold marks. The nerve! He ran away in 1918 and now he wants to be 'indemnified' with a measly 300,000. And he's not the only one. There are many more. They've all sued and they all seem to be winning. It's an outrage."

Cries of "bravo" and "action." Willy shared their indignation while at the same time he couldn't help thinking there was something funny in the idea of a republican people buttering the bread of the nobility it had chased out. . . .

"We need action is right," continued Helen with a stern glance at Willy. "Our party is considering a public referendum to expropriate all princes. Not a penny to any of them!"

The Youth Group unanimously put itself behind the party's decision. The next morning the Communist paper *Red Flag* came out with a similar proposition. This threw confusion into the ranks of the S. P. Could they make common cause with the competition?

To Willy these complications didn't mean much. At last he had found something worthy of a fight and he longed to get busy. To his surprise, the party secretaries advised the Youth Group to "lie low for a while," and Theodor didn't share his wholesale enthusiasm.

"Here you have it, Will," he said when, late one night, Willy, bubbling over with indignation, complained how the Youth Group was hamstrung by the party bigwigs. "This is a typical dilemma. To take away the large holdings of the princes—for whom I haven't a grain of sympathy, mind you—is a violation of the principle of private property. Most people in Germany won't stand for that. I, personally, am undecided, I admit. Should one take away, by violence, even from one's former enemies?"

For a second Willy was struck by Theodor's reasoning, only just now he didn't want to be talked out of his crusade. He recounted all the arguments supplied by Helen or Ferdy, and the debate ended in a stalemate.

124

Soon Willy got deeper into what his father called "the evil of politics." The Social-Democratic party leaders, as was explained to the young crusaders, favored a small token payment to the princes: in this way the cry of "bolshevism" which the nationalistic parties were sure to raise could be rendered ineffective. The Socialist Youth fought this. The Nationalists, they argued, led by their new boss, Alfred Hugenberg, a pathologically patriotic monarchist, would yell anyhow, and the progressives would only be repulsed by such soft-pedaling.

Weeks of uncertainty followed. Finally, after countless debates, the party officials reversed their second decision and reverted to their first: unconditional expropriation of the princes. Together with the Communist party—with which they usually disagreed on everything—they began collecting votes for the referendum.

Willy was startled to learn the long and exasperating ways of German parliamentarism. Two referendums were needed: No. 1 to decide whether there should be the final No. 2. For No. 1 only 10 per cent of all voters needed to sign a petition. The second, Helen explained, looking not too pleased, asked a "majority of all qualified voters"—about twenty million people.

Referendum No. 1 was quickly put through with the votes of both parties' registered members, and soon the date for referendum 2 was set for June 20, 1926.

For weeks Willy was engulfed in a stream of work. He neglected school, came home at all hours, and lost sight of Hal outside of the Goethe School—Hal having sworn never to join anything again.

In the spring all groups intensified their campaigns. The Democrats, the small party of old-fashioned liberals; the Catholic Center; the People's party, a spokesman for heavy industry; the Nationalists, and, of course, the National Socialists fought the expropriation bitterly. The *Frankfurter Zeitung,* for once, disappointed Willy by stating that interference with the rights of private individuals violated all ethical laws, and the other papers followed the same line, less subtly as a rule.

Many a night Willy spent at the smoky, barren Youth Group headquarters, folding pamphlets, mimeographing circulars, answering the phone. Occasionally he changed the wording of the circulars, most of which seemed stiff to him. In his opinion they would reach only those who were on their side anyhow. He began cutting out the complicated expressions which invariably went with the Scientific System. This got him into trouble with Mr. Haas, the secretary who functioned as intermediary between Youth Group and party.

Once before Willy had clashed with Rudolph Haas, a rotund, worried former metalworker who had been in the trade-union movement for decades. It was when the Locarno pact had just been signed—a singular triumph of Foreign Minister Stresemann. The French promised to evacuate the Rhineland and Germany obtained many other concessions from the Western Powers, who by now had what Theodor called a prolonged victory hangover. Willy had repeated Father's arguments to the group, and his praise of Stresemann who was really a pacifist. Mr. Haas, annoyed with the discussion, had stepped in.

"Keep out of foreign politics, you kids," he admonished. "That's too complicated for us. I hardly understand it myself. Study Marx, Engels, Bebels, and stick to union or local matters."

Willy, though rebuked, contradicted him but lost in the end. Mr. Haas told him to learn more about trade-union fights first.

Now, as Willy was to mimeograph Mr. Haas's circulars, he couldn't resist changing them. The supposedly inflaming pamphlets delighted in twisted, snake-like sentences which made them read like dry legal documents. Yet the author would tolerate no changes. He told Willy not to touch the phrasing, which he called "dignified," just mimeograph it. Willy did so, boiling.

When Reichspräsident Von Hindenburg unexpectedly abandoned his venerable reserve and publicly declaimed that the expropriation would "rob the German people of the foundation upon which their cultural, economic, and political life rests"; the nationalistic press celebrated the day with triumphant headlines. Wherever Willy went he saw the deadly effect of the old marshal's statement.

By a more intensified campaign the two pro-expropriation parties tried to scotch the chancellor's dictum. In April, although the Easter examinations were approaching all too rapidly, Willy started a house-to-house campaign.

Soon he discovered that canvassing was a most depressing occupation. He began in the Rebstock sector, an industrial neighborhood. He climbed narrow, angrily creaking stairs, walked through hallways smelling of cheap fried food, sidestepping noisy, unkempt children. He got a glimpse of the monotonous, fear-ridden lives of the women who even now worried lest their husbands lose their factory jobs.

What surprised him was that so few behaved as Ferdy and the Scientific System said they should. They weren't proud of being proletarians. Many swore by the *Frankfurt General News,* and told Willy if only the princely families would come back, life would be as pleasant as in the good old days of the Kaiser.

Occasionally he had to check himself; he got more interested in the people's dialect than in what they told him. Once he wasted a whole evening with an old harridan from Hamburg who taught him several juicy expressions used by seafaring men for whom, she

126

said, she had once kept a boardinghouse. Since her grandaunt had been a lady in waiting to the most gracious Duchess of Anhalt-Dessau, she was all out for the nobility and its God-given rights.

How Willy passed the Easter examinations for Lower Secunda he didn't quite know. Did Dr. Preiser help him once or twice by forming words with his lips or was he imagining things? He passed the examinations with a "barely sufficient." Yet instead of taking some days off during the vacation and visiting Hal, he started a new beat: he turned to the suburbs of Bockenheim and Roedelheim, the neighborhood of the "little people."

The small shopkeepers, city employees, and craftsmen in the drab streets opposed the expropriation violently. It fascinated Willy how the women managed to keep a genteel air although they had lost all their savings in the inflation. Their dresses were drab but painfully clean; they tended their conventional miniature gardens with loving devotion. Most of them loathed the Weimar Republic. They all seemed to despise the workers although their salaries often were below those of the skilled laborers. "A vote for expropriation is a vote for Bolshevism." So went the stock suburban answer. Or "A vote for expropriation is a vote against Hindenburg." And, surely, nobody wanted that. Soon Willy concluded that even a slight attack on the Venerable Symbol would cost him the sympathies of the suburbs.

To make his life more complicated, both Ferdy and Helen brought their troubles to him. Helen, dissatisfied with the heavy-handed technique the party officials applied to the campaign, began to drift toward the K. P. which Ferdy disliked intensely.

"Believe me, Will," he used to say, "there are many well-meaning idealists in the K. P. but also a lot of fanatics who remind me of Kurt and Hellmuth, only turned inside out. You know what I mean?" Willy did not quite know, but in order to reconcile them he defended Helen's point of view while to Helen he presented Ferdy's arguments. Both became angry with him and quarreled more violently than ever.

June 20, the day of the referendum, was hot and cloudless. Through the windows of Lower Secunda Willy caught sight of the blindingly blue sky stretched like a tight tent roof over the town. He yawned through the lessons, his mind still at headquarters, where he had worked late the night before while Ferdy and Helen carried on their running, nagging battle.

In the evening he crouched near the radio, impatient for the outcome of the referendum. As the final count came over the air Willy felt drained of all emotion. He sat in the living room, staring unseeingly into the garden while the faintly officious voice of the radio announcer repeated the results: the expropriation was rejected. Of the 20,000,000 voters needed, only 14,000,000 had gone to the polls. The German people by their own free will decided to give their former masters a lifelong tribute. Each year the Weimar Republic would pay millions and millions to Their Majesties in Exile. Apparently the Germans did not cherish their republic. They still clung to their overlords, the dukes, earls, baronets, and counts who had reigned over them for centuries.

All of Willy's efforts had been wasted. He didn't touch his food.

"You take everything too hard, Will," Melanie said. "You did all you could. You were like a racehorse gone wild. Remember my campaign to mobilize the Parents' Committee? I failed badly, but still I got over it. Come to think of it, you went through the same thing, only on a bigger scale. . . . Come on, eat your peach pie. You'll upset Anna if you don't."

Willy shook his head. As Hal always said, he was a bad loser. Right now he couldn't get his thoughts organized. He took the newspaper Father had spread before him.

"At least the party paper is honest," Theodor sighed, opening the *People's Voice*. The S. P. frankly admitted defeat, blaming on one hand the nationalistic propaganda which had used the President as a shield, and on the other the K. P. which should have accepted the "token payment" solution.

"You think that's true?" Willy asked.

Theodor looked at him for a moment. There was such unaccustomed tenderness, such compassion in his eyes that Willy had to turn away.

"I'm not sure, son," Theodor answered, unfolding the *Red Flag*. "At least it makes more sense than this here."

To Willy's amazement the *Red Flag* pronounced the result a "Resounding Victory for the Proletarian Forces." In heaven's name, why? How could they call a lost battle a conquest? He put the sheet down and walked out.

By now he had enough of everything. He decided to call Hal although it was eleven o'clock and the Petersen household usually went to bed at nine. The instant he turned toward the phone in the hall it rang.

"Your father should give you a stiff drink," Hal said. His voice sounded completely unruffled.

"Oh, it was to be expected, you know." Willy made a feeble attempt to sound unconcerned.

"Stop acting," Hal said. "I know how you feel, and I'm worried. You're becoming morbid and sour, Will. Quit the whole business. You aren't made for it."

"What do you mean?"

"I can't explain it. You told me to get out of the Wandervogel, remember? I didn't, at first. But you were right. Now, I say you're making a mistake, just like I did."

"I can't live the way I want and avoid responsibilities," Willy declared, but it sounded artificial. Before he went to bed he remembered he had read the phrase in one of Mr. Haas's pamphlets.

Of course Helen produced an explanation for the *Red Flag's* surprising announcement when Willy arrived at the Youth Group office the next day.

"It is a victory. In the last election both parties together pulled only about 12,000,000 votes. This time around 14,000,000 people went to the polls. This means 2,000,000 have come to our side. And if we had used all weapons ruthlessly, we'd have gotten the other 6,000,000."

"It's still not a victory," Willy insisted. He was suddenly very tired of arguments, quarreling people, headquarters, and the way the mimeograph machine was smeared with ink. He stared at the old-fashioned etching of the Founder, Karl Marx, who seemed particularly disinterested this afternoon.

"You don't know enough about dialectic materialism," Helen remarked acidly, and Ferdy snapped: "For heaven's sake, leave Will alone. There are several ways of looking at this."

"Not for me, not any more," Helen announced, pulling out a letter addressed to the Secretary General, Social-Democratic Party of Germany, District Frankfurt-am-Main. "I'm quitting."

"Fine," Ferdy said, looking as if he wanted to punch her. "Go on to those 'lumpen-proletarians,' that red-flag rabble."

"Will you see that Mr. Haas gets this note?" Helen asked Willy, ignoring Ferdy. She looked pale, and her behavior had something of a minor saint suffering gladly for a holy cause.

"I'm going home," Willy told her. "Why don't you mail your letter? Or don't you trust the mailman, either?"

He left her. As he went down the narrow stairs he felt very much like taking a long trip, to the French Riviera, leaving behind party offices, political quarrels, pamphlets, and schoolbooks, including the ancient Greek grammar which Preiser was hammering into the Lower Secunda with extreme vehemence. For tomorrow's lesson Willy had to translate two full pages.

Why, Willy asked himself as he turned into Reuter Weg, why should he study ancient Greek in the age of social upheavals?

In his room he found Theodor, engrossed in *Greek Grammar for Beginners,* by E. Bruhn.

"I've forgotten all my Greek," Father said. "It's a shame. I wish I could study it again with you. I decided to quit early today. Would you like to come for a stroll to Miquel Park?"

"Why, sure," Willy answered, a little startled. He hadn't walked to Miquel Park with Father for a long time. Miquel Park began where Reuter Weg and the city proper ended, and he had played ball there a hundred times.

Silently they walked up Reuter Weg. Within ten minutes they had left all houses behind them. A rush of memories overtook Willy. Here was the tiny farmhouse, of . . .

"Mother Ella," Theodor said. "Mrs. Winkler. One of my first patients—1906, 1914, and ever after. Do you notice something?"

Willy looked hard. Everything seemed as he remembered it of old. The decrepit but gracious farmhouse, left over from an earlier century; the large garden, now overflowing with flowers of all colors and smells; the long, pedantic rows of vegetables; the cone-shaped beehive . . .

"No bees, Father. That's it. Where are they? And no smoke from the chimney."

"Right. Bees and smoke belong to Mother Ella's house. It's empty now. She was moved out."

Theodor took Willy around the house where the road took a sharp turn. "Here, Will. Take a good look."

The vegetable fields showed gaping wounds. Two enormous cranes were digging a big pit, greedily mouthing the earth and spitting it out onto a hill to one side. Workers were milling around; the cranes were shoveling tirelessly, and behind their giraffe-like necks Willy could see other workingmen felling big trees, the large firs, oaks, and beeches which had made Miquel Park famous.

"They're killing our park," Willy cried out, stepping nearer. A piece of his childhood was being destroyed before his eyes.

Theodor drew him away. "We can still walk through Miquel Alley," he said. "It might be the last time."

Miquel Alley, a mathematically straight macadam highway, flanked by enormous straight-backed poplars, led far out toward Ginnheim.

"Our biggest chemical trust, the I. G. Farben, is going to erect its business office here," Theodor said. "They bought Miquel Park from the city—very cheap too. Two more streetcars will run up through Reuter Weg and Mother thinks I might get many more patients, all the employees with sour stomachs from too much I. G. Farben."

"It sounds awful," Willy said. "Our old street will be very noisy."

"Would you mind telling me what happened between you and Mr. Haas and the Socialist young folk?" Theodor asked without any transition. "If you don't want to talk, all right, and I'll tell you my new ideas concerning an all-fresh-fruit diet. But remember, I've

130

known party secretaries for years. Since I'm only your father, perhaps you . . ."

Willy realized Theodor wanted to help him. He didn't resent it; on the contrary. He felt guilty for not having confided in Theodor long ago. But he had wanted to find things out for himself. He gazed out into the summery fields and the faraway farmhouses of Ginnheim and then began to talk. He described how during his canvassing he had become more and more frustrated because the people didn't react the way he thought they should. As he groped for words, several ideas which had been simmering within him took on a clearer shape.

"I think, Father, the party is like an overgrown elephant. It can't move properly. Hardly anyone understands all its divisions, sections, subdivisions, locals, and sub-locals. Then everything and everybody seems to depend on the Central Secretariat. Any time Mr. Haas didn't want to do something, he said he must take it up with the 'higher officers.' Becker of the metalworkers and old man Schupp with his 'railroaders first,' are just the same. I thought it was a revolutionary party but it isn't. And the trade-union secretaries seem to be afraid of losing their jobs. As for me and Mr. Haas, he didn't like my changing his pamphlets and perhaps I was too fresh."

Theodor put his arm through Willy's. "How old are you? I'm afraid I never know."

"Sixteen," Willy said. If he had said nineteen, Father would have believed it too. "Why?"

"At sixteen you can't be fair. It's the privilege of youth. You remind me of myself, Will. I was very much like you at your age, only with one difference. I'm not sure whether it was an advantage or not."

"What difference, Father?" Willy asked. For once Father was like Hal, and Willy felt a sudden uncontrollable wave of tenderness for him.

"You have Mother's critical sense," Theodor said almost shyly, as if he didn't want to embarrass his son with a compliment. "Do you know, I was one of the first progressive doctors in Frankfurt and my family and almost everybody else turned up his nose as if I were stricken with an ugly disease. Your mother stuck to me, though. I was an uncritical, enthusiastic believer in progress through Socialism up to 1914."

"You mean when war came?"

"Yes. Mother, of course, predicted it, but I really believed that the united workingmen of all nations, with a sprinkling of us bourgeois in it, could prevent war, any war. Well, they didn't. I was more naïve than you'll ever be, son."

131

Theodor warmed to his story. He tried to paint a picture of the early Social-Democrats, why and how they had become what they were—or seemed to be. They were haunted by bad luck. They had been forced to take over after the war when they weren't ready. They took the blame for the entire ghastly heritage which befell the defeated nation: famine, strikes, the Peace of Versailles, the attitude of the Allies, the inflation, even the cold winter of 1917 was said to be the fault of the "radicals."

"And how some of us wished the Eberts and Noskes, the Haases, and Schupps were really more radical," Theodor said, as if reporting on a patient whom he had been treating not too successfully.

"In 1918 they promised to nationalize the mines but they lacked the courage. They didn't dare dissolve the big Junker estates east of the Elbe, either. This was when some of us left and founded split parties of which the K. P. is the only survivor. The S. P. leaders also missed out on the Army—let the Kaiser's old officers reorganize the Reichswehr. So the Reichswehr became anti-republican, anti-everything. A perfect reservoir for all militarists, and now a very powerful government behind the government. It's partly the S. P.'s fault, I admit."

Willy said he knew about the Reichswehr from his last days in the Wandervogel.

"It's all wrong," he added. "According to Marx, the workers must seize the power. They should have taken over the Army long ago."

"You couldn't make a single worker enter the Army in 1919," Theodor answered with a sigh, "and don't quote Marx to prove anything, ever."

"Why not? Everybody does. I know I don't understand all the books I plowed through, but I thought the Scientific System was foolproof. Something absolute, like physics."

"You can prove almost everything with Marx," Theodor said with an air of resignation. "The trouble is, he often changed his mind, as all theorists do, and, besides, you have to be an expert economist to decide whether the famous surplus theory is right or wrong."

Willy nodded. In a way Father was saying out loud the things with which he had wrestled. The surplus theory had always baffled him and the others in Helen's course, "Economics, I."

"I'll give you only one sample," Theodor continued, "because I don't want to lecture, and although it's called scientific, it's all rather fantastic.

"On one hand, so Marx goes, history moves in a certain direction. It travels like a train from one city to another, on a fixed schedule. Since it runs toward a certain goal, anyhow, one group in the S. P.

132

argues, why try so hard? In the end, the train will arrive at the station, capitalism will be finished, the Golden Age will rise from the ashes.

"On the other hand, Marx was all out for organizing the working-men, making them what he calls 'class-conscious,' and he admonished them to be 'ruthless' in their fight.

"So, according to your temperament, you can pick the one theory, take it easy, and wait; or the other, get busy, and be ruthless against whomever you consider your enemy."

"The train might get wrecked and never arrive," Willy said.

"Not a bad argument, son. I used it years ago when the party bigwigs told me to lie low. Another tough question: should the change from our present situation to the next one come slowly, in gradual stages, or fast, with a bang-up revolution?"

"I figured it would be fast, with a big fight, like in Russia," Willy ventured, though by now he wasn't sure of anything.

"You can prove both points with nice, fat quotes. The S. P. went all out for the gradual 'evolution,' and what happened? They didn't know how to go about it. How to reform the system in Germany without destroying it. They were like a physician, who, while trying to cure a patient, hopes at the same time to inherit the patient's money.

"Then, after the war, we suddenly found ourselves up against every-day problems we never dreamed about: foreign policy, education, religion, legislation, et cetera. Marx called these things 'super-structures' and thought they would straighten themselves out, once the economic foundations were properly laid. To my mind, he was dead wrong. God, think of our legislation! We got a republican government with brand-new laws, and not bad ones at that, but we never could reorganize the courts and get rid of the old anti-democratic judges. . . .

"Now, friend Haas thinks that's very unimportant. He's mainly interested in getting another 6 per cent raise for one of our unions. Tiny local victories make him happy and he never worries about the big things he doesn't understand. The K. P. has needled us for these things. Only, they seem to receive their directives from Russia, and by the time they put them into operation here, they don't fit the situation any longer. Incidentally, according to Marx, the Communists are all wrong. There couldn't have been a revolution in Russia."

"Why? There was one, wasn't there?"

"Marx was almost sure the industrialized Western countries were destined to start the upheaval first. Russia had no industry, therefore no workers and therefore no class to make revolution. Accord-

133

ing to strict doctrine, the United States should have had a revolution long before Russia,"

"Goodness," Willy said. The Scientific System seemed to be crumbling before his eyes.

"You haven't asked me the question I've been waiting for," Theodor said.

"All right, Father, why are you still with the Social-Democrats?"

"There is no other party to go with. At least we can prevent Hugenberg and his inane patriots from ruining the country. With all our faults, we are the only ones trying to make the republic a success—with a little help from the Center, the State party, and the reluctant People's party. Do I sound like an editorial in the *People's Voice?*"

Willy squeezed his father's shoulder. Eventually he would have to give up his faith in that absolute, foolproof something, the Scientific System. Nothing, so it seemed, was definite; the Scientific System wasn't scientific, Marx, the prophet, hadn't always seen true.

"The German Communists made even bigger boners than we did." Theodor continued his own thread. "They often started an uprising when nobody, including the workers, wanted one. Some of the K. P. fellows in Frankfurt are former S. P. members who got disgusted with us. I understand their reasoning. They're no happier now, though. Life with the Communists, I'd say, is as frustrating as life with us. The Communists always talk in extremes. Then when it comes to concrete questions in the City Council, such as how much credit to allow for new cheap houses for veterans, they quote Lenin and leave the figuring of the budget to us. Do you remember 1923?"

"I was thirteen then, Father," Willy said, "and the only thing I recall is the laundry basket with the million-mark bills which Mother and I lugged to the grocer."

"Well, in 1923, although the German workers weren't interested the K. P. proclaimed a general strike, uprising, barricades, all the trimmings—and then they called it off, all of a sudden. This happened several times, uprising on, uprising off, and the last time they forgot Hamburg."

"Forgot Hamburg? How?"

"Something went wrong. And so, in the early morning, some poor faithfuls, mostly dockyard workers, demonstrated all by themselves, seized a police station, and kept the surprised cops prisoners. The other workers went to work as usual, and party headquarters went mad. Someone had forgotten to wire the Hamburg branch that everything was off again. That's one sample, Willy, but of course I might be partial. No, since 1919 the K. P.

134

hasn't had a good man. And even if there were one, he would have to submit to a discipline very much like the one in the old Prussian Army."

"I wish all good people would get together," Willy said as they approached a huge, glum building, strangely familiar to him from earlier days.

Theodor sighed. "You're not the only one to wish that, son. Many of us 'progressives' in the party have tried for a united front. I'm afraid it won't work."

"Why? Don't the K. P. people see that the split is bad?"

"Some do. But most of them think of themselves as a kind of holy, lonely sect. They believe they must fight ruthlessly against the dissenters. This ruthlessness is dangerous. After a while you become ruthless even against those within your group who disagree on a completely unimportant point—such as where a new bridge over the Main should be built. In its overzealousness the K. P. often hits below the belt, just like Hugenberg or the National Socialists, and I think that's wrong. Besides, they have developed a secret lingo of their own which often doesn't conform to reality. This might have to do with their depending on someone in the Russian Central Office telling them how to act. You can't conduct a German party from abroad. It's too complicated—even from within."

"Everything is too complicated for me right now," Will said. They had reached an enclosure with a shingle: "Municipal Psychiatric Clinic. Entrance for Doctors Only." Through the dark fir trees Willy again caught sight of the workers and the cranes on the I. G. Farben plot.

"Willy," his father said, "this might not be the perfect place, but I want to impress upon you again: stay away from all politics and parties. The S. P. accepted me years ago, but I'm still an outsider. You'll always be one too. It's enough to belong to one minority."

Willy didn't understand.

"Your mother and I belong to two minorities," Theodor explained while they walked into the enclosure. "We are not accepted by the proletarians in the party: to them we are 'bourgeois.' And my colleagues, the physicians, the lawyers, the business people like Uncle Herbert, don't want us either. Most so-called academic Germans are crazily patriotic, clamor for a strong army, and worship Hugenberg. Since we don't, we are outcasts. You seem to be on the way to becoming one too. This means swimming against the stream and that, Will, makes for a tough and lonely life."

Willy nodded. Various incidents in his life began to fall into a clearer pattern: how he was never at home with his classmates—a few excepted—and how he had been an outsider in the Wander-

135

vogel and how, in a similar manner, this had repeated itself in the Socialist Youth.

He looked up, confronted by a huge, prisonlike building.

"Why, Pa, this is the Monkey Cage," Willy cried. "When I was little, Mother told me never to go near it."

The Monkey Cage was the slang name for Frankfurt's biggest institution for the mentally deranged. Willy meant to ask Theodor about minorities, but at this moment a big truck with an iron grille drove up to the entrance. The metal gate opened quickly and out rushed a group of agitated, shrilling women who reminded Willy of some of Shakespeare's witches. Several robust matrons were trying desperately to keep them in order. The patients resisted. A few simply remained at the gate, refusing to move, blinking into the sunlight in frozen and dejected postures. Others began beating themselves with their fists. One, a shriveled white-haired woman, fell on her knees and called upon the Lord.

An enormous man with a black beard appeared in the doorway.

"Professor Raeber!" Theodor said, stepping nearer. "What's going on? Where are you taking the patients?"

Two pallid elderly women who gave the impression of having been hidden in a cellar for years, now began to sing. In piercing yet dead voices they intoned a current hit about white lilacs in spring, inserting highly obscene verses and repeating the same words over and over.

"We must evacuate the patients within five hours," Professor Raeber shouted over the noise. "I. G. Farben is going to tear down the building tomorrow."

He started shooing the women into the truck, when from a side door another equally unruly batch suddenly appeared. Frantic, Professor Raeber called some husky male attendants, who hustled the women toward the truck. The women resisted. The attendants, called to action by Professor Raeber, began dragging the two singers, who kept on rasping out the same obscene words to the melody of white lilacs in spring.

Theodor rushed toward the attendants, held them off, and began talking to the women, soothingly and fast. Their song stopped abruptly, as if someone had turned off a radio.

They gave Theodor a vacant, lachrymose smile and then, with deliberate slowness, shuffled toward the truck, throwing coquettish glances back at him.

A chill ran over Willy as he watched the two approaching the truck, from which there still came loud and fearful outcries. The singers, by now the last ones outside the truck, hesitated in front of the truck door. Obviously they were afraid of the high steps. Professor Raeber, with studied casualness, stepped nearer, when

136

one of the attendants, a burly man with a head like a billiard ball, lost his patience and before anyone could stop him struck the women and tried to hoist them up into the truck.

With unexpected strength the two hurled the attendant back so that he staggered against the truck wheel. They kicked him, just once, and rushed toward the gaping crater with the towering cranes, defiantly shrilling their old sing-song. With unearthly speed they darted down the steep slope. Attendants, nurses, Professor Raeber, and, finally, Theodor and Willy, followed them.

The workers had just put down their tools, ready to go home. Their lunch boxes under their arms, they gasped as the two apparitions flitted by, singing loudly and holding on to each other.

"Stop them!" Professor Raeber yelled. "They are patients! Stop them!"

The two women, their hair flying loosely about them, clambered down the crater, falling, getting themselves covered with earth. But as if driven by an invisible motor, they recovered and began climbing up the cranes.

Willy stood there, petrified, while the workers began ordering them to come down.

Professor Raeber, though out of breath, implored them too.

"Be good, Maria and Henny." He coaxed them in the sweet voice of a governess persuading her charge to drink cod-liver oil. "We are only going to take you to a nicer place. Come down now and we'll give you something good to eat."

The two women stopped singing but climbed up farther. Like outlandish birds they hung on the crane's iron structure and Willy couldn't tell whether they had heard Professor Raeber or not.

Theodor offered to go after them but Professor Raeber refused his help, admonishing the attendants to get them down. When none of them obeyed, one of the workmen set the motor in motion. With a roar, the cranes started shaking; although Dr. Halder protested, Professor Raeber told the workers to go ahead, and slowly the iron necks began to descend, lowering the two women as if they were on some absurd Ferris wheel. The shaking of the iron structure proved too much for them. While still at a great height, they plumped to the ground, with a last piercing cry.

When Willy reached the crater's bottom, Dr. Halder was examining the two bodies. Attendants lifted them on two emergency stretchers made of rough-hewn building planks.

"One has a broken spine, the other a fractured hip," Theodor said bitterly as the women were carried toward the truck and the workers dispersed reluctantly. "I suppose you'll call it an accident, my dear colleague?"

"The attendants' fault," Professor Raeber replied. "Inefficient fools. I told them to watch the transfer with particular care. Never mind, colleague Halder, we'll take them to the emergency room. Of course, if one is rushed . . ."

"Why rushed?" Theodor asked.

"The directors of I. G. Farben promised to pay our institution a sizable sum if we evacuate speedily. The president's and vice-president's office are going to be where the old—er—asylum stood."

"I trust I. G. Farben will conduct its business in the same humane spirit as your institution," said Dr. Halder, taking Willy by the hand, "and I hope the ghost of the Monkey Cage won't disturb its transactions."

"I beg your pardon, dear colleague," Professor Raeber called after them, but Theodor and Willy had already left him. An early dusk had fallen, and as Willy turned back, the two cranes gave the impression of two malevolent petrified animals, baring their teeth. The truck with the iron grille droned past them as they walked by Mother Ella's deserted farmstead and reached the first houses of Reuter Weg.

12. DURING WILLY'S STRENUOUS LAST years political events formed a sort of underground accompaniment to his own life. Or, rather, he often imagined them like a second voice in a fugue, crossing and contradicting the first voice, his own existence. Although he became engrossed in innumerable new pursuits and his days were crowded, he couldn't help noticing the many illnesses which were befalling Germany.

His turning away from all political activity saved him in school. By staying at home every night and stubbornly cramming on E. Bruhn's *Greek Grammar for Beginners* and later Xenophon's long-winded *Anabasis,* he ultimately reached the level of his class, and even became second best.

As in all other subjects, Richter was first in Greek. In one respect, however, Willy beat Richter. When the Upper Secunda started studying Homer's *Odyssey,* Richter's logical mind became confused by Homer's overloaded and baroque verses, while Willy, without apparent effort, could disentangle them easily and make what he called "free translations."

Professor Preiser also invited him to a private seminar conducted every Thursday night at his old house in Ginnheim. Here the professor was interpreting Greek poets to a select group. This, in turn, led Willy to the poets of his day. Soon he, Oscar von Rainer, and Robbi—Hal declared poetry made him feel uneasy—spent long evenings discussing and squabbling over modern poets. Many of them, particularly those following the so-called "da-da" cult, which consisted of a sort of pessimistic baby talk, seemed to be determined to put as many obstacles in the reader's way as possible.

Unfortunately these discussions came to an abrupt end when Oscar von Rainer left Frankfurt at the close of the Upper Secunda term, to join his uncle's business in Hannsberg.

On a drab wintry Saturday afternoon Willy, Hal, and Robbi saw him to the station. At the last minute Hal had drawn for him a sketch of Willy, Robbi, and himself as they sat in the classroom.

139

"It's a good sketch. Thanks," Oscar said, putting down his bags. He seemed completely impervious to the din around him, and Willy again envied Oscar's gift for ignoring whatever he chose. The conductor began hurrying the passengers aboard.

"Good-by, fellows," Oscar said. For a fleeting instant he dropped his mask of aloof disgust. "I'll miss you in that Godforsaken hick town. Come and see me soon." He shook hands with the three and went in. As the train began to move out of the station, he stood in the window, very tall, fair, and too well groomed, and then the train took him away.

As his heritage, he left to Willy Siegfried Mahl of Lower Tertia, who took private lessons in Latin, French, and German, three afternoons a week, ten marks. Right now Willy wanted some money of his own.

Shortly before Oscar was scheduled to leave, Willy had asked his mother whether he could take speech lessons from Walther Taube, the leading actor of the Frankfurt Playhouse. Melanie, looking almost guilty, refused his request.

"I know this won't please you, Will," she said, "but we have less money than last year—despite all the I. G. Farben employees and their nervous stomachs. I know most people are making good money nowadays but we aren't." She put her hand over her right breast and looked out of the window.

"Uncle Herbert certainly is doing fine," Willy said.

"Never mind Herbert," Melanie said. "There's something else you must know. Please don't tell Father. I've been taking some treatments from Father's friend, Dr. Stein. Father is not to be told. Promise?"

Willy nodded slowly. He had noticed how Melanie left quietly every afternoon around three without ever mentioning it; also, the few times they had been shopping together she had been loath to carry even small bundles.

Now, she had averted her face, and he knew she did not wish to be questioned. For a brief moment an onrushing fear gripped him. It must have shown in his face because Melanie smiled and said:

"For heaven's sakes, it's nothing serious. I'm getting old, that's all. But you'll have to earn the money for your lessons yourself. I wish, though, you'd start saving a little, Willy."

"Why, Ma? I mean what for?"

"Father and I think you shouldn't enter the acting school right after the Goethe School. We'd rather have you study one or two terms first, in France and England, if we can manage. Remember Grandfather Pallavant's plan for you? How I wish I had that fund for you now, Willy. It would solve all your problems."

140

Willy hesitated. He hadn't worried much about what he was going to do after school.

"You don't have to decide anything now," Melanie said. "Only, if you can, save some money. Incidentally, acting school isn't cheap, either."

Thus Siegfried Mahl had entered Willy's life as the source of Willy's first earnings. Three afternoons a week, from three to five, Willy labored through Siegfried's homework, trying to be forebearing and not to be upset by his pupil's extraordinary stupidity and perpetual whining.

Siegfried Mahl, Jr., was fat, maddeningly slow, and lived in constant fear of his mother. Mrs. Mahl, a cadaverous lady, fond of horses and strict discipline, refused to accept the fact that Siegfried simply wasn't bright. She made Willy uncomfortable the moment he entered her house, and it seemed to pain her physically when she paid Willy his ten marks, on Fridays, at five minutes past five.

For two years Willy patiently steered Siegfried past the worst dangers of German, French, and Latin composition. He decided to skip the lessons from Mr. Taube. At the end of his last school term he had saved four hundred marks, half of which he deposited at the Creditbank while the other half was kept in Melanie's sewing cabinet. For reasons he couldn't explain to himself, he liked having some ready cash on hand.

Toward the end of Willy's last school term Mrs. Mahl announced she could pay him only eight marks, times being what they were and with Bolshevism practically on her doorstep. Willy was too preoccupied to quarrel with her. The whole year of Upper Prima was one big refresher course for the graduation exams. Sometimes Willy asked Hal or Robbi to take over the tutoring because he was too fed up and, besides, Siegfried seemed to grow steadily worse.

Hal was the envy of the Upper Prima, and for a very simple reason: his course was already charted. He would enter the Art Academy in Frankfurt—or somewhere else if his parents could afford it—and study painting. Most of Willy's classmates hadn't yet decided what to do, and right now they found no time to worry about it. They stuffed their heads with the reigning dates of emperors, presidents, and statesmen, chemical formulae, Latin, Greek, and French grammar, and other seemingly endless facts which they would forget the moment they left school.

Most of the others had vague plans: Gerhard Pueschel was going to be an athletics instructor, a policeman, or might join the Reichswehr; Kurt Schupp was inclined toward economics while, of all people, Franz Duester manifested a profound interest in the law. Robbi's future was all mapped out by his parents and, as he con-

141

fided to Willy, he couldn't defy them because it would make them unhappy. One term in Grenoble, France, one term in Italy, and finally apprenticeship in his father's jewelry shop. Most of the others in Upper Prima would attend some university though they didn't have any special interest or talent—it would keep them from looking for full-time jobs which were becoming scarcer and scarcer.

There began for Willy and Hal feverish months of wading through facts, rattling off names and dates to each other night after night, while the world outside was preparing to make them feel unwelcome once they had ceased being pupils. Any time Willy glanced through a newspaper or talked to his parents, he had a sinking feeling in his stomach, and only by the utmost effort could he get back to his books.

For, as the year 1929 went on, the air of hopefulness, of mushrooming buildings, crowded factories, increased production, began to disappear. On his way home one day in April Willy found himself face to face with a long queue of people, mostly young, bitter-looking men, caps back on their heads, small booklets in their hands; the new unemployed waiting for their insurance.

One night Willy simply couldn't go on cramming. For the hundredth time he had rehearsed the outlines of world history only to find how true old Preiser's summary was: as a whole, history was enough to make you retch.

He went into the drawing room and sat in Mother's chair near the garden window. Perhaps Ferdy was right, after all: weren't the world's crises getting bigger and worse? Mother often had described her childhood to him. When she was a girl in the eighteen-nineties life stretched before her like a quiet, well-tended street, unexciting but safe. Nobody ever dreamed of inflation or crises.

"Is that you, Willy, sitting there in the dark?"

Melanie switched on the light. "I'm glad you stopped working. You look done in. Do you like my hair? It's washed, but I still haven't got a bob."

"It looks like whipped cream," Willy said, getting up. Although he was only five feet eight, he was still a head taller than Melanie. "Promise me never to cut it short, Mother." He kissed her hair. It smelled of lilac shampoo and it also preserved a whiff of the sweetish-hot fumes of Mme. Albersheim's beauty parlor where he had accompanied Mother when he was younger.

"Look at this." Melanie unfolded a copy of the *Red Flag*. "I only hope Father won't see it, though some dear friend is sure to tell him." Willy looked over her shoulder.

The *Red Flag* denounced the increasing unemployment—two millions by now—as caused not only by capital (the usual source

142

of all evil) but by the real enemies of the German workers, the Social-Democrats, who from now on would be unmasked wherever feasible as "Social-Fascists."

From there on the editorial went all out, as if it had made a surprising scientific discovery. Ruthlessly, it declared, it would go on unmasking the archenemy, the Social-Fascists who, in reality, were a tool of the Big Bankers and the Industrial Czars. Even worse: because they feigned to protect the working class, because they were enemies in disguise, they were doubly dangerous.

Next to instalment 21 of "Lenin's Life, Translated from the Russian," Willy found a violent attack on Frankfurt's Theater Commission for not including a single "revolutionary drama" in the repertoire and "poisoning the public's mind with such opiates as *Five Frankfurters,* a comedy glorifying those supercapitalists, the Rothschilds."

Together with the other members—two from the People's party, one Center, one German National party—Dr. Halder was accused of "fascist leanings." The paper denounced his efforts to provide sick funds for the trade unions as "a blind." Like all upper-class physicians, he was interested only in exploiting his patients. . . .

"They must be mad," Melanie said with a sigh. "But it's the new line. We are Social-Fascists, Willy, in case you didn't know."

Willy was furious. "Can't Father sue? Or do something? I'm just in the mood to go over there and kick . . ."

"Don't be childish," Melanie said in a matter-of-fact voice. "They have been given the line and some of the poor fools might even believe it. You'd only get a black eye, and how would that impress the professors at graduation? The *People's Voice* will answer them, although they might as well not bother."

Willy never found out whether the *People's Voice* answered. However, some days later, after the last class, Gerhard Pueschel sauntered over to Willy's bench while he and Hal were gathering their books, too exhausted to talk. Pueschel, by now a clumsy six-footer, with the face of an athletic baby and brilliantined blond curls, grinned sheepishly.

"Look, Willy, what they say about your old man."

He pulled out a copy of the *Frankfurt Observer,* Only Certified Organ of the German National-Socialist Worker's Party, Section Frankfurt. The certified organ, Willy knew, was the old scandal sheet *The Lantern,* edited by the same man, Deputy Sprenger, the former plumber.

Hal and Willy went through the paragraphs Pueschel had marked with a red pencil. They assailed Theodor Halder in almost the identical terms as the *Red Flag,* with one slight difference. Where the Communist paper had accused the Theater Commission of

143

neglecting the revolutionary drama, the *Observer* observed the dearth of truly national plays dealing, for instance, with the patriotic Free Corps fighters. They accused Theodor and the other members of "cultural bolshevism" for putting on such outrages as "Wall Street's propaganda piece, *Strange Interlude,* Tolstoy's communistic the *Living Corpse* and the Rothschild apotheosis, *Five Frankfurters."*

Hal burst out laughing and, surprisingly enough, Pueschel chimed in. Willy had noticed Pueschel's illogical behavior before: he admitted having joined the Hitler Youth in Lower Prima and, occasionally, when Preiser gave him a low mark, he muttered something about the nation's awakening which would eliminate such teachers. Yet he was on the most friendly terms with Robbi Goldschmidt; also he had often begged Willy to come down to the gym and, for the benefit of the boys, give his imitations of the teachers and of the different dialects of the Frankfurt region, which Willy had perfected during the last years. Willy had always refused.

"Tell me, Gerhard," Willy said, "do you think my old man is as bad as all that? Do you believe this trash? At Tolstoy's time there wasn't any Communism in Russia, see Neubauer's *Modern History,* Volume Three. . . ."

"Aw, it's just talk to get people excited," Pueschel said. "Lots of hot air. I know your mother is a wonderful woman. Remember the amphitheater? So your dad must be swell too." He laughed heartily, then whacked Willy on the back. "Christ, that seems ages ago, doesn't it, chum?"

Pueschel sat down, and a brooding expression came into his too-blue eyes.

"You are all all right, and so is Robbi Goldschmidt. I keep telling my mother, not all Jews are bad, just some. Robbi never lets a fellow down. Only yesterday he helped me with those damn French verbs. Robbi's a pal."

"So we're all all right?" Hal said, slapping Gerhard's back just as hard. "Why the heck are you wearing this, then?" He dived into Pueschel's shirt and pulled out a tiny swastika on a silver chain.

"Hey, leave that alone, Petersen," Pueschel said, not at all embarrassed. "Nice silver work, isn't it? You see, the Goldschmidts are the exception to the rule. After all, I've known Robbi for years."

"Almost nine years," Willy intercepted. "We've put up with you for over eight years."

"Is it that long?" Pueschel took the *Observer* and pushed it into his coat pocket. As usual, he wore a loud sports jacket which he thought made him look like a boxer in an American movie.

"You know what?" he said, glancing over the cheerless class-

144

room, the dirty, chalk-smeared blackboard, the empty benches, "I'm almost sorry we'll be through here so soon. I'll miss you guys."

He stopped, groping for words, and Willy realized, to his amazement, that Pueschel was getting sentimental.

"I got the blues when Rainer left." Pueschel continued his outburst of intimacy. "In a few weeks we'll all be scattered to the four winds. Makes me feel awful. You two know what you're going to do. Petersen is going to paint and you, Will"—he made an almost affectionate pause—"Will, you're going to be famous. An actor. Or a movie star. And you won't know me any more then."

"What in hell!" Willy exploded, but Gerhard, in a feast of humiliation, went on: "I'm no good at anything. Sports, yeah. Or perhaps I'll make a good cop. Or I can handle that junk shop of ours in the old town with the 'Lorelei' playing til! you go crazy. The Hitler Youth? Is that what you wanted to say, Will? Aw, nuts. Gives me a kick to march with them or yell at somebody or smear words on walls. Something to keep me busy so I won't have to think about myself, or how I'm going to earn my living and how much more you kids have got. And my storm troop thinks I'm good!" He laughed, a thick, choked laugh which Willy had never suspected Pueschel of being able to produce.

"Sure, I'm good! A strong guy with all the muscles in the right places. And a lot better than the party riffraff they've got, those little jerks who think the swastika is going to make 'em big shots one day. Or the girls, those quick-lay brigades.

"No, I'll miss the stinking old school." He stopped abruptly and walked toward the exit.

At the door he turned toward Willy, giving the impression of a fierce dog who has lost his master. "Promise me one thing, Will."

"All right, Gerhard," Willy said.

"At the graduation party, will you do all your numbers? Bruhn, Preiser, Noll, the Taunus farmers, the hicks? Do Hitler and Goebbels if you want to, I don't care. I want a graduation party I can remember all my life."

Pueschel wasn't the only one to lose his balance. During the past three weeks in school Willy never stopped being startled by the thick streams of sentimentalism and good fellowship in which the Upper Prima wallowed.

They began recounting long-forgotten school incidents, savoring every detail. Melanie's fight with the departed Lattau, her victory in the amphitheater made her a kind of class Joan of Arc, and Willy couldn't prevent his mates from ordering an elaborate bouquet, to be sent to Melanie after graduation.

For once Franz Duester left his place at the bottom of the social ladder. The boys teased one another how he had explained "the thing" to most of them. The consensus—with Richter slightly dissenting—was that they should be grateful to Franz because he had told them outright how everything functioned, and at an early age too! Hal was approached, with Professor Preiser's approval, to make a sketch of all of them in the classroom with the teacher in front.

"If you can find time, Petersen," Dr. Preiser had added anxiously. By now he was as worried as the Upper Prima about the exams.

Shortly before graduation Willy gave up coaching Siegfried Mahl. The fat boy manifested no emotion whatsoever when Willy announced his resignation. Mrs. Mahl, the *Observer* in hand, immediately told him he had been by no means satisfactory and he also had poisoned Siegfried's mind with radical ideas, as she had not failed to notice.

"I wish I could impress anything on Siegfried's mind," Willy answered, "whether Latin grammar or radical ideas doesn't really matter."

Of course it was lost on Mrs. Mahl who, he discovered later, had cheated him out of one lesson. He forgot all about it in autumn, when the first examinations began.

The boys were led into a huge paneled hall especially reserved for this day. Behind a large screen painted, as Richter insisted, with phony Chinese letters, waited several chamber pots for emergency use. Two teachers, seated on a high platform, were watching the class, which was divided into groups A and B, each with different problems so the boys couldn't receive help from their neighbors.

The air was sticky. Director Bruhn wouldn't open any windows during written examinations, as if this would decrease the solemnity of the occasion.

Willy, as exhausted as all the others, never knew how he got through the three days. He did very well in Latin, Greek, French, German, and history, but muffed three out of four of Hagen's mathematical problems. For the German composition—an appraisal of the characters in Goethe's *Faust,* Part One, he filled more than thirty pages, finishing before everybody else, including Richter. Professor Preiser nodded at him imperceptibly, after he had glanced over the first pages.

At one o'clock, on the third day, when everything was over, the results appeared on the bulletin board: all had passed the final exams. They were to be matriculated tomorrow. Like almost everybody else, Willy hurried home, went to bed, and slept through until the next morning, the day of graduation.

146

The day was wet and gray. The huge auditorium of the Goethe School, decorated with plaster-of-Paris busts of German emperors, Greek poets, and assorted composers, was filled with parents and relatives in their Sunday best and slightly intimidated. The Upper Prima, in blue serge suits, was seated on the raised rostrum, facing the guests.

The school orchestra began with Brahms's "Academic Festival" —a piece Willy disliked intensely—and then Director Ewald Bruhn mounted the speaker's dais to wish the pupils Godspeed.

He reminded them of the manifold things they had learned, of the classic education they had been fortunate enough to receive and which would be a solid, never-wavering foundation for their future. Only once did Director Bruhn touch on what really lay ahead of them, as he admitted that times were not what they used to be. But no matter to which field of endeavor they might turn, what they had acquired in the time-honored Goethe School would serve them well for life.

Did Director Bruhn really believe that the knowledge of Greek grammar, chemical formulae, or trigonometry was going to matter? Willy wondered, while his eyes roved over the tightly packed rows of the auditorium. In the fourth row he spotted Theodor and Melanie. Sitting there, they appeared almost like strangers to him, and it struck Willy that they had aged, their hair nearly white, and that they bore themselves with an air of weary courage.

Not far off he spotted Mrs. Goldschmidt and Hal's mother, and the enormous Wagnerian woman next to Mrs. André must be Mrs. Pueschel. For a second Willy had a pre-vision of Gerhard Pueschel in about twenty years, when he had put on several layers of fat. At the end of another row sat Maria Reger, smiling at him when his eyes met hers and giving him a bad conscience: he had neglected her during these last months. He would call her up for another theater date next day.

And then, as Director Bruhn reached the last part of his speech and the musicians began rearranging their music, Willy recognized Mrs. von Rainer. She sat there, tiny and wrinkled and as if excluded. She had come for the graduation although her Oscar had left school two years ago and could never graduate. Now she was crumpling a handkerchief in her hand and fighting back the tears. Her eyes were wandering over the assembly hall and Willy guessed that she was memorizing every detail so she could write it to her son in Hannsberg.

"May you all find in whatever profession you choose the happiness, the brotherly spirit, and the profundity you enjoyed in this, Frankfurt's oldest school," Director Bruhn concluded. "But before, for the last time, you walk down the steps of your school, permit

147

me to follow the ancient tradition and introduce the new teachers and the new pupils, our new Sexta."

A procession of embarrassed ten-year-olds walked up to the director and, as he read their names, shook hands with him. For a moment Willy almost expected to see among them himself, ten-year-old Willy Halder, step up to start life in school. Hal nudged him sharply and whispered, "Wake up. Here comes our cue."

"We regret to see Professor Preiser leave us to take a position at Frankfurt University, as associate professor for classic languages," the director announced.

A wave of applause, started by the Upper Prima, swept the auditorium, forcing Professor Preiser to stand up and take a bow. The director frowned: this obviously had not been on the program.

Richard Hagen was also leaving, and the Upper Prima, previously informed of this event, greeted him with a thundering salvo.

There followed the introduction of the new teachers; Professor Bruhn rattled down some unknown names, shook the hands of some nondescript elderly men, when, suddenly, a wave of excitement went through the Upper Prima and captured the hall.

"It gives me special satisfaction," the director droned, "to welcome Professor Eberhard Lattau back into our fold."

Professor Lattau stepped up, jolly, rotund, and rosy, though his left eye was twitching worse than ever. The class did not applaud him. They remained stiff, looking straight ahead, and it seemed to Willy as if one could hear the silence spread over the hall.

Then the school orchestra hastily intoned the national anthem and graduation was over. Since the big party, with Professor Preiser as lonely guest of honor, was to start at eleven after they all had gone to see an Austrian operetta, *The Edelweiss King,* the boys didn't bother to say good-by now.

Theodor and Melanie were waiting outside for Willy. They pressed his hand, without saying anything, and then Theodor hailed a taxi. As they rode through the streets Willy had walked so often, twice a day and sometimes more, he was overcome by the feeling of losing something irretrievable, which he had thought he would never experience and which he had found silly in the others. . . .

He had never liked school. The fear of mathematics had spoiled too many years, and with the exception of Preiser's lessons, the Goethe School hadn't given him much. Now that he was free, it appeared he had lost a shelter. He was nineteen years old now and nobody would set up a curriculum for him. He was, as Bruhn had said, his own master, supposed to be grown up and bravely facing the world, armed with the wisdom of eight years of classical education.

148

He took Melanie's hand and Melanie bent toward him and kissed him.

"I looked over the other parents and decided I liked you two best," Willy said.

"Shouldn't I give you a good portion of fatherly advice now?" Theodor asked, but before Willy could answer, the cab, with a sudden jolt, came to a stop.

They had reached one of Frankfurt's most famous squares, the usually quiet Rathenau Platz. Now it was filled to overflowing with a huge, noisy crowd, pushing toward a big white building while policemen tried in vain to keep the people back.

"The Creditbank," said the driver, turning toward them. "God Almighty, the Creditbank is broke and they've closed it."

"Impossible," said Melanie. "They can't do that. Why, we . . ."

From a boy yelling, "Extra, extra," the driver bought the *General News* and showed them the headlines: Panic Grips World's Stock Exchanges as Stocks Tumble. Frankfurt Creditbank Closes. Others Follow.

"God Almighty," repeated the driver, "look over there." He jerked his car around and Willy recognized the sedate palatial building of the National Bank. Two cordons of policemen surrounded it, like a choker, and he could hear the savage protests of the crowd.

"Open the doors!" they shouted. "Let us in! We want our money! Open the doors, quick."

"A real crash," Melanie said in a toneless voice. "Another panic."

"That New York crash started it," the driver said, while cautiously backing away. "What's going to happen now? Another inflation? Where to, did you say, madam?"

"Sixty-six Reuter Weg," Willy answered. "There goes two hundred marks' worth of Siegfried Mahl."

The cab hurried past Opern Platz up Reuter Weg. With a glance at Theodor, who had averted his eyes so they couldn't see his face, Melanie said:

"Thank God for my sewing cabinet."

Theodor finally turned to her and Willy: "Your sewing cabinet?"

"I put half of what I saved in there for no particular reason," Willy said with pointed lightheartedness. "So I'd have some money after graduation."

"A nice graduation we offer you boys," Dr. Halder said, "a graduation into bankruptcy. That's how much, driver?"

"I don't know, Doc," the man said. "God Almighty, I'm all mixed up."

149

Unquestionably the Upper Prima's graduation party wouldn't have taken the course it did if the closing of the banks hadn't shattered almost every household in Frankfurt.

From the moment the boys met in front of the Opera House, a mood of desperate giddiness overtook them. For Willy, the idea of going to an old-fashioned Viennese operetta on the day of a bank crash was grotesque. Perhaps because both plot and music of *The Edelweiss King* seemed taken out of moth balls: there was the Baron disguised as a farmhand amid the elderly chorus farmhands who always kept ten feet away from him; there was his sweetheart, coy Annerl, pretending she didn't see through the clever disguise, which sent her into ripples of coloratura laughter throughout three acts.

The Upper Prima, in conventional stiff white collars, giggled loudly through *The Edelweiss King*—only Richter took it seriously —spoiling the second act love duet between the disguised baron, sung by a Wagnerian tenor who shouldn't have worn leather shorts, and Annerl, who kept throwing anxious glances at the conductor. Yet the figure which impressed Willy most was Sarek, the Bohemian peddler, billed as a "rattrap man," who provided the comic relief. He spoke the harsh dialect of the Czech-Austrian borderlands, adding Slavic endings to many words, rolling his *r*s and his eyes, and was given to sudden outbursts of fury.

His function—as far as Willy could determine—was to sell all kinds of gadgets and traps to the farmers, providing them with time-honored jokes and helping the plot along between songs. With his tiny mustache, darting eyes, and furious, hissing, and sputtering language, he bore a striking resemblance to Adolf Hitler. Whenever, during the years to come, Willy listened to the National-Socialist leader, he saw the Bohemian vendor of *The Edelweiss King* darting about the stage, blustering furiously, and peddling his traps. While Willy watched, he began working out his imitation and thus missed most of the ballet treasures of the last act.

The graduation party, in the second-floor ballroom of the Red Anchor near Antonio Platz in the Old Town, gave Willy a chance to try his new act. The Upper Prima, intent on ignoring the bank crash, drank steadily from eleven to one o'clock. None of them, except Franz Duester, was up to it. Even Kurt Schupp, who had prepared an orderly speech, was swaying, and managed only the first part. They sent two telegrams to Oscar von Rainer, and when Willy revealed Hal's big drawing of the entire class, Pueschel started to sniffle. Several others were equally moved, partly because of the liquor, partly because of their coming separation.

For half an hour Willy regaled them with his little skits, imitating all the teachers he knew how to portray, and the boys responded as if they had never heard them before. Around midnight Hal announced that, on Pueschel's special request, Willy was going to impersonate another personality.

While he shouted, sputtered, banged his fists, and stamped around the room, Willy wasn't sure whether he was impersonating Hitler or Sarek, the rattrap man. The two had fused. He mixed in long Latin words, mispronouncing them carefully, praised Pueschel for being blond, Duester for being sexually so productive, and proved that all evil in the world was caused by one group alone. "A secret conspiracy of calumnious mountebanks," he called it, glaring madly at the Upper Prima and spitting the syllables at them. This, it suddenly came to him, Hellmuth Handler had done when he made his coup with the Wandervogel, and Hellmuth, too, blended into the monster Willy was creating.

"The secret conspirators are—the bicyclists," he pronounced triumphantly. The bicyclists were ruining everything. Down with the un-Nordic velocipedes. It was an old gag to Willy, but the Upper Prima thought it hilarious and roared and drank more.

After Dr. Preiser had left, the gaiety mounted. They forced Willy to down several toasts, and from there on everything became foggy. Many had left, so much Willy knew. At the end there were only a few, with Robbi sleeping happily under the table.

They left the Red Anchor singing. Dimly Willy recognized Antonio Platz with its satyr on the fountain top. Time seemed to turn back as Duester led them into the Golden Pheasant. As if he hadn't moved since Willy last saw him, there stood Heinrich, the bartender, with his protruding yellow rat teeth. Was a clock striking three as they went up the narrow staircase? And was he supporting Hal or Hal helping him?

It was the nasty look of the bedroom which sobered Willy a little, though not enough. By now he knew that life was repeating itself and that he stood here in one of the bedrooms of the Golden Pheasant where Duester had taken him years ago and from which he had fled. Through the window again wafted the musty smell of cider from the thousand cellars of the Old Town.

This time he was the sailor whom he had watched in the next room but he was also Willy. Or was he? The girl waited on the bed for him, looking very soft in the light of the pink lampshades. Someone had pressed a tiny package in his hand and the woman showed him how to protect himself, perhaps because he was young and shy, and Willy went through everything as if it were something quite ordinary. Only one thing he knew clearly while he waited for Hal and the others downstairs in the deserted bar: he was as grown up as Duester or as Hugo Lammer, before whom he had once almost failed. How he remembered that awful summer—the damp cabin smelling of tar and heat and his haunting fear that he wasn't and never would be ready. The fear was banned for good. Stepping out into the morning, all the dizziness left him very abruptly.

A wan light was creeping over the gabled roofs of the Old Town as Hal and he walked away. The twisted alleys, the dark lanes, the narrow-breasted houses were still asleep, and their steps sounded much too loud. Hal had taken his arm. He once grinned at Willy and asked, in a low voice, as if afraid to wake the Old Town:

"Everything all right, Will? Were you careful?" Willy nodded, and they marched toward the Main Station. At this hour the huge place was deserted. Only a porter was picking up scraps, and he seemed to move as if in a trance. Yet the third-class waiting rooms were full of people, sleeping on benches, looking ragged and hungry.

They sat on the bench next to Track 10 where the first train to Cronberg was due at five-fifteen.

"Graduation into bankruptcy," Willy murmured. He had suddenly remembered it, and with Hal he didn't need to explain. "That's what Father said this morning. Half of my Mahl money was in the Creditbank."

"I can't believe we are grownups now," Hal answered, absent-minded. "I'd like to paint the station now, empty and asleep, with the tracks out there catching the light. Mother had her savings in the National Bank."

They looked up. A boy about their own age, in spotty pants, a black shirt, a greasy cap over one ear, stood before them.

"Could you spare a nickel for coffee?" he added, without looking at them. They gave him twenty-five pfennig and a thin grin spread over his weasel-like face. "Thanks, fellows; if there's anything I can do for you, I'll be in the third-class waiting room. Today and tomorrow, probably."

"What's he doing here, Hal?" Willy said. "He can't be older than we."

"A tramp," Hal answered. "One of the juvenile delinquents, as they call 'em. I see them every day in the waiting room here. They're tramping from town to town, looking for a job, or just tramping. Say, Will, does your father think we'll have another inflation?"

Willy looked out toward the tracks, which seemed to be hurrying into infinity. How often had Hal and he sat here, building beautiful and childish dream castles.

"I don't know, Hal," he answered, "but he's scared of what's coming."

152

13. EVEN IF WILLY HAD TRIED TO ENTER the Municipal Acting School it would have refused him: there were too many ahead of him. The next term at Frankfurt University didn't start until spring, and Willy found himself with a few empty months on his hands. Since Hal's art academy—at which he had managed to obtain a fellowship—also opened its new season around April, Willy spent a good many days at Cronberg.

The two boys were more exhausted than they had realized. The first week end after graduation Willy and Hal did nothing. Though they slept more than twelve hours every night, the unnaturally mild autumn air made them drowsy.

They were sitting in the Petersens' garden one Sunday afternoon when Hal received a phone call. He appeared excited and embarrassed when he returned.

"What's the matter?" Will inquired. "Who called?"

Hal hesitated. Then he plumped down in the grass at Willy's feet and told him about Ilona. Hal and she had met while registering at the academy. Ilona Rushenka was born in St. Petersburg and had come to Frankfurt as a child. Her father, a former White Russian officer, insisted he was one of the few not claiming to be at least a cousin of the late Czar.

Ilona and Hal had started exchanging sketches, arguments, and kisses, and Hal admired her caricatures, which were better than his.

"She's blond, with green eyes," Hal concluded, "and I feel like a heel for what happened on graduation night."

"Don't tell me she has a short temper, rolls her *r*s, and carries a volume of Dostoevski around," Willy said with a pang of what he knew was unfair jealousy. After all, Hal could make friends with anyone without consulting him.

"She's intelligent and wonderful to talk to," Hal answered. "I was afraid you wouldn't like her because in many ways she's just like you."

153

For a moment they looked at each other. It occurred to Willy that Hal had grown more and more to resemble his father, the taciturn, sunburned farmer Petersen who looked as solid as the trunk of one of his apple trees. By now Hal's freckles had settled down to a peaceful pattern, his red hair had lost the carrotty sheen. Although Willy liked the old color better, its brown-red made Hal less conspicuous. Through Willy's mind flashed the innumerable instances when Hal had gone his own way, quietly, answering to no one, and how he, Willy, had felt shut out. It was about time he let Hal go his own way, particularly since Hal never interfered with Willy's life.

Ilona arrived later that afternoon and was duly introduced to Willy.

Fortunately he didn't have to pretend he liked her. He really did. Willy had never met such a girl. She talked exactly the way he did and, besides, her temperament drew him irresistibly to her. Ilona took it for granted that he was, so to speak, Hal's oldest possession, and she did not attempt to establish between her and Hal a common field of interest which would exclude Willy. She avoided talking shop but, to Willy's delight, did some quick caricatures. They, like his imitations, attempted to capture the characteristics of a person and exaggerate them. Although Ilona only rarely gave him a chance to finish a sentence, they understood each other perfectly while Hal sat there, whittling a dumb-looking sheep's head, letting them throw half-finished and often nonsensical sentences at each other.

"I gabbed too much," Willy whispered to Hal before they left to take the last train back to Frankfurt, "but she just made me go on."

"Don't be an ass," Hal said. "I was afraid you two wouldn't get along. Thank God, I was wrong. Besides, you won: she carries a volume of Dostoevski with her."

The volume, *The Idiot,* was printed in such fine type that Ilona couldn't read in the dim light of the Cronberg local. The two talked about everything under the sun and not once did Ilona emphasize how fond she was of Harold or treat him to one of those very personal confessions with which girls always embarrassed him. Ilona also gave him an idea.

"You simply can't sit home and mope until the new term. You know what I would do?"

"Of course I don't, Your Highness," Willy said. "Or is it Your Excellency?"

"I'm the only White Russian girl in Frankfurt who insists on being called simply princess," Ilona declared. "Besides, never joke with Russians about their former rank. All *émigrés* are touchy. My

154

idea, in case you care to listen, is to get work as an extra in the Playhouse and the Opera, if you can get in, and learn how things are done."

"You mean I should wear historical costumes which never fit and shout 'The King is coming?' Sounds stupid."

Ilona simply smiled, and they understood each other.

Melanie thoroughly approved of the idea—to Willy's surprise—but they argued awhile about the proper procedure.

"Why couldn't I call Busch?" Melanie asked. "After all, your father helped him get in as a director. It will save you a lot of red tape."

Willy remained stubborn. "I want to try by myself. Fritz Peter Busch might say yes because of Father, but he won't like it."

Melanie gave in, pointing out that, no matter what, he would always be known as Theodor's son, and good luck.

In the big, drafty waiting room of the Playhouse office Willy found Maria Reger. She seemed very grown up and carried herself with a certain tense manner which Willy diagnosed as the current style among young actresses-to-be. It had been started by a young star from Vienna, who always gave the impression of a frightened and intellectual deer.

"Congratulations on your graduation," Maria said, looking over his head. "I went to your commencement but you never so much as wrote me a line. Mother thought you were probably too busy with your little self."

"I really was busy," Willy answered, slightly taken aback. "How does your mother know what I'm doing?"

"Oh, Mother knows everything," Maria cried enthusiastically, forgetting her current style. "She managed to get me into acting school. I'm here to speak to Director Kordan right now. I'm so happy."

"Congratulations," Willy said. "You can turn your nose up at me. I'll be an humble extra while you'll be a real 'member of the staff.'"

Before Maria went into Director Kordan's office she bent over Willy and said: "Please call me. I simply can't call you, you know."

Willy decided he would, but then he was propelled into F. P. Busch's office. Busch was tall, thin, and overpowering. He interspersed his sentences with foreign words, and the moment Willy entered the super-modern office he had the feeling that F. P. was classifying him the way an experienced zoologist classifies a minor beetle.

"Hm. Young, slim, dark, sensitive," F. P. declared, instead of a greeting. "What do you want here?"

155

"I want to be an extra so . . ."

F. P. laughed heartily, then stopped abruptly in the middle of a cascade.

"Of course you want to be an actor. You figured this is the way to break in. You're wrong. What do you know about the stage?" He shook his mane of white hair and circled around Willy, who began to enjoy it. It was a scene from a play F. P. was improvising.

"What would you like to hear, Mr. Busch? Shall I be the over-awed young man with aspirations? Or shall I be brazen so you can roar?"

Willy roared the last word, and F. P. stopped.

"Aha. You want me to see you aren't stupid. Most actors are. They must be."

"I shall try to live up to your expectations," Willy said, "if you let me get in a word or two."

"Sit down," F. P. declared in a flat voice. "What's your background?"

As he talked, Willy knew Melanie had been right: he'd always be Dr. Halder's son.

"Why didn't your father call me?" F. P. said promptly. "After all, we fought together to get *Strange Interlude* past the loggerheads in the commission."

"I guess I wanted to strike out for myself. Please give me a chance, Mr. Busch, so I can see how things are done backstage."

F. P. nodded. He shuffled some papers, then suddenly relaxed, assuming such a natural air that Willy wasn't able to figure out whether F. P. was being really himself or whether he was playing the part of a man at ease. In later years Willy was to discover that F. P. himself didn't know. He stylized every episode of his life into a scene and the exaggeration had become part of his nature.

Willy was hired to start the next week in *Goetz von Berlichingen,* at two marks a night, and if he wanted to see F. P. at work he could attend rehearsals of the new Georg Kaiser play, *October Day,* starring Henrietta Rauh.

As he turned to leave, F. P. remarked over-casually: "Other people work differently. You know Mrs. Reger?"

Willy said he only knew her daughter.

"We were ready to accept Maria into the school because she is talented. The judges, Mr. Taube, Mr. Impekoven, and Miss Einzig agreed. Then Mama Reger began putting on pressure. Well, see you soon."

He looked deeply into Willy's eyes—figuring, Willy was sure, who was next on his schedule—and Willy was dismissed.

He felt elated. The elation sustained him during the performances of Goethe's *Goetz,* in which Willy appeared as Young Guardsman. He felt at home on the huge playhouse stage, in the crammed, smelly dressing room whose walls seemed to be covered with cold cream, and in which the extras, mostly theater enthusiasts like himself, were forever exchanging dreams about their brilliant though remote acting careers. They relished the regular actors' innumerable intrigues, plots, and counterplots to the last detail.

He ran into Maria quite often. One night he persuaded her to take a walk along the Main River. They sat on a bench, discussing Henrietta Rauh, Frankfurt's character actress. The river murmured past them, unconcerned and lulling. Slowly Willy felt himself soften, as though a chemical change had taken place within him. An urge sprung up to be close to Maria, and he slid a timid arm across her shoulders. It was good to sit here, while the city lights formed an irregular pattern in the darkness, like the flash bulbs on a huge telephone switchboard. As he pressed Maria's shoulder to him, he felt peaceful and sheltered. He just wanted to sit there while her body, so much softer than his, leaned confidently against him. He wanted to be nice to her, to make her feel as good as he did while they watched the lights go out here and there like signals, with a special meaning only for them.

"You aren't listening at all, Will," Maria complained. "Miss Rauh says my profile is perfect for tragic parts. Look."

She turned a very straight and unyielding profile against the night. Willy relaxed his pressure against her shoulder. The lazy happiness slowly trickled out of him. Why did she want her profile admired now? Or was he again too sensitive?

"A very good profile, Maria," he said. "But you need more than a profile to be as good an Antigone as Miss Rauh."

They discussed Miss Rauh for some time, then Maria declared she must go home. She put her arms around Willy and kissed him. She kissed ardently, with an abandon Willy had never expected. Yet in some way he couldn't define the urgency of her kiss excluded him, as if she just followed her desire to be kissed. It was a possessive and at the same time a blind embrace.

Before they parted Maria invited him for dinner. It was high time he met Mother. Willy accepted for the following Friday.

He was a little apprehensive when he rang the bell of the Regers' dignified but faintly neglected house in the Westend, which on the outside kept up the pretense of being a one-family mansion although it had been divided into several tiny apartments. On Melanie's advice he brought some flowers, which Mrs. Reger accepted as a fitting tribute, owing her and her daughter from every male visitor.

157

Mrs. Reger, stately and exuding chiffon, wore a perpetual thin smile, but her face reminded Willy strongly of a boiled potato into which a child has set two pieces of coal for eyes. Somehow she was one with the living room, which featured velvet-covered sofas and silk cushions. Its walls were spattered with gravures of forgotten ballerinas and actresses, and Willy couldn't find a single picture of a male anywhere. His apprehension grew as, during the excellent dinner, Mama Reger directed the conversation with a steely hand. She seemed convinced that she and her daughter were unique, living on a far higher plane than other people. At regular intervals she praised one of Maria's many outstanding qualities. Willy expected the girl to squirm but instead she beamed. In turn, when Mrs. Reger retired for a while after dinner, Maria launched a campaign of praise for "Luli." Luli had brought her up, scraping and saving, after Mr. Reger died, leaving them very little— out of sheer malice, it seemed. Mother had taken her present exhausting job so that Maria could have everything—could even attend Mlle. Chautemps's Pensionat pour Jeunes Filles, in Lausanne; and now Luli had helped Maria to pass the examinations of the acting school. . . .

Willy's uneasiness increased even more when Mrs. Reger, having rested and put on another chiffon cloud, began elaborating the perils and vicissitudes of two women living alone. For twenty years Mrs. Reger had been working for the City Welfare Bureau, helping the poor. Yet everybody was against her, in the office as well as on the many committees where she served out of a sense of duty. As the afternoon went on, more and more undeserved enemies peopled Mrs. Reger's tales—mostly women and all socially far below the Regers. Several boys were also mentioned who had quite often enjoyed Mrs. Reger's "old-fashioned hospitality," but suddenly, with a show of very bad behavior, had stopped calling. Mrs. Reger ended up by accusing the boys of having harmed—or almost harmed—her Maria.

Willy left, confused and depressed. He had found a new Maria who considered it her main duty to form a phalanx with Luli against the many intruders threatening their hectic unity.

The next evening, after *Goetz,* however, Maria smiled at him as if nothing had happened. While they sat in the Theater Restaurant munching sandwiches, Willy couldn't resist the temptation to say:

"Don't get mad, Maria, but it made me uncomfortable to hear your mother sing your praises all the time. As if I was expected to say every five minutes how wonderful you were."

Maria vehemently denied that Luli had ever praised her at all, and then jumped at him with unconcealed fury:

158

"Luli and I are very close. We have to fight against all those awful people. You as a man can't understand it. Don't criticize her. I won't have it! I won't have it!"

Maria's voice had lost the soft timbre of the acting school and she looked exactly like Luli, with only the chiffons missing.

"All right, Maria. I won't bring it up again. Forget it," Willy said.

After a while Maria regretted her outburst, and as they said good-by in the hallway of her house she kissed him breathlessly, as if she would never let him go.

When next he saw Hal, Willy tried to describe the situation but Hal was no help. As a matter of fact, he hit on a most unfortunate idea: Willy must take him and Ilona to the Regers' soon, since Ilona was much better at sizing up women than either of them.

They overrode Ilona's protests, and the next Sunday afternoon the three of them set out to visit Mrs. Reger who, in her own words, was only too glad to meet any friends of Willy's. . . .

From the moment Ilona entered the living room Mrs. Reger put up her defenses. When she offered her tea, she sounded as if Ilona were an undeserving welfare case. Maria treated Ilona as a rival of long standing. Mrs. Reger never addressed her directly, devoting herself almost exclusively to Hal. To hear his judgment of her paintings, she took him into the other room, from which her aggrieved and reedy voice could be heard clearly.

They stayed for what seemed to Willy a long time, while he and Maria sat in silence, playing with the spoons in their teacups. Ilona had started browsing through the Regers' bookcases. When Mrs. Reger reappeared, she walked quickly toward Ilona.

"Do you read German fluently, Miss—Rushenka," she asked, "or do you have to read our literature in translations?"

"I read them in German," Ilona said. "I came here as a child."

"How nice," Mrs. Reger answered. "I can't read Russian writers. They're so—well, so crude and passionate. Do you think they reflect the character of the people?"

A silence followed which, finally, Willy broke with considerable effort.

"Goodness, it's much later than I thought. F. P. is expecting me at the theater. Let's go, kids. Good-by, Mrs. Reger. Thanks for the tea. Good-by, Maria; see you at the playhouse."

The three left, and for a while none of them said a word. As they walked along Bockenheimer Strasse, Ilona took Hal's and Willy's arms.

"Willy," she declared, "Maria's a prisoner. Don't you get the setup?"

159

Willy shook his head. "Not entirely. But there's something between them that frightens me."

Ilona decided she wanted to relax, on a hard seat, please, and they sat down on a bench in Opern Park, which at this Sunday-afternoon hour looked as if all the inhabitants had fled in panic.

"I'm going to give you my opinion, Will," Ilona began, "even if it hurts. You are lucky. You haven't met women like Luli Reger. I have. The women in magazine offices, the women with big jobs in the fashion industry—many of them are like her. Petty monsters. Luli is a jealous one to boot. She owns Maria completely. She persuaded her long ago that only Mother knows what's good, that all outsiders are evil. Maria may be a nice kid, but she's blind. Mother still holds her in a baby carriage with steel bars."

"Maria didn't mind kissing Willy," Hal said. "And in a grown-up way too."

"Don't be embarrassed, Will," Ilona said. "I've been around more than you, and I hope you can kiss Maria away from Mother. But mothers have many weapons, and I'm afraid she'll win."

"For heaven's sake, the girl must learn to lead her own life," Willy said, and Ilona answered: "I have an inkling you aren't the first to try, Willy."

Ilona proved to be a shrewd guesser. The next night, as Willy and Maria sat on their bench, close to the slowly breathing Main River, Maria told him about how vulgar Edgar had been, a boy in high school, and what trouble Mr. Jackel, a middle-aged businessman, had caused. Maria talked on, innocently proud of her previous beaux. Without being aware of it, Willy played with her hand. He felt reluctant to kiss her, reluctant to confide in her, and he was depressed by her self-preoccupation. While she spoke—always about herself or Luli—Willy heard Mrs. Regers's voice through her. Luli was with them all the time.

He couldn't go on, he had to think his way through all this. He took her home early that night and when he kissed her good-by in the hallway the impression swept over him that he was kissing a complete stranger.

In a long letter Oscar von Rainer invited Willy and Hal for a visit in Hannsberg.

"It might help overcome my boredom," he wrote. "Not that Hannsberg is quiet. It's loud, dirty, and rough, but I'm bored nevertheless, since none of these hold any attraction for me. You can stay at our house—it's too big anyhow for Uncle Erich, Aunt Frieda, and me. The meals are good, the weather is crazily mild this fall, so come up, now that you have time."

160

"He's lonely," Willy said, putting away the letter. Hal and he were sitting in Willy's room, looking out into Reuter Weg. A loud sun made the streetcar rails glitter and the leaves on the trees were still parading a rich green color.

"A round-trip ticket costs about thirty-forty marks," Hal said.

"It's a lot," Willy admitted. From the moment Oscar's letter had arrived he knew he wanted to accept the invitation. It might be good to get away from Frankfurt, from Maria, from the confusion and unhappiness she brought him.

"What do you say if we hitchhike? We'll dig up our old outfit, pots and everything. This is our post-graduation trip, the one we had planned so long, to Norway or India."

"To Hammerfest," Willy took up their old, half-forgotten game, "the northernmost city. Remember? In any case you need new pants. You've grown too fast."

"I saw a pair of sea-blue corduroys," Hal said, "and this is a good pretext to buy them. What do you suppose our parents will say?"

Theodor had no objections. They'd run into boys from all walks of life, he said, the kind they'd never meet at a university, and it might be a valuable experience. Melanie objected strongly; many of the tramping youths were riffraff, and the two might get into trouble.

This time she lost. The Petersens raised no objections—what the doctor decided was all right for Willy was all right for Hal. Melanie extracted several promises from them: they must wire her if they got stuck, they must look up Theodor's friend, Dr. von Erb in Hildesheim, and they had to write regularly—she compromised on post cards—every two days.

Joyfully, Hal bought his sea-blue corduroys. They could still use the sleeping bags, windbreakers, knapsacks, and other utensils from their Wandervogel days. Willy contributed a first-aid kit, while Hal carried the maps in an elegant leather pouch. He added his big whittling knife, planning to carve some figures on the way and sell them to the farmers, if possible.

Thus, at seven in the morning they set out in the unnaturally mild September weather which, the meteorologists insisted, would last long this year. Near Ginnheim they thumbed their first ride with an elderly couple driving to Bebra. The couple disapproved of two boys from the "better classes" hiking all the way up to Hannsberg since the road was swarming with "dirty, job-shirking unemployed." They deposited Willy and Hal at Bebra, at an untidy youth hostel.

From then on Willy and Hal discovered it wasn't easy to thumb a lift. Two salesmen who took them for a short stretch explained why: too many assaults recently, too many unscrupulous youngsters took advantage of those who offered them a lift.

Erny, the first experienced tramp they met in a deserted hay barn that night, denied this. Erny wore extremely ragged clothes but his baby face shone with kindness and his blue eyes radiated candor. Not more than eighteen, he had been on the road many months—he couldn't remember for how long—and he bristled with road lore.

"Never trust the old-timers," he warned, as the three settled down in the hay. "By the way, have you something to eat, comrades? Haven't been able to filch a thing today."

Slightly reluctant, Willy handed him some bread and sausage. Erny accepted the food as a tribute to his wisdom. Soon they all went to sleep after having decided to set out together for the city of Fulda early in the morning. Willy and Hal, tired from the long hike, overslept. Hal was still asleep at nine o'clock when Willy woke up. He looked around. No Erny.

At a glance Willy guessed what had happened. It was remarkable how much a single boy could carry. Erny had stolen the two sleeping bags, which they hadn't used in the barn, all the food, the leather pouch for the maps, and their extra clothing, graciously leaving them one pair of socks and one shirt each. While Willy was rummaging through the knapsacks, Hal woke up. He first refused to believe Erny could be a thief, then was seized by a fit of fury. All morning Hal muttered about the "chiseling bastard" while they walked on over the bumpy roads.

The landscape became increasingly hilly and ugly.

"These meadows make me sick; look at the coal dust on the trees," Hal commented sourly. "Remember: we won't sleep in a barn if there's anyone in it. We might wake up without our pants."

As it turned out, Hal couldn't live up to his resolution. After wandering three days without getting a single ride, the two looked as dirty as anyone on the road. One night they spent in a forest near Fulda. The hard ground made their bones ache so much that from then on they accepted gladly any hay barn, crowded or not. At least Hal had found a good piece of oak wood in the forest and transformed it into a miniature lamb.

That evening Willy took the carving to the first farmhouse he could approach without being bitten by a dog. The woman opening the door scrutinized him with a cold face. Like many farm women she appeared at the same time immature and very old, and she declared she'd have to call her husband. Willy heard her shriek, "Anton!" through the house in a piercing, dead voice.

Willy was lucky: Anton Herder liked the lamb. He turned it

162

admiringly in his thick gnarled fingers which reminded Willy of beet roots, and said he'd take it but pay no cash. In exchange Gerda, his wife, would give them a meal and they could sleep in the hay barn.

Willy hurried back to get Hal, and soon they stripped as much as they assumed farmers could stand, and cleaned themselves thoroughly under the pump in the yard. The meal was served in the gloomy kitchen. Its mainstay was potatoes—farmers, Willy had noted before, seemed to thrive on them. However, Gerda also served some boiled beef with cabbage and a cup of Kornfrank afterward.

While Gerda started cleaning the dishes, Anton showed the boys his farm. As Hal grasped immediately, it once had been a well-kept place, comprising several acres of land, a huge orchard, roomy stables, and a large chicken coop. Now the stables were almost empty, only five pathetic chickens cackled in the coop, and the fields were badly tended. Anton's output, he said, had fallen off steadily. Anton and Hal carried on a knowing shoptalk while Willy listened, watching the farmer. He was a heavy man of undetermined age with features which seemed built of several heavy wood blocks and which, as a rule, remained as impassive as his wife's. Yet while he talked to Hal his eyes occasionally lit from inside with a fierce and quixotic light.

When they returned to the kitchen, Anton took a bottle, three thimble-sized glasses, and a bunch of brochures from a cupboard.

"You fellows are no tramps," he said gravely. "It's a pleasure to talk to you."

He bowed in a very old-fashioned way and poured the white liquid into the glasses. "Kirsch," he announced. "Old Kirsch. Go easy or it will burn your throat."

He gulped his own, however, without any visible effect, and poured himself a second. Then he told them what had happened to him.

It wasn't a new story—most farmers told the same—but nevertheless it struck Willy that to a farmer the loss of land or cattle meant much more than the loss of property to a businessman. Every farmer Willy had met looked upon his acres, his house, his animals, not simply as pieces of salable property. They were part of his daily existence, almost as it were of his body, and their loss filled him with undying bitterness.

"I couldn't pay my mortgage last year," Anton said, "and just when crops were bad, the bank wouldn't extend the loan. Said they had trouble themselves." Anton laughed a short, defiant laugh. "Trouble! A bank! All banks are filthy rich. They could have tided me over, but no. They took away my best cows, my

163

oxen, and the good layers among the hens. One day, I tell you, the banks will be destroyed. The Lord's fire will fall from heaven on the moneylenders, as the Bible says."

"Don't talk so loud, Anton," said Gerda, who had shuffled into the kitchen. "You woke me up." She sat down, a little removed from the men, the sleep still on her face. "What's it all about?"

When her husband told her, her face lost its blankness. An immense hatred filled her eyes as she began telling, in a rattling voice, how everybody had betrayed the farmers. All Weimar parties were rotten, catered to the cities, the banks, the moneyed people. . . .

She went on with her litany, interspersing it with learned-sounding phrases which, Willy suspected, were lifted from some book and which to him seemed like garish tropical flowers growing incongruously in a drab cabbage patch.

All these high-flown clichés told of "the farmer's sacred mission to renew the nation's vitality."

Pointing to the brochures, Anton said: "We're the backbone of Germany. Blood and soil are what make a nation. You know, these here books opened my eyes. When the time is ripe, we'll get rid of the moneylenders, cattle dealers, Jewish-international banks. We'll get back our livestock, our chickens, and our land." He stopped, overcome at the prospect.

"That's our ticket all right," Anton Herder continued. "All my neighbors are deep in the red. The Hitler party is a farmer's party. And don't let them tell you we farmers are stupid. Our day will come."

While listening, Willy glanced around the room with its furniture gone to seed, its old-fashioned calendar, its gaudy oil painting which had been elegant fifty years ago. It dawned on him that for the first time the Herders were being told they were better than the city people whom farmers secretly had always considered superior. Now farmers had a "sacred mission." They believed they were better than all the others. He'd never argue them out of anything. . . .

The two boys slept long next morning but Gerda fed them a huge breakfast, assuring them her husband had enjoyed their talk last night.

"You shouldn't hike this way," she added to Willy, almost maternally. "Even for a city boy you are too fine."

Hal kidded Willy about this during the next weeks when things began to take a dismal turn. The Thuringian Mountains between Fulda and Eisenach—their next goal—seemed to scare motorists; only once could they get a lift. Thanks to Hal's carvings they were a little better off than the other hikers. Many farm women liked Hal's animals, and so Willy and Hal often got a warm meal while the others had to shift for themselves. Also, most of the women took to Willy. When they had closed the deal, they usually asked more questions than the boys cared to answer, and Willy often invented wild stories to satisfy their curiosity. It was useful to pretend to be students—apparently there had been many so-called "work students" on the road during the summer, looking for jobs.

Farmer Friedrich Schmitt, near Muehlhausen, for instance, had hired several of them and though, in his opinion, city folks were a pest, these students had done a good job. After having talked with the Schmitts for a while Willy couldn't help agreeing. The students had converted farmer Schmitt from a devout Catholic into an equally pious believer in the gospel of the new prophet Adolf Hitler.

Friedrich Schmitt's farm lay near an immense dark forest which, as Willy and Hal had approached, took on a more and more malevolent air. Willy was grateful to Mrs. Schmitt for persuading her husband to let them stay in the barn—he dreaded the idea of sleeping in this "Forest of Shadows" as it was called.

"Too many people have lost their way in it," farmer Schmitt explained almost proudly during dinner. "My wife won't let our children gather wood there. Gunnivor, so the legend goes, lies in wait there, ready to kill human beings and eat them, bones and all."

"Who is Gunnivor?" Hal asked, and Mrs. Schmitt said: "Don't spread those awful tales, Father. You'll frighten everybody." She crossed herself and glowered at her husband who, unperturbed, explained about Gunnivor.

The legend went far back to the times when the Thuringians and Saxonians had been Christianized by force. The Franks from the west had killed thousands, forcing the remaining people into slave labor. The Saxonians and Thuringians had become Christianized, but they hadn't given up their old pagan gods. The gods, led by Gunnivor, had gone into hiding. . . .

As farmer Schmitt described the ritual, worship, and the awe-inspiring appearance of Gunnivor, the man-eating dragon god, it seemed to Willy as if these battles had not been fought a thousand years ago, but recently, perhaps during the last world war. To Friedrich Schmitt, Gunnivor was as real as the forest outside or the unpredictable weather or the saints in which he had once believed. As dusk fell slowly over the forest, it seemed as if its trees were imperceptibly advancing toward the farm, to occupy it, planting their root feet right here in the kitchen floor.

For a moment Willy could almost understand farmer Schmitt's faith in Gunnivor, and a chill ran over him.

"In the Thirty Years' War," Mr. Schmitt concluded, "two hostile

165

regiments went into the woods to fight it out. But no shot was heard. No soldier ever came back, and the church chronicle says their bodies were never found. Gunnivor . . ."

"Don't you ever tell this to the children," Mrs. Schmitt broke in furiously. She put a big hunk of cheese on Willy's plate, saying: "I declare, you look peaked, my boy. Are you cold?"

Willy said it was a little chilly, and Mrs. Schmitt at once proposed they should sleep in the attic room instead of the drafty and eerie barn.

Friedrich Schmitt agreed and offered the farmer's universal medicine against everything, a strong Kirsch, which Willy gulped down. It made him warm inside and a trifle dizzy, so that he thought he didn't hear right when farmer Schmitt suddenly asked:

"What do you fellows think about Point 17?"

Hal tried to come to Willy's rescue by saying they were very tired and perhaps they'd better go up to the attic but Mr. Schmitt insisted on informing them that Point 17 of the National Socialist party program demanded a thorough agrarian reform and the abolition of ground rent. This proved that Adolf Hitler was the farmer's best friend.

Friedrich Schmitt spoke of the party with the same awe with which the *Red Flag* referred to the Communist organization. "This Hitler may be a foreigner," he declared, "but he and the party know what we need. I've learned the difference between creative and rapacious capital. I know."

Willy blinked at Mr. Schmitt and tried to understand the roots of the farmer's faith.

"Creative Capital" was one god, a benign one. Not all capital was bad, as the Communists preached—who appeared as dangerous heretics to be burned at the earliest moment. Industry, small business, craftsmen, farmers, they were all creative, producing for everybody's benefit. Rapacious Capital was evil and, unfortunately, much more powerful. All banks were rapacious. They didn't produce, they just held and lent money and drove the farmer from the farm, the craftsman from his shop if he couldn't pay. Rapacious Capital was Jewish, since all banks were Jewish, and it was international, an equally sinister quality. A gigantic ogre, it spread over the whole globe, holding Germany in bondage. Interest slavery, those reparations Germany must pay America and the Allies, they were the work of the arch fiend, Rapacious Capital, set to destroy Germany. . . .

As the words droned on, it swept over Willy that to the farmer Rapacious Capital meant another, a world-wide Gunnivor, out to devour Germany. They were both dragons; you couldn't understand them by thinking, you must slay them. In this new mythological

166

world created by the messiah Hitler arguments didn't count because Faith had rendered the Believers invulnerable against the bullets of reason. Schmitt and Herder and the other farmers had accepted the sham gospel which exalted The Peasant as much as Marx's Scientific System had exalted The Worker. . . .

Fortunately Mrs. Schmitt insisted they go to bed now and led them up to the attic. The bed was roomy enough for three, and Willy soon fell into a deep sleep under the heavy red-checked featherbed.

At five Mrs. Schmitt woke them up. Willy could hardly persuade himself to wash under the outdoor pump, whose water was positively icy. When they dried themselves, Hal said:

"Let's take it easy today. Just stroll along. I want to catch the light over the meadows and make a sketch of the Forest of Shadows. Can you beat it, Will? Schmitt really believes in dragons. I didn't get the business with that Rapacious Capital, but to him it's a kind of monster too. The way he talked it sounded like something out of——"

"*The Eye of Lo-Fo,*" Willy broke in. "By Maximilian Kern. You're right. It is funny."

Yet Willy didn't really think it was funny, and his attempt at banter didn't deceive Hal. He looked somewhat pinched. Mrs. Schmitt, apparently more at ease now that her husband had gone to work, stuffed him with breakfast. She had lit a candle under a wooden Madonna which, Willy could have sworn, hadn't hung there last night. Probably Mrs. Schmitt had remained a good Catholic and was fighting an unceasing battle against her husband's new beliefs. She seemed a little lost as she sat there, much too worn out for her years, gazing out at the forest, dark and massive before her door.

"Would you like me to make a quick sketch of you for keeps?" Hal suddenly offered. To Willy, it seemed exactly the right thing to do. Mrs. Schmitt had been nicer than all the others and deserved something extra. Now she was blushing; what would her husband say? But Hal finished the sketch while she was still protesting. She accepted the drawing with hushed awe. Then, as they were leaving, she forced four good-sized sandwiches on them and made the sign of the cross over them.

"If you're in Nordheim, near Goettingen, look up my sister, Mrs. Fleck. God bless you, boys."

The sun had begun to warm up the fields and the air grew milder. It was so transparent they could see the faraway church steeples of Goettingen and the white smoke rings left by a locomotive racing northward. Around noon Hal stopped opposite a softly curved hill and plumped into the thick grass whose blades

167

showed yellow tips, reminding Willy of a woman's painted finger-nails.

They ate two of Mrs. Schmitt's home-cured ham sandwiches and Hal started sketching while Willy just lay there, staring into the sky. He must have fallen asleep because he leapt up with a jolt when Hal suddenly shook him, pointing toward the rails.

"Look. There, near the tracks. It's moving."

Willy followed Hal's direction. He was right: something was lying there. It resembled a huge package, thrown out from a train.

They hurried toward it.

"My God, it's a boy, and he's alive," Willy said. "Don't stare, Hal. Let's take off these dirty rags."

Willy had never seen a similar getup. The boy's head was wrapped in a cloth bag with two slits for his eyes, which were closed now. His legs seemed swollen because of several lengths of cloth tied around them, filthy with coal dust and oil. Around his waist were wrapped similar enormous layers dripping with black grease. When they removed the head bag, they found his face covered with a thick cake of dirt. It reminded Willy of an American film actor made up as a Negro.

Underneath the layers of rags the boy wore a pair of brown corduroys and an old shirt, army style. After some searching, Willy and Hal discovered a brook and began cleaning him. Willy had to use almost his entire cake of soap. As they took off the shirt, Willy's eye fell on the label: "Goodwill Reformatory, Erlangen, Bavaria," it read.

"A reformatory boy," Willy ventured. "Probably escaped. Looks as if we need some coffee to revive him."

The inordinate amount of cold water alone brought the boy back to consciousness. At first he was frightened, then he accused them of having stolen his clothes, finally, given a Schmitt sandwich, he settled down peacefully and told them his name was Rolf Ebers.

"How did you get so oily?" Willy wanted to know. Rolf looked at him contemptuously.

"By riding the rods, of course. It's an old trick. You must cover yourself from head to foot, otherwise you choke from the oil, or freeze to death. I hadn't enough clothes. That's why I jumped off."

Willy nodded. He knew many were riding this way, tied to the axle of a freight car. If they relaxed, they'd be crushed. Rolf had ridden more than eight hours because he wanted to get as far away from Goodwill as possible.

He was eighteen, hardbitten and cynical, with a curious code of right and wrong all his own. Twice he had escaped from a reforma-tory, once knocking down a guard. He had been in jail, of course, and admitted proudly to having "pulled some stunts" with several

168

former Goodwill inmates who had graduated into the world of adult, respectable crime. He longed to work with them. He was not unlike an ambitious medical student pining for further studies with an outstanding professor.

Like a stray dog forced to survive a hostile neighborhood, Rolf was extremely quick-witted. Within a short time he found out that Willy and Hal weren't real migrants. Yet instead of acting superior, since he considered himself so much tougher, he developed a curiously protective attitude toward them, particularly toward Willy. He never tired of watching Hal carve his wooden statues, and when he heard how Willy charmed the farm wives into giving them meals and lodgings, something approaching admiration crept into his manner.

After a few days Rolf made a deal with them. He would accept the hay barns Willy and Hal got for them. But if they were offered a room, they must accept it and forget about him—he'd always find a place to sleep.

In Nordheim, Willy looked up Mrs. Schmitt's sister. Farmer Fleck's hay barn turned out to be a blessing, since the rains started shortly after they reached Nordheim. Mrs. Fleck, also a devout Catholic, was so happy to have direct news from her sister that she let Willy and Hal stay as long as they wished, if they'd help a little around the house. One of the Fleck children owned a box of water colors and on Mrs. Fleck's insistence Hal began to paint a Madonna—and, in a crude way, it resembled faintly the "Madonna of the Forgiven Sinners" in Frankfurt. After a few days Willy told the Flecks about Rolf. They accepted him, too, though they didn't like him.

During one of the endless evenings, when Hal was working in the house on his picture, Willy got into a fight with Rolf. They were lying in the hay barn and Willy asked him not to swear in the presence of the Flecks. Rolf cursed and grumbled, saying nobody could order him around. Finally Willy, to his own and Rolf's surprise, began shouting at him and Rolf turned his back and went into the other corner of the barn, sulking.

After a while he came back and said Willy was right: it made little sense to insult the people who fed you and where would they go in all this rain?

"I'll tell you something, Will," Rolf went on. "They forced too much religion down my throat. First at home. My father was killed early in the war and from there on Mother went to church every morning. But she gave me away, nevertheless, when I was thirteen."

He paused, and Willy, since this was expected, asked: "What do you mean 'gave you away'?"

"I was sure you wouldn't know," Rolf said with faint triumph.

169

"She gave me to Mr. Gerngross, the locksmith, as an apprentice. I worked, lived, ate, slept there. God, how I hated that man! He was out to get me the moment I set foot in his house. I slept in the store's back room with a dirty potato sack for a blanket. I got up at six for the watery chicory and bread crusts his wife gave me as breakfast. I worked from 7 A.M. to 8 P.M. If anything went wrong, he beat my behind with a birchwood whip. Three floggings a day was routine, like the soggy potatoes at dinner. He had to break me, he said. Caning a boy like me was his God-given duty."

"I can't believe it," Willy said. "It sounds like a hundred years ago."

Rolf looked at him almost pityingly. "You don't know life, Will. But it is true. You've seen the scars on my back."

Willy admitted he had, but he'd not known where they came from.

"Why didn't you ask me?" Rolf said, as if Willy had committed a breach of etiquette. "The worst thing was I and the two other fellows there had to pray with him and his wife. Unclean reprobates, he always called us, and then he'd beat the hell out of us."

Rolf stopped and opened the door to the hay barn. The darkness stood outside and the sheets of rain built an impenetrable wall around them. Rolf closed the door.

"We're lucky to be here," he said. "And with the Fleck woman giving us decent meals—I could stay here forever."

For Rolf, Willy knew, staying in this hay barn with his friends meant home and security—a luxury he was hardly able to enjoy. Since he wouldn't let Willy see this, he used the foulest language possible as he described how he and the two other apprentices finally had run away with Gerngross's cash, been caught by the police and sent to Goodwill, a reformatory near Erlangen in Bavaria. This was his third escape. Life in Goodwill, according to Rolf, was not much different from life before. They were beaten regularly by the guards, and if they broke one of the innumerable institutional rules, they were put into a dark cellar on bread and water. Since Goodwill forced the boys to attend a church service they didn't understand, Rolf had developed a boundless hatred of everything religious. That Mrs. Fleck, an ardent churchgoer, should be nice to them, confused him but didn't shake his outlook.

His outlook was very simple; like most of his kind, he hated everything, religion foremost, and since the future was hopeless, to "be smart" and "pull stunts" was the only way to go about living.

"Find work? Me?" he retorted when Willy ventured a timid suggestion. "Without proper papers? With a police record, as a runaway from Goodwill? Most of us guys never find regular work. That's why we're on the road."

170

When Hal came in later, he told them how many of his friends had joined the Communists because "they were going to change everything." But when the K. P. hadn't, they had drifted away. Rolf still occasionally used expressions from the *Red Flag* repertoire but he didn't know what they really meant. He just loathed everything, the Weimar Republic, the rich, business, cops, and society in general.

The next day, just as Hal finished his Madonna, the rains stopped. He left it for their hosts—though Willy considered the picture much too good to hang in the lonely farmhouse. They said good-by to the Flecks, Rolf thanking them politely—which Willy considered a personal success. After they figured out the best road to Hildesheim, Rolf stopped.

"I'm going the other way, fellows. Good-by and thanks for——" He stumbled, apparently not used to the new emotion which had overcome him.

"What's the matter, Rolf?" Willy asked. "Don't you like us? Or do you think you're better off alone? Well, you aren't, and you know it."

Willy had fallen into the scolding inflections of Big Anna. Hal, in the same tone, added: "You're giving us a dirty deal, Rolf, leaving us alone now."

"If a cop catches me, you'll be in for trouble," Rolf argued. "No need to get you involved."

"Nonsense," Willy said. "You're much safer with us. Besides, you know all the tricks of the road and can teach us a few more. So we are really safer with you too."

This last argument was out-and-out flattery. Yet Rolf, saying, of course, if they needed him, he'd get them to Hannsberg safe and sound, accepted almost greedily.

From the moment he laid eyes on it, Willy disliked the Mueller house. It was the last one in a seemingly hostile village. Dusk was falling as Willy approached it. The Mueller dogs were growling and Willy, standing there in the chill air, staring into Mrs. Mueller's suspicious face, had gathered all his strength and managed to get her interested in a Madonna which Hal, on Rolf's advice, had tinted with garish colors. The Muellers gave the three a scanty meal and allowed them to sleep in the barn.

Rarely had Hal and Willy seen such a decrepit farmhouse. Cracks ran along the walls, spiderwebs hung in the corners, and the smell of dogs was all over the house. Their only child, an idiot called Hermann, glowered at them during the meal, which had to be doled out to him bit by bit. The idiot in turn fed the dogs, obviously considered his equals at the table.

171

In the barn, far away from the house, several planks were missing in the ceiling and on the sides. The only friendly feature was a pair of farm horses, who seemed to enjoy the visit of someone other that the Muellers. A weak kerosene lamp near the water troughs shed some yellowish light, and after prolonged arguments Mr. Mueller let them keep it.

Willy was chilled. Through the holes in the walls a constant draft of cold air struck them; the nearby trees smelled damp and resinous. The hay was hard and dank—a combination achieved only by the poorest grade. As it grew dark, a loud, hostile rain prattled on and through the roof. How Hal managed to wangle a blanket out of the Muellers, Willy never knew. Hal and Rolf wrapped him in it and they huddled close together to keep warm.

The next thing that reached his consciousness was a flashlight shining in his eyes. Someone was shaking him rudely, ripping off his blanket, fumbling through his pockets. He heard shouts, muffled noises, and, fully awake, saw Rolf holding back a group of boys, Hal's carving knife glittering in his hand.

In the stingy light of the kerosene lamp Willy discovered Hal wrestling with someone. By now Willy was awake enough to realize that a boy was yelling at him. He wore a lumber jacket, and a mane of black hair covered his eyes.

"Give me your knife," the boy yelled. "Come on. Hand it over."

"Leave him alone," Willy heard Rolf's voice. Rolf was trying to edge toward him, still thrusting his knife at the group which was led by a youth with a completely shorn blond skull.

From somewhere a scene swept over Willy, a scene from a military play called *Mutiny*. In the second act, the Prussian officer (Mr. Taube of the Frankfurt playhouse), had kept the rebels in check by talking loudly and coldly.

"Will someone be kind enough to explain what this nonsense is all about?" Willy said in a thundering yet snarling voice—surprised that his cold hadn't muffled his vocal cords. "Or do you want farmer Mueller to kick us all out into the rain?"

A moment of silence followed which Willy utilized to lift the kerosene lamp and glance around. Incredibly enough his shouting had impressed the gang.

"They went after me with a knife," Rolf said, breathing heavily, but Willy shouted: "Quiet! Who's your leader?"

Whether this, too, was a line from *Mutiny* Willy didn't know. Anyhow, it worked. Slowly the tall fellow with the shorn skull stepped forward and planted himself before Willy, looking straight into his eyes. He reminded Willy of a great Dane, trained to jump at strangers. At this moment the horses began to whinny nervously.

"You'd better order one of your men to feed them some hay, but

172

gently," Willy remarked in the tone of a general conferring with an admiral during battle. "Farmer Mueller is mean. I know him."

"Fritz, give the horses some hay and keep them quiet," the great Dane commanded. One of the boys went over to the troughs.

"We need this barn," he continued in a gruff, high-pitched voice. "We can't have no strangers around squealing to anybody about us."

"I'm Willy Halder, student at Frankfurt University," Willy said politely. "These are Hal and Rolf, my companions." He made a sweeping gesture.

"My name is Gunther Ewers," the great Dane said after a moment's hesitation, extending an enormous paw, and Willy knew his act had been successful. All of a sudden the chill came back, and he had to sneeze. Rolf solicitously handed him the blanket, and Willy wrapped it around his body as if it were royal purple.

Hal, a slight bruise on his cheek, offered Gunther Ewers a cigarette. This settled it. Ewers lit it and inhaled with an almost obscene greediness.

Hal and Rolf forced Willy to lie down, planting themselves at his side.

"He's sick," Hal remarked to Ewers. "Why the heck did you have to fight us? There's enough room in the barn for all of us."

"Have a Schnapps, Willy." Rolf offered his flask.

"Where in heaven's name did you get Schnapps?" Willy wanted to know.

Rolf grinned. "Sneaked into Mueller's parlor while you were in the kitchen. Nice job, eh?"

"Don't let the gang see what you've got," whispered Gunther Ewers. "They haven't had liquor for a long time." He himself took a deep swallow.

Willy confirmed Gunther's suspicion that one couldn't trust Mueller and that the gang had better leave the barn early in the morning, hide in the forest, and come back, in case the rain lasted. Gunther called the boy who had attacked Willy. His hair, Willy discovered, didn't fall over his eyes by chance. It was combed over the forehead to hide an enormous scar, running from the hairline to the nose, resembling some hideous lizard.

"This is Karlheinz, my adjutant," Gunther explained. Karlheinz clicked his heels and was told to stay up and wake them at four while Gunther took a long-needed nap.

"Something's foul," Rolf whispered to Willy after Gunther had retired to a protected corner. "I'll watch out. Just in case."

Willy should have protested, but he was too weary. His throat ached and before he dozed off he wondered how, with his cold, he could have shouted as loud as he had.

173

When day broke—the Ewers gang had sneaked out before—it was so dismal that Hal asked Mr. Mueller to let them stay in the barn. The farmer agreed, but he gave Hal and Rolf a lot of work. Obviously Mr. Mueller let them do all the dirty jobs he had saved for such an occasion. Rolf and Hal didn't mind—it kept them busy and warm. Mrs. Mueller served a better meal this time, including a hot beef broth for Willy. The meal revived him. Once back in the barn, Rolf said:

"I can't figure out the Ewers gang. They are no reformatory boys. And they aren't just migrants who have joined forces by accident. They're runaways too. That's why they jumped at us. If one of us guys comes into a barn and finds others there, why, he's friendly. We're all brothers on the road."

"Karlheinz clicked his heels," Willy said. "But they're too young to be Reichswehr soldiers."

"Let's beat it as early as possible," Rolf said. "I don't trust 'em."

Yet the rain forced them to stay. For several days they had to share the barn with the strangers. Though he protested, Willy wasn't allowed to work with Hal and Rolf.

On what the Ewers gang was living, Willy couldn't fathom. They looked worse each night as they slouched in. Willy usually kept some morsels of food for Gunther and fed him, apart from his gang. It was exactly the technique to win a dog's confidence. One night, after Willy had provided him with some hot coffee, Gunther broke down and told them his story, almost too fantastic to be true. Willy believed Gunther only because he was mentally unable to invent anything.

They were fugitives. Rolf was right. They had spent more than a year hidden from everyone in the old fortress of Hameln, near the Weser River, as trainees of the Black Reichswehr, an organization which officially didn't exist. The Reichswehr paid its bills, though irregularly. The boys had been lured into this secret army by promises of good pay, good food, and regular training. They would be the shock troops in the coming civil war, they were told. They'd have uniforms, money, guns, and girls.

After a few months they all knew that they would die if they stayed in Hameln. No outsider ever entered the fortress. The boys couldn't visit the village near by. They were at the mercy of two sergeants, both with a good-sized criminal record. If someone disobeyed, he was flogged, or thrown into a cellar for many weeks. One of their pals had died there, but they had discovered his body only weeks later. Gunther's best friend had contradicted the sergeant on a day when the Reichswehr pay failed to come through. The sergeant had hit him. In desperation the boy had grabbed an iron rod and attacked the sergeant. The sergeant simply shot him the

174

same night, and Gunther was ordered to throw the corpse into the nearby river, after the identification marks had been removed.

"What a rotten deal," Willy said. "But why did the Reichswehr let all this happen? That way they'd never get extra soldiers."

Gunther didn't know. It appeared to Willy as if the Reichswehr had tired of its own bastard. Since the funds could never appear in any book, the Reichswehr had to falsify the records. Nobody knew the boys' whereabouts. At their induction they had been ordered to write a fictitious address to their parents. Legally, the occupants of Hameln didn't exist, and if it had burned to the ground, none of the boys' parents would ever have known where their sons had died. The parents of Gunther's friend who was shot didn't yet know he was dead.

Corruption had saved Gunther and his friends. After Karlheinz had been branded on the forehead by one of the sergeant's creatures, Gunther had begun organizing his group. About this time they heard through the caretaker's wife that the sergeants had embezzled money. Both were called to Berlin on a Wednesday night, leaving their stool pigeons as guards. The caretaker couple, frightened by the disappearance of too many boys, agreed to play along with Gunther. They brought in a keg of liquor which the guards couldn't resist. Gunther's gang fled, not without knocking down their worst enemies and gagging the caretakers so they wouldn't be suspected. They still had not written home, none of them. They feared the Reichswehr officials might catch them through their parents.

For several weeks they had been tramping on the road, and the fear of being betrayed, drummed into them as members of an illegal army, never left them.

"I'm at the end of my tether," Gunther admitted. "And I want to see my mother. I wouldn't put it past those guys to have written her a phony story that I had run away to join the Navy and got killed abroad. It's been done before. You don't believe me, do you?" he added.

Through Willy's mind flashed the picture of Hellmuth Handler taking over the Wandervogel, and the Reichswehr officers instructing him and Ferdy in machine-gun practice. It had happened long ago, in the Bergstrasse.

"I believe you," he said. "You needn't worry about us. We won't talk. I think it's safe to go home."

"What makes you think so?" Gunther asked.

"There are too many of you," Willy explained. "You said yourself that officially you don't exist. No records, nothing. If they mobilize the police, they would have to admit the existence of the Black Reichswehr Center in Hameln. They won't let the police in on that. The Prussian police are under Severing, a Social Democrat."

"I hate the Social Democrats," Gunther interrupted, not quite logically. "They kept the funds from the Reichswehr. I hate this sissy republic. You know, one should burn this whole country, just destroy everything."

"Never mind," Hal said. "I would go home if I were you. Sounds like the right thing to do."

Gunther said he'd think it over, and went into his sleeping corner. The next morning the rain had stopped. Hal, Willy, and Rolf left the Mueller farm. Willy never saw the Black Reichswehr boys again and never found out where they had gone. He collapsed after they reached the city of Hildesheim.

Hal's head seemed to approach and recede, recede and come nearer, and then it began to rotate like a mechanical whirligig Willy had owned as a child. He closed his eyes, opened them again. He was in bed, in a clean white bed, in a strange room.

"Take it easy, Will." Hal's voice was like a familiar, warm touch. But Willy's head was bursting, as if stuffed with farmer Mueller's hay, and his cheeks burned.

"We are in Hildesheim at Dr. von Erb's, your father's friend," Hal explained. "And don't say 'Where am I?' You simply passed out with fever and I brought you here. Rolf went on. Sends you his regards."

A woman came into the room. She was large and soft, her white hair wound around her head in the most complicated ringlet and curl arrangement.

"This is Mrs. von Erb." Hal introduced her somewhat sheepishly. The woman smiled and gave Willy something hot to drink. It tasted of a thousand nourishing things. Willy closed his eyes again and for a moment he pretended to be very small, lying in bed at 66 Reuter Weg, after Melanie had told him a story. . . .

As the days went on, Willy slowly recovered. Hannah von Erb and her husband, Friedrich, a tall, taciturn man, treated him like a son. Their own son, Baldur, showed up only sporadically, slept on the couch of what Willy considered his room, and once asked Willy whether he had gone through the chest of drawers. Willy, truthfully, denied it. One afternoon, while dozing, Willy had the distinct impression of Baldur hiding something under the bed. Later, when he looked, he found nothing. However, Baldur bought a steel cabinet with a lock and transferred the contents of the drawers into the cabinet. Willy pretended to be asleep that night and with one eye watched him filing away mountains of papers. Baldur, a thin, tall. scraggy-faced youth, proudly wore the fencing

176

scars still sported by many members of Germany's feudal fraternities, and there was something furtive about him which reminded Willy of the jackals in the Frankfurt Zoo.

Hannah von Erb took scrupulous care of Willy—apparently she bestowed on him all the tenderness Baldur rejected. Hal thought so too. When Willy started walking around a bit, Dr. von Erb told him he must go home, not continue to Hannsberg. Though he was only a psychiatrist, he could diagnose Willy's illness as an insidious virus grippe, made worse by exhauston.

Willy was crestfallen but Hal didn't show any surprise. "I have already written to your mother," he confessed, "and she sent the money. I didn't tell her how sick you were, but she guessed something anyhow."

"What about you?" Willy asked. His weakness, so he had noticed, had made him oversensitive, and he often guessed what people were going to say or what they tried to hide while talking. "Why don't you go on to Hannsberg?"

Hal protested: it was no fun going alone and Oscar was more Willy's friend than his, anyhow. They argued back and forth during the next days, until a letter from Oscar decided the issue. Oscar was sorry about Willy's mishap but implored Hal to visit him, promising the most glorious opportunities for "proletarian" paintings in Hannsberg's factory districts.

"Our leather workers look exactly like those on all modern canvases, romantic in a grimy way," Oscar added.

When they had finished reading the letter, Willy said: "I can go home alone as soon as the Von Erbs let me. I wish you'd look up Oscar. I spoiled the trip for you by getting sick. Hannsberg isn't so far now."

This Hal had to admit. Finally he had his corduroys cleaned—they had faded to the blue of a light summer sky, Hannah remarked—and got his other things ready. The night before he left Dr. von Erb took a look at his knee. He had been told about the operation Theodor Halder had performed years ago. A fascinating shape, Dr. von Erb declared. The bone was completely deformed but there was enough kneecap to function if Hal didn't strain it. He even took some X rays because such cases should be recorded.

Willy was sent to bed early while Hal and Hannah talked on for a long time. Willy guessed that Hal urged her not to send him home too early—an unnecessary reminder, since Hannah would keep him here as long as she could.

Hal woke Willy early next morning. "Write your mother today," he said. He handed Willy a bundle of bank notes. "Your mother wants you to take a second-class ticket."

Willy protested that third class was much more fun, but Hal wouldn't take back the money.

"Have you enough to get to Hannsberg?" Willy inquired. "You're not going to hike, are you? It's too late for that."

"Don't worry, Will," Hal said. "I got money from Mother. I'll write you soon." He gave Willy's arm a short squeeze and then turned abruptly. Willy heard him in the hallway, thanking the Von Erbs for all they had done. Through the window Willy followed him with his eyes. Hal's hair was almost red-blond and his corduroys were too light—they would get dirty soon.

As if she guessed that Hal's leaving distressed him more than he cared to show, Hannah took Willy to Grottler's, the most fashionable tearoom in town, and made him eat two huge *meringues glacées*. Grottler's was the utmost in provincial elegance, with potted palms multiplied by unending mirror columns, and marble walls, floors, and table tops. An anemic orchestra played the overture to *Mignon* and other sweetish pieces, befitting the rich pastry and, so Willy thought, even outdoing it.

On their return they found Baldur. He didn't say a word during dinner and he looked gray.

In the middle of the night a noise awakened Willy. Baldur had opened the steel cabinet and was throwing letters and file cards on the floor. Willy watched him ruffling through the letters in an uncontrolled frenzy. Finally Baldur began tearing them to pieces and throwing some of them into the wastebasket. Then, changing his mind, he took several bundles to the kitchen, where he stealthily lit the stove.

Willy's curiosity was aroused. He leaped out of bed and looked at the fragments in the wastebasket. The file cards, all with a big *C* on top, contained detailed descriptions of people of military rank. One of the letters still in the drawer dealt with money to be paid and "a plan which necessitated hiding the materials." He heard Baldur move in the kitchen and rushed back to bed.

Baldur repeated the procedure for quite some time, while Willy lay, pretending to sleep. His vague suspicions were verified when, a few hours after Baldur had left, an extremely polite plain-clothes man asked for Mr. von Erb. He searched Baldur's room, asking many questions which the Von Erbs and Willy answered as well as they could.

From Commissioner Berndorf's hints and from what Willy knew he could pretty well piece together the story. Baldur had been an active member of the "Organization Consul," abbreviated O.C., a secretly operating clan whose aims were amazingly simple: to fight the "revolutionization of Germany," to instal nationalist governments, and to "eliminate" outstanding liberal personalities. They had been very successful in carrying out the last part of their program. Recently, arrests had reduced their activities considerably.

Willy wasn't too surprised about the O.C. He remembered Gunther Ewers's story of the Black Reichswehr, and he also remembered a remark of Theodor's long ago: in Germany, the best people were either killed, driven into exile, or died early from worry.

Hannah von Erb did not try to shield Baldur. His evil deeds had caught up with him, she said, and she was not the one to stand in the way of the Lord's justice. After Commissioner Berndorf had left, her husband took her hand and turned to Willy.

"I'm a patriot, Willy. I belong to the German Nationalists. I know your father thinks different. But we're both for decency in politics. American gangster methods in politics—that's the end. Sorry you were exposed to all this. Well, I'd better get back to my book."

"Don't mind me," Willy said. "At least I know why Baldur rummaged through those papers in the middle of the night. What book are you working on?"

"Oh, don't you know?" Hannah said. "My husband is writing about the mentally sick in Germany. Statistics and all."

"Too many of them are running around free," Dr. von Erb said. "You'd be surprised in how many high places . . ."

"Never mind, Friedrich," Hannah said, trying to prevent her husband from embarking on his favorite theme. "To hear you talk, anyone would expect the insane to put the normal people away one of these days."

Hannah sounded lighthearted enough, but the same night Willy heard her sobbing in the next room while Friedrich von Erb tried to console her. She had renounced Baldur but she couldn't help crying about her son who had thrown in his future with a gang of fanatical assassins.

As Willy lay there in the darkness while the file cabinet glittered coldly in the light of a white moon, something seemed to constrict his throat, holding him in a tight grip. Between sleep and wakefulness his mind began to spin feverishly, conjuring up a procession of distorted faces. He couldn't move, and his heart beat too fast as he watched the figures move: Hellmuth Handler and Professor Lattau gesticulating near the camp fire while a procession of youths approached with torches. Suddenly running toward him was Rolf with Gunther Ewers's Black Reichswehr boys, their faces covered with blood. As an insignia they all wore deep scars on their foreheads, like Karlheinz. Then Willy found himself transported to the fortress of Hameln. In a cellar a boy was bleeding to death, his mouth open for a cry of agony. But no sound came.

179

Somehow he escaped from the dungeon. Almost at once he encountered them again, marching toward him in close formation. This time Hal was at his side and they were running away under a brilliant, stinging sun with rays like cannon shafts. The pursuing army was running, too, led by a giant Hellmuth whose scar shone like an illuminated stigma on his forehead. Willy began to sweat, and then the sun vanished quickly, the light fled, and black birds with enormous wings spread over the skies, darkening out everything.

As if out of a pit there rose farmer Schmitt's Forest of Shadows. Willy stumbled past the high firs toward a dull roar in the center. The thousand feet behind him were running, too, in sharp rhythms like an army of tap dancers. Then Willy reached a friendly clearing, where a clear brook sauntered through high green grass. Squatting there, immense, immobile, and with the head of a monstrous crocodile, sat Gunnivor, the dragon. Someone jerked Willy aside—it must have been Hal—but the others marched forward with banners fluttering under the fir trees, toward Gunnivor, who slowly opened his jaws.

Sweat was trickling down Willy's sides as he sat up. The steel cabinet still glittered inimically. He tried to laugh it off, the dragon out of Wagner's *Siegfried,* the boys with Karlheinz's scar, yet he couldn't. The fear remained after the phantoms had gone. He was wide awake now. He still wasn't quite well, and of course this might be the source of it.

The vision finally left him, as he calmed down, for he was young and his body demanded sleep. Yet in the years to come it was to return to Willy many a night, repeating its first appearance in Hildesheim and spreading a fine film of dread over everything Willy attempted in the clearer light of the day and robbing it of its purpose.

Never before had 66 Reuter Weg seemed so sweet. On his return, Willy found the tea table laid, with many delicious plum tarts Big Anna had baked for the occasion. Theodor sent his patients home early and they settled down to a prolonged *Kaffeeklatsch.* It included dinner and a Chaplin movie at the UFA Palace which made Willy and Melanie rock with laughter while Theodor had to be told what it was all about: he was as bad at understanding films as Willy at math.

During the following week Willy took Melanie for long walks during which they watched with fascinated disapproval the rapid growth of Frankfurt's first skyscraper, the I. G. Farben administration building.

180

A postcard from Hal, marked Lehrte near Hannsberg, indicated that he had hitchhiked, after all. In an upsurge of suspicion, Willy sought Melanie.

"Did you send Hal money for a second-class ticket, Mother?"

"No, I didn't. Mrs. Petersen and I just had enough for third-class."

"The fool," Will said angrily. "He must have sold his ticket to make me go home second-class. Here." He showed Melanie the greenish-colored card from Lehrte. "If he had taken the train he'd be in Hannsberg, not in some Godforsaken village."

Willy phoned Ilona, who listened patiently and told him not to worry. Hal had hitchhiked from Hildesheim, it was true. He had written her about it in a long letter from this place, Lehrte, including two sketches he had made. He was all right.

Ilona made a date with Willy to see another American film—like most young people in Germany they had become enamored of them and couldn't get enough—but Willy had to cancel it because the same afternoon F. P. Busch called him to come to the playhouse, "without delay," because there was a nice part for him in Karl Hergert's new drama, *The Void*.

"A nice part" was the usual F. P. Busch exaggeration, as Willy discovered during the five days of hectic rehearsals left before the *première*. *The Void,* a complicated and allegorical play about an automobile racer's love for speed, space, and a mysterious woman, took place in a plushy Riviera gambling casino. At the end of Act II, after everybody had left the huge hall, Willy, as a young blind Chinese, had to grope his way across the entire stage—the morning light seeping in with sickly effect—to find his old mother dead in an armchair. He had to hold her in his arms, murmuring a few poetic, senseless words, before the curtain descended.

Miss Mathilda Einzig, who usually played gossipy mothers-in-law, querulous scrubwomen, or haughty old dowagers, was to be his mother. She was a short, round, gray-haired woman of around fifty who, offstage, was never taken for an actress. Yet she possessed an infallible grasp of every part and as a comic had no equal. F. P. left the details of the scene to her. Willy learned more from Mathilda in these five days than he had ever learned before. Step by step she built her character, perfecting every nuance of speech and movement. One afternoon, when Mathilda didn't like what he was doing, she rebuked him, breaking into broad Frankfurt dialect. Willy apologized, making his speech even broader. The listening stagehands snickered and Miss Einzig said: "Why, that's good!" Coming from her, the undisputed master of South-West dialect, this was a high compliment.

181

A few hours before the première Friday night she came into the extras' dressing room (strictly against regulations) to check his make-up.

"More eyebrow pencil," she said. "And stay away from Miss Reger, Willy Halder. I could be your mother, so I can be frank. She is not good for a youngster like you. How would you like to do a radio skit with me next week? Strictly dialect, strictly trash. You as Heiner, my feeble-minded son. Think it over."

She left a bewildered Willy. He had talked to Maria several times, when they sat out the endless hours during which they weren't needed in *The Void*. She seemed more quiet and hadn't mentioned Luli once. . . .

He went backstage and waited, with mounting anxiety, for his cue. When, finally, he made his entrance, all stage fright suddenly left him. He did everything as Mathilda and he had worked it out: lightfooted, yet a bit unsure, he inched his way across the stage which seemed gigantic now, and spoke his few lines in an incredulous, monotonous voice as he held Mathilda in his arms—Mathilda who even managed to give the illusion of slenderness.

After the curtain had fallen, F. P. was enchanted, and one of the old stagehands slapped Willy's back, saying, "Nice work, young Mr. Halder. Give your father Hans Borchardt's regards. Treated me in 1911." The old man smiled at Willy, who didn't know what to say, particularly since the stage now resembled an anthill invaded by wasps. He turned, and his eyes met Maria's. She had overheard the stagehand, and for a second her face showed an unconcealed jealousy though her mouth formed a hearty smile.

"Nice going, Willy," she said, drawing him away. "Let's go somewhere after the performance."

At her insistence, Willy took her to the fashionable Café Laumer on Bockenheimer Landstrasse. He ordered a drink, but Maria would sip only tea—liquor was bad for her figure, Luli contended. She was sweet and submissive, and after a while Willy knew something was wrong. She wanted to tell him something and didn't dare. From the next table floated the laughter of a group from the playhouse. Willy was aware of Mathilda's keeping an eye on him. Maria began to "act"—the moment she felt watched she began to slide into a role, and Willy decided to leave.

Silently they strolled under the trees of Bockenheimer Landstrasse which had turned a dry autumn brown. Heaps of leaves rustled under their feet like dry paper. Willy took Maria's arm and waited. He waited for the tender urge, the old desire to hold her and enjoy her softness, but it didn't come. He waited for her to open her mind, but she had withdrawn. She chattered much too rapidly about the theater, and pointedly avoided mentioning Luli. In the hallway he kissed her good-by, as usual. She yielded willingly, her hands stroking him, and he knew that secretly she wanted him to go further. Yet at the same time he felt that, in some way, she was betraying him.

As he entered the apartment a dim light shone under the living-room door. Melanie sat in her favorite chair, the light shining on her white hair.

"Why aren't you in bed, Mother?" Willy said, kissing her. "It's late, you know. You need your sleep."

This is what Melanie used to tell him when he was younger, and it had become a standing phrase ever since Willy had started coming home late, while Theodor and Melanie went to bed early.

"Sit down, Will," Melanie said, putting down her sewing.

"What's the matter, Ma? Has something happened?"

Melanie sighed. "An improbable scene took place here tonight. Perhaps I should have warned you. While you were away, Mrs. Reger sent me a letter, asking me to visit her to discuss a question concerning her daughter and you. I didn't answer it. I decided to wait until your return. Tonight she walked in, uninvited. You don't have to defend yourself, Will. I don't believe you were threatening to seduce her innocent daughter. But Mrs. Reger is dangerous and, I believe, not quite normal."

Willy gasped. Had Maria known, while he was kissing her, that at the same time Luli was launching her underhanded attack?

"She talked without pause for an hour and a half, covering herself with laurels for what she had done for Maria," Melanie continued. "Every man, it seems, is after Maria, and she must be protected. Mrs. Reger ended by boasting about her connections with the police department. Has she any grounds for legal action, Will? Maria is still a minor."

"She hasn't," Willy said. Something turned cold and heavy within him and he wanted to vomit. "It simply never came to it. I can't believe it, Mother. Do you suppose Maria knew?"

"Not in the beginning, Ilona and I figured," Melanie answered. "Yes, I called her after Mrs. Reger had left—Ilona has common sense and knows everybody concerned. By now, of course, Luli has reported to her daughter a grand spectacle of motherly bravery, making our house seem a den of sin. Don't take it too hard, Willy."

Willy wasn't sure whether he took it too hard or not. He was hurt and furious. If Maria had known about Luli's visit, it would explain her behavior on the night of the première. As if it were a living yet separate part of him, pierced by a bullet, his affection had died when Melanie told him the story. He had never known how affections could die, how fast a chemical change could take place within oneself.

183

Since Willy didn't address Maria during the next days, since she studiously avoided him, he never found out the truth. Also Mathilda Einzig occupied much of his time with the rehearsals for the radio show. She had planned another for next week. She constantly hovered about Willy, and he suspected her of knowing the whole story.

The inanities of Mathilda, the vegetable woman, and her moronic son, Heiner, pleased the audience as well as the director of Frankfurt's municipal station, Dr. Ernst Schoret, who invited them to do a whole series on the same order. A contract was to be signed soon. Willy would be paid well, and both Theodor and Melanie were immensely proud of him.

Monday morning a long-distance call came through from Hannsberg. Willy jumped out of bed, certain it was Hal, who hadn't written for quite some time. It was Oscar von Rainer. The wires crackled, and Willy could barely understand him. Hal hadn't shown up at all. Even if he had hitchhiked, he should have been there four or five days ago. Oscar sounded embarrassed, declaring he just wanted to check. The three minutes were over before Willy could say something sensible, and Oscar hung up.

Willy never knew what made him do the things he did that morning. He went through his morning rehearsals with Mathilda with complete calm; he ate lunch with her and answered all questions correctly, though somewhat on a second plane. All the time an indefinite apprehensiveness was growing within him. It brought back the choked feeling that had once paralyzed him in Lattau's amphitheater. He was scared. He called Ilona, couldn't find her, telephoned several of the agencies handling her designs, finally found her waiting in one of them on Goethe Strasse.

"I must go to Hannsberg," Willy said as they walked out. He had not planned to say it, something deep within him had made the decision. Ilona agreed—she wanted to go with him but this was impossible: Oscar couldn't put up a girl. She gave him some money, the rest he took from his radio skits. He sent a special delivery to Mathilda, calling off the next shows. He packed his bags the same night.

Neither Theodor nor Melanie attempted to stop him. Melanie put some warm underwear in Theodor's old battered suitcase, went with him to the station, insisted on his buying a sleeper, and paid the difference. She wired Oscar that Willy would arrive at 7 A.M. This would warn Oscar to be at the Hannsberg Station before going to work.

"I hate to mention this," Melanie said before the train left. She glanced over the busy, gloomy station, holding her hand over her right breast. "It's Father's idea, but he's right. You and Oscar must

184

check up on all the hospitals in Hannsberg. Hal might have had a minor accident and be unable to get in touch with anyone. I'll talk to Mrs. Petersen tomorrow."

Willy thanked her. He had completely forgotten about Mrs. Petersen—again he cursed the egotistical streak in him which always came forward when he was upset.

"I should have done it, Ma," he said, but Melanie said this was a woman's job.

"Send us a wire as soon as you know," she called out while the train began to move. Willy smiled back at her, then went to the porter to find his bed. He slept only a few hours, and the train seemed to stop interminably in many obsolete small towns. In between he dreamed of Professor Lattau and sometimes, as he woke up, the railroad stations where they stopped seemed to resemble the amphitheater with its choking fumes.

14. A FAT CLOUD OF BROWNISH SMOKE hung over Hannsberg as the train pulled in. Oscar, conspicuously elegant among the early morning crowd of overalled workers, got a taxi and they went to his uncle's mansion, a soot-covered gingerbread monstrosity, half Gothic, half Greek, in Hannsberg's best neighborhood, on Kaiser Allee.

Willy had to be polite to Uncle Erich and Aunt Frieda, who looked surprisingly alike, both rotund, sixtyish, and complacent. They seemed to worship Oscar—they had no children of their own. Would Willy mind sharing Oscar's room?

"Hal wrote me to meet him," Oscar began as soon as they were alone in his room. He showed Willy a post card. "This is the last one. He sent me quite a few."

Willy went through the cards, mostly bad reproductions of drab North-German villages. On the last one, postmarked Willingen, Hal instructed Oscar to meet him at the Hannsberg Station, in the third-class waiting room, on October 3 at 9 P.M.

"Oscar," Willy said, "be frank. What could have happened?"

"He could have gotten stuck on the road." Oscar hesitated. "But then he'd have dropped us a line. My theory is he fell ill between Willingen and here."

"Have you started . . ."

"No, I waited for you."

Oscar then left for his shoe factory. Although weary, Willy took a streetcar back to the Main Station, found a train to Willingen, and arrived there around noon. Willingen was a small place and in contrast to the coal-blackened streets of Hannsberg it seemed neat and optimistic. He inquired at the only hospital. Hal wasn't there, and there hadn't been anyone fitting his description.

"Hundreds of hitchhikers are coming through this town," the nurse told him. "We had a few here, some pneumonia, some fractured ribs, some sick with exhaustion. But no redhead, no one from Frankfurt. Perhaps the police can help you."

Willy's first visit to a police station established a pattern for all his following visits. At first the officer seemed friendly enough. When he heard Hal had hitchhiked, he became disgruntled.

"Too many youngsters on the road without papers. Too many delinquents. We can't watch out for them. They should stay home."

No hospital or police station had any record of Hal Petersen in the four villages between Willingen and Hannsberg where Willy inquired the same day. He arrived at Kaiser Allee much too late and found Uncle Erich and Aunt Frieda waiting dinner for him. Willy apologized. He was exhausted and couldn't eat much. They soon went up to Oscar's room.

"Don't run off so long without letting them know," Oscar said after they had gone to bed. Their heavy wooden beds stood far apart in the large room with its Gothic window ornaments and heavy velvet drapes. "Dinner is a sacred routine here but they'd never start without their guest."

"Sorry. I won't do it again," Willy said. "Hal must have arrived here in Hannsberg. Tomorrow I'll phone all the hospitals here and if we don't find him, I'll go to the Missing Persons' Bureau."

"Let me do the phoning from my office," Oscar said. "If necessary, I can take the afternoon off and we'll go to the bureau together. You can do some sightseeing in the morning. Not that there is much to see, but look around anyhow. Only don't get lost in our 'Little Venice.' "

Whenever, in earlier days, Willy had wandered through a strange town he had been filled with a strange expectancy, which made every detail of the town appear much more extraordinary than it could possibly be. In Hannsberg nothing like this happened. Victoria Platz, the town's center, was a busy thoroughfare, flanked by officious and sullen buildings in the "Imperial Gingerbread" style of Uncle Erich's mansion. The streetcars clamored through the streets asthmatically, jangling their bells; wherever Willy went he was confronted by huge chimney stacks from which billowed fat black clouds, falling greedily over the city, covering everything with a greasy film. Willy's hands went clammy and gray after half an hour as he wandered away from the town's center toward the suburbs.

Apparently this had once been Hannsberg's Old Town but it could never measure up to Frankfurt's. The few really old buildings, hemmed in by rickety four-story brick dwellings, each exactly like its neighbor, had lost the aura of history which gave those in Frankfurt a sort of dignity. As Willy went farther, following an instinct he couldn't analyze, the streets grew worse.

The houses stood like rows of petrified cripples. The poor paint had rotted off their fronts; they bent to one side and their window openings gave the impression of cavities in a set of teeth. All were

187

narrow, all were dyed the same grayish-black color of coal dust and poverty. Children had chalked dirty words on the walls, and wherever windows were broken they were mended with a layer of newspapers whose print had run.

A shabby, listless crowd filled these streets—the young unemployed men with sharp, dull faces, and the housewives, sickly and shapeless as their houses. At certain moments the streets seemed to take on the quality of a stage set to Willy: the endless rows of diseased fronts were almost too uniform to be real. From time to time there appeared a veritable dwarf among them, a one-story dwelling which its neighbors seemed determined to strangle. The diffuse light of a cloudy October morning was further darkened by the coal dust in the air.

Willy stopped at a crossing. More people were milling around in a sort of squalid industriousness. Soon he knew why: the basements had sprouted shops, selling secondhand clothes, secondhand furniture, secondhand everything. The houses above the basements were just as secondhand, and Willy was sure they were for sale too. By now he was aware of a sweetish smell of coal, old clothes, and disintegration, and it made him want to turn back. Yet something drew him farther, toward the water of the Leine River which he saw glittering at the end of the secondhand row.

A canal, spanned by small bridges, separated him from a peninsula, black with houses. They were like big flies gathered around a carcass. While Willy stared at a signpost announcing "Little Venice," someone tapped his shoulder.

"Want to buy a jacket, mister? Cheap too. You can have it for one mark."

The young man, his cap down over his forehead, presented a shabby sports jacket. His few chipped teeth showed while he spoke, and when Willy waved him away, he vanished silently in the crowd.

The smell of putrefaction was so strong that Willy hesitated to walk farther. Here all the rotting houses had merged into one decrepit structure that seemed ready to fall into the dark river as soon as someone touched it. Through opened windows women were throwing garbage into the river. The steep house walls, rising directly from the riverbank, seemed like prehistoric rock formations, and the women, as they leaned out, were like cavedwellers left over from another age.

In the restaurants with incongruously opulent names, Grand Restaurant Italia, Bar and Grill Venezia, sat old men and women, their empty coffeecups before them, staring into the dirty nothingness outside. To Willy, these houses wore their cankers proudly, and the buying and selling in the basements had the feverish activity of a sham stock exchange. Several times someone stopped Willy,

188

offering a silver watch, a pair of pants, shirts, five pounds of beef-steak from the French Army supplies in the Rhineland, complete with "official certificate."

When Willy looked up he had the feeling the houses were so infested with their disease he'd never get out without catching it. In many a room a subdued red light was fighting pitifully against the day, and more than one woman asked Willy whether he wanted her—only one mark, since this was morning, the slack hour.

He reached the end of the peninsula. From there Little Venice resembled a gigantic garbage can, inhabited by innumerable rats, scampering greedily through the leftovers. One day they would gnaw through the walls and it would all totter into the river. On the other shore of the Leine, Willy saw long green reed grass, and he crossed another bridge leading to it. There, however, the path ended, and a sign warned passersby of the Leine swamp. The grass wasn't tall enough to hide the cans, rags, broken pieces of metal and china thrown into the swamp. There was even a man's sports jacket, half swallowed by the muck but looking almost new and with only a few darkish spots.

He turned, walked back and out of Little Venice. He felt ex-hausted. For a moment he paused in front of a secondhand clothing store, staring at the display. In the glass he caught the reflection of a boy sauntering up to him.

"Nice stuff they've got," the boy said in a high, childish voice. Willy turned angrily. He didn't care to talk to anyone; his only impulse was to flee. But the boy was too incredible to be ignored. In a second Willy recognized the make-up—they used that shade for "juveniles" on the Frankfurt stage—the blackened eyelashes, the overred mouth. The boy withstood his stare, smiling in a foolish effort to be coquettish.

"You don't like me?" he said in the tone of a five-year-old who has been denied a lollipop. "I'm not your type? You're a stranger here, I can see that."

Willy relaxed. He had heard of men selling themselves, but he had never met one. This pitiful child, trying to appear seductive, somehow dispersed the spell which Little Venice had cast over him.

"No, I don't want anything," Willy said amiably.

"Can't you be nice and buy me a cup of coffee and a bun? I'm hungry. I'll show you around. The real places."

Willy shook his head. Glancing into the shop again, he realized that, incongruously mixed with the dirty threadbare stuff there lay two or three clean jackets, vests, and trousers.

"All right, Duke," the boy said without rancor. "If you ever need me, you'll find me at the Main Station. Third-class waiting room. Almost any night."

He sauntered away, with a lisp of his hips.

"Wait!" Willy ran after him. "In the Main Station, you say."

"Sure, handsome," the boy said, mildly astonished. "Why, everybody's there. Buy me a cup of coffee and a bun, please."

"I'll buy you two cups and three buns," Willy said, "if you tell me about the station." *Nine o'clock, Main Station,* Hal had written on his last post card, marked Willingen.

The boy took him to a halfway decent place on the outskirts of the Old Town. His name was Ronny, he declared, and he looked exactly like his twin sister, Lonny, who was in the same profession. He shoved her photo across the table to Willy.

Ronny happily munched his buns while he explained to Willy that the black-market dealers, the pimps, the girls and boys of his profession regularly gathered at the Main Station. Once in a while the cops raided the place, but on the whole they left everybody alone. As if he were deriding a rival football team, Ronny complained about "the competition," the runaways, the bums, ready to go with any "better-class gentleman" who approached the station late at night.

An idea began to take shape in Willy's mind: what if someone recruiting for the Black Reichswehr was collecting boys in the station? Though Hal was usually not easily moved, he might have been taken in.

"Black Reichswehr?" Ronny made him order some more Danish pastry. "I know them all. Usually beaten up and bruised, the poor dears. But they're runaways. Not recruits. I don't think they recruit 'em any more."

Willy got up and telephoned Oscar to tell him he'd be late. When he returned, Ronny had wrapped the Danish pastry in a napkin and put it in his pocket.

"I'll be at the Main Station tomorrow around nine," Willy said. "With a friend of mine. There's something in it for you, so don't worry," he added as Ronny opened his mouth.

"You're looking for someone, aren't you, handsome?" Ronny declared. "And if you don't want to talk to me, just look the other way. I never speak to a gentleman in the station unless he greets me first. It isn't proper."

Oscar had telephoned every hospital in Hannsberg but nobody resembling Hal had been registered—Hal's red hair simplified the search. Although Willy was exhausted, he insisted on accompanying Oscar to the Bureau of Missing Persons the same afternoon.

As they rode in the streetcar to Victoria Platz, Oscar said: "I made an appointment with the only man with some brains, Commissioner Hegner. He's recently arrived from Berlin. He's much younger than the old codgers here, and they resent him because he's not a Stahlhelm man."

Oscar showed no surprise over Willy's conversation with Ronny and agreed to go to the station to meet him.

"I'm afraid we won't find much ourselves," he added. "Everybody knows the Main Station is full of thieves, pimps, underworld characters, and black-market businessmen. Don't mention Ronny to the commissioner, Will."

When they got off at Victoria Platz, Willy broke out: "I hate this town, Oscar. I wish I'd never heard of it."

Oscar stopped. The aloof flippancy had gone from his face. He put his hand on Willy's shoulder.

"It's my fault. I've kicked myself a hundred times for asking you to come up here. Willy—you realize you might be in for a shock."

"I know, Oscar," Willy interrupted. He stared at the pseudo-Greek columns of the police building and he managed to speak as calmly as Oscar.

"It's not your fault; I sent Hal here from Hildesheim. I insisted . . ."

He couldn't go on, and then they were swallowed by the police building whose hallways turned and twisted as if built to baffle the intruders. They had to wait in Mr. Hegner's anteroom, together with an old farmer couple. The woman sat, her face stony and wrinkled, her eyes fixed on the brown wall, while her husband tried to console her. Two big, healthy police officers, in their chipper green uniforms, were whispering to each other, ignoring the visitors and from time to time breaking into hearty, manly guffaws.

Commissioner Hegner was so huge and athletic that at first Willy took him for just another police bully. Yet as he began asking about Hal—his habits, character, looks—as he made the boys talk, Willy realized that Friedrich Hegner played the part of a bully only for the benefit of the other policemen.

While Willy sat there, reporting on their meeting with Gunther Ewers's Black Reichswehr boys, on his illness in Hildesheim, as he met Friedrich Hegner's grave eyes, the intuition rushed over him that something evil had befallen Hal and that Hegner, too, suspected it. For a second the floor seemed to recede from under Willy, the floor and the chair and the file cabinets, and he closed his eyes. His hands clutched the chair.

"Drink this glass of water," the commissioner said, as Willy opened his eyes. He had risen and stood before Willy. Willy drank it. Oscar had gone to the window. Willy looked up at the man before him, seeking his aid in a task for which he himself was pitifully equipped.

"Willy," Friedrich Hegner said, "I'll be frank. It's hard to take, but there it is. More and more young people have been missing in and around this town for the last year. Mostly boys, but some girls, too, always very young. Most of the boys came here to get jobs in our potash and artificial-rubber factories.

"You know about the Black Reichswehr, so I don't have to softpedal this. We've been hampered by the War Department, by military big shots everywhere. I should have about fifty investigators. You know how many I've got? Three. When I came here from Berlin five weeks ago I found some people had come to this department ten, twelve, fifteen times. They always were sent away when they complained about their missing children."

"I know the Hannsberg police," Oscar said. "They are overage, inefficient, and splendidly corrupt. You don't have to apologize for their blunders, Commissioner."

"No, but I'm paying for them," Mr. Hegner said, getting out a huge pile of papers. "Here. Just one case at random. Grete Marlock was a very young girl, working in a factory. She seemed to have accepted gifts from men. She disappeared three months ago. Her parents, who wouldn't speak to her when she was with them, have been here a dozen times. They claim they saw some woman wearing Grete's dress.

"I wish I could crack the black market. You know, the occupation army in the Rhineland will be sent home soon. So the boys are selling frantically—it's almost like the inflation in 1923. The stuff is second-rate, inferior grades of meat, coarse flour, army blouses, and trousers. Hannsberg is just in between the Rhineland and Berlin, so lots of stuff is unloaded here. And Little Venice buys it and resells it."

"I saw the shops," Willy said. "They had everything. Above all, a lot of secondhand men's clothing."

"You catch on fast, Willy Halder," Commissioner Hegner said. "The trade in secondhand clothing is unduly brisk. I'm trying to trace the clothes. I've found certain leads but I can't make them public yet. Perhaps I can tell you soon. And I promise I'll keep an eye out for your Hal Petersen. But for heaven's sake don't you two get into trouble. Everything I said is strictly confidential. Give me a ring in three days."

Oscar and Willy thanked him and left. The two policemen in the anteroom gave them disapproving glances. Willy somehow knew they loathed Hegner.

From the moment Willy stepped out of the pompous building onto Victoria Platz, a fog of unreality enveloped everything he did. He moved as if following orders from some secret center within him. A black, all-consuming anxiety began to fill him.

192

Throughout the following days, with their swift succession of merciless blows, a feeling of being tossed like driftwood by an onrushing surf never left him.

That night the vision revisited him. Again he saw farmer Schmitt's Forest of Shadows—the straight dark fir trees guarding Gunnivor's residence. Only, the trees had changed: they resembled the rotting houses of Little Venice neatly arranged around the clearing, and in the middle sat the dragon, just as in his first dream, in Hildesheim. This time, too, Gunnivor's features seemed blurred.

When at last the slovenly morning crept into their room, Willy knew he mustn't let himself go. Above the fear which seasoned everything he touched lay the impression of having been taken to the second act of a play and of now trying to reconstruct what had gone on before. To their surprise, Commissioner Hegner called around noon inquiring about the clothes Hal had worn and telling them he had received more help from Berlin.

Shortly afterward Aunt Frieda handed Willy a special delivery from Theodor—good old Aunt Frieda, who sensed the boys' state but couldn't figure it out and tactfully left them alone. His father advised Willy to talk to Professor Ernst Tressler, of the Hannsberg Institute of Engineering. A philosopher, journalist, and choleric, Theodor wrote, but a fighter for the right cause. He enclosed a note to the professor. Willy went the same afternoon.

At first Professor Tressler showed no interest in receiving a visitor. For a long while Willy waited in the half-lit drawing room of the house which was built in a half-Gothic, half-Spanish style and stood directly opposite a railroad track. From time to time the shrill whistle of a freight train split the silence.

"I'm very busy, young fellow," Professor Tressler said when he finally came in. He was a tiny old man with a fiery expression. A bush of gray hair fell over his forehead. He eyed Willy suspiciously from under his old-fashioned spectacles.

When Willy told him his story, Professor Tressler's eyes behind the thick lenses suddenly softened.

"Wait here," he demanded. He went away, then reappeared with a stack of papers. "How old are you?"

"Nineteen," Willy said. A week ago he would have enjoyed this eccentric. Now he only hoped he wouldn't have to take another shock. "What are these papers?"

"I hope for the best," Professor Tressler said. "I hope your friend is fine. But I demand action!" He pushed one sheet toward Willy. "The first of my series. It will come out tomorrow, in the Social-Democratic *Courier* if they dare, those softies. It's all based on ads in other papers. Look."

Pasted together were clippings from other Hannsberg journals, all

193

inquiring about missing persons. Anxious parents promised rewards, describing the clothes their Hans or Erich or Trudi or Gretel had worn when last seen. No girl was more than eighteen. The boys' ages ranged from sixteen to twenty-eight.

"This town!" Professor Tressler shook his fist at the railroad yard. "Industrious, Prussian, conservative, respectable on the outside. On the inside? Rotten. My faculty tells me to keep quiet. But I must find out where these poor children have gone. They can't all be in houses of ill fame. Have you seen Little Venice, Mr. Halder?"

"Yes, I have," Willy said. "What——"

"They must burn it down!" Professor Tressler shouted. "It's a boil on the town's body, a stinking sore. But they're afraid. The real-estate owners, respectable people, members of the Stahlhelm, good patriots. Go home, Mr. Halder. Let the police do the work. And me, an old man. You're too young."

"I'll stay until I find out," Willy said. "I'm ready for anything."

This was a poor lie and, of course, Professor Tressler saw through it. Then the old man slowly took another paper.

"Have you read today's *Courier?*"

"No, I haven't. Please tell me why I should."

"I can't," said the professor almost tenderly, turning away. "You mustn't get into this."

"I'll see it anyhow, Professor. Please." In an odd reversal Willy felt he should console the old man, who seemed too feeble for the crusade he had set himself.

As the professor finally shoved the paper across the table and Willy slowly went over the column marked in blue pencil, the blessed feeling of unreality, of playing a scene, swept over him so strongly it saved him from suffering the full impact of the blow.

"While playing near the Leine River not far from Little Venice," the article reported, "a group of children found bones they believed to be those of a dog. An investigation at the police laboratory, however, proved them to be parts of a human skeleton or, to be more exact, of several skeletons of young persons. Commissioner Hegner has sent out several search parties to comb the shores." Willy put the paper down.

"It's time for your lectures, Professor," a woman, apparently the housekeeper, said, appearing at the door.

Tressler nodded mechanically, and Willy thanked him and left. He never remembered how he got to Kaiser Allee.

He fell into a leaden sleep during the afternoon, managed to sit through dinner with Uncle Erich and Aunt Frieda, and then he and Oscar set out for their date with Ronny.

194

What he really expected Willy didn't know. He simply followed an impulse: Hal had asked Oscar to meet him at nine at the station, and he hadn't shown up. Willy wanted to see the station at nine. Perhaps life, in its incredible negligence, would give him a hint.

The boys wandered through the overcrowded waiting rooms, with their acid smell of poverty, up and down the long, noisy station. Within a short while Willy saw how a black market operated. The station was crawling with young girls and men, all shabbily dressed, all out to sell something. The familiar ferret-faced, half-grown boys from Little Venice were there whispering to Willy and Oscar about smart suits, well-preserved shoes, warm sweaters, or their younger sisters. The girls seemed to have reserved one part of the waiting room where they occupied the benches, one next to the other, gaudily and poorly painted. Ronny and about six other boys, flashily dressed, sauntered along, mostly in twos, flirting with those men who weren't looking for girls or black-market merchandise. Patrolling from one end to the other was one beefy, officious policeman who majestically ignored everything that went on.

In the hallway to the washroom Willy and Oscar saw many a suitcase being opened hastily, displaying for the onlooking customers sugar, meat, jackets, sweaters, socks, all for cash only.

They passed Ronny and motioned him to come over. Ronny was obviously pleased to see them, or to show before his friends what nice-looking young gentlemen had chosen him. But he wanted to leave.

"I'm going to meet my sister at Warm Hugo's," he declared, as if he had an appointment with royalty. "The air is thick here. They raided it some days ago, I heard tonight. And Lumber-Fritz arrested two kids yesterday. Took them to the station too."

"Who's Lumber-Fritz?" Willy inquired.

"Oh, we call him Lumber-Fritz because he's as big and strong as a lumberjack. He is thick with the cops, a kind of private dick. But he also sells old clothes and sometimes he puts you wise to a raid, that is if he likes you."

Ronny laughed. "He plays both sides, I guess. He's crazy too. He goes for very young girls—and roughnecks. Can you imagine? And when he's drunk he sings Christmas carols."

Willy and Oscar promised to be at Warm Hugo's later, and gave him fifty pfennig so he could order something there. He left satisfied, without giving his pals a glance.

Willy looked after him. The light, filtered through the station's glass cupola, tinted everything a yellow-greenish shade. The whole station gave the impression of an underwater anthill crawling with insects, all of them blind yet senselessly active. Only the boys dozing in the third-class waiting rooms were motionless. They had no plans, no business, no hope. Some of them were Black Reichswehr boys, runaways or tramps, but the majority were simply the unemployed who had hiked to Hannsberg to find jobs. There weren't enough jobs, there never would be, and now they were derelicts, in a strange town which didn't want them and tossed them out like garbage.

"Listen, Will," Oscar said. "This is all too familiar and depressing. It won't do us any good watching these sorry people. And I must say I can't imagine Hal ever having had anything to do with anyone here."

Willy agreed, "He had nothing to sell, either. He knew he was going to meet you—so he wouldn't need money. And I know he would never have accepted an invitation from one of the——"

"Look," Oscar said. "What a huge man. That could be Lumber-Fritz."

The man, more than six feet and with enormous shoulders, approached with incongruously short, fast steps. Several of Ronny's crowd flocked to him, and he talked incessantly to them, never stopping for breath. His red, blank face was well-fed, the face of a healthy businessman who likes his daily beers. A small dark mustache hung over very large lips which he incessantly moistened with a darting movement of his tongue—like that of an overgrown nervous snake. His shining, small black eyes reminded Willy of Adolf Hitler and, with that, of Sarek, the rattrap vendor. Only this man had a better, ruddier color. The gang left him, laughing, and the man disappeared in the third-class waiting room. In a short while he came out again, with a skinny, hungry-looking blond youth who carried a battered suitcase. The boy grinned sheepishly while Lumber-Fritz nodded his head, greeting every second person. Two of the girls sauntered up to him and Willy could hear them giggle. The man patted their cheeks and handed out some bills whereupon the girls immediately went into the second-class buffet. Seen from the back, Lumber-Fritz seemed another person. He walked like a heavily muscled woman, not like the rugged outdoor type. His fat white hand, with its thick, hammerlike thumb, held the boy's elbow—was he arresting him or taking him home?

The two stopped as Lumber-Fritz turned to another youth, a short, broad boy in a miner's outfit. Since he stood near, Willy could watch the big man's face as he talked. The boy began squirming, took out his wallet, presenting some papers. At the same time Lumber-Fritz had grasped his arm. A sensuous expression clouded his face so that he looked like a cross between a prize fighter and a woman in ecstasy.

Willy felt chilled. The huge man let the miner go and left, followed by his blond escort. Willy grabbed Oscar's arm.

"Right," Oscar said. "Let's go. God, this Lumber-Fritz is like a jellyfish with fangs."

The Warm Hugo in the heart of Little Venice was cozy in a grimy way. Willy found himself talking most of the time to Lonny, Ronny's twin sister, who confusingly resembled her brother, but was more intelligent. Ronny, proud of having introduced them, kept to his friends. The Warm Hugo, filled with smoke and kitchen smells, served beer, coffee, and a surprisingly large variety of sweets. To people like Ronny and Lonny it was "business" office and second home. It was a place where half the people went late at night to find someone congenial—for a reasonable sum—and the other half to be found; yet an air of hearty respectability hung over it, as if the Warm Hugo were the sort of beer garden where bank tellers and their wives went twice a week for a card game.

After some minutes Willy told Lonny that he didn't want to take too much of her time and pressed three marks into her hand, under the table. Lonny put them in her black bag and gave him an almost genuine look of gratitude from under her senselessly mascaraed eyes.

"I knew you didn't come here for a pickup," she said. "Why did you go to the station? It's a bad place."

Without hesitation Willy told her. Despite her loud make-up, her silly professional mannerisms, Lonny possessed a certain home-grown shrewdness. She confirmed Commissioner Hegner's report: some of her own friends had simply vanished. She had read about the bones in the river, though she could hardly bring herself to mention it. When Willy asked about Lumber-Fritz, Lonny nearly upset her beer glass. Lumber-Fritz was the worst of all, a stool pigeon for the police, she said, who, at the same time, sold horse meat, old clothes, and other stuff on the black market.

"He also has a detective bureau called 'Lasso,'" Lonny went on. "He arrested me once because he said I didn't have a real 'license.' Then he promised to let me go if I would send him some chickens—you know, girls under age.

"I called his bluff," Lonny declared, a note of triumph in her voice. "I said: 'I know plenty about you which the police will be interested to hear.' He got scared. He's chasing every young girl in Little Venice, you know. I can't tell you what he asks them to do. You're a gentleman."

Willy assured her he didn't want to know any more about Lum-

197

ber-Fritz. Lonny added angrily that he was also after the young roughnecks, and that it was typical of the Hannsberg cops to have a type like him as an informer. . . .

They left Warm Hugo and, for some reason he couldn't define, Willy promised the girl to come back in two days. The night was very cold, and a swollen yellow moon hung over Little Venice. Only a few women were walking around, hoping against hope for a customer. What really caught Willy's attention in that basement window he never found out. He was walking with Oscar, too weary to talk, too benumbed to think, when his eye fell on the display in the secondhand store. He stumbled down the rickety stairs. He stared at the merchandise, barely visible in the uncertain opalescent glow of the winter moon.

He wasn't aware of Oscar holding his arm; nothing registered except the things in the window which pierced his mind like a knife.

There stood one of Hal's wooden figures, a dark-brown young lamb, tagged "1.50 marks." Willy would have recognized it in a thousand. Nearby, on top of a stack of other clothes, lay Hal's seablue corduroy pants, more washed out now, nicely cleaned and creased. "Two marks," the tag announced.

Willy wanted to open his mouth, to cry out that Hal had worn these when he left Hildesheim, but no sound came. He stared at the wooden lamb, at the blue corduroys with their neat creases until they started whirling around him. A choking hand seemed to close his throat. A tide within him mounted and then, in an enormous onslaught, washed over him, burying him underneath, and blanking out the world.

The next morning the case broke. After a doctor had given Willy a strong bromide, Oscar wired Dr. Halder to come to Hannsberg. The Hannsberg police succumbed to Commissioner Hegner: they couldn't hush things up any longer, particularly since the appearance of Professor Tressler's first article, which shocked all of Hannsberg into a state bordering panic.

In dry, angry words Tressler reported on the thirty-odd youngsters who, in the span of one year, had disappeared; on the skeletons swept ashore by the river in several places, first discovered by children playing in the sand; on the still-recognizable human bodies, decapitated and half-swallowed by the swampland near Little Venice. All belonged to either very young girls or halfgrown boys, as the medical experts unanimously agreed.

Again and again anxious parents had gone to the police, begging for help. The Hannsberg officials had sent them away, vaguely promising investigations. Among the missing youngsters were runaways from the Black Reichswehr, Tressler explained, boys whose official whereabouts could not be divulged, who could disappear without a trace.

Theodor, who arrived the next day, decided to keep Willy under sedatives with Aunt Frieda watching him faithfully. Thus Willy did not at first hear about the arrest of a certain Friedrich Haarmann, known as Lumber-Fritz, accused of having murdered an unknown but enormous number of young people. As the *Courier* revealed, Lumber-Fritz had utilized his unique position to the fullest: as a police informer of long standing he could easily approach his victims, threatening them from his official position. Simultaneously, he protected those who, for some reason, appealed to him, and denounced those who might have become suspicious, for petty crimes he knew they had committed. Considered a plain-clothes man by the crowd in the third-class waiting room and in Little Venice, he could always arrest the young unemployed by asking for their "working papers," which none of them ever had.

Desperately the police officials fought to keep up the pretense that Haarmann had never been on the pay roll, but Professor Tressler presented such a tight case that no one in Hannsberg believed their denial.

Sometimes Haarmann had simply promised candy to school-girls, cigarettes to adolescent boys who aroused his desire. He took them all to his room in one of Little Venice's oldest houses, over-looking the river and furnished with a closet the height of the wall. Why he killed some of them, but let others go; whether he, later on, killed his partners only to sell their clothes Tressler could not explain. From Theodor, whom Commissioner Hegner had asked to act as medical adviser, Oscar heard that Haarmann, in the frenzy of his love-making, bit through the throats of his victims, without knowing what he was doing. Afterward he severed their heads with a large butcher knife—the heads of all the skeletons were found separated from the bodies, in a manner described by the experts as "extremely skillful."

Haarmann hid the bodies in the closet. After dark he threw bodies and heads into the river, sometimes directly from his window. On occasions he went to the quagmire near the Leine River in the early hours of the morning. The bog had swallowed most but not all of them. . . .

Although a group of influential citizens threatened the *Courier,* hinting the revelations might harm Hannsberg's business, the professor disclosed more and more details: how, as a profitable side line, Haarmann had done a thriving business with his victims' shoes, wallets, belts, and, sometimes, their flesh. Lumber-Fritz had sold an inordinate amount of "horse meat," at cheap prices, to the restaurant Our Little Angel in Little Venice. The meat was

199

neatly cut, white, and of a peculiar taste; Haarmann insisted, during the entire trial, that it was black-market merchandise from the occupation army in the Rhineland. But according to the medical experts, these pieces, of which they found some left in the restaurant's storeroom, had quite another origin.

This article brought about the end of the meat black market. Hannsberg lived in a frenzied state. Yet the pressure against Tressler increased. Haarmann had provided several members of the Stahlhelm and the National Socialists with desirable young companions. The list of his clients was found among his belongings. Together with Hegner's superiors, these organizations used every means to prevent the "mad Jewish professor," as they labeled Tressler, from getting at their members' names in Haarmann's book.

"Tressler will ruin his career," said Theodor to Oscar after he had returned from another meeting with Hegner.

"Some people in the Reichswehr ministry are leaving no stone unturned to keep the Black Reichswehr out of the trial. But Tressler won't give in, and I admire him for it. He says if a country permits its boys to leave their parents for an unknown destination, one can't be surprised if they are killed by an insane murderer, or, as Tressler calls him, a werewolf. . . . Tell me, Oscar, how well do you remember Hal?"

"Do you think you've found . . ." Oscar asked, and Theodor nodded.

"I want this cleared up before Willy regains consciousness. I'm afraid that's the least we can do."

Yet, mercifully, Oscar was spared looking at Hal's remains. Dr. Halder was able to identify Hal by the deformed kneecap bone on which he had operated years ago. As the trial opened a few days later, the name of Hal Petersen was added to the thirty-eight boys and girls of whose murder Fritz Haarmann was accused. He admitted to thirty-four.

It wasn't necessary to give Willy all the details, Dr. Halder decided, after he had stopped giving him sedatives. Willy had to live through it, Theodor thought, and the less he knew about the fantastic and noxious details, the easier it would be. Outwardly, Willy remained surprisingly calm when he was finally permitted to go out again. He even ate some of the food Aunt Frieda put on the table. He spent most of his time with Professor Tressler. He was so quiet that Oscar and Theodor began to wish for a breakdown—he couldn't swallow all this silently, calmly, with that unnatural control he had assumed.

Only after two weeks had passed did Willy talk to Oscar about it. They were in Oscar's room that night, each in his old-fashioned bed, and the distance between them seemed so enormous that Willy was afraid his voice wouldn't carry. Now that the first numbing shock was wearing off, as an anesthetic wears off after an operation, he had to talk about it, about everything, for days and days. The sensation of living in a kingdom of unreality, of taking part in some archaic play whose heroes were destroyed by a barbaric, dismally ignorant fate, while he survived, against all reason, was the only thing that sustained him in the following endless, dark weeks.

"It's clear, now, Oscar," Willy said, looking at Oscar's blond head barely visible in the dim room. "Haarmann arrested Hal for not having working papers, just as he arrested all the others. Then he sold Hal's blue pants. And the lamb he found in the pocket . . ."

"You mustn't discuss all this," Oscar said. "Your father is terribly worried about you, Will. Try to forget it. Anything I might say to you is useless. My words are weak—you know there are no words for things like this."

"You don't know Gunnivor," Willy said, more to himself than to Oscar. "A monstrous old pagan god some farmers believe in. I believe in him now too. Gunnivor sits in the forest and waits for his victims to come. Then he destroys them. You know what Tressler says? He says a country where a Haarmann can work unhampered, a country where a mass murderer is hired as a policeman, is corroded and finished. It's a sign that the insane are stronger than the sane."

"Willy, it's morbid," Oscar said, almost imploring. "Don't listen to Tressler's stories. He is a fanatical eccentric."

"But he's right. I thought there are no monsters, no dragons in our time. It's wrong, Oscar. We have werewolves in this age of radio and electricity. Gunnivor is alive. His name is Haarmann, or somebody else, and he is out to kill. Oh, Oscar, I don't want to live any longer. I'm all choked inside, empty and dumb."

Oscar wanted to answer, but then he heard Willy crying. It was the first time he had cried since he was sure of Hal's death, and Oscar let him go on. Willy had held back so long, Oscar was afraid something in him would burst and destroy him bodily. There was no consolation for Willy. He had to pass through the darkness, and Oscar resolved not to say the conventionally smooth words, ever.

When Theodor entered the room, around midnight, Willy was still weeping, shaken by an uncontrollable spasm that held him until he was weak and spent.

"We'll go home tomorrow," Theodor whispered, putting his arm around Willy's shoulders. "The trial is over. Haarmann will hang."

Dr. Halder looked at his son, so incredibly young in the old-fashioned bed, much too young to know the vortex of life that had opened before him.

"There is nothing I can say to you, son," he said, "nothing real, nothing that would mean anything to you. Except that nobody can help you, Willy, but yourself. And that we all love you very much."

15. YEARS LATER, WHEN WILLY THOUGHT back on these first weeks of 1930, he couldn't recall all the nights of wakefulness and despair. It was hopeless to try to describe to anyone that gigantic black vacuum within him. Yet when he looked in Melanie's eyes, when he talked to Ilona who was always there when one needed her, he realized he mustn't let himself go. It was bad enough to torture himself; he must spare those around him. After his one talk with Oscar he never discussed Hannsberg with anyone.

What Willy always remembered was the night Ilona brought Mathilda Einzig to the house. Mathilda, Willy saw at a glance, had been told and would never ask a question. She carried a huge brief case and began pulling out typewritten sheets.

"I found an imbecile son for our radio skit, Willy, but he wasn't imbecile enough. Schoret has a new series, dramatizing the youth situation today. Not a dialect part. Are you very busy?"

Willy hesitated. He didn't feel like reading a part, acting, doing anything. Yet there was Melanie, bent over her sewing, avoiding his eyes, and Ilona, busily leafing through the scripts. They had arranged it with Mathilda, of course. They wanted to help. As he realized how he had worried Melanie and Ilona, as, almost physically, he felt their affection floating toward him, he gave in.

"I'm not busy, Mathilda. But I won't be much good."

"Look at the first script tonight," Mathilda said. "Be at my place tomorrow morning at nine."

"So early?" Melanie asked. "Willy often sleeps——"

"My other rehearsals start at eleven," Mathilda interrupted, "and I want to work on your son before we get to the station tomorrow."

When Willy saw her to the door, she said: "Your friend Maria Reger is doing nicely. The girl is really talented."

"I've forgotten her, Mathilda," Willy said. He hadn't thought of her since Hannsberg. But it was nice of Mathilda to lie for his sake.

The next morning she coaxed, cajoled, scolded, all but literally whipped him. She got him so exhausted that, for the first time, he

203

slept a few hours that night without waking up in a sweat. And, almost against his wish, his mind began dissecting the sentences, determining the high lights, working out the inflections. He was touched by Mathilda's wisdom. She had given him what appeared to be a rather sad role, a young student defeated in his search for love and jobs until the very end when both suddenly materialized. In his present state Willy couldn't have attempted a dialect part. But this essentially phony radio play couldn't be taken seriously, cried out to be played for "ham," and thus sent his mind in a different direction. Trash was refreshing, and that was what Mathilda had counted on.

After the performance, Mathilda took Willy to Director Emmery Schoret. Seventy-five marks for the work was not enough, she declared, whereupon the director began clamoring for the dialect skits Mathilda had promised long ago, and congratulated Willy on his performance. If they'd go on the air with two comic pieces and a serious one every month, he'd pay more.

"I don't know whether I can do a dialect piece next month," Willy said. "I might not sound funny enough."

"Let him rewrite his parts," Mathilda demanded. "The man who did these doesn't know Frankfurt."

They left, and Mathilda squeezed his hand. "Don't do anything you don't want to do, son," she said, and turned abruptly.

Willy took the scripts home. Melanie was still up, in her usual place, reading *The End of Capitalism,* a then very popular tome by F. Fried.

"You sounded fine," she said. "I wish it had been longer. Mr. Fried's capitalism and its end bores me. Mathilda was excellent, too, but if you don't mind, the play itself——"

"It was dreadful, Mother," Willy said. He smiled at her, and he saw how happy it made her to see him smile again.

"But the seventy-five marks I got aren't so dreadful," he said. "I'll buy you something."

"Seventy-five?" Melanie sounded incredulous. "You know, Father has to treat, let me see, over twenty Sick Fund patients to earn that. You won't buy anything for me, Will. This will be your university fund. Can you get more work?"

Willy pointed to the bundle of scripts. "They asked me to look these over. Comic dialect pieces. For Mathilda and me, called *Dopey's Holiday.* I'm to be Mathilda's stupid son, a stooge with the worst Old Town dialect."

"You can't imagine how much it would help," Melanie declared, putting *The End of Capitalism* aside. "Father worries about your university fees, which your radio sketch could easily pay."

204

Willy opened the first manuscript. "Erna, a hefty market woman selling vegetables on the Old Town Platz," the directions went, "explains to Heiner, her not-too-bright son, how to sell cabbages while she goes for a cup of coffee."

"That's Mathilda's star role," Melanie interrupted. "You'll have a tough time living up to her, Will."

Willy handed her seventy marks. "Keep them for our fund, Mother. I'll do as many Dopeys as they give me."

Melanie kissed him good night and said: "Father will be proud of his imbecile radio son, but don't be surprised if he doesn't show it. He feels he should let you keep all you earn."

The next day Willy spent over the scripts. Here and there he changed the lines to make them better fit the type of Old Town yokel. After Melanie had left for her usual afternoon treatment, Anna asked Willy if he would open the door for the patients this afternoon. She intended to buy a special sort of apple for Frau Doktor, which she could find only in Ginnheim, and did Willy mind?

The afternoon threw Willy back to days long gone. When he was smaller, he had enjoyed helping Anna, throwing open the waiting-room door with an elegant flourish, and involving the patients in what he considered beneficial chitchats. Now this thrill had faded and it was just a job. Of course he couldn't help observing Father's patients. One could guess the degree of their sickness by the pace at which they clambered up the stairs.

There were far too many this time. How could Father treat them all between three and five, even between three and seven? Often they turned up in couples, particularly the old ones. A few smiled at him, remarking they remembered him, but most of them remained stolid and somewhat sour.

In the middle of the afternoon Theodor came out, an expression of disbelief on his face.

"It's just as well Anna isn't here," he declared, falling into an easy chair. "You know who's going to be my patient? Deputy Sprenger. Anna hates our National-Socialist City Council leader. She calls him a scoundrel, a blackmailer of the first water. She'd throw him down the stairs. He's an epileptic, you know, with ulcers. Recently, during a meeting, he had an attack after one of his tirades, and since I was the only physician there, I had to treat him. I gave him an injection and he calmed down. Now he has the nerve to call on me."

"He printed nasty things about you too," Willy said.

"More than once," Theodor said. "Well, a doctor has to treat everybody. But why pick on me?"

He went back, and Willy heard him open the door to his office, saying, "Next, please." The more fashionable physicians had nurses, but the Halders could never afford a nurse.

Deputy Sprenger announced himself in a loud voice, stamping up the stairs. He seemed to be made of two shapeless flour sacks: one for the body, one for the head. What was left of his blond hair was plastered in thin strands over his pate; but out of the general shapelessness sprang the most prominent eagle beak Willy had ever seen. He remembered the caricatures of Jews in Mr. Sprenger's own *Observer;* his nose was taken straight from there. There seemed to exist a mocking law of nature, Willy mused, which made so many of the race-maniacal National Socialists resemble those they attacked.

"Heil Hitler and good afternoon," the deputy said, breathing heavily and taking off his overcoat with the golden swastika on the lapel.

Willy didn't know what moved him, but of a sudden, falling into the role of Dopey Heiner, he drawled: "Ach, good afternoon. What do ye want, mister?"

For some reason, Willy's stupid expression pleased Mr. Sprenger. Automatically adopting the Old Town brogue, he explained he was Deputy Sprenger, N.S.D.A.P., and had an appointment with the doctor.

"Who are you?" he added.

Willy stared at him, heavy-lidded, and stuttered: "Ei, ei, ei. I'm Daddy's son. You must wait a little, just a little."

"I telephoned beforehand." Mr. Sprenger's voice began to rise. Willy, in the same sleepy fashion, repeated:

"You must wait a little, just a little, just a little."

By now the deputy realized that he had to do with a mentally underprivileged young man, shrugged his shoulders, and let himself be led into the waiting room where, to Willy's satisfaction, only the most uncomfortable chair was free.

About an hour later Theodor threw open the door between the office and the living room, a door rarely used and hidden by a brocade curtain.

"Quick. Get me some more cushions," he shouted. "He's having another attack."

On the office floor lay Deputy Sprenger, his arms and legs beating the floor in an irregular fast tattoo, his eyes turned inward, foam on his lips. He still resembled a sack, now an obscenely quivering one. His head was supported by Theodor's only office cushion. Willy put two more cushions under his arms, two others under the legs. Mr. Sprenger gave the impression of an unduly swollen roach seized by a gay dancing fit.

Theodor rolled up Mr. Sprenger's sleeve and put the needle

into his arm. After a while the convulsions subsided. Dr. Halder lifted the receiver and made a short call.

"I'll send him home by ambulance," Theodor said. "He got all worked up when I told him that, in his condition, he must avoid excitement, and he should give up politics and go back to plumbing. Incidentally, he asked me whether I had a moron opening the door."

"Good," Willy remarked. "I was trying out my radio program. He seemed to be the right guinea pig."

"Pig in any case," Theodor murmured, glancing out the window. "Goodness, Willy, look at the ambulance."

Underneath the red cross of the car Willy read: "Frankfurt Municipal Jewish Hospital."

The bell rang and Willy admitted two enormous, white-clad stretcher bearers. They greeted Theodor with a friendly "Hello, Doc, what's going on here?" and lifted the deputy on the stretcher. Theodor threw Sprenger's vest and jacket over him.

"How did I get the Jewish hospital ambulance?" Theodor asked.

"Oh, that's just the car, Doc," one of the men said. "We're from Saint Francis, near Opern Platz. You called us, didn't you? We got the car a month ago and haven't had a chance to repaint it. D'you mind, Doc?"

"I don't," Theodor said, smiling, "but the man you're supposed to carry is Deputy Sprenger, of the National-Socialist party."

Willy watched the two bearers. At first they didn't seem to get it, then they exchanged a quick glance, keeping straight faces.

"Sprenger? The fellow from the *Observer?*" the first one said. "Doc, it's a pleasure to take him home in this jalopy. Shall we drive past the *Observer* building?"

"Sorry, no," Theodor said. "Better get him home to his wife quickly. Glauburg Strasse 321."

They took Sprenger downstairs. As they descended Willy could hear the men giggle like basso grasshoppers.

He would use the inflection he had tried on the deputy for the radio rehearsal. It had worked spectacularly, and for a moment the pressing weight within him seemed to have lessened.

Only after many weeks did Willy realize the state of self-suspension in which he had been living for so long. Now, as winter turned into spring, as his radio work kept him more and more busy—Mathilda fussed over every script as if it were Shakespeare —it seemed as if his senses were returning from a leave of absence. He again began to notice the world around him; he opened up a little to other people.

One evening in March, after Ilona and he had sat through an

207

empty and glittering UFA film and settled down in the smoky Café Toni, it struck him suddenly that Ilona's calm cheerfulness rang false. It touched him deeply. Ilona had lost as much as he, yet she respected his refusal to discuss Hannsberg, though she must want to know everything about it.

Also, she was a link with Hal, a living link. Hal had loved her, and now she owned a part of Hal just as he did. Willy cursed himself while he sipped his red wine; he had been so immersed in himself that he had become indifferent to other people. At the same time the idea came to him that Ilona and he should console each other, that it might help both of them, and that, in this way, he somehow would be a second Hal. Of course this was not only abstruse but disgraceful. It also made him aware of how much he needed affection, love, everything a girl could give him. . . .

"Does Mathilda think we're having an affair?" Ilona asked, as if she had been thinking with him. "She's as jealous of you as if she were your mother. And you and I have been together too much. I'm not able to get along with new people and you and I were so close because of . . ."

Toni's was the wrong place for Ilona to cry but she couldn't help it. Willy turned away, listening for a moment to the chatter of voices, staring into the air thick with smoke and filled with the bitter aroma of Toni's Café Espresso. Toni's had become the rallying point for Frankfurt's young bohemians, most of whom knew Willy and Ilona. Willy hoped Ilona wouldn't be embarrassed by Kurt Marland glancing at her from the neighboring table. She wasn't. She hid her face behind a large pocket mirror and set to powdering her cheeks.

When she emerged, she took Willy's hand and squeezed it very quickly.

"Sorry," she said. "It's the first time. You know most of these people, too, think you and I are having an affair. I thought about it, Will, but it would be wrong and destroy everything."

Ilona was one of the few girls who could speak of sex, libido, and such things, as was the fashion among the Toni crowd, without showing off how "broad-minded" she was. It was inevitable, then, that Ilona, too, was being pushed toward the idea of their having an affair. It was good to know she didn't think it was monstrous. She simply considered it wrong for them. And the way she had squeezed his hand was exactly like Hal. For a second Willy saw two schoolboys standing at Gate 10 of Frankfurt's Main Station, while the Cronberg train puffed impatiently. He felt Hal pinching his arm as a good-by gesture. It always hurt a little but you knew, for a long while, that Hal had been with you. . . .

208

"I dislike Kurt Marland," Willy said, changing the subject. He glanced at the next table, where an ardent discussion was proceeding. "What's his political creed at the moment?"

"Still pacifism," Ilona answered. "What was it before?"

"A new brand of radical conservatism. The good old families together with the Reichswehr should form a medieval government of the elite, romantic but stern. That was three weeks ago. Now he's crusading for a world-wide anti-war organization."

"He's a clever charlatan," Ilona said angrily. "Frankfurt is full of them. They all want to prove that conventions mean nothing to them. So they invent a new set of unconventional conventions. Incidentally, Kurt and his clique dislike you too."

"Why?"

"Kurt thinks you shouldn't have turned your back on politics."

"Politics is a mess," Willy declared. "Father says we are going to get that Center man, Bruening, as chancellor. Do you think he can invent jobs for all? I have enough of parties, Ilona."

"I'll tell you another reason they dislike you," Ilona went on. "They're envious because of 'Dopey Heiner.' It's successful. They can't forgive you that."

She stopped. Kurt had sauntered over to their table. He was so tall, almost six feet five, that only a few people ever became aware of his perfectly symmetrical face with its smooth baby skin. He would have been handsome, as the male UFA stars were handsome, if his black lashless eyes hadn't been too narrow and too cold. They resembled those of an anaconda Willy had once watched at the zoo. Now Kurt brought over a girl with frizzy dark hair, who kept twisting her handbag.

"This is Friedelgunde Fischer," Kurt introduced her. "She writes for the *General News*. She is going to enroll at the university. Thought you might like to meet her, Will."

They had no choice but to ask the pair to join them. Soon Friedelgunde involved Willy in a discussion on which courses to take. Her interests, she emphasized, were the same as his. Everything Friedelgunde said or did had too much heat, Willy decided, while listening to her denunciation of Professor Schatter's course on German Literature, I. According to reliable sources, it was duller than dull.

"Ah, but Professor Naumann is different. I sneaked into a course when I was still in high school. A genius. And so good-looking!"

Miss Fischer beamed a pair of ecstatic blue eyes at Willy, fluttering her lashes. She talked so vehemently that the neighboring tables heard every word. She launched an all-out attack on Willy, shooting words like "dadaism," "psychoanalysis," "expressionism," "libido" at him, while Kurt watched with icy interest. When Ilona and Willy finally managed to leave, Kurt whispered to Willy:

"She isn't good-looking but easy to get. Even Toni had her."

"I'm afraid our tastes are not the same," Willy couldn't help answering. "Toni and you can take turns."

He walked Ilona home—she lived near the Goldschmidts in a tiny house on Hoch Strasse. After a while Ilona asked:

"Did Kurt, by any chance, try to pass Friedelgunde on to you? It's considered the great sport among the Toni crowd. It's none of my business, Will . . ."

Willy took her arm. "He did, Ilona, and of course it's your business. Friedelgunde's approach was dazzling. She asked my opinion on everything, mainly sex, and pretended to be overwhelmed by my cleverness."

"I'm afraid you're going to see a lot of her and her sort," Ilona remarked as they turned toward the silent, narrow-gabled houses of Hoch Strasse. "The university seems to be crawling with them."

Willy had been looking forward to his studying as much as he could to anything at the moment. The university, a sprawling group of pseudo-Gothic sandstone palaces, stretched out over several blocks at the end of the Westend, just where it deteriorated into the drab suburb of Bockenheim. It had no campus but was blessed with numerous glum offices and haughty marble statues of famous scientists.

During the first days Willy did nothing but stand in line to get his papers. Every student received a green notebook in which he wrote the courses he was going to take. After this, one had to pay the regular fees, plus innumerable extras. On Theodor's advice Willy started out early, but even so he spent endless hours getting everything straightened out. The murky university hallways were crowded with young people in a perpetual search for this or that special office, and it all reminded Willy of one of the early Keystone comedies in which too many Kops chased a man who was just escaping around the next corner.

Finally Willy had his courses together and went to the bursar's office. Altogether, his fees amounted to 200 marks—just the sum he had saved from Siegfried Mahl's private lessons.

"Do you wish to pay in one, two, or three installments?" asked the young student who apparently was being broken in by the real bursar, a weary-looking man, scribbling figures in a large tome.

"I'll pay the whole thing now," Willy said.

For a moment the young student looked at him incredulously,

and the old man stopped writing. Willy began to suspect there was something criminally wrong in paying the whole amount.

Then the young assistant laughed, almost embarrassed. "All right. Fine." Lowering his voice, he added: "Most of the fellows pay in installments. They save the money while working and pay us in dribbles."

For the first time in his life Willy felt what it was to have more than others. Of course he had sweated enough with Siegfried Mahl, but at home, hidden in Mother's sewing bag, lay more, the salary from his radio skits. It filled him with a certain self-confidence; yet he almost had a guilty conscience when, during the coming months, he heard the other students talk about how to earn something extra.

Toward most professors, Willy soon discovered, he had to assume a lenient attitude to endure them. Their first lectures were crowded: that was when they signed their names in the green notebooks as proof of the student's attendance. Since they had to sign again only at the last lecture, and kept no attendance records, the students were free to skip the sessions in between, and many did so. Despite the confusion of Willy's first weeks of academic life, he noticed how often the older students cut classes to gather in one of Bockenheim's spacious taverns, drinking huge quantities of beer and discussing everything but their work.

Willy couldn't blame them. He had taken as few courses as possible during his first term, because two or three mornings a week Mathilda expected him to rehearse and rewrite their broadcasts. Even of these few courses, only one or two gave him anything. He was forced to attend at least one weekly lecture by the head of the department of German literature, Professor Ferdinand Schatter, a pompous little man of about fifty who bore such a startling resemblance to a frog—he even wore green suits—that Willy expected him to croak when he opened his mouth. Perhaps it would have been more interesting had he really croaked—his "Introduction into Modern Literature" was overloaded with musty philological details or pedantic arguments. He efficiently killed all interest in any subject he was teaching, and, besides, the students could read everything in Professor Schatter's book, as he never failed to point out discreetly. Although a freshman, Will had managed to get into the "Intermediate Seminary" on the "Development of the Novel," but there Ferdinand Schatter, acting before a small but attentive audience, was even worse.

Within the first three months Willy got to know several of the students. He couldn't help it if most of them knew of his radio job through Friedelgunde, official gossip of the department. The only person with whom he became friendly was Wolfgang Brosig, a member of a Catholic youth organization. He was a boy with one of those honest ugly faces Willy always liked. Wolfgang succeeded one evening in breaking down Willy's reserve and they went to a small café in Bockenheim for "a talk and a glass of milk"—Wolfgang never touched alcohol. Wolfgang criticized the "Frog" as frankly as Willy, and after a while Willy told him his new theory.

"Language students can be divided into two groups," he declared. "The grasshoppers and the ants. The ants are the future schoolteachers, earnest and deadly industrious. The grasshoppers just want a degree and then go into journalism, or the theater, or something equally irresponsible. As far as I can see, I'm the only grasshopper in the Frog's 'Intermediate' crowd."

Wolfgang, sipping his milk, agreed: the ants outnumbered the grasshoppers. He himself was a sort of grasshopper, too: he wanted to reorganize the Catholic youth theater in Germany.

"Don't judge the ants too harshly," Wolfgang added. "According to statistics only three out of ten will get a teaching job after they've finished. So they throw themselves into their work because only those with top ratings will make it. Tell me, are you going to join a ladder?"

"What's a ladder?" Willy inquired.

"I always forget you're only a freshman," Wolfgang said, grinning. "Anyhow, a ladder is a fraternity, feudal, elegant, or otherwise. You drink far too much with them, meet 'the gang,' and later on they help you to get jobs. If you study law they're a 'must.' The old judges and district attorneys hand out jobs only to fraternity brothers. But they're after us little fry too."

One evening a few weeks later, when Willy came in from one of his broadcasts, Big Anna, with an expression of distaste, announced there were two "stiff" gentlemen waiting for him in the doctor's waiting room, and besides, dinner was ready.

The two gentlemen, it turned out, represented the Alemannia, one of Prussia's "most honored fraternities." They introduced themselves as Otto von Fritsch and Gert Wagener. With their dueling scars they reminded Willy of Hellmuth Handler or Kurt Renner of his Wandervogel days.

The Alemannia's motto, the two elucidated, was simple: For Honor and Fatherland. How this motto was put into practice, however, was something else. Every morning at eleven the members met for a friendly get-together and an early beer; their rallying point in the university was in the main hall under Humboldt's bust, and one could always find a drinking companion if one didn't care to attend a course. Nobody in the fraternity cared much about

212

attending anything, it seemed. Willy was informed of the "comradely" meetings on Friday nights (beer again) and the unique institution of the "crammers": those members who had devoted themselves more to the comradely pursuits during the term would be helped through their examinations by extra instructors. These would cram into the Alemannian heads in a few weeks what the brothers hadn't learned in two terms of beer drinking.

The old feeling of acting a part again seized Willy as he stood there in the old waiting room, staring at Boecklin's loathsome "The Isle of the Dead" (why didn't Father remove that thing?) and listened to their clumsy attempts to make him join the fraternity, at five marks a month—an extremely high amount in 1930.

Politely, Willy declared he was honored by their offer but his work kept him too busy to join anything.

"Incidentally," Willy said. "Didn't your office tell you before you came? My father is a Social-Democratic deputy. I guess that's hardly the Alemannia's political line?"

Von Fritsch and Wagener appeared dumfounded. If they had one ounce of humor, Willy thought, they would have joked about their inefficient office, but they simply looked at each other for help. Their code didn't cover such a happening. Finally, Wagener clicked his heels, bowed, and said: "Sorry to have taken your time. Good-by." Von Fritsch likewise bowed elegantly, and they disappeared.

Anna, in an enormous apron, opened the hallway door and said in a voice to shake the whole house: "Dinner's getting cold, Will. People always come at the wrong time!"

Anna disliked the gentlemen from the Alemannia as much as she disliked those from the Berengaria, the Hannoveriana, and others who presented themselves later on. Fortunately, the National-Socialist students, abbreviated N.A.S.T.U., left him alone. This was gratifying; at least they seemed to know who would make a likely prospect and who wouldn't. Willy didn't find out until later that he had a friend there.

One afternoon, as Willy was hastening through the dim corridors to his seminar on "Theory and Practice of the Theater," someone stopped him. A heavy paw fell on his shoulder, he smelled the faint odor of lilac brilliantine, and then recognized Gerhard Pueschel's beaming baby face.

"Why, Willy, where are you rushing to? How are you? Come, have a beer with me."

"Goodness, Gerhard," Willy said, gently removing the paw, "I thought you wanted to become a cop."

"Aw, I changed my mind," Pueschel said. "Franz Duester and

213

I are studying law. His brother Erwin gave me a part-time job, and law is a soft touch, anyhow."

"Sorry, Gerhard, but I have a class now. Aren't you working in your parents' shop?"

"Shop was sold," Gerhard said. "Nobody would give us credit. Say, do you ever hear from Robbi? Or Oscar? Or Petersen?"

It was the first time anyone had asked Willy directly about Hal. The people next to him knew what had happened, and Melanie and Ilona had erected a protecting screen around him so that nobody ever referred to Hannsberg. Now Willy just looked at Pueschel, stupid as ever, brilliantined, and with a large swastika in his lapel.

"Yes, I'm a storm trooper," Gerhard said. "Don't glare at me. If it weren't for me, they would have tried to get you into the N.A.S.T.U. I told 'em it was no good. I always listen to your broadcasts, Will. You sound just as good as in school. Well, what about Petersen?"

"He is dead," Willy said. He didn't look at Gerhard, and it sounded false in the murky corridor. It hurt him almost physically because he tried never to think about Hal, and now he was forced to say it aloud—to Pueschel, of all people.

"I'm sorry," Gerhard said, his tiny mouth wide open. "I didn't ——" But Willy had left him and hurried toward the theater seminar under Professor Gottfried Pfeiffer-Belli.

There were only about ten students in the seminar, but Professor Pfeiffer-Belli's regal manner made them feel as though they were five hundred. He was a huge, stout man with a fleshy mobile face, combining the mannerisms of an actor who has played before royalty with those of a wealthy dilettante who has devoted his life to the curiosa of the stage.

Since Willy loathed pompousness and that overzest for detail in which most of his professors wallowed, he didn't expect to like Pfeiffer-Belli. But after a few sessions he changed his mind. The grand manner, he discovered, was genuine. Gottfried Pfeiffer-Belli had played Hamlet and Lear before kings and emperors; he had managed many of the innumerable small German theaters which, before the Weimar Republic, were endowed by stage-loving princes and which now struggled along on municipal funds. Gradually the professor made Willy appreciate the grandiose gestures of the previous century, the frankly theatrical, florid style which had survived only in the opera—and Willy liked it.

They began by discussing Schiller's *Kabale und Liebe,* and Willy got along beautifully with the old majestic actor who was a much better teacher than most professors.

214

Of the other students he noticed mainly Mr. Rundt. Pimply Alfred Rundt was given to long confused speeches about "intuitive conception," "semi-historical perspectives," and his own large and humid soul. If the professor was annoyed he didn't show it—his patience seemed unending.

To Willy's great satisfaction, Mathilda thoroughly approved of Pfeiffer-Belli.

"You know, old Gottfried was handsome once," she said one morning. "Please give him my regards, Willy."

Willy did so the next time before the seminar started, and an enormous smile came over the professor's face, like fat spreading over a hot frying pan.

"I knew you were acquainted with dear old Mathilda," he said. "My son told me about the—hm—plays in which you and she are appearing. I'm sorry, but it is against my principles to listen to the air waves."

"We aren't really doing a play," Willy stuttered, "it's more like a sketch."

"Don't let it spoil you," the professor implored Willy. "Radio teaches the young people to be natural. What a dreadful misapprehension! You must expand your emotions in the theater, not compress them into any life likeness." He stopped and expertly changed his tone. "Give my regards to dear Mathilda."

Willy nodded. The rest of the group had gathered around them, listening, slightly bewildered, to the conversation. There was among them a new girl with copper-colored hair leafing through Willy's Reclam edition of *Kabale und Liebe*.

The professor motioned the students to their seats and began:

"We are going to have a new member today. I am only too glad to welcome Miss Arlène Duval. Miss Duval is one of the French exchange students our government has asked to visit German universities. I consider it an honor that she has chosen my seminar. Nothing more taxing than to study the theater in a foreign tongue! May I ask you whether you're familiar with *Kabale und Liebe*, Miss Duval?"

The girl had just discovered she had taken Willy's copy and was giving it back to him with a whispered, "Thanks." Now she said:

"I read it in French, Professor. Thank you for welcoming me. If my German isn't as good as that of the other students, I hope you'll forgive me."

Her voice was clear, and although it wasn't an alto it gave the impression of one. Her accent was almost unnoticeable. As the seminar went on, it became apparent to Willy that Miss Duval knew more about the theater than all the others put together, and

215

that she saw through Mr. Rundt's learned double-talk in no time. The professor and the students forgot that the girl was using a foreign language. To Friedelgunde Fischer's dismay, Professor Pfeiffer-Belli made her read the ingénue parts. When they discussed the characters, Willy found she always made sense. Arlène Duval fought all attempts to give the characters more significance than necessary, and at the end of the seminar she opposed Mr. Rundt in the most friendly manner when he burst forward with some dim "philosophy of despair" which he insisted Schiller had anticipated.

How it came about that Willy decided to walk home instead of taking the streetcar as usual, whether he really followed Arlène Duval or ran into her on the corner of Westend and Bockenheimer Landstrasse, he could never remember. Summer had almost come, and the plane trees on the avenue were breaking forth with a lush green that made the leaves appear lacquered. According to German concepts, all French girls were supposed to be brunettes, but Arlène Duval wasn't. Under the rather ghostly arc lights of Bockenheimer Landstrasse, her hair shone like antique gold. He finally overtook her, and she smiled at him.

He said hello, and they began talking. At first Willy tried to show off his French but he soon stopped. Arlène's German was so much better, and, besides, she had come here to practice it. They went into Badendieck's Book Cabin on Opern Platz and purchased a tattered copy of *Kabale und Liebe* for Arlène. After sauntering through Opern Platz and up Reuter Weg, Willy discovered she lived only a few houses away, at Mrs. Sigbert's.

This was the beginning. He saw Arlène the next day and some days later, and he fought the temptation to be friendly. He didn't want any new people in his life. Yet every Tuesday and Friday they met in the theater seminar, and it was inevitable that he walked her home. Not once did she ask a personal question. She was content to discuss dramas, the tricks of staging, and what in heaven's name Mr. Rundt meant when he embarked on his endless flights of fancy.

Arlène was highly suspicious of everything high-flown or confused. She almost made Willy believe that any problem could be solved if one applied an ounce of common sense. She was good for him—he was ashamed to admit it, but she was. When he talked to her his mind became easier. And his dreams lost some of their nightmare quality. Willy had reconciled himself to the fact that again and again he would wake up in the early hours of the morning, drenched in sweat, because he had just run through Hannsberg, searching for Hal, or been confronted by a fantastic monster sitting in a clearing and looking like Haarmann or, sometimes, like Lattau. Not once did he mention his dreams to anyone.

Being with Arlène made him feel as if this "night side" of his world might vanish if he simply ignored it. Her sharp and concise mind allowed for no hidden dangers, and, knowingly or unknowingly, she directed him toward the practical tasks of their studies.

16. IT WAS AN AFTERNOON IN JUNE, shortly before the long vacations which changed everything. It began with Melanie's asking Willy to accompany her to Dr. Stein at three o'clock. She had never done this before, and though he was supposed to attend Professor Naumann's class on *The Minnesingers,* he immediately decided to drop it and go with her. Melanie carried herself too carefully erect and Willy knew this meant she didn't feel well.

Although there existed a direct streetcar connection, Melanie took a taxi to Dr. Stein. Once inside, she said with an unexpected urgency: "Willy, my boy, Dr. Stein wants to talk to you. Promise not to repeat to Father whatever he tells you."

"We've had so many secrets together before, haven't we, Mother?" Willy answered, and Melanie, grateful for the chance, smiled at him, a smile that frightened Willy.

He then sat in Dr. Stein's waiting room under Boecklin's "Isle of the Dead"—apparently a "must" for Frankfurt physicians. It seemed absurd that he who had so often opened the door for Theodor's patients should be sitting in another doctor's room. It was somehow as if he were on the other side of a mirror. He forced himself to open *Cosmos, The Illustrated Nature Magazine,* and read the childish pieces on ingenious weasels and venturesome gophers and nature's marvels in general. He sat there only an hour but it seemed to stretch interminably.

When Dr. Stein, a small, soft-spoken, white-haired man with rimless spectacles, called him in, Melanie had left.

"We had better talk alone," Dr. Stein said. "You've grown, Will. I've known you since you were little. How old are you now?"

"Twenty. What is——"

"Sit down, my boy." The doctor drew up a comfortable chair. He himself went back behind his large desk with its many islands of pharmaceutical samples—the same ones Theodor always received from the factories.

"It won't be easy for you to hear what I have to say, Willy. But I have no other choice. I've known your father since we were

218

students in Paris. He's a wonderful man and an idealist, so much so that he often refuses to face the realities."

"I never looked at it that way," Willy answered. The old doctor obviously wanted to take his time, and Willy tried not to show his anxiety. He must stay in character, as Mathilda always admonished him, the understanding, reasonable, calm son.

"It is fortunate that your father is sometimes so blind," Dr. Stein continued. "Your mother is ill, Willy. It is not dangerous, but it might become so. Your father, though he is an excellent diagnostician, hasn't noticed it, and your mother doesn't want him to. But you're old enough to know. We might have to operate on your mother in about three to six months. Perhaps we won't have to—I'm trying out a new treatment and she seems to react favorably. There is a small malignant growth in her right breast. If it increases, I must take her to the hospital."

Willy nodded. The pharmaceutical samples on Dr. Stein's polished desk seemed to reiterate their names to him, and he hoped all this wasn't real and would vanish. But of course it didn't.

"X-ray treatments might stop cancer in its initial stages," the doctor went on. "But if it doesn't, we have to amputate the breast. Such operations nowadays are much less perilous than they sound. Only the convalescence takes a long time. Your mother says your father must go on with his work, so you have to bear the burden of knowing, young Mr. Halder. Your mother is a very brave woman. . . ."

Willy left Dr. Stein's house in a daze. The streets were still warm, but a breeze had sprung up and the afternoon had an incongruously festive air. Whether Mother was right in keeping her illness from Father, he couldn't decide. He made up his mind to stay home with her more often, to take her to a theater, a movie, to do anything for her. All these were silly little moves which couldn't erase the merciless and indisputable fact that sooner or later they'd take her to the hospital.

For a second he thought of going to Mathilda; but now, at five, Mathilda would be at the acting school, teaching pronunciation and voice. As he walked through Opern Park he suddenly felt worn out, as if someone had hit him or given him a drug. He sat on a bench, and it was there that Arlène Duval, returning from the university, found him.

She put her books on the bench and sat next to him. She didn't ask questions, and Willy was grateful. She just sat there, patiently. What made Willy finally talk to her he couldn't figure out, neither then nor in the years to come. It was probably the light which fell on her hair, making it—how could he have missed that?—resemble Hal's.

Perhaps he had no right to burden Arlène with what weighed on him. But as she listened, Willy read in her eyes that it did concern her, that she liked to be burdened. It was against all the rules to tell her so much about Melanie, and several times Willy wanted to stop. But Arlène made him go on. As if it were the most simple thing, she had taken his hand. Her grip wasn't soft, like Maria's had been. Her slender fingers were almost as hard as a boy's, and from her touch a wave of comfort, of affection, of understanding flowed into his body.

Dusk was spreading slowly over the square, and the lanterns in front of the Opera House were being lit as Willy told her further about his daily fight to forget Hannsberg and all that had happened there. He made no attempt to describe his "wound"—this he knew would be a waste, since he couldn't express it to himself. Arlène refrained from any sympathetic remark. She nodded from time to time, she held his hand firmly while she gazed at the dark silhouettes of the trees whose tops caught the brilliant illumination of the Opera House. Finally Willy stopped. The noise of cars driving up the ramp reached him—people were going to the opera as they always did. It was late, and Melanie must be waiting.

He looked at the girl. Her nose, with its unexpected tilt, was too small. Her eyes, large and dark, had lost their coolness. They held him now, tenderly, and it seemed as if he had known her the way he had known Hal and needn't be ashamed to be weak.

"We had better go home, chéri," she said. He took her arm, instinctively holding her close. A tide of emotions surged up in him, thousands of waves tumbling over each other. She was a solace, a foothold in the flood which threatened to swallow him. It was not necessary to say it—such things always sounded silly—but walking with her up Reuter Weg under the darkening summer sky, it seemed as if the same blood was running in their veins and they had become one.

It took Melanie only a short while to accept Arlène. Occasionally Willy even experienced pangs of jealousy when he heard them talking together—they understood each other by allusions and abbreviations which he didn't grasp. Ilona, Big Anna, Mrs. Sigbert, the grocer, and the milkman, even Emil, the delivery boy from the apothecary, not only accepted but fussed over "the new French girl." Melanie made it a rule to have Arlène over for dinner after Pfeiffer-Belli's seminars. When the classes stopped in the summer, Melanie insisted Arlène keep on coming, and Anna always prepared something "extra special" for these occasions.

"Willy eats more when she's around," was Anna's grudging comment.

220

Thanks to Friedelgunde Fischer, who had taken an immediate dislike to Arlène, the seminar and the Toni crowd were enlightened about everything. Most of the students in Toni's, with meaningful grins, thought Willy extremely lucky to have a French girl. At first Willy was furious. But Arlène and Ilona—who had introduced Arlène to the whole Toni crowd—made him see how absurd it was to fight the popular notion about Frenchwomen, a myth to which even the Toni intelligentsia religiously adhered.

"Dopey Heiner" did not survive the summer months. The station director, Mr. Schoret, occasionally gave Willy a small part which was miserably paid, compared to the steady income his vegetable-market moron had provided. In vain Willy tried to persuade Mr. Schoret to let him do something other than dialects; he was typed, once and for all. Besides, he was a student, and there were many jobless actors who would do any part for very little money.

Chancellor Bruening declared an emergency in July, quoting a paragraph in the Weimar constitution which, learned jurists argued, he had hardly a right to use. As the summer went on, Willy understood why it was an emergency. The crisis really hit the country, and no end seemed in sight. Like many other physicians, Theodor was served notice by the Workers' Benefit Sick Fund that he could not count on fees for special services, such as urinalysis, metabolism tests, et cetera. Unlike many physicians, Theodor continued to do for his patients what he thought necessary, regardless of payment, which meant that many flocked to him, keeping him busy late into the night.

In earlier years, Melanie would have found a way to stop him. Now she let him go on. At least it kept him from overworking for the Social-Democratic Election Committee of which, reluctantly, he had become a member. The elections, scheduled for September, spurred all parties, but particularly the National Socialists, to heavy activity.

Willy did his best to ignore them. He and Arlène spent practically the whole summer at the Mosler Baths, sunning themselves, devouring textbooks, preparing for the next term. But, even so, he couldn't help seeing and hearing what went on.

By now, in the summer of 1930, the storm troops were efficiently organized and drilled. With swastika banners and brassy tunes—mostly adapted from Communist songs—they marched through Frankfurt's streets, preferably on Sunday. They organized mass meetings in which a minor saint of the Frankfurt hierarchy, or, sometimes, the uppermost deity, the Fuehrer, would exhort the crowds, and in which no opposition speaker ever had a chance to say a word. Occasionally the Communists tried it, and it always ended in violent fights in which the Brown Shirts and Black Shirts

221

inflicted serious wounds on their enemies. The police never found the guilty ones.

Loud-speakers began to appear near the Opera or on Haupt-Wache, and a rasping gramophone voice, with a Bohemian accent, promised the German people jobs, money, peace, a place in the sun—in short, everything if they voted for the N.S.D.A.P.

Occasionally a loud-speaker from a boat on the Main River would carry the election propaganda into Mosler's island, and it always made Willy squirm.

"What did they say this time?" asked Arlène one afternoon after the disembodied and sepulchral voice had stopped. "I don't always understand them."

"The Communist party this time," Willy answered. "You're better off if you don't understand it. They called Bruening a 'hunger chancellor,' denounced businessmen and Social Democrats as Fascists, and ranted against the Young plan—just like the Hitlerites."

"Why does it upset you so, Willy?" Arlène asked. "It's simply an election campaign. They don't mean much."

"It doesn't upset me . . ." Willy started, but checked himself. He didn't want to deceive Arlène. Of course he wished there were no elections. He didn't know why, exactly, and he didn't feel like discussing it now. Arlène didn't insist—she never did—and to divert him, she told him about herself. Her life hadn't been extraordinary at all, she reported, yet Willy listened with fascination to her account of Professor Duval's unconventional household.

For a long time Arlène had lived in Strasbourg, in Alsace-Lorraine, but she wasn't born there. She had given up explaining this to people because, she said, when someone asked why she spoke German so well and she answered she came from Alsace-Lorraine—which had been German before the war—they broke into understanding "Ah's" and "Oh's." It was a hopeless enter-prise to point out that she had been born in Paris and that it was through her father, a language professor at the Sorbonne, that she had learned German.

"Everybody in Strasbourg spoke French," she went on. "The Alsatians were glad to be French again for a change. Father taught me German, and when the talkies came, Mother learned it quickly too. It might come in handy for movie contracts, she said."

"Is your mother an actress?" Willy asked. Arlène had never mentioned her before.

"You've seen her. She uses the stage name Camille Ronay."

"Why didn't you ever tell me?" Willy cried. A few years ago Camille Ronay's films had conquered Germany. Willy and his generation had fallen for her the way they had surrendered to

Buster Keaton and Gloria Swanson and Charlie Chaplin, who brought something into their lives Germany simply couldn't produce.

He kissed Arlène's hand. "This is for your mother. Now I understand how you learned so much about acting."

"True and not true," Arlène said. "It's more complicated. I rarely see Mother at work. Half a year she spends with Father, running the house like any housewife, and half a year in the studio. She never talks shop at home. Then, when she makes a film with Jacques, her director ever since I can remember, she leaves the house at six and comes home late at night, dead tired but usually satisfied with her work. In the meantime Aunt Claudine, who is sixty-six years old, takes over. Even now that Mother has worked for so long in the theater and the movies, Aunt Claudine considers both hotbeds of immorality."

Arlène, it appeared to Willy, had led a much more regulated life than he had. Everything had taken its course, as it should. Even her mother's film activities were governed by a level-headed business sense and didn't disturb the Duval home life.

"Doesn't your father mind your mother's working so hard?"

"Not at all. They're as happy together as your parents. Perhaps even happier. My father isn't as—distrait as Dr. Halder. He, too, is an Internationalist and a pacifist, but it's less of an ordeal in France than here."

"Father once explained to me how he had always belonged to at least two minorities," Willy said. "That was when I quit the Socialist Youth ages ago."

"Why did you?" Arlène inquired in the casual tone which indicated she really wanted to know.

"I'm not born for politics," Willy said heatedly. "Father thinks so too. I want to—— Oh, Arlène, what do I want to do?"

"Let's go for another swim," the girl said, putting her small and surprisingly cool hand on Willy's back. "And then we must attack that seventeenth-century poetry."

"The season has begun with a vengeance," Melanie told Willy one day in September. She gave Arlène and Willy a subscription to the "Museum Galas," a series of symphony concerts, presenting outstanding guest artists. They drew a segment of Frankfurt society passionately devoted to music.

For Arlène's sake Willy wished he knew the women who nodded to him as he and Arlène strolled through the large gilded foyer during intermission. They usually inquired about Mother, and would he please send her their regards? He never could identify the women, all of whom apparently knew him from old and who

223

were dressed with an old-fashioned regal splendor which seemed deliberately to ignore what went on outside the concert hall.

It was Arlène who, after one of the Galas, discovered the garish poster next to the announcement of the coming "All-Brahms Festival," proclaiming the personal appearance of Adolf Hitler at a mass meeting in the Hippodrome on September 13, admission fifty pfennig ("Unemployed and War Veterans Free"). On the bottom it read, "Wake up, Germany," and the Hippodrome tavern would serve beer for ten pfennig afterward.

"I've never seen that man," Arlène said. "Father keeps asking me about him. Please take me there."

Willy couldn't refuse, though he loathed the idea. He was sure he'd be bored, listening to the old litany. He was proven utterly wrong.

When they arrived an hour late at the Hippodrome (seating capacity, 8,000) a band was playing march music. The enormous hall was suffocating in banners. On the walls, erect and arrogant, stood special storm-troop squads in neat uniforms and shiny high boots which Willy always associated with a certain type of Old Town prostitute. The light was diffuse, dimmed by the flags' red, black, and white cloth. On the dais, which was hung with operatic-looking golden swastikas, sat the guests of honor and the other speakers, trimly uniformed and blinking in the spotlights. Every ten minutes the music stopped, a man walked to the microphone and announced, in a hushed voice, that the Fuehrer's plane had reached such and such a spot on his whirlwind trip to Frankfurt.

The shabbily-dressed crowd, a curious mixture of housewives, young ruffians, teen-age girls, and contented elderly couples, sat patiently, staring at the stage where no performance took place. After a while Willy could feel the expectancy mounting, and it was almost palpable. The crowd politely applauded minor gods like Deputy Sprenger, the epileptic plumber, whose speeches against the city administration were filled with vulgar invective, but who was only a time-killer, and knew it.

Yet the elderly couple next to Arlène didn't seem to mind the endless wait. Their eyes never left the rostrum and, as time went on, they appeared connected to it by strong, invisible threads. Again and again the Fuehrer's plane was reported approaching the Frankfurt airfield—the coming of the savior was by now a certainty.

For more than three hours they sat there, stolid, with blank faces, until shortly before midnight. Then the orchestra stopped unexpectedly. The men on the dais rose. Three spots high-lighted a runway, and the long-awaited, the thousand-times-announced, the great magician appeared.

224

No prima donna ever received more applause. No king's subjects ever lay more prostrate before him. Hitler, with a wave of his hand, quelled the thunder and launched his sermon.

Yes, Willy thought, he still sounded like Sarek, the rattrap vendor. He still used the same violently illogical phrases, the same superlatively insane twists of reason, of history, of common sense; he roared and stamped and threatened. But by now, Willy recognized, he had mastered his craft. What this craft was, Willy couldn't define while against his ears thundered the charges against the rotten republic, the greedy allies, against everything and everybody opposing him. It was, perhaps, a process of hypnotizing, of bursting open the tunnels of the subconscious of the huge shapeless mass before him, annexing their hatreds and fears and throwing them back at them with a power they lacked and worshiped.

No, this was no speech. Once Willy had been to a film in which a Negro evangelist conducted a revival meeting. The faces of the black people had changed to terror and then to belief, and one after another had stepped forward, fallen to the floor, confessed his sins, while the congregation clapped hands or stamped to the glory of God. Hitler did not make his parishioners step forward to beat their chests. For they were not sinners, but the victims of sinners. He made them proud of being of an elect race. Yet after he had lifted them to the mountains, he dropped them back into the pit as he depicted the abject misery awaiting all of them.

He knew what scared them, because he was one of them. There had been no happiness in the last eight years. No job was secure, nothing was secure since the Enemies had launched the inflation, since the whole world was bent on destroying Europe's "heartland." The conspiracy's magnitude became apparent, even to the most inert, as the prophet of a new kingdom shot his unending hyperbolic phrases at them. He made them relive the secret terror which had undermined their lives, had undermined them ever since the republic of swindlers and crooks had come into existence. The republic was against personalities; the republic wanted a majority to make decisions. Wrong, criminally wrong! No army could be run this way. He knew, he had been in battle, he had been blinded but by a miracle regained his eyesight. Only one man could bring salvation, one chosen instrument of God.

Hitler didn't slow down when he began spreading his promises, like a golden mirage, as Moses has shown the Hebrews the land of milk and honey. Willy marveled how this harsh, rasping voice managed to sound gentle and soothing as the prophet returned the small stores to the little people, found work for the unemployed, canceled the farmers' debts, and banished poverty forever. It

225

wouldn't be easy ahead, though—he knew his Germans better. Tireless effort, honest sweat, he demanded. The workers of the fist and the brain would unite for a better future.

He himself had devoted all his strength to his beloved country, giving his all. And tomorrow was the hour of destiny. Tomorrow, at the polls, the German people would decide whether to choose a life of slavery and fear or the new path, the new faith, the liberator.

He held them there, the storekeepers, the aged couples, the office girls, and the young unemployed men. Their ecstatic surrender flowed to him. When he stopped, they fell back into drab reality, exhausted but enraptured, for they had seen the promised land. . . .

"I'm frightened," said Arlène, hurrying away from the Hippodrome while the singing of the crowd wafted after them toward the dead chimneys of the Rebstock factories. "I've never been scared before, but now I am."

The election results the next day sent a wave of alarm through the town. With 107 candidates in the parliament—they had only twelve before—the N.S.D.A.P. was now the second strongest party. The Communists, too, had increased their number from fifty-four to seventy-seven. Yet, after the initial shock was over, life in Frankfurt seemed to go on as before. Bruening stayed on as chancellor, sullenly supported by the Social Democrats who declared they had no other choice. In the Frankfurt city parliament the N.S.D.A.P. remained a minority and, anyhow, so the business people assured each other, as soon as the crisis was over they would lose all their votes again. In the university the N.A.S.T.U. boys showed up in brown shirts. Then, after the university senate declared the wearing of uniforms within the university grounds illegal, they took to parading suits which looked like uniforms but weren't.

Willy's former schoolteacher, Professor Preiser, implored him not to miss the inauguration address of the new philosophy professor, Paulus Hillden who, incidentally, had been instrumental in enforcing the ban on uniforms. Willy went, and from then on he and Arlène became "Hillden partisans."

Willy could never explain precisely what Hillden meant to him. The professor called the new attitude a "belief-ful realism"; people in England and America spoke of a religious socialism, but Willy and Arlène didn't care about the label. Paulus Hillden saw the world and its history in a deeper perspective than anyone Willy had ever encountered. He admitted the fatal flaw in the Scientific System which had accepted the materialistic basis of

226

the order it attacked, and he made Willy see the demonic forces of the present time. The world now was an invitation to anarchy. Even the rich were tortured by a foreboding that the forces they had let loose would, in the end, destroy them. Mankind, Hillden liked to say, had reached the state of the sorcerer's apprentice, unable to stem the satanic powers it had conjured up.

Willy and Arlène knew it would take them a long time to comprehend all of Hillden's theories. He had been a minister before turning to philosophy, and often, in the seminars, he soared into metaphysical heights where Willy couldn't follow him. Occasionally he called in a young instructor to conduct the seminar with him, and Willy always looked forward to the appearance of Dr. Walden-Arditi, though for nonscholastic reasons.

Dr. Walden-Arditi was the essence of a type Willy had met before: the superbrilliant radical who could explain anything, any time, and lived under a compulsion to be desperately original. Dr. Walden-Arditi was fond of "X-raying everyday life," and he X-rayed, with equal zest, eating habits, modern music, the coal industry, Greek philosophers, and women's hats. In many respects he followed a school which declared utter despair the root of all existence and which, in the Germany of the twenties, found many addicts. Willy always wondered why these "despair-happy" people didn't commit suicide, since existence was sheer pain, and one could never know anything for sure. Dr. Walden-Arditi, a fat young man with an almost bald head and a pale blond baby face, relished despair the way a cat relishes catnip, and he liked to embark on scintillating explanations in which, at the end, everything canceled itself out.

Toward the end of the term, in December, Willy couldn't avoid being late for the Hillden seminars every Friday. Mathilda had revived their old radio serial, and it went on the air at eight, just when the class started. The listeners, so it appeared, had clamored for Dopey Heiner—to Melanie's and Willy's delight. Thus he could earn all his tuition fees for the next term, and probably something extra. Dopey Heiner had acquired several brand-new idiocies which endeared him to the listeners: he was forever munching a raw carrot, attempting to involve his impatient mother in inane political discussions, mixing up everything, and thus providing Mathilda a chance to go into her best number, loosing a flood of Old Town invective at Willy who mistook them for compliments. . . .

The new Dopey was an outright success. F. P. Busch sent a congratulatory telegram and even Professor Pfeiffer-Belli unbent to tell Willy that, according to his listening son, the moron had become even more sublimely moronic. The only one never to comment on his success was Theodor. It would have been nice to hear a complimentary comment from Father, but Willy knew that Theodor, since the election victory of the N.S.D.A.P., had been striving to re-activate the Social Democrats of South Germany, though with no particular effect. . . .

Theodor also tried to get the Social-Democratic party bigwigs to fight back when, in December, the storm troopers scored another success. For several days Frankfurt's elegant UFA Palace had run, with singular success, *All Quiet on the Western Front,* hailed by the critics as one of the few sincere American films. At the end of the first week's run, in the middle of the last Friday showing, two women in the audience suddenly began to shriek. Several others followed, jumping up from their seats and rushing to the exit, screaming. White mice were scampering over the thick red rugs of the UFA Palace's orchestra and three gilded balconies. White mice were appearing in many of the theaters which featured *All Quiet on the Western Front.*

Simultaneously, the N.S.D.A.P. arrogantly demanded a withdrawal of this "American-pacifist poison." The S. P. trade-union leaders declared that this wasn't an issue worth fighting for; the hesitant Center, the weak liberal state party also retreated—particularly since nobody could think of a practicable scheme to prevent an ununiformed Nazi from entering a theater with a brief case full of white mice. Shortly before Christmas the film distributors withdrew the film. . . .

To Arlène, this was sheer cowardice. She got quite incensed at Willy's indifference and they quarreled quite often.

"I'm too busy," Willy inevitably answered. "Papers, examinations, Dopey Heiner with three rehearsals—I have hardly time enough for you and Melanie."

This Arlène had to admit. She proposed that they cut out the theater seminar after Christmas but Willy stubbornly refused, backed by Mathilda, who, on her part, was after him to drop everything not concerned with the theater, mainly Paulus Hillden.

As the term approached its end, Willy was so exhausted he often missed the early morning courses. In one of Ferdinand Schatter's seminars he nearly fell asleep, and only Friedelgunde Fischer's shrill giggle saved him from closing his eyes. Of course it didn't escape Schatter, who assigned Willy a particularly difficult paper for one of the last sessions.

After one of the Friday seminars, Paulus Hillden took Willy aside and asked whether it was getting too difficult: he had noticed Willy wasn't following the seminar with the same interest. Willy explained about Dopey Heiner which, surprisingly enough, the philosophy professor found highly interesting.

228

A week later, when Willy rushed into the seminar, breathless and flushed from the broadcast, a portable radio was standing on the seminar desk and everybody, including Hillden, was grinning.

"We decided to forego Hegel's *Philosophy of History* this evening," Hillden declared, while Willy began to blush in happy embarrassment, "and watch the workings of a simple mind. Mr. Halder, could you summarize Dopey Heiner's philosophy?"

Hillden's eyes were twinkling, and Willy realized that Hillden had put up the radio as a gesture of friendship, not ridicule.

"Dopey's philosophy can be summarized easily," Willy began, and then, falling into Dopey's dialect, continued: "I'm clever, I am nice. Why are all other people such dumbbells?"

"Very satisfactory," Paulus Hillden declared while the seminar giggled and Arlène pinched Willy under the table. "A typical subjective philosophy, influenced by the neo-impressionist school." Whereupon they went back to Hegel.

After the seminar, Hillden asked Arlène and Willy to stay for a moment.

"Mardi Gras will be here in three weeks," he said, offering them cigarettes. "I'm planning a little party, right here in the seminar. Willy, could you get together some kind of show? You may make fun of everybody, including me. Do you sing, Miss Duval?"

"Of course she does," Willy answered. Arlène was always humming French chansons though she pretended she was unable to sing them properly.

"For you, I'll try," Arlène answered promptly. Willy was delighted. Almost any other girl would play coy, so the professor would have to beg her at least three times, and then, at last, reluctantly she'd surrender. Arlène said yes or no when she meant it.

"I'll take you to Von Rhyn right away," Hillden said, directing them toward the hallway. Kurt von Rhyn, the president of Frankfurt University, gave only one course, a philosophy of history which was quite famous because once he had made history. He had been in the diplomatic service for many years. He had published his books on philosophical problems while working as an attaché in Moscow, between lunches with Lenin. His diplomatic colleagues had wagged their heads because no German attaché did such things. Now, his less popular colleagues liked to point out that no diplomat should be a university president.

Hillden led them into the enormous office where they found Von Rhyn buried in papers. He was tall, sparse, and with an almost white mane of blond hair. He seemed glad of the interruption.

"Paulus's idea to have a party right in the seminar intrigues me," he said. His friendly, offhand manner was very much like Oscar

229

von Rainer's, only much more perfected. "It has never been done before. Of course they'll call me a radical again." He sighed, then smiled at Arléne.

"You've chosen a most unfortunate time to visit Germany. I'm glad you're not studying law or medicine, though."

"Why is that?" Arlène asked. The old diplomat was flirting with her but Arlène knew how to handle men over fifty.

"I presume that over half of the medical and law students either belong or will belong to the N.A.S.T.U., our lovely Nazi students' group. Do you think we can risk a philosophical fete without interference by a noisy Brown Shirt?"

Arlène thought they could. The president told Willy that tomorrow he would post an official bulletin on the blackboard, asking for writers, singers, and other talent.

It was arranged that Pfeiffer-Belli and Dr. Weber, head of the music department, would assist Willy. Mrs. von Rhyn and Mrs. Hillden would take over the buffet. The president insisted on an only slightly alcoholic punch. This would stimulate the spirits without arousing them too much.

"We are a dignified institution, after all," he said. "Wait until Schatter hears of the feast. He'll bust. And our National-Socialist colleagues . . . Well, Paulus, what will they say?"

"They'll accuse us of corrupting the national spirit," Hillden answered. "But they'll do that anyhow." He turned to Willy.

"Between us, we suspect half of our faculty of either having joined Hitler's ranks or flirting with the idea of soon doing so."

"And Frankfurt is a liberal town," Von Rhyn added with a scornful smile. "I have hired three Jewish professors since I became president. Quite a daring thing to do; and I appointed Paulus here, whom the storm troopers don't understand and dislike. In other universities many of our brethren are jumping on the bandwagon . . ." He stopped and turned to the window where the lights of Bockenheim were flickering timidly.

"Anyhow, you get a show together, Halder. And let Mademoiselle sing as many numbers as she can." He rose and saw them to the door.

The university seemed almost deserted. At the end of the corridor a light shone from under one of the classroom doors. Kurt von Rhyn stood outside his office, listening.

"Felix Brentano, labor law. One of the brilliant new professors who worry me. Wrote a passionately anti-nationalistic book." He stopped.

Willy heard the noise too. There were faint steps somewhere nearby, steps of people who didn't want to be heard. Before he had time to think, the bell rang, the door opened, the students

230

swarmed out, laughing, chattering, and disappeared. The class-room door was left open. As if on a stage, Willy saw the figure of a small, slightly stooped man gathering his papers, when, suddenly, from the other side of the corridor there came the trampling of heavy shoes. A group of about ten men rushed into the classroom, slamming the door behind them.

"They're beating up Brentano!" Hillden cried. "Come on, Willy." Willy ran toward the classroom, trying to keep Arlène back. He was dimly aware that Von Rhyn had disappeared into his office.

Willy threw the classroom door open. On the floor lay Professor Brentano, motionless. One burly blond youngster was showing another, darker one, how to kick him in the loins.

"Dirty Jew," they shouted. "We'll teach you to spread lies about us."

Willy threw himself at the nearest of them, but two others attacked him at once, hitting him so hard that he reeled.

"Stop at once!" Hillden thundered, pulling the biggest one off Willy. Some of the gang looked up and hesitated.

"This is criminal assault. I'll have you expelled," he blazed at the burly blond leader.

"This is none of your business, Professor," the man said. "I'm the N.A.S.T.U. leader. My order stands."

"I'm Professor Hillden. I'll have you arrested." Hillden tore into one of Willy's assailants. By now Willy had fallen to the floor, the blood trickling from his mouth. Arlène had sent a second attacker to the floor by kicking him with her sharp heel. She had seized the ink bottle, and as the N.A.S.T.U. leader began to force Hillden into a corner, she threw it at him, hitting him on the head. The glass broke, the dark liquid spilled over his face, blinding him for the moment. Willy, though half-conscious with pain, could see her holding a sharp instrument against one of the gang lunging at her. The man, with a loud yell, fell back. And then a police siren sounded outside. The men looked up. The door swung wide open. In it stood Kurt von Rhyn flanked by two university watchmen.

"Good evening, Mr. Henkel," Von Rhyn said, addressing the blond leader who was still trying to wipe the ink out of his eyes.

"A nice mess you've gotten yourself into. The police must be entering the building this very minute."

The two watchmen lifted Professor Brentano and laid him on two chairs they had pulled together. With Arlène's help Willy scrambled to his feet. Paulus Hillden's glasses were broken. Only Arlène was unhurt. Despite the loud throbbing in his head, Willy heard heavy steps coming nearer. One of the gang made a desperate effort to pass by Von Rhyn. The leader opened the window and looked out.

231

"Go ahead, Mr. Henkel," Von Rhyn said politely, "it's only six stories high."

Then a swarm of blue-clad policemen filled the room.

"Book them for criminal assault, officer," Von Rhyn said. "I'm ashamed this had to happen in my university."

"We'll get even with you. Just wait," Henkel yelled, as the policemen took him and the others away.

Professor Brentano had regained consciousness. His face was covered with blood, and he tried to suppress his groans.

"The ambulance will be here any minute," Von Rhyn said. Paulus Hillden began wiping Brentano's face with a clean handkerchief. Von Rhyn turned to Willy. "What about you? Are you all right?"

"I guess so," Willy answered, "thanks to her."

"Nonsense," Arlène said. "I used my nail scissors and the idiot thought I had a knife. I never heard of ten students attacking one professor."

"It is one of Hitler's proud achievements to have introduced gangster methods into everyday academic life," said Von Rhyn. "Let me call a taxi and take you all home."

The two bumps on Willy's head remained for some time, but, altogether, caused him fewer pains than the show he had promised to put on. Night after night Willy, sometimes assisted by Professor Pfeiffer-Belli, patiently listened to the aspirants in the drafty room of the music department. After having suffered through many loud, confused juveniles, coy ingénues, surrealist poets, and ear-splitting sopranos, Willy decided on three people, all, surprisingly enough, members of Hillden's seminar.

Gerhard Winter, small, quick, blond, with the features of a fashionable archangel, possessed a high tenor voice, originally trained for church work. He also had a flair for the grotesque and later helped Willy write some of the skits, making them much more inane than Willy would have dared. He could also paint and rig up stage sets.

Therese Braun, a pupil of Mathilda, was Willy's main discovery. She had played old women from the time she was seventeen—she could do nothing else—and only later had she decided to study languages at the university. Her father made her do it, she explained to Willy. Old Mr. Braun owned The Emporium, one of Frankfurt's biggest dress stores. "The one with the worst dresses," Therese insisted. Willy was relieved to have someone who knew more about putting on a show than he did, and who immediately took over many of his duties.

Therese Braun's features were completely indefinite. She looked

232

like someone else each day, despite a rather prominent nose and very heavy black hair which, she said, could never make up its mind whether to curl or not. She was self-conscious about looking "oriental," and Willy had to reassure her regularly she did not have Jewish features. Once she got over this, she worked with unceasing energy.

The strangest of the three was Elena Franzen, a girl with a pixie-like face, long arms, and hair falling over her shoulders like the branches of a weeping willow. When Willy got around to interviewing her, she announced primly that she would dance. A waltz. And where was the accompanist? Professor Pfeiffer-Belli, without uttering a syllable, went to the piano and played the old-fashioned *pièce de salon* she had brought called "Viennese Violets."

Her dancing, Willy was sure, would be irresistible. She overdid every conventional step. In between she stopped unexpectedly, waving her chiffon handkerchief and saying in a tinny baby voice, "Oh! the lilting memories of Vienna," then went on again.

What they needed was an accompanist. Professor Weber hadn't sent anyone. Arlène played adequately but didn't like accompanying in any case, particularly when she herself sang. She decided on a few numbers her mother had done—with no voice, as Arlène said— in two of her early films, among them *"Au revoir, chien noir,"* and *"Les horribles dimanches."*

One night, coming home late, Willy found Melanie in her favorite spot, reading.

"Where can we get an accompanist, Mother?" Willy asked. "He must be a student who knows how to support amateurs, and who can fill the empty spots with something like 'Rhapsody in Blue.'"

Melanie thought for a while. Then, as if trying to recall a forgotten face, she said slowly:

"Ferdy Rohn. Do you remember? You were a Wandervogel and he taught you the pitch pipe and later you quit together before—— Sorry, Will."

"It doesn't hurt any more, Mother," Willy said, sitting down at Melanie's feet as he had done as a little boy. "I remember Ferdy and how we left the Wandervogel before Hal did. You don't have to be afraid to mention Hal, Mother. Arlène and I talk about him so often she says she almost feels as if she had known him."

"I'm glad," Melanie said, stroking his hair. "I'm very glad. Well, Ferdy was here to consult Theodor several times but he thought he'd remind you of something you want to forget, so he never went in to see you. Anyhow, you're hardly ever home. He's studying music, you know."

"How crazy," Willy cried. "Why didn't they send him? Why didn't he come for an audition? He's good, you know."

233

Willy phoned him early in the morning and Ferdy visited the Halders' the next evening. Three nights a week he played in a night club but he would arrange his schedule so he could squeeze in the revue, he declared. He looked haggard, with brownish circles under his eyes. It took him and Willy a while to rediscover the common ground they had lost. The rehearsals, however, soon accomplished this, and Willy found himself arguing with Ferdy as if they were still roaming through the woods. From his employer, Ferdy wangled permission to use the café in the mornings as a rehearsing place, and they worked there intensely, from nine to twelve. The place smelled of stale ashes. Charwomen, handkerchiefs over their hair, were running about, mops and brooms were constantly in their way, but finally they had the program ready. They went to the seminar the night before to prepare the stage and see how it sounded there.

First, Gerhard, Ferdy, and Willy rigged up a stage—a rather small and precarious affair. Therese had procured several baby spotlights and switches, and "borrowed" a green plush curtain, plus rings, from the Emporium. It took them hours to get the stage ready. As dressing rooms, they had to use the university washrooms, but this didn't disturb them. Kurt von Rhyn had kept his promise: a tinny piano had been brought up from the music department. They went through the numbers once more; they all sounded completely flat. Around four in the morning they staggered home. Willy left a note for Big Anna not to wake him before five in the afternoon.

When Willy entered the seminar around six—the party was to start at nine-thirty—his crew had arrived safely but confusion was mounting. Fortunately, Mrs. Hillden showed up early, armed with two enormous boxes of prepared sandwiches. She turned out to be a quiet, efficient woman with the patience of the experienced social worker who can soothe anybody's nerves.

Soon Willy needed more help: not a single ticket was left, they needed more chairs. In despair Ferdy called on his friends of the Free Students' League. His call saved the day—only Willy was too busy to notice it. Around eight six students of the league fought their way through the crowd. Therese immediately assigned them to their posts—coatroom, ticket takers, and the others to help with the show.

In the meantime, Gerhard Winter and Ferdy hammered at their sets, Willy once more went through his skit with Therese, Elena Franzen had fled into the ladies' room. Only Arlène appeared completely serene and unruffled, in a wine-red taffeta evening gown Willy didn't even have time to admire. Therese finally rushed backstage. The seminar was more than full. It was time to start.

234

Suddenly Willy realized he hadn't been on stage since the trip to Hannsberg. Yet the old, ineradicable excitement stirred within him and he remembered the night when he had seen *The Tempest* and wished he could be on stage himself one day. . . . Then the seminar lights were switched off, the spotlights went on. The audience quieted down. Ferdy began playing. His mock overture mixed pseudo-Wagnerian tunes with children's songs, then stopped abruptly when Willy came forward to introduce the show.

Willy's nervousness vanished the moment he faced the audience. He had collected a number of quotations and favorite expressions from the works of the professors present, and he twisted them around, adding silly footnotes and academic flourishes. The audience was warming up—he could sense it. Then he announced Elena Franzen who, during her dance, lost her many violets and at the end got entangled in her own train. The audience giggled happily.

Therese, as Frau Hoffmann, fishwife from Old Town, giving the listeners a piece of her mind on the political situation, was a hit, too, and the audience became quite noisy.

But Ferdy calmed them down. With a few chords of music he created the right quiet mood for Arlène's appearance. The baby spot fell on Arlène's face as she stepped before the curtain and, with a sense of happy surprise, Willy realized how much she resembled Camille Ronay. It was impossible to explain what exactly Arlène did with a song. She was like a child who enjoys singing for herself. There was a grain of sadness when she reported that the poodle Fridolin, her *chien noir,* had died because he had eaten too much chocolate; there was an infinitesimal trace of annoyance as she told about the long Sundays in the provinces, where nothing ever happened. . . . As he listened to her backstage, a surge of affectionate pride welled up in Willy and he again wondered why a girl like Arlène had chosen him, who could give her so little. . . .

When Elena had finished the last number ("Dance of a House Mouse As Seen by the Dance Tragedienne Mary Wigman"), the audience cheered and couldn't get enough. . . .

Now that it was over, Willy's head ached. The two bumps started hurting again. The suspense was gone; the familiar sense of depression overtook him. All he wanted was to go home and sleep.

"Don't get low, Will," Arlène whispered as Willy sat down on one of the backstage chairs. "Now you think it was all senseless. Don't let it get you." She put her small, dry hand on his face and kissed him lightly. " *'Un succès fou,'* Mother would call it. Come on, I'm hungry. Let's get a sandwich."

Willy took her hand. Gerhard was rolling up his backdrops but Willy didn't care. "You know me too well," he said. "I must bore

235

you with my fits of black mood. But it's partly my head. It still hurts."

"Why shouldn't it?" Arlène answered. "One can recognize the two bumps very distinctly. And don't think the audience didn't see them."

She took Willy's arm and dragged him to the buffet. The rest of the evening Willy could never quite remember. He thanked the six students from the Free Students' League, all of whom said it had been more fun than they had expected. Then he remembered he must arrange for the removal of all props the next day. But Therese said she and Gerhard would take care of everything, and not to mind.

Arlène and Ferdy hailed a taxi and took Willy in between them.

"You always got tired quickly," Ferdy said. "I remember when you went on the first trip with us. You went out like a light."

"Well, we did it," Arlène said. She put her arm around Willy, who leaned his head against her shoulder. "We did it, and they ate it up. And you, Will, didn't give yourself a single juicy part. Don't think we didn't notice."

"Do you like my girl friend, Ferdy?" Willy said sleepily. "Do you think she has any talent?"

"If she weren't French, the Free Students' League would ask her to become a member," Ferdy said. "We haven't many like her." The taxi had reached Opern Platz and Ferdy got out.

"I like to walk home," he said. "See you soon."

The cab rode through the silence of Reuter Weg and came to a stop before sixty-six.

"Melanie is still up," Arlène said. She kissed Willy. "Good-by, Will. What are you thinking?"

"Wait a second, driver," Willy said, giving the man a mark bill. "I'm thinking of you and whether you'll be with me when the black dream comes, the one that doesn't let go, about the forest and the people who get killed."

"You won't have any dream tonight," Arlène said. "You mustn't fall into the pit after you've made so many people happy. I'll be with you and I'll try to be in your dream too."

They got out of the taxi, in the uncertain light of the coming morning, before the rusty iron gate of Willy's house.

"My landlady will think God-knows-what. *Au revoir, petit chou,*" Arlène said. She looked around, kissed him quickly on the mouth, and walked away. Her hair under the street light showed for a second, gleaming and silky, and in perfect order.

236

17. WHILE AN ATMOSPHERE OF TENSION began to spread over Frankfurt, N.A.S.T.U. leader Henkel and his nine helpers went on trial for their assault on Professor Brentano. Previously, the University Senate, an independent body, had expelled them, which led to the distribution of new, violently worded N.A.S.T.U. leaflets. The magistrate's court, finding them all guilty of criminal assault, meted out the maximum penalty. Despite the *Observer's* outcries, the next higher court of appeal affirmed the first decision. Arlène and Willy had to testify—the defense making the most of the fact that Arlène was French and, therefore, prejudiced against "national-minded" young Germans. The N.A.S.T.U. appealed again, and in November the highest court revoked the decision: the sentences were too harsh, since Professor Brentano, in his writings as well as his lectures, had given vent to ideas which to many a "true German" bordered on the treacherous.

"The effect of Harzburg," Kurt von Rhyn told Arlène and Willy. He had called them to his office the moment the news reached him. Harzburg was a tiny spot in the wilds of the Harz Mountains, once renowned for the annual gathering of witches, where recently the German Nationalists under Hugenberg and the Hitler troops had joined forces and formed what Von Rhyn called "an obscene alliance to crush everybody and everything sane in Germany."

"The judges in Prussia are getting jittery. Ordinarily, they're stanch burghers with some sense of decency. Now that Hugenberg has sold his party to the Mephisto from Bohemia, they must prove they are upright super-patriots." Von Rhyn made a sound of disgust. "How can I run this university peacefully? And what, Mr. Halder, shall I do with the backdrops from your show which are still in my office?"

"I'm sorry, Professor," Willy began, but Von Rhyn interrupted him. "Never mind. I think we'd better store them in the catacombs. Here, I'll show you something."

237

He opened an inconspicuous wall door behind a big desk. A narrow metal staircase spiraled down.

"My private exit," Von Rhyn said. "Built so the president can slip out unnoticed."

Willy and Arlène took the pieces of canvas and followed Von Rhyn. The staircase, twisting in busy circles, led into the boiler room. Kurt von Rhyn walked toward the end of the cellar and pointed to a corner.

"Leave them there," he said. "Too bad we won't need them any more."

Then, passing the big furnace, he opened a miniature door. A ribbon of light fell on the coal-dusted floor. "Do you know where this leads?"

"Goodness, it's Bockenheim," Willy said. "We must be at the other end of the university."

"Right," Von Rhyn said. "My predecessor, who was given to drinking, had the staircase and the extra exit built so he could slip out when he was loaded."

When they had returned to the president's office, Von Rhyn asked:

"Tell me, Willy, have you joined any group?"

"I haven't joined anything," Willy answered. "I have no time."

"The Reichsbanner started a recruiting campaign to rally all anti-Nazi forces. Some of our students went in. On the other hand, the N.A.S.T.U. has been banding together with many of the feudal fraternities." He glanced at some papers and sighed. "There'll be more fighting in our academic temple. You know what I had to do with Brentano? He's so badly hurt, he won't be able to lecture for a long time. I gave him a leave of absence. I feel like a coward. Perhaps I am . . ."

Apparently he had forgotten they were there. For a moment the perfect composure of the aristocrat faded, the Oscar von Rainer-like aloofness which gave his enemies no opening for attacks.

Arlène had risen. "We must be off, Professor von Rhyn. Naumann's class on minnesingers."

Von Rhyn didn't say anything, just stared out of the window, and silently they left.

Professor Naumann's classes on medieval poets at first promised to be a welcome change of diet after the stodgy Schatter lectures. Hanns Naumann, Schatter's partner and most bitter rival, resembled a mature matinee idol. His elegant bearing and his beautiful, almost sensuous voice lured Frankfurt's fashionable matrons into his public lectures. Years ago the tall, silver-blond professor had published a volume in praise of modern pacifist German writing. But

238

now he experienced a change of heart. In his most flippant tone he declared one day how medievalism was being reborn in Germany right now, and indulged lingeringly in veiled allusions to the "spirit of national awakening," which would produce a new national art. He frequently attacked the authors he had glorified in his first book, and Willy and Arlène listened with morbid, angry fascination as he interpreted the minnesingers, poets dead for more than five hundred years, transforming them into prophets of the hordes who cried "Germany, awake!"

Willy and Arlène couldn't skip his class; if they were to pass their examinations they needed both Naumann and Schatter. To Arlène, Hanns Naumann was as interesting as a beautiful poisonous snake behind glass. Besides, she occasionally managed to embarrass him. For some unknown reason the professor often addressed her in his seminar, and Arlène, having received a sizable amount of information from her father, was able to argue him into a state of anger. It would do Willy no good later, when his paper was being examined, but he wouldn't tell her that.

One evening in December Ferdy Rohn invited Willy and Arlène to his working place, the Café de Paris, for a drink. His boss, Mr. Berger, the fattest man Willy had ever seen, hovered about, his protruding sad eyes glued on Arlène who gave him her most conventional smile.

Willy knew that Ferdy had joined the Reichsbanner Black-Red-Gold, and its offspring, the more active Iron Front, whose so-called Hammer Groups were organized to check any uprising of storm troopers. Arlène had been seeing Ferdy quite often, and Willy had an inkling of what they were trying to accomplish.

"I guess I don't have to beat around the bush with you, Will," Ferdy began, after the boss himself had set the drinks before them. "Never mind Berger. He assumes all Frenchwomen are wicked and is therefore fascinated by Arlène. Pay no attention to him. I rather wish you were helping me a little in the Iron Front."

"I was afraid you'd come to that," Willy said. "But you know that politics and I don't agree."

"Sure, sure," Ferdy said. "I also know that probably the Iron Front crowd would dislike you as much as they dislike me. After all, I'm an artist too. And what am I doing? Playing piano in a night club. But that's not the point. You don't know what's going on, in Frankfurt and everywhere. The storm troopers are starting a little civil war, just for fun. They're breaking up meetings of all parties they don't like, and they've begun blackmailing Jewish store owners. Ask Mrs. Goldschmidt."

"Hannah Goldschmidt?" Willy asked. "Robbi's mother?"

"Yes, your old friend Robbi's mother," Ferdy said. "Her husband had trouble with one of his best workmen, a foolish engraver who stole some silver from the workshop. Father Goldschmidt didn't call the police; he simply dismissed him. Ever since things have been happening. One day the store windows were smashed. A few nights later somebody broke into the store and destroyed several valuable plates. Then Mrs. Goldschmidt received a threatening anonymous letter, advising her to sell the store to an Aryan owner, and hadn't Arthur Goldschmidt better hire a bodyguard?"

"I can't believe it," Willy said. "What did the Goldschmidts do?"

Ferdy shrugged his shoulders. "Arthur Goldschmidt did the wrong thing: he appeased them. He took back the man he had fired, and from that moment on everything has gone smoothly."

"I must go see them," Willy said. "I had no idea. I only heard Robbi was in Rome, studying."

"Look, Willy," Ferdy said. "You can't stay aside, doing nothing. Not someone like you. You should go into the Free Students' League or join the Iron Front. Even if it isn't any fun."

"Ferdy is right," Arlène said. "Even if you have to skip one of Schatter's silly seminars."

"They don't want me," Willy said. He should have been angry with Arlène for siding with Ferdy, but he couldn't be, because he knew she was simply following her conscience. "I don't fit into any organization. I don't fit anywhere where there are too many people."

"My God, you yourself got beaten up when they attacked Brentano." Ferdy was almost shouting. "You're in it already, whether you want to be or not. You fought back, you aren't outside any more. And times have changed since we were together in the S. Y."

"Sorry, Ferdy," Willy said. "I just can't start again with politics." Perhaps Ferdy was right; but, even so, Willy couldn't throw himself into any "cause."

The three soon went home, Ferdy and Willy sulking, while Arlène pretended she had had an interesting evening in a fashionable night club.

A few days later, on a cold December night, Willy took Arlène to call on Mrs. Goldschmidt. The old house on Hoch Strasse seemed to receive him with a smile of recognition, as if it were only yesterday that he and Robbi had read plays together.

In the large living room with its red-brown wood panels sat Mr. and Mrs. Goldschmidt, alone, playing cards. They had aged. Mrs. Goldschmidt's hair was completely white and her smile, as

240

she rose to greet him, made her appear even more melancholy than Willy remembered her. He soon found that she was carrying on an unending argument with her husband. Arthur Goldschmidt, though much heavier and with bluish bags under his eyes, had preserved his cheerfulness. He didn't mind letting "an old friend" hear what he and Hannah were squabbling about.

"She doesn't want Robbi to come back to Frankfurt, this year or next," he complained. "My wife thinks Germany is no place for Robbi. And she is afraid one day something will happen to me and my business." Arthur shook his head. "My business friends and I say this whole Hitler party is nothing but hot air. They'll calm down, they'll come to terms. It's only the few rowdies who make all the noise."

Mrs. Goldschmidt served Arlène and Willy her incomparable hot chocolate. "You always liked this, Willy, didn't you?" she said. "And here are some of the biscuits you used to enjoy."

For Willy the hot chocolate conjured up the picture of Robbi limping up and down his room after he had bought all the Reclam plays on which they never worked.

"I don't want my son to know what happened in the workshop. It would only upset him," Hannah Goldschmidt said without any emphasis. Willy sensed she had argued this out with her husband so often it had become an established routine. "My husband says I have become morbid," she went on, "and, Mademoiselle Duval, perhaps I have. I sit here in the old house where Robbi grew up, all by myself, and suddenly this uncontrollable fear comes over me. I begin to despise the street, the grocer, the delivery boy, all the faces around me. They all seem to be enemies. Not open enemies, Willy, but hidden ones. One day they'll come out with it: they'll want our house, our silver, everything . . ." She stopped, and Willy saw that she had begun to cry.

"Forgive me," Mrs. Goldschmidt said, and left the room.

Arlène put down her porcelain cup, and the small sound broke through the silence and brought back the old reality.

"My wife is in a highly excitable state," Arthur Goldschmidt said quietly. "The doctor thinks it will pass. She even speaks of my selling the business and going away. Why, I've lived in Frankfurt for over fifty-seven years."

"I'd love to see Robbi," Willy said slowly, "but perhaps he's better off where is now. I'd let him stay there. Or send him to France for a while. Until his mother feels it's safe here. Of course it's none of my business . . ."

Arthur patted Willy's shoulder. "You've always been a sensible fellow, Will, even when you were small. Perhaps I should send Robbi to France."

241

"Why couldn't he study in Paris?" Arlène said. "My father will be glad to help him. L'Ecole des Beaux Arts would be just right for him. All the most famous jewelry designers graduated there. Robbi could stay in our house too. It's empty, now that I'm gone."

"Thank you very much, Mademoiselle Duval," Mr. Goldschmidt said, beaming. "My wife will be happy to hear this, and the exchange of the French franc is even better than that of the lira."

"I'll write my father as soon as you've decided," Arlène said, rising.

Before they left, he showed Arlène the little square garden with the stone cistern and the statues. Arlène agreed: even now, covered with snow, its trees barren, it managed to look transplanted from the Mediterranean.

Perhaps it was the garden, perhaps it was because Arlène suddenly declared she didn't feel like going home and studying, that Willy decided to take her through Old Town. He almost felt like a tourist himself—he hadn't been there for such a long time. Arlène wasn't shocked by the Antonio Platz satyr, as Willy had feared, since, she declared, she had seen such things in France and Italy before. As they wandered along the twisted alleys, she took Willy's arm, admiring the narrow-gabled houses, the signs over the taverns saying: "Built 1557," the seemingly indestructible wooden beams along the house fronts. It was clear and cold and the roofs carried old-fashioned bonnets of gray-white snow. Without really wanting to, Willy tried to lead her to the Golden Pheasant—but he couldn't find the place. After a while he discovered that the restaurant had closed. A young man in a leather jacket, standing motionless on the street corner, said it had gone into bankruptcy, and could Willy spare a cigarette?

Willy gave him a few and the youth couldn't thank them enough. If they were tourists, he'd show them around for twenty-five pfennig, as long as they wished. He betrayed no disappointment when Willy told him they needed no guide. He nodded, lit his cigarette, went back to his corner, and continued staring into nowhere.

The "Madonna of the Forgiven Sinner," on the other side of the street, was still there, smiling in her wooden gown with its neat folds, sweet and forebearing. Snow covered the chipped gold of her crown and the three fingers holding the child against her.

"She seems so cold and forgotten here," Arlène said, "and she's beautiful."

"Hal always wanted one day to do something as beautiful," Willy said. "Perhaps he would have . . ."

An enormous wave of memories flooded over him. But now

they didn't drown him. Arlène was here, and she had fortified his bastion against the past.

She pressed his arm, and he could feel her small breast, soft and firm and reassuring. Overhead, the sky spread like black translucent glass and the stars seemed to radiate the cold. Slowly Willy became aware of a growing uneasiness. It wasn't because of the old houses —they were asleep and they hadn't changed ever since he could remember, with the cathedral steeple haughtily overshadowing them, as it had always done.

He glanced around, and at the same moment he knew Arlène had felt it too. For a cold December night there were too many people milling around Old Town. On every street corner stood groups of four or five men, talking in low murmurs. None of them wore winter coats. Shivering in their short army or leather jackets, all of them presented the same blank expression he had noticed on the young man who had asked for a cigarette.

In a rush, a vision of Hannsberg came to Willy—Little Venice, the boys at Warm Hugo, the peddlers, the pimps: here they were, in Frankfurt, too, the unemployed young men, staying up late because they had nothing to do the next morning but sleep. They hated to go home to their scolding wives and mothers, and they craved one another's company. They moved from one corner to the next, from beer cellar to beer cellar—they reminded Willy of fish in an aquarium, swimming around in circles, sometimes banging their heads against the glass.

"I once saw a hospital garden," Arlène said, hurrying away a little faster, "where for hours on end the injured and the lame would circle arm in arm around a fountain. This is like that. How much unemployment insurance do they get?"

"Just enough to starve not too obviously," Willy answered. "At dinner last night Father said the country's Christmas present to its young people is seven million unemployed."

"They give me the shivers," Arlène said as they passed the Church of Saint Catherine. "I can hardly blame them for anything they may do. Probably some of them wear the brown shirt because it's the only clean one they've got."

"You know what Father told us last week?" Willy went on, as they reached the Hauptwache, Frankfurt's main center, where life, of a sudden, seemed normal again. "A book has come out, written by a Social Democrat, mind you, in which all crises are called something natural, like birth and death, against which one mustn't do anything. Let them be unemployed for a while, and then the crisis will pass. It's in the nature of the system, and no man, no party can or should do anything about it."

"That's plain silly"—Arlène was quietly furious—"to make

243

unemployment a God-given necessity. And I still think you should join the Free Students. It's the least you can do."

Willy couldn't ignore the two elections, the first in March, the second in April, in which Paul von Hindenburg (aged eighty-three) competed with Adolf Hitler for the presidency of the Reich. After it had become impossible to push through their own, a more moderate, less aged candidate, the S. P. supported the old Junker. The K. P., with undying zest, put up Ernst Thaelmann, its own candidate, but of course everybody knew the real race was between Hitler and Hindenburg and that Thaelmann was just a "symbol."

Willy, too, cast his vote for Hindenburg, but he didn't approve of him. There was simply no one else to vote for. That was the trouble with politics: it always forced you to decisions you really didn't want to make.

When finally Hitler was defeated, Theodor couldn't conceal his surprise at the attitude of his colleagues.

"Old man Schupp and the other trade-union people are really contented and calm," Theodor told Melanie the night after the election. Minister Groener, with the help of Chancellor Bruening, had just banned uniformed S. A. and S. S. troops from the streets. "I'm happy about the ban—it was high time—but happy about Hindenburg as president? My God!"

"Mathilda and I got into trouble," Willy said, polishing one of the Pallavant silver spoons. Every spring Melanie cleaned and rearranged the family silver. "We had cooked up a harmless Dopey Heiner joke about Hindenburg, but you should have heard the indignant telephone calls afterward. Director Schoret had fits and Mathilda had to promise him never to mention old Hindenburg again."

"I wish you could see the cocky Mr. Sprenger now," Theodor said. "Since he has become a member of the Theater Committee, he talks 'culture.' Recommends plays by the impossible Hanns Johst or a thing about that underworld character Horst Wessel they love so much."

"Did he ever pay his bill?" Melanie asked. "After all, he selected your office for one of his fits. Does he show any gratitude at least?"

"Gratitude?" Theodor repeated. "Mr. Sprenger shows his gratitude in many ways. He attacks me whenever he can, and after the meeting he comes over, smiling sheepishly, and asks for free medical advice on his new symptoms."

"I'll send him a bill with teeth in it," Melanie said. The putting away of the silver seemed to have exhausted her. She sat down a bit heavily and Willy detected, for the first time, a faint quiver of her lower lip, an involuntary contraction as if something was hurting

244

her. Yet when he met her eyes they told him not to take any notice in front of Theodor.

Was his father really so preoccupied with his work that he didn't see the change in Mother? Ever since his visit to Dr. Stein, Willy had become conscious of Melanie's efforts to put up a good front. Dr. Stein hadn't called him since—obviously the X-ray treatments worked out all right. But Melanie had begun making up her face with infinite care, rouging her cheeks and renewing it more than ever before. She also went to the hairdresser quite often, and she had stopped going to the theater or to the Museum Gala Concerts. Whenever Arlène or Ilona came to visit in the evening, Melanie urged them to stay on, and during the last months it had become apparent that she was afraid of going to bed early.

He wished Father would call him in for one of those long talks they used to have when Willy was younger, and tell him that Mother was not well. But Father never did. Should he tell Father, although Melanie had implored him not to? He was often tempted, particularly when Theodor casually mentioned what treatment he had prescribed for one of his more complicated cases. Father's cases had always been something impersonal to Willy. He never connected them with people he knew. They existed, so to speak, only in their special realm, Father's office. Now Willy flinched when Theodor praised the progress in tumor and cancer operations, and tried to direct the conversation into other channels. On the other hand, perhaps Dr. Stein was exaggerating.

The doorbell rang, and Willy jumped up.

"You are jittery, Will," Melanie said. "Who is going to take you where?"

"Probably Therese Braun," Willy said. "We're going to stay here for a change. Is there anything to eat or drink in the house?"

How thankful Melanie was for the company! It almost pained him. She went into the kitchen and Willy could hear her talking to Big Anna.

"Look at my new face," Therese called before she had reached the landing. Willy was nonplused. Therese had dyed her hair a burning red. She wore a hat of such enormous size that even her nose looked tiny, and she had flung a long fur scarf over her shoulders with calculated carelessness, the way opera stars liked to be photographed in the Frankfurt *General News*.

"The famous opera singer Elma Shrill-Quaver," Willy complimented her.

"Madame Shrill-Quaver has brought you a present." Therese gave Willy a mysterious, seductive smile, straight out of the movies, and swept into the kitchen.

There was no stopping her. Both Melanie and Big Anna admired

245

her outfit and Therese, sniffing the air, declared she smelled heavenly sweets, dangerous for a woman of her size and position.

"Miss Therese, you aren't big, you're just round," Anna declared, whereupon Therese discovered that Anna had definitely lost weight.

Melanie insisted they wait in the living room, and soon Big Anna rolled in the tea wagon loaded with pastry and a chocolate soufflé, fresh from the oven.

In between countless cups of tea Therese ate every bit of the soufflé, and then started to talk rapidly. She had come to propose to Willy. Not what he thought—she laughed a kind of coy old spinster giggle that always amused Melanie—but to propose a business deal. She had figured it out, pored over it for hours, and gotten Siegfried Braun, owner of the Emporium, on her side.

Would Willy be ready to start a cabaret with her, a satirical night club with the kind of program they had put on at the university?

"Don't contradict me," she protested, before Willy had opened his mouth. "And don't tell me you have too many papers to write. Your doctor's degree can wait. Everyone has one nowadays. But you can do something better: you can hold an audience."

Therese smiled at Melanie. "Your son may not be so funny as I, but he has a certain—well, I'll call it charm, though it sounds like a phony ad. Anyhow, Dad is willing to put up the money. He even considers it a good investment. Ferdy will be in charge of the music. Will, you'll be master of ceremonies and write the texts with me and Gerhard. You and I are in charge of the whole program, do you hear me? Gerhard is going to paint what little we need. Elena has three new dances ready. Arlène's French songs can never miss. We also need, perhaps, one more girl and one man. . . ." She stopped, finally exhausted.

"Where shall all this take place?" Willy inquired.

"All taken care of, Willy. I found a place, a bankrupt restaurant in Old Town. Nothing is going on there. We'll make it fashionable to go to our place, christened by me The Porcupine."

"I like porcupines," Melanie said. "But Will's too young to start anything so big."

"It isn't big," Therese insisted. She had it all prepared, including a statement from her father guaranteeing the expenses for the first months and a lease for the ground floor of the Golden Pheasant.

"Goodness," Willy said. "That place has an evil reputation."

"After it has been repainted, redecorated, and renamed, it will get a new reputation. Ferdy is willing, so are all the others, if you're with us. We need you."

"What about the university?" Willy asked. Therese's enthusiasm was contagious, and his imagination had begun to conjure up all sorts of programs.

"We'll take enough courses to keep registered. Then, when things are running smoothly, we can take more. Father knows the license commissioner. We can have the Golden Pheasant for practically nothing. You can even keep on with your radio program, Will."

"Dopey Heiner will go a summer vacation pretty soon." Willy hesitated. "After the trouble with Von Hindenburg, Mathilda isn't sure whether we'll continue next fall or not."

"We have all summer to get the program into shape," Therese stated. She rose and rearranged her fur piece. "What do you say, Mrs. Halder?"

"I say, go ahead, children, and try it," Melanie said. She seemed almost as eager as Therese. "But you must leave out politics completely. After all, 13,000,000 Germans voted for that man Hitler some weeks ago."

"Yes, but Father says the ban of the storm troopers is the first step in curbing them." Therese's optimism was not to be shaken. "We'll keep out of politics, don't worry."

"I must talk to Hillden. I'm sure he won't like the idea," Willy said when Therese finally left, after having kissed everybody, including Big Anna.

"Talk it over with La Arlène," Therese called from the stairs. "I must have your answer in three days."

Willy had chosen a bad day to consult Paulus Hillden. He had been so busy discussing Therese's plan with everybody, there were so many papers to be written for the end of the term, that he wasn't conscious of the primary or so-called "Laender" election of April 24. In many states the Nazis scored a success, but their main triumph was in Germany's biggest state, Prussia. With 162 members they moved into the Prussian diet—the strongest party. The Bruening Cabinet, alive only by an unhappy alliance between the Social Democrats and the Catholic Center, lost its last real stronghold. At the university, the swastika appeared in more and more lapels. Willy was dimly aware of all this but he pushed it away: he had to give Therese an answer.

His appointment with Hillden was for the day after election. He found the professor standing at the window, gazing out into the little University Park drowned in a vicious April rain.

When Hillden turned to him, Willy could hardly bear to look into his eyes. All at once he seemed old.

"I'm feeling pretty low today, Willy," Hillden said, lighting a cigarette. "You don't realize what this election will lead to. Our liberal minister of education will be fired. They'll force on us all the

247

nationalistic professors which Von Rhyn up to now has been able to avoid. It may mean the end of academic freedom. Well, you wanted to ask me something?"

Automatically Willy found himself repeating Therese's arguments, leaving out that they hoped to make a bit of money: you simply couldn't mention money in Paulus Hillden's presence.

To Willy's surprise Hillden approved highly of The Porcupine. Willy could take up philosophy later, any time, and a Ph.D. wasn't worth much anyhow.

"You might even do some good," Hillden added. "Ridicule can be a deadly weapon. And I think Frankfurt is the right place."

"Why?" Willy inquired. "It never occurred to me that Frankfurt is anything special."

"But it is, Willy. Fankfurt has always had to balance the north against the south, the east against the west. It's a tolerant town. And the people have a good-natured humor I often found missing in the north. No, Frankfurt and the whole south are much better. Go ahead with your Porcupine."

Willy thanked him and left. As he hurried across University Park, his collar turned up to protect himself from the lashing rain, someone stopped him. Willy first noticed the high boots, the black raincoat. Then, under a semi-military cap which had become fashionable for the N.A.S.T.U. students, he recognized his old schoolmate, Franz Duester.

"I have my car here, Willy," Franz said, as if he had always had one. "I'll take you home."

Later on Willy cursed the April rains—he never should have gotten into Duester's enormous black car adorned with a tiny swastika flag. Franz hadn't changed much. Only the rings under his eyes seemed darker and he looked as if he had just left the bed of a woman with whom he had spent two days and nights and still wasn't satisfied. Black curls stuck out from under his open black shirt. Only then Willy recognized the regular storm-trooper uniform under his raincoat.

"Pueschel is S. S. too," Franz remarked, driving fast through the sheets of rain. "We in the S. S. get the better girls. The S. A. is for small fry. We read about you in the *Observer,* Will. Bad things too."

"I didn't see it and, frankly, I don't care." Willy had no idea what the *Observer* had written about him. "Will you please take me to Opern Platz?"

Franz drove slowly, reminiscing about school, about their days together at the Mosler Baths. It was all long past, he declared, and his present political work was much more important. His tone belied him. It told Willy that Franz, like Pueschel, often dreamed

248

of the wonderful schooldays. He also asked, rather timidly, about Melanie.

"She's fine," Willy lied. "And how's your brother? I remember he used to visit us when I was a kid."

"Erwin has married again," Franz said with distaste. "An over-sexed widow. I give it four months. He is rolling in dough. Import and Export. We live on Hoch Strasse now, did you know? Opposite Robbi Goldschmidt's house."

They had reached Opern Platz. Franz seemed reluctant to let Willy go. Apparently he wanted to say something and didn't know how. Willy decided to encourage him.

"Do you sometimes listen to the radio?" he asked.

"I and Pueschel always listen to Dopey Heiner." Franz turned toward him after he had brought the car to a stop, and in his eyes Willy read the same obsequiousness he had shown when Willy had treated him badly in the Goethe School.

"A pity you're not one of us," Franz murmured, looking the other way. "Do you know a girl called Friedelgunde Fischer?"

"Yes, she's in the seminar. Why?"

"Do you know a fellow called Kurt Marland?"

"Not too well. He studies law, doesn't he? Why, Franz?"

"Nothing. I just wondered." He opened the door. "Well, you'd better get out here so the crowd in Toni's won't see you leaving my car, Will. I'm almost glad Robbi Goldschmidt isn't here."

Confused, Willy jumped out of the car and hurried into Toni's. He found Therese surrounded by a large crowd. Kurt Marland, in his ferocious yet completely cold manner was lecturing Therese on the coming elections.

"I must talk to you, Therese," Willy said, not taking off his coat. "Alone."

Kurt Marland's lashless eyes examined Willy calmly while Therese put on her complicated rain outfit. Some months ago Kurt had joined the Free Students. He proved to be a hard-working enthusiast, ardently recruiting new members. As Arlène had told Willy, he had been elected treasurer. It was possible that Duester had met Kurt in one of the law seminars. But why should Franz mention him and Friedelgunde to Willy? And why should Kurt know a storm trooper like Franz? Kurt hadn't been to school with Franz. In fact, nobody knew where Kurt came from.

Therese dragged him away and they rushed to the Café Falk, a rendezvous of shopping matrons, where the pastry was richer and the coffee weaker.

She was overjoyed with Willy's acceptance and ordered two glasses of schnapps. Tomorrow she would sign the necessary papers. They arranged a first meeting of the "Porcupine Associates" for the next night at Therese's house. Of course they would have to stay in Frankfurt during the summer and work out their program.

"Here's to The Porcupine," Therese declared, downing her schnapps. "See you tomorrow night."

The rain soon stopped and Willy ran over to Mrs. Sigbert to fetch Arlène. She approved of Willy's decision.

"Of course Father wants me to come home to Paris this summer," she said. "But I guess I can talk him out of it. Do you think we can find something for Ilona to do? I saw her recently. She isn't too well."

"I've neglected her," Willy confessed. "It always happens. I get too involved in my own doings." He then told Arlène about the incident in Franz Duester's car.

"He might have met Kurt in one of the law courses," Arlène said thoughtfully. Her eyes narrowed a little. "But why should he mention Friedelgunde, that ugly duckling? She doesn't study law. Let's have a look at that piece in the *Observer*."

They went into the university library and plowed through two months of *Observer* back issues a job equal to cleaning a latrine, Arlène declared. Finally she found the piece. It deplored the violation of the university's dignity by a "radical and orgiastic cabaret program," presented in the "sacred room" of the philosophical seminar. Willy was accused of having authored "lewd, tasteless sketches, smacking of French bedrooms," and how long would the authorities tolerate such undignified doings? It was a long piece of outrage and it was written "by our regular correspondent, F. F."

Arlène dragged Willy from the library, just in time for the theater seminar. They decided to let Professor Pfeiffer-Belli know their suspicions: that Friedelgunde Fischer, the awkward, coy girl, so bent on being everybody's friend, was the *Observer's* university reporter. She had been at the party—Arlène remembered her. Her initials tallied, and the piece, Arlène added, had something of her perpetual gushing.

Professor Pfeiffer-Belli shook his head incredulously when Willy and Arlène told their story. Nevertheless, he lifted the receiver and phoned the *Observer* office, asking for Miss Fischer. The office at first denied having a Miss Fischer. Then, as the old actor, with brazen naïveté, asked how he could reach his dear old friend Friedelgunde, who signed her column F. F., and whom he hadn't seen for so long, a second telephone operator broke in, informing him that Miss Fischer didn't work in the office. She was a regular contributor, however, and they'd gladly forward mail to her. . . .

Neither Arlène nor Willy had his mind on Goethe's *Faust*, the seminar's topic for the evening. Mr. Rundt double-talked almost

250

uninterruptedly, and the professor let him and Friedelgunde run the show. For the first time Willy was glad when the seminar was over.

As he and Arlène hurried home through Bockenheimer Landstrasse, while a sudden clear sky mirrored itself in the black puddles of the afternoon rain, Willy said:

"So Duester's hint was correct. Pfeiffer-Belli clinched that fast enough, didn't he?"

"That can mean only one thing," Arlène said. "There is something fishy about Kurt Marland too. It may sound melodramatic, Will, but he might be a stool pigeon, planted in the Free Students by the N.A.S.T.U."

"My God! He's been writing pacifist articles ever since I can remember," Willy said. "It sounds so—improbable."

"We must warn the Free Students in any case," Arlène said. "I'll speak to Ferdy and to Lisl Farner, their chairman. Perhaps you should see more of Franz Duester, Will."

The Free Students, so Ferdy reported to Willy in May, were checking up on Kurt Marland, but it looked as if in this case Franz had given Willy a bad steer. Willy forgot about the whole incident because Therese needed him fourteen hours a day. To be co-director of The Porcupine demanded every ounce of his strength.

When Chancellor Bruening resigned and an unknown named Franz von Papen became chancellor, Willy wasn't even interested. That day Therese and he went shopping for secondhand furniture.

In June the ground floor of the Golden Pheasant was almost finished. There was to be no bar, only small tables seating two or four. Gerhard had decorated the walls with murals depicting scenes from popular operas as they were done in the nineties—blond, over-corseted sopranos leaning against Gothic pillars, while sinister, equally corpulent contraltos lurked in corners, thirsty for revenge.

At the same time storm troopers again appeared on the streets in slightly altered and much cleaner uniforms. Chancellor von Papen, so Uncle Herbert Lange explained, had no choice but to make this concession to the belligerent Nazis.

One S. A. troop held its meetings not far from The Porcupine. Every night when Willy went home, dead tired from getting the place into shape, he heard them bellowing their repetitious and bloodthirsty songs about Germany's awakening. More than ever the S. A. men seemed to strut in the streets. Willy noticed that Therese took his arm whenever they passed them. One day one had strolled into The Porcupine and inquired what was being planned here. Gerhard Winter, with his blond, innocent smile, had explained in the simplest terms—it was always safe to as-

251

sume the lowest possible I.Q. among the awakeners of the new Reich. The S. A. man was pleased that "something is being done in Old Town." There was no reason for Therese to be afraid, Willy thought, but she refused to go home alone at night and one of the boys always had to take her. She also confided to Willy that the two new members, needed by The Porcupine, should be blond, if possible.

"People nowadays are inclined to think that everybody dark-haired is Jewish," she said to Willy one night, after they had passed a car with a loud-speaker, admonishing Frankfurt's citizens to vote for Mr. Sprenger and Mr. Hitler.

"Too many elections. Bad for our show. Stirs up the people," she went on.

"Never mind elections," Willy said—he had said it often to her. "We still have a lot of work to do."

Toward the end of a hot day in July, when Willy was describing to Melanie over dessert his ideas for a satire on modern drama, Theodor stormed in unexpectedly.

He fell into his chair, breathing heavily, as if he had run all the way home, and his white hair was disheveled. He threw his brief case onto the dinner table—a thing he had never done before—and some papers tumbled out.

Willy wanted to leave. He felt almost guilty to see Father in such a state.

"Von Papen has deposed Severing, the Prussian Premier, and Grzesinski, the Berlin chief of police. He's declared himself Reichs Commissioner of Prussia, and has given Von Rundstedt, the Reichs-wehr general, supreme authority over Berlin and Brandenburg. It's an illegal coup, a putsch, and my colleagues . . ."

"What did Severing and the others do?" Melanie asked.

"They resisted, but not enough," Theodor cried. "Severing said he'd yield only to force, so Rundstedt sent some soldiers around to their office—and they yielded."

"Sorry, Father, but I have to leave. We have a meeting at eight-thirty," Willy interrupted. He hurried out without looking at anyone. Politics, always politics! It depressed Therese; it hampered their progress. The only thing was to ignore it and go on living.

At the Golden Pheasant he found all of them in a black mood. Only Gerhard was painting away blissfully—always so absorbed in his work that nothing touched him.

"It looks grim," Therese said, shaking her red curls. "New elections in eleven days, today this thing in Berlin. Everybody's upset . . ."

252

"We can't stop every time something happens," Willy cried angrily. They turned to him, startled. Even Gerhard looked up from his canvas. Arlène smiled.

"It's July now, and we haven't half of the program ready," Willy went on. "Elections or no elections, we must get done. Therese, what about the spotlights? How near ready is the stage? I tell you now: we'll make it a law to ignore politics here. Do you hear me, all of you?"

Yes, they agreed readily, for they, too, wanted to be reassured and encouraged. Therese, recharged like a new battery, went into action. Hans Feld, an F. P. Busch disciple, a wizard of stagecraft, had already finished half the stage and bought baby spots and footlights for half price. Leininger, the agent, had found a good bookkeeper who was so enthusiastic about the whole thing that in addition he agreed to take charge of the box office in the evening —a wonderful chance to get away from a nagging sister at home.

At eleven a man and a girl appeared, slightly intimidated by the disorderly state of the place: the two new prospective members Therese had invited and then forgotten. The auditions were held on the half-finished stage by the glare of two naked bulbs.

Inge Bart was the perfect magazine-cover girl: petite, ash blond, blue-eyed, with an angelic face. She had brought some music which she put on the piano Ferdy had acquired a few days ago, gave him a radiant smile, and began, in a conventional lyric soprano, one of the current hits, "Your Eyes Are Blue as the Skies."

Willy was disappointed: she sounded like any night-club performer. Yet slowly it dawned on him that Inge Bart's lovely face and honeyed voice were only disguises: she ran the song into the ground. She quavered and quivered, putting the sentiment on inches thick, and at the end she unexpectedly broke into a rowdy version of what really happened "that day in June when our hearts were in tune," with a voice as beery as a truck driver on a binge.

When she finished, they all broke into applause, whereupon Inge read *A Poem to Be Said by a Serious-minded High-school Graduate on Commencement Day*. Her success made it tough for the second candidate, Manfred Wagner, a tall, muscular boy, originally trained as an acrobat. He gladly did somersaults, splits, and incredible leaps that shook the tools backstage.

They persuaded Manfred to sing. He sang an Italian aria in a loud, still-rough tenor that shook the house. Manfred exuded masculinity and confidence from every pore. Next to him even Therese appeared feminine and helpless.

In the ensuing hasty conference, held without Inge and Manfred, Arlène pleaded for Manfred whom Willy didn't like.

253

"We need one strong, unsophisticated man," Arlène explained. "He's the perfect foil for the others. He can dance and sing, and he's the right man to leaven the whole program." Willy gave in, and both Inge and Manfred were accepted as new members.

In the July elections the Nazis gained 230 seats out of 607 in the Reichstag. Often, when Willy got home, Melanie and Theodor would still be up, talking in low tones, and Ferdy again and again canceled rehearsals because of his activities in the Iron Front. But Willy, ignoring everything but The Porcupine, threw himself into his work. Therese, too, worked untiringly, particularly after Von Papen issued a decree against the S. A. terrorists in August. Manfred had fallen in love with everything and everybody. He installed spotlights with Hans Feld, helped Gerhard build the box office, and was around whenever help was needed. No job was too small—or too big. Surprisingly enough, he didn't try to charm any of the girls—he and Inge were engaged, and that was that. If Therese had fallen for him, she got over it quickly.

As summer turned into fall, The Porcupine's program slowly began to take shape.

They had set the first of October as opening day. The stage lights were installed; the curtain, decorated with Gerhard's fat angels, double-headed ladies in tights, reading dogs, and typewriting cats, was greeted with applause when the "team," as Therese liked to call their group, first saw it. Mr. Dingel, their bookkeeper, had developed into general business manager, taking charge of the printing of tickets and innumerable other tasks for which Therese and Willy had no time. Coatrooms were upstairs—awkward, but it couldn't be helped. The gentlemen's and ladies' rooms, in turn, hid in the cellar—tiny establishments on whose walls Gerhard had lavished his most extraordinary paintings.

Strangely enough, in this fall of 1932 a change occurred in Frankfurt's mood. Imperceptible at first, it grew stronger as time went by and bolstered the Porcupine team: the National-Socialist party seemed to be losing ground. The storm troopers had stopped their arrogant parading and looked worried and shabby. At the university the N.A.S.T.U. lost half of its members, while the Free Students gained. For the first time in many a month the moderate parties could hold meetings without being attacked.

One night in September, Theodor told Melanie and Willy that Mr. Sprenger had been voted down in the City Council, point by point, and that for some time now the other Nazi deputies were like sheep without a shepherd.

"The *Observer* is in bad straits," Theodor added. "Half of the advertisers are pulling out." Rarely had Willy seen Father so

254

happy. "I don't know what happened. The S. P. bosses don't seem to understand it either. It's a trend. They're beginning to beg for contributions."

"Indeed they are," Melanie said. "I had tea with Hannah Goldschmidt today and she told me about Mr. Reichert, who is foreman in their shop and an old Nazi party member. A few days ago he offered Arthur Goldschmidt a sort of insurance contract. If Arthur would contribute 500 marks to the Nazi Workers' Fund, the foreman would guarantee no harm would come to the Goldschmidts, even if a Hitler government takes over."

"A Hitler government?" Willy repeated incredulously.

"You've been out of touch for some time, Will, haven't you?" Theodor said. "Von Papen offered Hitler the vice-chancellorship in August but Hitler refused. All or nothing was his motto. So Von Papen and old Hindenburg dissolved the Reichstag. At least you've heard that?"

Willy lowered his eyes. "I haven't, Father. The only thing I look for in the papers is our publicity."

"Incidentally, what did Arthur do?" Theodor asked before retiring to his studio.

"He told the foreman he didn't need insurance. The Nazis were on their way out, and his family had lived in Germany longer than Hitler's."

Theodor was satisfied and went into his office to "bring his files up to date"—a task which was never achieved.

"When is your opening, Will?" Melanie asked, taking up the sewing of one of Willy's costumes which Ilona had designed but couldn't make.

"First of October, Mother. Didn't you know?" Willy asked. Melanie's face was half-averted and he was dimly aware that she was aiming at something without wanting to disclose it directly.

"I almost wish it were earlier," Melanie said softly.

Willy left his chair and sat down at her feet. Under the rouge and powder her face appeared drawn and, so Willy realized with a shock, a little swollen.

"You're in such a state of excitement, it must be hard for you to wait until October," she added, stroking his hair gently.

Willy accepted her explanation, although hidden somewhere in his mind a nagging doubt remained and, before falling asleep, he resolved to talk to Dr. Stein again.

But then Therese telephoned at eight in the morning to summon him to another "emergency" meeting; he had to check the galleys of their program; the *People's Voice* desired an interview—and he forgot about the doctor.

On the way down to Old Town Arlène and he heard the rattling of collection boxes, a noise which was to follow them in the following weeks wherever they went. A strike had broken out in Berlin. In unexpected accord, the Nazis and the Communists sponsored it, soliciting funds together. The S. A. and S. S. troopers who previously had broken up Communist meetings with a vengeance now stood shoulder to shoulder with their former enemies. Since many S. A. troopers had dyed their brown shirts during the last weeks, it was hard to tell which party was begging for "Pennies for the Strikers, Pennies for the Strikers."

The day before their opening Arlène stopped Willy as they passed the beer cellar where the storm troopers used to hold their meetings. A dirty "FOR RENT" sign dangled across the boarded-up door and the oversized swastika flag had vanished from the building.

"They've closed up," Arlène said. "They probably couldn't pay the rent. It's too good to be true."

In a way, the opening of The Porcupine was a repeat: it was like the show at the philosophical seminar, only on a much more elaborate scale. The last-minute confusion and hysterics were on a more elaborate scale too. Therese and Arlène had to calm Elena Franzen with two huge glasses of brandy. The waiters, as nervous as if they were to appear on stage, were treated to whisky, and Mr. Dingel had to be persuaded not to sit in his tiny box office until seven. After all, they opened at nine-fifteen.

Backstage, Therese delivered a magnificent pep talk. She radiated confidence. She reminded Elena not to step too near the rear, where the planks were uneven. She admonished Manfred not to outsing the others, and proposed a toast to the "untiring music master," Ferdy, who had written or arranged all their music.

At nine Mr. Dingel was sold out. Willy decided to set a precedent and start almost on time, at nine-twenty. Outside, crowds were angrily clamoring for tickets—a sweet noise.

The show started with Elena's violet dance, taken over from the old show. It put the audience in the right giddy mood. Then followed Willy's pet number: a parody on the new dramas of "blood and soil." At that time Germany was being swamped with innumerable farm plays, all dealing with country life, all written by playwrights imbued with Hitler ideas. Without exception they praised rustic simplicity for three long acts. They inevitably featured old Grandmother in her rocking chair, predicting evil if "the modern world" ever invaded the village; inevitably, the farmers were taciturn and ponderous; in between came lyrical outbursts, lauding the beauty of the soil, of cows, or chickens. Willy and Therese, assisted by Gerhard, who had contributed the most

256

grotesque touches, had concocted a parody, calling it "The Dung-heap."

The skit was a field day for Therese as eighty-year-old Granny, spouting dire predictions, calendar platitudes, and ancient super-stitions in a cackling voice. Willy and Manfred were rival farm-hands, while Inge, with braids so heavy they seemed to drag down her head, was the no-good daughter, introducing "newfangled contrivances" on the farm. Willy, using his broadest dialect, ex-changed threatening dialogues with Manfred in which none of them ever uttered more than short ejaculations. Therese's last speech, augmented by a garish sunset, the while Manfred could be seen through a window, burying Willy's corpse in a huge dung-heap, brought down the house.

After Elena's never-failing mouse dance, Arlène appeared. She had added two numbers in German to her repertoire, and to Willy's great joy she impressed the audience much more than she had the students. They forced her to repeat the song about Fridolin, *"le chien noir,"* and about the long Sunday afternoons when noth-ing happened. Finally, she sang them in German, with an accent that seemed to delight everyone.

The rest of the program went as smoothly as if they all had done it for years: Therese's solo number, as "Mrs. Hoffmann from Old Town," giving pithy comments on politics, taxes, and the neigh-bors' love lives; the opera take off with Manfred's tenor brightly shining; Inge's high-school graduation poem, for which Ilona had made just the right ill-fitting black dress usually worn by Frankfurt suburban girls, and at last the finale.

The curtain came down for the last time, and while the audience reluctantly went home, Mr. Dingel began counting the intake. They had made it. The weeks of arduous work had not been in vain. Old Mr. Braun was more than satisfied, and so were the people stream-ing backstage to congratulate them. Leininger, the agent, promised to look into touring possibilities.

Long past midnight, after everybody but Arlène, Therese, and Gerhard had left, Willy realized that neither Father nor Mother had shown up. From experience he knew that this was the mo-ment when the depression caught him and this time he battled against it as hard as he could.

"Come on, Therese," Arlène said. "We'll take you home."

"I think I'll have a drink with Gerhard somewhere," Therese said, her face glowing. "I'm proud of everybody, including myself. I want to talk to Gerhard about the last number."

"I think——" Willy began, but Arlène interrupted. "Please take me home now, Will. I can't stand on my feet much longer."

They left The Porcupine, smiling at Gerhard's sign of a very

257

bristly, sly beast over the entrance, and walked through Old Town. It was strangely quiet. The old houses always seemed more asleep than those in Frankfurt's new section. On the corners a few of the unemployed young men were still talking. By now they knew Arlène and Willy, and they nodded. One came over and thanked them—he had earned a good-sized tip by showing the way to the many people who couldn't find the place. The storm troopers with their rattling boxes had disappeared, and far away one could hear a boat horn on the Main River. All at once Willy remembered the graduation morning when Hal and he had walked away from the party toward the station. He pressed Arlène's arm.

"Have I treated you badly these last days, Arlène?" he asked. "Was I too busy with a thousand things?"

"Don't be silly," Arlène said, kissing him quickly on the cheek.

"I did neglect you," Willy persisted, not quite logically, and hailed a taxi although Arlène said it wasn't necessary.

"I'll come up for a cup of coffee," Arlène said when they had reached Reuter Weg, and Willy knew she understood he was worried about Theodor and Melanie.

On the dining-room table they found a letter for Willy. As he read it, still in his overcoat, his heart hammered and he found it hard to breathe. The same dread, choking sensation that had gripped him when he suddenly saw Hal's corduroys in the window in Hannsberg surged up again. An old wound had been ripped open.

Arlène took the letter from him. "Dr. Stein wouldn't wait any longer," Melanie wrote, "and they are going to operate tomorrow. That's why I couldn't come to the opening. I thought of you all this time and I prayed for your success. You know how much I wanted to come, but Dr. Stein wanted me there at least twenty-four hours before the operation. Father knows now, of course. We had to tell him everything. I'll be away for several weeks, so look after him. Dr. Stein will let you know when I can see visitors. I hope it may be soon. My love to you and Arlène."

Willy fell into a chair—he didn't realize it was Mother's chair near the window. A torrent of fear, of despair and remorse rushed over him. He should have guessed when Melanie said she wished the opening were earlier. For his sake, she had waited because she was afraid he couldn't go on being "funny" if he knew she was in the hospital. He should have called Dr. Stein, he should have watched over Mother, and he had failed.

He buried his face in his hands and, irresistibly, the tears welled up in him. He hadn't cried since Hal's death and this, too, brought back a rush of memories as if they had lain somewhere, waiting to

258

attack him—the miniature lambs, the crippled houses of Little Venice, the headlines in the Hannsberg papers. . . .

"Don't cry, Willy." Arlène had put her arm around him. "You'll see her in a day or two. We'll telephone the hospital tomorrow morning."

Willy took her in his arms, but the shock subsided only gradually. Arlène didn't leave him that night and they lay awake until the uncertain light of the October morning crept in through the window.

18. HOW HE MANAGED TO KEEP GOING during the next days Willy never knew. According to Dr. Stein the operation had been successful so far—but he wouldn't let Willy see her. It was impossible to ask Father for details. Theodor sat at the dinner table, his eyes heavy from lack of sleep. He wasn't really there. He kept repeating "Melanie is all right. You mustn't worry." Arlène, who shared the Halders' meals, agreed: One mustn't talk to him about Melanie. So, during the meals the three carried on an unreal conversation about new books or plays.

Although Big Anna ran the household as efficiently as ever, 66 Reuter Weg had changed. Without Melanie it was simply a place to eat and sleep. For Willy, a part of his life, the foundation on which it had rested for so long, was slowly falling to pieces. How much had been taken from him he couldn't as yet guess. He felt unprotected, like a sleeper who suddenly awakens to find all the covers flung off.

After the initial shock Willy managed to get hold of himself. This, he admitted, was Arlène's doing, and he felt closer to her than ever before: as close as he'd been to Hal. She also possessed some of Hal's characteristics—his sobriety, his fearlessness, his talent for adjustment. According to her the only thing to do was to continue with The Porcupine.

Willy didn't quite know what to do. He hated to go on stage. The "company" had behaved perfectly. Therese, bringing him their regards, had immediately offered to close the show for a few days and recast the sketches: Manfred and Gerhard could take over Willy's numbers and she would "emcee" the show. Willy hesitated; then Dr. Stein made the decision for him. Melanie was worried he might stop and begged him to carry on.

The same day Willy went down to the place. They all squeezed his hand warmly and from then on acted as if nothing had happened. Only now Willy saw the reviews. Nearly all the critics had liked the show very much. The *General News* discerned some "traces of radical influence," but benignly conceded they were a minor detail. The *Frankfurter Zeitung's* Dr. S. D. devoted a long

260

essay to it, much longer than the usual brisk review, in which he explained that a new form of entertainment had been born in Frankfurt, something as necessary to German culture as salt to meat, something unpretentious, without the dangerous urge to be "deep."

Willy was certain not one third of the readers understood Dr. D.'s article, but they did understand that they should buy tickets. . . .

The *Observer* had not been invited—by unanimous vote of the team. Yet the day after the *Red Flag* had printed its verdict of a "thoroughly bourgeois but harmless time killer," Friedelgunde Fischer was seen buying a ticket—the cheapest, incidentally. In the next issue the *Observer* ran a major attack, signed F. F. Two things particularly incensed F. F.: the take off on the "blood-and-soil drama," which it called "a slap in the face to all decent Germans," and Ferdy's music.

The Porcupine members looked at one another in amazement, as Arlène read aloud F. F.'s battle cry against America. To fill in at one point Ferdy usually played a long excerpt from the "Rhapsody in Blue," together with some Zez Confrey and Jerome Kern. This was "degenerated Negro-Bolshevist art, alien to German blood, obscene, dollar-minded, and destructive." F. F. demanded "German music for German ears," and foresaw dire effects if these German ears were exposed to Gershwin over any length of time, and ended by stating that this "Negro-Jewish-American-Bolshevist cacophony," like the whole program, must be seen as a political onslaught against the Fuehrer's sacred principles.

If anything, Friedelgunde pushed Willy into carrying on with all his strength.

A week after the operation Willy was finally allowed to visit Melanie, in the Hospital of the Holy Spirit. As he entered her room, which smelled of disinfectant and suffering, he found her lying motionless in the high metal hospital bed. Her face, her hair, and the pillow seemed of the same white color, but she smiled at him faintly as he sat on the chair at her left. He struggled to keep calm and not let her see his emotions.

"They read me your reviews," Melanie said in a small voice. "It made me happy. As soon as I'm out of here, I'll be down, if you're still going."

"Oh, we'll be there a long time, Mother," Willy said. "Mr. Dingel says people are ordering weeks in advance."

With an effort Melanie stretched out her hand and Willy took it in his, stroking it softly. Her palm was sweating and, feeling it between his own cool hands, he knew that the pain was still stabbing at her—her hand betrayed what her face tried to hide.

"I've been thinking a great deal," Melanie said. "About us, and you, when you were little. Other boys never knew what they wanted, but you did. I remember when you started imitating your uncle Herbert. You weren't more than seven."

"I don't remember that," Willy said, drying her palms with his handkerchief. "I can remember how I mimicked our French teacher, Mr. Noll, and how you bawled me out for my bad French."

This time Melanie's smile seemed real, and it warmed Willy. Perhaps for a second he had succeeded in making her forget her pain.

"Do you know about your cousin Hans?" Melanie went on. "He joined the Hitler Youth after the Wandervogel, and now Uncle Herbert wonders whether it wasn't a mistake. They wrote me a note—Aunt Helen hopes you won't get involved too much with 'theatrical folks.' "

The nurse appeared in the door and Willy had to leave. He kissed Melanie on the forehead and wandered slowly through the immaculate hospital hallways, bright and antiseptic and busy. The hospital's garden was deserted now, and the first snow covered the large, bald tree branches.

From then on Willy visited Melanie every day. Each time they let him stay a little longer. Since Theodor usually visited in the early morning and late evening, Willy went around four o'clock, after Melanie's prescribed nap, and they had tea together. The only thing that interested Melanie more than the happenings at The Porcupine were the oncoming elections, set for November sixth. It grieved her that she couldn't cast her vote. She could hardly wait.

When, on the seventh of November, Willy arrived with flowers from the company, Melanie had got so excited about the news that she had slept badly.

"We must avoid undue perturbation," Nurse Brenner declared primly as he entered, and Willy was tempted to ask her how one went about it.

To celebrate, Melanie had ordered chocolate cake for Willy. The Hitler party had lost 34 seats in the Reichstag. They had decreased from 230 to 197 representatives, and though they were still the strongest group, the loss bolstered the prevailing Frankfurt saying that "the swastika robbers are finished." The Communists had risen, of course, and how any government could function with the two extremist parties shrieking their lungs out the more sober people didn't know. But it was the first defeat for the

N.S.D.A.P., and even the usually unemotional Social-Democratic papers sounded a new note of regained confidence.

Melanie was quite touched by the company's flowers—after all, she knew only a few of the team. For the first time she seemed to enjoy the tea, and Willy began to hope that she would soon be her old self. Dr. Stein's last reports sounded favorable, too: he was almost sure Melanie could return home soon.

One afternoon a few weeks later Willy had asked Arlène to pick him up at the hospital, and when Melanie heard about it she insisted on seeing her, although Nurse Brenner was unfavorably disposed toward visits by "anyone but the closest relatives."

Arlène stayed only a short while. When she left, she didn't say anything, but took Willy's arm and together they walked through the white, desolate hospital garden to the streetcar stop.

"Mrs. Goldschmidt wants to see me," Arlène said finally. "I wonder what she wants. Your mother hinted that she is more nervous than ever." Arlène shook her head, then changed her tone. "I forgot to tell you, Mr. Dingel computed our salaries today. You're going to get 800 marks, and if we keep going on our present speed we should each average around 200 a week."

"It's fantastic," Willy said as they climbed into the old streetcar. "I'll be able to send Mother to the Riviera as soon as she's better."

The streetcar was rattling through the monotonous alleys of suburban Bockenheim when Arlène suddenly said: "Yes, send her to the Riviera, Will. And when we have finished with the show—it can't go on forever, after all—I want you to visit us in Paris. And stay with us. For a year at least."

Willy said that the government—the new one under General Schleicher who had kicked out Von Papen—didn't approve of people leaving the country except on urgent business.

"That's just it," Arlène said. Then, as they walked toward the little restaurant where the team often ate dinner, she added: "I'm afraid if you wait too long you'll never get away."

"You're more pessimistic than I, Arlène," Willy said. "That's unusual."

Arlène didn't answer, and Willy knew something was wrong. When, as if by chance, Therese dropped in to say hello, it became apparent that something was being kept from him. Willy never forgot the moment: they were sitting at the little table, Therese in her immaculate tailor-made costume, incessantly playing with her rings; Arlène, her auburn hair falling over her forehead, trying to calm down Therese. Only Willy paid attention to the food.

"We didn't want to bother you, Willy—" Therese began picking at the beans on her plate—"but we must soon decide what's to be done."

"What is it?" Willy asked. "Are we losing money? Do the police consider us lascivious?"

"All right, then," Therese sighed. "Storm Number 13, Squad 4, of the National-Socialist party, Frankfurt, offers us its protection." She pulled out a letter and read: "As you no doubt realize, The Porcupine (formerly The Golden Pheasant) is situated in a neighborhood in which robberies, burglaries, and worse crimes are not infrequent. Knowing this neighborhood quite well—our meeting place used to be next to your establishment—we want to offer you protection so that your many visitors won't be molested. A squad of three or four S. A. or S. S. troopers (not in uniform, of course) would be sufficient. In exchange we'd appreciate a contribution of about 30 marks per week to the party's welfare fund."

"Those rotters," Willy said, filled with a cold anger. He couldn't finish his food. "Therese, call an emergency meeting after tonight's performance. For everybody, including Inge."

Inge, though admittedly too sleepy after a show to think at all, stayed this time. Ferdy proposed to hand the letter over to the police, but Therese objected. Finally they took a vote—they decided to reject the offer of Squad 4, Storm No. 13. Against Therese's vote, the letter would be given to the police, after a copy had been made.

A few days later Willy and Therese called on Deputy Police Commissioner Hartung, a former trade-union leader, a member of the Social-Democratic party for more than twenty years and, according to Theodor, a good though a trifle cautious man.

Willy found Mr. Hartung somewhat more than a trifle cautious. Sitting in his spacious handsome office in the Police Building, opposite the Goethe School, Mr. Hartung, a large man with a florid face, explained that the main thing in times like these was to avoid trouble.

"Your father is aware of it, young Mr. Halder, just as much as I. The Schleicher government is not kindly disposed toward us Social Democrats. Even if the Hitler party has lost many members, they are still very strong. I'm sorry, but I couldn't spare enough policemen to protect your night club."

He looked over a list. "Your next precinct is Number 16. I'll ask Lieutenant Mangold to keep an eye on you."

The commissioner hesitated. "Is there anything controversial in your program, anything politically dangerous?"

"No," Willy said. "Unless you think American dance music is unpatriotic and corrupting, as the *Observer* did."

Hartung didn't think so, though he himself preferred choral

264

works for male voices, as performed by his Lieder Club, the Frankfurt Leather Workers' Union Choir, of which he had been a member for many years. . . .

With these reminiscences Mr. Hartung dismissed them, having promised precisely nothing.

On their way to the hospital, in the decrepit old Bockenheim streetcar, Arlène and Willy met Friedelgunde Fischer on the platform. It was in the beginning of December, on a cold and dim wintry day. Recognizing them, Friedelgunde blushed a deep crimson and looked the other way.

Arlène, cool and friendly, went over to her and said: "Why are you attacking us, Miss Fischer? Please tell me."

After a pause Friedelgunde stuttered: "Attacking you? I? Why, what an idea! I'm too busy at the university. I haven't even seen you there for quite some time."

"So you didn't write in the *Observer* about our show?" Arlène went on. "So sorry. We must have made a mistake. I thought I recognized your style. It's so unmistakable."

Friedelgunde squirmed. "I don't know what you're referring to," she said, and she seemed to realize how unconvincing she sounded. She left the car at a forlorn square in deepest Bockenheim where, Willy was sure, she had not meant to get off at all.

Bockenheim looked careworn and soured in these chilly December days, with the darkness falling early. Some shops displayed Christmas trees in their windows, but even the trees appeared undernourished and listless. Over the noise of the streetcar Willy could hear the rattling of the boxes, the voices of young men asking for contributions for the strikers in Berlin. There was no escaping the chattering boxes in this winter of 1932. The eyes of the young men asking for pennies betrayed unconcealed hostility— to them, Willy was one of the lucky ones. With his new blue overcoat, his white muffler, and gray gloves, he definitely seemed a young man of comfortable means; Arlène, no matter what she wore, always gave the impression of being stylishly dressed—it was mostly a trick of using scarfs and gloves, she said.

Surely Willy had worked hard, put more of himself into the cabaret than into anything he had ever done before. But he had a bad conscience for having a job, even for having Arlène. Now, as they left the streetcar, he couldn't help seeing the men sitting in the beer cellars, playing cards, or simply leaning out of windows, staring into the bleak December dusk. Neither Bruening, Von Papen, nor Schleicher, it seemed, had changed anything.

Melanie was reading when they entered. By now, she said, she was enjoying the hospital. At last she could read the books she had wanted to read all her life. When tea was brought in, she reminded Arlène of Hannah Goldschmidt.

"She asked for you again," Melanie said. "Please go see her. I must warn you, Arlène. She's off balance; she cries easily, and she may ask you to run some impossible errands for her. She won the battle with Arthur, though. Robbi is not coming home for Christmas—he's going to Paris."

"Fine," Arlène said. "I'll write Father tomorrow."

Before they left, Melanie said: "I hoped to be home by Christmas, Will, but the doctors want to give me some more treatments. You must celebrate without me."

She sounded peaceful enough as she sat there, propped up comfortably, her book—Stendhal's *Le Rouge et le Noir*—on the night table next to her. But all at once Willy felt chilled in the warm hospital room. As if a picture had been smashed, a picture that he had seen hanging on a wall for a long time, his dream of Melanie and himself, sitting in the warm Riviera sun, suddenly went to pieces. He had meant to talk to her today about the Riviera, to ask her also what presents he should buy for Theodor and Big Anna, but now he couldn't speak about it. He was almost glad when Nurse Brenner came in to take her temperature, "just for fun"—Nurse Brenner's jokes sounded staler than ever today, and she did not reprimand him for eating too much cake, as she invariably did on other days.

If Arlène had noticed, she kept it to herself on their way back to town. She was going to Mrs. Goldschmidt right now, she declared, leaving him at Opern Platz. It was a pretext not to talk about what they both felt, Willy was sure. Something had again gone wrong with Mother. Big Anna knew it, too, though she wouldn't say a word and insisted he lie down and rest, so he'd be in good form.

Usually Willy managed to relax before the show, to gather enough strength for the next hours when he had to be on his toes every second. But now as he lay stretched out on the couch in the living room his nerves were taut, and he knew he'd only become tenser if he kept trying to relax. He went to the phone and called Stein. The doctor was noncommittal and in a hurry to get to another case. Willy decided to go to The Porcupine earlier—there was always something to do there. Downstairs in the mailbox he found a brown envelope, addressed to him personally in a scrawling, primitive handwriting. It contained the latest issue of the *Observer* with another vicious indictment of The Porcupine.

They had a full house that night. Although most places of entertainment did poorly these weeks before Christmas 1932, The

Porcupine was filled to the last seat. Arlène and Willy hardly noticed it. They had enough trouble getting through their numbers without letting the others see their mood. Somehow Willy felt like a clown and an impostor as he stood there in front of Gerhard's crazy curtain, telling humorous anecdotes or kidding himself, the cabaret, and the number that was to follow.

It was during the "Follies of 1932"—which had been made to look even more ridiculous thanks to the enormous ostrich feather fans which Gerhard had given the girls and behind which they coyly hid that Gerhard whispered something in Willy's ear. Willy didn't understand because Ferdy was hammering out the old hit, "Chicago," but he noticed that the door stood open and that Mr. Dingel was not sitting in his box office. The "Follies" ended. After a short intermission Willy went before the audience to announce the last number. Then he dashed backstage to put on the uncomfortable armor with the helmet whose falling visor cut off his speeches at strategic intervals. Where was Mr. Dingel?

Willy wanted Gerhard to close the door but couldn't find him. He wasn't needed in this number. The curtain went up. Inge began a plaintive monologue, was interrupted by Manfred, in armor, threatening to seduce her. Willy, dashing onstage, went to her rescue, challenging Manfred to a duel.

While he talked Willy noticed that the waiters had disappeared. He heard whispers. Heads were turning. A man was loudly demanding a drink. Then, suddenly, something was thrown into the room, exploding with a loud report. A deafening clatter of falling furniture followed and the tramping of heavy boots. Willy stopped. Inge had fallen into a chair. Manfred was feverishly trying to get out of his armor. There came the piercing screams of women and then a biting, choking gas began filling the hall, a thick, white vapor that made people cough and gasp for air. Willy wanted to stop the people, who now were rushing toward the exit in a panic, shouting and screaming. Someone managed to pry open the emergency door —Willy dimly recognized Therese's figure through the asphyxiating clouds.

Arlène, a handkerchief to her lips, took his arm. "The storm troopers," she whispered, coughing. She was pale under her makeup. "They threw stink bombs. God, here they come now."

Willy never knew how the people had fled—without the emergency door they would have trampled each other to death. While the fumes started slowly to rise, a group of black-shirted troopers marched on stage. Another group began to smash tables, chairs, and glasses systematically and efficiently, as if it had been rehearsed.

Willy couldn't extricate himself from his costume and had to face the troopers clad in armor and trying to keep his visor from falling over his face.

"You'll pay for this," Willy began, as the four S. S. men planted themselves before him. His whole team was on stage now. Only Gerhard was missing.

"I'll do the talking," the man said, while the second group kept on smashing the chairs against the tables. "Your waiters are in the kitchen under guard." He stood close, his face almost touching Willy's. He was a wolfish fellow, with the face of a depraved athlete, and Willy realized that he was enjoying the situation.

"I'd like to knock hell out of you," the man said. "You're Jews and Bolshevists. You've been playing nigger music and attacking us. We don't want your kind of stuff in this town. Do you hear me? Don't try to come back. We'll be there, throwing our eggs."

He pushed Willy, who stumbled backward and would have fallen if Manfred hadn't held him. Manfred stepped forward, but before he could open his mouth the leader hit him straight between the eyes. A second trooper held Manfred's arms, a third kicked him in the groin. Helpless, Manfred doubled over, blood trickling down his face.

"That's enough," the S. S. leader said calmly. They let Manfred go. By now there wasn't a chair left in the house. The floor was covered with broken bits of china, wood, and glass; even the imitation marble tops were split.

"You can't get away with this," Willy yelled. "We'll open again. You can't do this."

Before he could finish the three troopers seized him. They held him in a firm grip, and tried to twist his arms. But, incredibly enough, the armor proved its value. They couldn't get hold of him. They hammered at him, but it didn't hurt. Willy only hoped Arlène wouldn't start anything. Then, as they realized they weren't getting anywhere, the leader hit Willy on the chin, just once. For a second Willy's world went black, and his knees gave way under him.

"Don't try anything," the man said. "We'll wreck your place the minute you start again."

"You'll pay for this, you rats," Willy managed to stutter. But it sounded muffled, and something was wrong with his jaw.

The S. S. man stepped forward. "So you won't give up, eh?" he said. "I'll show you." He motioned one of his assistants to come over, but the man hesitated.

"Aw, Karl, let's go," he said. "The smell in this place is awful. They can't start again. We did a thorough job. Look." He pointed through the open kitchen door. Heaps of broken glasses and dishes

268

lay on the floor; kitchen chairs, tables, bottles, pieces of china were scattered as if a bomb had hit the place.

Willy recognized the voice of the second man. It was Pueschel, his baby face flushed.

"They're through, Karl," Pueschel went on. "Let's go have a drink. That godawful stink will stick to our clothes if we don't beat it."

"You're right, comrade," the man called Karl said. He motioned to the other troopers. One gave the unconscious Manfred a last kick. The troop from the kitchen filtered in and Karl said:

"You'll find two of your fellows in the men's room. The cashier and a blond fellow. He started yelling, so we shut him up."

Karl marched away, his men following him in military fashion. Pueschel was last. He lingered, and when the others had left he rushed over to Willy.

"I couldn't help it, Willy. I did what I could. If you hadn't talked back Karl wouldn't have hit you. Why didn't you pay those 30 marks?" Pueschel shrugged his shoulders. "I tried to stop them, but nobody can stop Karl's squad. Sorry, chum."

"Go away, Pueschel," Willy said. "Your pals are waiting. I don't need your sympathy."

"They'll be back if you don't give up," Pueschel said, almost plaintive. "And let me tell you: without me they would have beaten you all to pulp."

He walked away past the heaps of broken furniture and glass, as if he had walked past debris all his life. Willy heard him shout "Heil Hitler!" as he joined the squad outside.

Gerhard and Mr. Dingel had to be transferred to a hospital. Gerhard's head had a deep gash and an X ray showed his skull was fractured. Fortunately, Mr. Dingel was only numbed by the shock and recovered quickly. They both had been knocked down, then put into the washroom, under the guard of a storm trooper.

Theodor's old friend, the lawyer Dr. Hirt, proposed to file a suit against Squad 4. Together with the letter they had a solid case of blackmail and assault, he asserted. Yet even if there was a chance to win the case—which, Arlène figured, would take months and months—Willy knew he was beaten. The Porcupine had been killed. People wouldn't take the chance of being tear-gased a second time.

On Theodor's orders Willy stayed in bed for a few days. His jaw was dislocated but not broken; Dr. Stein came and with one quick movement set it so fast Willy felt almost no pain. Willy's main worry was Melanie. Fortunately he was able to speak to her on the phone—they had installed one in her hospital room—and

269

assure her he was fine. He also promised her not to revive the cabaret.

Again Therese proved her efficiency. She visited Willy the second day. She was amazingly quiet, but Willy saw how deeply she was shocked. Yet she wound up the business. She returned the money to the ticket-holders, sent notices to the papers, paid each company member two weeks' salary, and went about collecting insurance. Without telling anyone, she had previously insured The Porcupine against all possible damage. The Frankfurt Life Insurance Company disputed the claim: acts of political vandalism, in 1932, were, like acts of God, beyond anybody's control, they stated, and therefore the company wasn't liable. But her father's lawyer would keep after them, Therese assured Willy, and at least they would get some compensation this way. She also reported that Gerhard and Mr. Dingel were improving rapidly and that Manfred, Inge, and Elena had been offered jobs in a night club, provided they use other material.

The first day Willy was allowed to get out of bed, Ferdy Rohn visited him. He apologized for not having come earlier—he had been too busy.

"Willy," he said, sitting down and lighting a cigarette, "you mustn't take this lying down. In a way, we almost invited it. They even warned us—remember the *Observer* articles? Remember Franz Duester's talk about Kurt Marland?"

"What has Kurt Marland to do with it? And, incidentally, how did you manage not to get hurt? Where were you?"

"Oh, they broke one or two of my ribs," Ferdy said nonchalantly, "and then left me lying under the grand piano. By the time I came to, you had left. Neither you nor they could see me, because of the heaps of broken stuff around the piano. Much later Therese returned and took me home. Nothing serious, the doc says. I started on my old job at the Café de Paris last night."

"You mean we simply forgot you?" Willy said. "I certainly didn't act like a hero, did I, Ferdy?"

Ferdy smiled, then grimaced. "I mustn't even smile, Will. It hurts. Twenty armed storm troopers against four fellows and four girls. No, you did what you could; I guess we all did. Now for Kurt Marland. Or don't you want to hear?"

"Go on," Willy said.

"Well, at first the Free Students laughed at your warnings. Then Lisl Farner, the head of our group, began to wonder. She set to work. Well, after a while she found out. Kurt was planted by the N.A.S.T.U. to report back to them everything we did. Your old schoolmate Duester did us a great favor shooting off his mouth, though we believe he had personal reasons for disliking Kurt. Lisl

270

Farner wants to thank you. Friedelgunde Fischer, of course, is the informer in the Germanic seminar. The N.A.S.T.U. has one of its people in each seminar, in each university department—even, we think, in Von Rhyn's office."

"I don't believe it." Willy stared at Ferdy. "Why should they do that?"

"Sometimes it takes you damned long to face facts, Will," Ferdy said angrily. "Are you blind? Or deaf? Or are you purposely playing deaf and dumb? The N.A.S.T.U. hopes to take over the university the day their party takes over in Frankfurt. And the party has stool pigeons in the government, in the labor unions, everywhere. It's organized spying on a large scale. A part of their warfare. Don't you see that?"

"But they lost in the last elections."

"That doesn't mean anything!" Ferdy almost shouted.

"Maybe you're right, Ferdy," Willy answered softly. Looking into Ferdy's familiar, frowning face, he suddenly remembered the early days when Ferdy had explained politics to him. First he had followed Ferdy, worked for the expropriation of the princes. Then he had retreated, in disgust. He thought he had found where he belonged, thrown himself into his studies, his radio work. Finally, after months of arduous labor for The Porcupine, came success, sweet and rewarding. Now it was all gone. He had tried hard to ignore what went on around him, but no matter what he did, he became entangled again and again. There seemed no escaping a new religion that demanded submission in all fields, even in something as remote as a night club. He had fled, Willy admitted to himself, he had fled politics, and it had caught up with him again.

"For the first time we've got Social-Democratic and Communist students, Catholics of the Center party, a few of the People's, and even the State party with us, besides the many who are unaffiliated," Ferdy went on. "For the first time it looks as though we're all together."

"You asked me once, or even twice before, and I said no," Willy said. "This time I'll go with you."

"Fine," Ferdy said, getting up. He hesitated for a moment, gazing at the map of Europe over Willy's bed. "Let me tell you, Will. Lisl Farner, our chairman, has no use for the arts. She's a wonderful girl, works like a horse, and it was she who got the S. P. and K. P. students together. But she considers anything like our old Porcupine—well—frivolous. She's also angry at the Social-Democratic bigwigs who won't give the Iron Front enough arms while the N.A.S.T.U. is getting them from all over. Since your dad is a councilman, she might be prejudiced against you."

"Never mind, Ferdy," Willy answered. "I'm prepared."

He paid three marks in initiation fee and promised to be at their next meeting, the Saturday before Christmas. They talked a little longer, and when Arlène came in she found them sitting in the dark, reminiscing with a sort of disgusted nostalgia about the old Wandervogel days.

Arlène switched on the little table lamp. "You look pale and thin, Willy," she declared. She kissed him on the forehead. "Have you finally given in?"

"I have," Willy said, "though perhaps it doesn't make much sense. You think a handful of students can change things?"

"Of course they can," Arlène said. "Do you know the whole university is talking about us. And, can you beat it, Pueschel sneaked up to me when nobody was looking, and asked how you were doing."

Arlène stopped for a second. Then she went on: "Willy, I wish I could be home for Christmas. But it's too late now. After what happened to us I feel I've had enough. For the first time."

Pointedly tactful, Ferdy left soon. Arlène saw him to the door.

Willy walked slowly to the window. Snow had begun to fall, thick, isolated, soft flakes, carelessly covering Reuter Weg with a blanket that deadened every sound.

He felt Arlène's light hand on his shoulder. She stood next to him, gazing into the street.

"Incredibly peaceful," she said. "Just what the doctor ordered for Christmas." Willy put his arm around her and together they watched the flakes gliding down, sometimes illuminated by a sudden spark from a streetcar.

"I never told you about Hannah Goldschmidt," Arlène said. "Come, lie down. I promise not to touch your jaw."

Willy stretched out again and Arlène sat next to him, holding his hand and, from time to time, stroking his hair.

"Mrs. Goldschmidt has had new locks put on every door in the house. Arthur, who intercepted me the minute I entered, told me she receives treatments from a nerve specialist. She is certain her house will be taken from her, she lives only in visions of future disasters. She seemed very disappointed when I told her I wasn't going home for Christmas."

"Why?" Willy wondered. "Did she want you to take along a Christmas present for Robbi?"

"Not quite. She asked me to smuggle out six fabulously precious pieces of jewelry and deposit them in a bank vault in Paris. I'd receive a commission, of course. She wants to have something outside of Germany. Arthur says it's just her imagination; there's no earthly reason to do such a thing. Incidentally, it's illegal."

"She sounds like a sick woman," Willy said slowly.

272

"I don't care whether she's sick or not," Arlène said. "I felt so sorry for her I went to Monsieur Delacroix at the French Consulate, an old admirer of Mother's. He's going to Paris over the holidays and was quite willing to take the jewels—his diplomatic baggage won't be inspected, of course. He demanded a very high commission, and I got the impression this wasn't the first time he's done a job like this. Arthur first chafed at the high price. Then, when he realized what it meant to Hannah, he gave in and told me he would have paid twice the price, if only it helped his wife."

There was a knock at the door and Anna announced that Inge and Manfred wanted to see the "sick maestro." They brought flowers—quite unnecessarily—and Willy assured them it was perfectly all right for them to take a job at any night club. Later on Elena Franzen and Therese appeared and didn't leave until Anna threw them out, saying the doctor and Willy both needed their rest. Arlène would call on Willy early next morning: they were going to the university to find out how he could make up for lost time. There were only two days left before the Christmas vacation.

It was Christmas, more than anything else in this winter of 1932, which brought home to Willy the feeling of an inexorable change in his life. The Halders celebrated Christmas in Melanie's hospital room. Willy had bought a small tree and Arlène and he trimmed it while Melanie watched, leaning back on the cushions and smiling at them. It gave Willy a twinge to look at her. There was no denying her face had changed. It was extremely white and quite swollen.

Like many families in Frankfurt, the Halders celebrated on the evening of the twenty-fourth. There were presents, as usual; they ate a special hospital dinner, and in the neighboring rooms they could hear the visitors talking and laughing. Melanie knew all about her neighbors—she was living in the hospital world now, a separate kingdom of nurses, doctors, orderlies, where small events took on the aspect of great importance.

Theodor said little. He sat on the chair next to Melanie's bed, patting her hand, absent-minded, trying to hide his worries, trying to fall in with the general Christmas spirit of joy and lightheartedness. Melanie, in an almost bantering way, told them several stories concerning the rivalry of two doctors on her floor.

And while Willy listened to her, his eyes on the slightly flickering wax candles, he realized he had to strain his ears to catch Melanie's words. Her voice had lost its resonance, although she didn't seem to be aware of it. He turned to Arlène, but she had averted her eyes, staring out into the hospital garden whose darkness was broken by a gigantic tree with colored electric bulbs. Willy had an urge to go over to his mother, kneel before her bed, and kiss her hand and thank her for all the things she had done for him. But this would only upset her. As he looked at Melanie, she stopped talking. Her hand was on her throat, and in her eyes he could read how she struggled with the pain.

When Nurse Brenner entered and, after admiring the nice presents and the nice tree, tactfully hinted it was time for Melanie's injection, Willy felt something almost like relief. And he knew that Melanie, too, was waiting for them to leave.

Contrary to Ferdy's prediction, Willy got along splendidly with Lisl Farner, the Free Students' chairman. They never argued about anything theoretical—Lisl, a specialist on economy and philosophy, knew so much more that Willy didn't even try. But, to his surprise, he discovered that Lisl thought he had a certain something she found rare among the members.

One night between Christmas and New Year's, after they had discussed a rumor that the N.A.S.T.U. had acquired a certain number of machine guns, Lisl said:

"I don't mean to flatter you, Will, but I think you have a knack for handling people. I heard you talking with Herb Simrock. Well, you and I know he's an orthodox believer in the Scientific System, K. P. version, and a choleric to boot. But you got around him by not getting into an argument, and he actually grinned once."

"I'm ashamed of it," Willy admitted. "I imitated Dr. Walden-Arditi's latest sermon of the Danish philosopher S. Kierkegaard's philosophy of voluptuous despair. By now the doctor isn't so fond of dialectics, and Herbert and I are convinced he's making of Kierkegaard, his pupil Heidegger, and the whole school of elegant despair, a clandestine storm troop of philosophy."

"Walden-Arditi is an intellectual juggler," Lisl said angrily. "The trouble is he's so clever he can quote Emerson to prove Hitler, and vice versa. Then he'll show them both up as wrong, and put up another deity only to destroy it the next day."

She sighed and glanced around the meeting place, a large back room of the Bockenheim restaurant, The Peacock, decorated with murals depicting gay hunting scenes. They were alone, sitting on the dais, Lisl with a glass of beer before her, which, somehow, didn't fit her at all. Willy didn't like beer and stuck to Rhine wine which cost more but didn't leave him with a hangover.

"Well," Willy said, "you didn't mean to discuss Walden-Arbiti with me, Chairman. Or did you?"

Lisl smiled. She was a small girl of such extreme blondness that most people never came really to study her features because their eyes stopped at her silver-white silky hair. Her face was that of a young athlete on a classic Greek vase, almost hard, with greenish-blue eyes. Yet, at the same time, like Paulus Hillden's it was that of an idealist, anxious to change this earth into something better.

"You've been with us only a short time, Will. Do you think I'm a fool?"

The question left Willy baffled. He had never assumed a girl like Lisl, who had organized the non-N.A.S.T.U. students at the university, could ever nourish any doubts.

"Don't tell me things you'll regret tomorrow," he said, quoting Mathilda, who had said this to him when, long ago, he had wanted to tell her about Maria Reger. "To me you represent 'the fighter for the right cause.' Unerring, a bit like Joan of Arc."

"For heaven's sake, skip it," Lisl cried. "All right, I organized the group. I brought together the fighting K. P. and S. P. students on a highly intellectual plane, away from party lines. Through Wolfgang Brosig, your old pal, I got some of the liberal Center, and then came the many who wanted a roof over their heads. The storm troopers are still begging in the streets and the trade-union people are convinced that Hitler's bankrupt. Willy, do you understand what's going on behind the scenes?"

"No, I don't. I think the only man who does is Von Rhyn," Willy answered. "As far as I can figure out, Von Papen is double-crossing Von Schleicher and also trying to make the Nazis appear respectable—and it's all a mess."

"How are your old schoolmates Pueschel and Duester these days?" Lisl went on.

Willy turned it over in his mind. "Subdued, but not so downcast as those begging storm troopers in the streets. Of course I see little of them. Pueschel has a bad conscience because he helped wreck our Porcupine and I haven't talked to Franz for quite some time."

For a while Lisl kept her clear eyes on the hunting murals. Then she said: "Will, I want you to give a talk at a trade-union meeting early in January. Yes, you! All non-Nazi groups must band together, just like our small students' league. Pueschel and Duester aren't as down and out as those begging in the streets, because they're in the know. They know Hitler has been out and back in a hundred times. They're biding their time. You must make the old trade-union people see the danger which they like to think has passed. Do I sound like a professional Cassandra, Willy?"

"Don't forget, Cassandra was right," Willy sighed. "I give in. Let me have all the material. I must rehearse. After all, Lisl, I'm not a worker, just a frivolous entertainer. If I remember correctly, the old fighters for better wages, hours, and working conditions always were such inveterate realists that they never guessed what would happen two months later."

275

19. THE LAST DAYS OF 1932 AND THE FIRST months of 1933 carried Willy along at an ever-increasing speed. He didn't attend many courses at the university, because his work for the Free Students took up as much time as had his work for The Porcupine.

The events in Old Town had endowed Arlène and him with a certain ambiguous fame. In Hillden's seminar complete strangers came up to him to assure him how sorry they were he had had to stop; on the other hand, Professor Naumann was said to have made some rather acid remarks about young people who thought they must attend a university while they really belonged in a circus. Repeatedly President von Rhyn invited Arlène and him for a bit of lunch in his office, but he avoided talking politics and instead told them entertaining anecdotes of his stay as ambassador in Russia in the days after World War I. Willy noticed that Von Rhyn was writing several important-looking letters by hand instead of calling his secretary—apparently he had been warned. Lisl suspected the girl had been planted by the N.A.S.T.U.

Whenever there was a mountain of work to do, Willy managed to cast aside the worries, to forget the blows he had received. The hectic preparations for The Porcupine had been good medicine to get over Hannsberg—although his many sleepless nights warned him the wound hadn't closed. Now, when day broke, he managed to push aside the memory of The Porcupine's defeat by busying himself with the work for the Free Students. He wrote pamphlets, sent reminders of membership dues, distributed leaflets in the university. Professor Schatter was exceedingly angry when he discovered them in the sacred precincts of the Germanic seminar, but neither he nor Friedelgunde Fischer ever caught Willy.

Since she was French, Arlène couldn't become a member, but she stood by Willy, as always. She virtually lived with the Halders, and sometimes, during one of their cheerless dinners, Theodor asked her advice about some practical matter, exactly as he had always asked Melanie. Since Melanie's illness, Father had given up

276

all political activity. He stayed at the hospital until the nurse made him leave. He seemed to carry a burden too heavy for him, and he hardly noticed what went on around him. Long before Dr. Stein admitted it, Willy had guessed that Melanie's illness had spread to her throat. They had to increase her morphine ration week by week.

Melanie had asked Willy, pointedly and expressly, to go ahead with his work for Lisl. Although her voice now sounded perpetually hoarse, as if she had bronchitis, her mind worked perfectly, and sometimes it seemed to grasp things faster than when she was well. She asked him to tell her about his speech for the trade unions at which Willy was to represent the Free Students.

So, since it seemed to please her, Willy rehearsed his speech before her. Then, about a week after New Year's, he found himself seated on the dais of the Hippodrome, together with representatives of every union in South Germany, no matter whether they belonged to the Social Democrats, the Communists, the Center, the State party or none at all. An immense crowd overflowed the hall: mostly respectable-looking, middle-aged people. It occurred to Willy how all mass meetings invariably carried an element of deception: they managed to give the participants a feeling of being much stronger than they really were. Now, looking over the black, red, and gold flags, the militant banners of the Iron Front whose strapping uniformed young men policed the hall incessantly, Willy couldn't help thinking that it appeared as if the trade unions still held the powerful position they had enjoyed five years ago. It was the wrong setting for the play, he said to himself, cursing his habit of seeing everything in stage terms.

The union leaders on the dais, conscientious and often pedantic men, with a tendency to refer constantly to the glorious past, read their prepared papers as if they were scientists reluctantly explaining new discoveries to a lay audience. Often an unfortunate absence of vigor condemned what they said to an early death. Proudly many of them recounted the strength of their organization, their membership, their funds. A common front against Hitler was good, they asserted, but the main thing was to keep the union organization intact, and to avoid hasty decisions. The economic crisis which, Willy knew, had cost them thousands of paying members, was bound soon to make room for prosperity, according to scientific economics. . . .

While Willy listened to them, the material Lisl and he had gathered seemed to turn sour. They had prepared a historical survey of the Fuehrer's party, from Beerhalle Putsch up to now, with figures and charts. Figures? Charts? A few minutes before he was due to step forward a million ideas raced through Willy's head:

277

Friedrich von Erb, in Hildesheim, telling about the insane slowly pushing out the sane and putting them away; the reformatory boys, the Black Reichswehr fugitives on the road; the unemployed on the cold corners of Old Town and in Little Venice. . . .

Willy heard someone call his name. The chairman introduced him to the audience as a member of the Free Students, an "inter-party group combining all the progressive elements." To Willy's alarm he also credited him with having been that famous local character, Dopey Heiner. When Willy stepped forward he heard the audience chuckle: they expected him to be funny.

He disappointed them. Contrary to the custom of many of the Free Students, he hadn't dressed like a worker: he knew when he couldn't fill a part. Slowly he put down the prepared script and looked over the rows.

He told them about his trip to Hannsberg, about the desperate young boys on the road, about the farmers, Herder and Schmitt and Mueller, and how they had turned to the new religion. What he told them was absolutely personal, unorthodox, unlike the usual pattern of trade union speeches. Yet after a while he felt he had them in his grip. Their upturned faces had surrendered to him. Perhaps it was theater, but he didn't care. The students were a small part, he admitted, the Free Students even a smaller part of the part. But they had started something new, something above parties. They all had to work together, because only unity of all, the Social Democrats and the Center, the Communists and the trade unions, the undecided and the strong, could prevent the reign of the ruth-less, the violent, the inhuman. Yes, he admitted, the Hitler Youth Center on Kaiser Strasse had been closed; yes, the *Observer* was al-most bankrupt. But this was deceptive.

He ended on this warning note: if they failed to create a new unity they might perish.

As the applause rushed up to him and the chairman made him come forward again and again, he knew he had moved them. Mak-ing a speech for a mass audience, Willy thought, was like being on the stage under F. P. Busch's direction. The suspicion pierced his mind they might have taken his speech as a performance. The resolution of the "immediate founding of a united front of all groups opposed to the criminal violence of the Hitler party" seemed to belie this. Perhaps, after all, he had done some good.

As he walked out into the chilly January wind, he knew one thing: he hadn't planned to paint so ominous a picture of storm and defeat. It had come from his inmost depths, somewhere where he stored these things, and only now, after he had said them aloud before thousands, did he realize he had told them nothing but his own hidden fears.

278

When he reached home, there was a light burning in the living room: Arlène and Ilona—whom Willy hadn't seen for months—were waiting up for him with something which Willy recognized as the kind of hot chocolate Mrs. Goldschmidt used to serve. M. Delacroix, he was informed, had returned from his trip to Paris. The jewels had reached Robbi, the commission had been paid, and Hannah had taught Arlène how to make her special chocolate.

"I'd rather have wine," Willy said as they settled in the kitchen. "I'm exhausted."

After he had given a description of the meeting, Arlène pulled out a note.

"Monsieur Delacroix had news for me and for you, too, Will." She handed him the note. Camille Ronay was inviting Willy to stay at her house for the Easter vacation.

"I'm making another film in two languages and if you're all my daughter writes me you are, perhaps there'll be a part for a young man like you," Camille Ronay wrote in a fine, firm handwriting.

"Don't tell me you must work for the Free Students," Arlène cried before he could open his mouth, and Ilona remarked: "I'm going to study in Paris next term, Willy."

Willy had to laugh at the obvious alliance of the two. It reminded him of the traditional female conspiracies in operas: Arlène (contralto) and Ilona (soprano) persuading him to go to Paris. Ilona then told him it would take ages to get a passport, and he'd better start soon.

The next morning he went to the Central Police Office on Goethe Park, opposite his old school. Its chief, Dr. Puttkammer, after a call from Theodor, had referred his request to his assistant, Dr. Hassler, who appeared to be the result of a marriage between a lawbook and a goat. Also, Willy recognized him as one of the people who used to stand around with Gerhard Pueschel under the big clock at the university. If Dr. Hassler recognized him, too, he didn't bat an eyelash. He kept Willy waiting in the dingy anteroom of the huge drafty building, he found fault with the passport picture Willy had brought along, he wasn't satisfied with this and that, and it became obvious that he wanted to prevent Willy from getting the passport.

For a subaltern to act against the wishes of his superior was unusual in any German official institution and while Dr. Hassler requested a triplicate of Willy's university matriculation card, it occurred to Willy that he was probably involved in a feud between aggressive Dr. Hassler, in private life a storm trooper, and old, benevolent Dr. Puttkammer, in charge of passports since 1925 and a Social Democrat.

"I've been invited by Madame Camille Ronay, the famous French actress, to make a picture in Paris," Willy lied after he had discovered the photos of several movie celebrities on Dr. Hassler's wall. "Didn't Gerhard Pueschel tell you?" He showed Dr. Hassler the latter part of Camille Ronay's letter which, by a lucky accident, he had kept in his wallet.

Dr. Hassler's cold eyes flickered. He took Camille Ronay's note and studied it. His fingers were loath to part with it.

"Camille Ronay? The actress who made *Le Grand Jeu?*" he asked "Can you get me an autographed photo of her?"

Willy was taken aback by Dr. Hassler's frank request. In the old days, Frankfurt officials couldn't be bribed, neither with money nor gifts. Dr. Hassler was asking for a collector's item—one autographed picture of Camille Ronay was probably worth a good many autographed photos of German UFA stars. It was a good thing he hadn't said anything; suddenly Dr. Hassler whispered, "Come into my office." Willy followed him through long, echoing corridors into a small room filled with file cabinets.

Dr. Hassler, his eyes animated by an unbecoming fire, showed Willy album after album of film-star pictures, all autographed: German, Austrian, American, Swedish, Danish, French women, smiling brightly and unnaturally. While Willy looked them over, Dr. Hassler began putting stamps into a passport blank. Without interrupting his inspection of the collection, Willy handed him his passport photo.

"You're a friend of Gerhard Pueschel?" Dr. Hassler asked. Now that Hassler had given himself away, Willy felt on safe ground.

"Nice collection you've got," he remarked. "Not quite complete, though. Gerhard and I have known each other for years—about ten years to be correct."

"I haven't seen Gerhard for quite some time. He's in another department," Dr. Hassler remarked, fingering rubber stamps. Willy remained motionless. Did old Puttkammer know that his second in command was a storm trooper?

Dr. Hassler held a passport in his hand. "We can make it valid for three or for five years. It costs a bit more for five."

"Make it five years," Willy said. He didn't know why, but something made him do it. "I'll send you a photo of Madame Ronay, Doctor. Autographed. I'll be staying at her house, in case you have some more requests."

"Every night I look over my little harem," Dr. Hassler murmured, taking the money Willy handed him. "Every night. They really come to life, you know. Much better than the real women. . . ." He looked out on Goethe Park where some little boys were throwing snowballs at one another. "One of the few missing is Ronay. Mail it to me, soon."

"First thing," Willy said. The passport lay on the green baize-topped office desk. All at once it had become a thing of overwhelming importance.

"Here's my address in Paris." Willy copied it from the letter, then handed it to Dr. Hassler, who gave him his passport. It was brown, new, and imposing-looking. With an abundance of stamps and officious-looking flourishes, it certified that this was Willy Halder, born in Frankfurt-on-Main.

"Perhaps Gerhard and you can come over to my place and look over my entire collection," Dr. Hassler remarked as Willy rose. "I have a unique gathering of beautiful women there." His palm was moist as he shook Willy's hand, and he looked as if he had fever. Willy thanked him and said it would be a pleasure to look the girls over.

He was tempted to run through the Police Building—the long corridors always seemed to extend an invitation to shatter their stony peace with loud, jarring footsteps, but he kept his pace and walked away without looking back.

Goethe Park, wrapped in snow, presented itself chaste and cold. The shed behind which Pueschel once had beaten Richter still stood there, though a little dilapidated, and he passed the bench where Franz Duester had taken him when Willy's nose wouldn't stop bleeding. His old school building seemed almost cheerful in the sharp winter sunlight. For a moment Willy was tempted to walk in and sit down in one of the classes. Silly, of course—nobody would know him except perhaps Professor Lattau.

He turned toward Bockenheim. He'd surprise Lisl at the Free Students' headquarters where she was surely mimeographing and invite her for lunch at a good, bourgeois restaurant.

The elections, toward the middle of January, in the tiny state of Lippe-Detmold showed the Hitler party again on the increase—they gained about 17 per cent, and this helped the "Member Committee" of the Free Students in their recruiting campaign. Several liberal Catholic student fraternities of Frankfurt University announced they were willing to discuss a merger, and Lisl was overjoyed.

The radical group, led by Herb Simrock and his buxom and usually quiet girl friend, Paula Graber, wanted to "put conditions to them" before even discussing their coming to the meeting. It took all of Lisl's authority and Willy's maneuvering to make them accept the possibility of a large Catholic group joining them. They kept muttering about "religion as an opiate" and confessed to what Paulus Hillden called an old-fashioned materialism, 1870 vintage.

Finally the meeting was arranged. Lisl welcomed the visiting fraternities, led by Willy's old colleague, Wolfgang Brosig, in the back room of The Peacock. Willy couldn't help admiring her. For once Lisl had not put on her usual severe black dress, but an elegant brown one, softened by a huge lace bertha which gave her a decidedly aristocratic look—all to the better, Willy decided.

After Lisl had explained the purpose of the Free Students, and of this meeting, Wolfgang Brosig announced that he and his friends would retire to another place to discuss the question of a merger. They left, only to reappear in a short while. Then Wolfgang said:

"We young Catholic students know that the differences between us are as big as ever. But essentially we take the same stand toward human affairs as you do. Surely the time has come to stress what we have in common instead of what divides us. We're ready to join you under the condition that we can remain a separate unit."

While he spoke, Willy had noticed Herb Simrock passing a paper among his close adherents. Willy was just ready to rise and move they unconditionally accept their guests' offer, when his eye caught Lisl's. Herb had put the note before her. Her face was white and tense and she stared at Herbert, whose head was still bandaged—he had been wounded in one of the many fights between the N.A.S.T.U. and the Communist students that had recently started outside the university. Herbert avoided her eyes and kept his head down. Arlène who, as a guest of honor, sat next to Lisl, rose slowly.

"*Mes amis,*" Arlène began, and then catching herself, continued in her singing, overprecise German, "I'm only a guest here. I should refrain from mingling in your affairs. But I must speak now. I was so happy to see that tonight a step was made toward further unity. Herbert Simrock, do you insist in having your motion submitted?"

"I insist," said Herbert without looking up. He resembled a man whose most secret obscenity had suddenly been exposed.

A flurry ran through the hall. It subsided to a deadly quiet, however, when Lisl rose and in a monotonous voice read: " 'We, the undersigned members of the Free Students' League, demand that our organization declare itself in complete agreement with the pronouncement of the German Communist party that Germany is still in the throes of interest slavery; that the capitalist world is still forcing undue reparations on her. Neither the cabinet of barons under General von Schleicher nor the Social Fascists who held our land in bondage for so long have done anything to remedy

282

this. Only a real revolution, led by Germany's proletarian forces, can free our country.' There follow the signatures of thirteen of our members, headed by Herbert Simrock."

Lisl put the paper down. For a second nobody moved. Then Willy, furious, jumped up and turned on Herbert.

"This is precisely what the super-Nazi Alfred Rosenberg submitted to the Foreign Affairs Committee yesterday. And the K. P., together with the National Socialists, passed it. The people who attacked and wounded you voted with your party. Don't you see through it? Must you play their game here?"

"That's a lie!" shouted Herbert's girl friend Paula, and from then on there arose such shouting and name-calling that it took Lisl an immeasurably long time to bring the meeting to order.

Finally Wolfgang Brosig made himself heard. "We apparently came at the wrong moment. I'm afraid I must retract our offer of joining you."

He rose and left, followed by his group. He closed the door softly, bowing to Lisl. Willy would never forget the expression of bewildered dismay on her face.

"Congratulations, Herbert," Willy said loudly. "Nice work."

"I protest!" Herbert Simrock jumped up. "This facetious tone is an insult. I demand that Willy be called to order. I demand a vote on our petition."

"I protest against the use of the term 'Social Fascist,' " Willy declared, equally loudly, when Lisl had given him the floor. "Herbert, you're much too intelligent to fall for clichés like these. You know damn well that the Social Democrats and the other liberal people are no Fascists, you know it as well as I."

He pointed to his old friend Ferdy Rohn. "Ferdy has worked in the Iron Front against the swastika boys longer than many people in his room. And you call him a Fascist?"

"Rather Hitler than the Social Fascists," cried Paula furiously. "They're throwing dust in the workers' eyes, making them impotent for the day of the real revolution."

"Dust never made anyone impotent," Willy remarked in his loud "aside" stage whisper—one of Mathilda's oldest tricks.

Paula Graber turned on him, blazing. "You little Fascist," she said, red in the face, groping for words. "You bourgeois actor, you . . ."

"Quiet!" Lisl pounded the gavel. Herb Simrock pulled Paula away from Willy. "Quiet! Herbert, will you change the word 'Social Fascist' in your petition?"

All eyes turned to Herbert. There was still a red spot on the bandage around his head. He kept his eyes down. He waited a long while, during which time seemed to stand still and Willy, for the hundredth time, counted the hounds in the hunting murals on the wall.

"I can't," he finally said.

Lisl again pounded the gavel. "Will those in favor of Herbert's petition please raise their hands?"

Willy counted quickly. Not only the K. P. people but several others who belonged to no party had raised their hands. It was about even, as the second check—those against it—proved.

"Under the circumstances we can't remain with this organization any longer," Herbert announced. "We're going to establish our own Red Fighters' Group. Those who are with me, follow me."

He walked out, looking at no one, while Paula threw Willy a last angry look. A great many followed them. Paula slammed the door.

Lisl stepped down from the rostrum. She suddenly seemed listless, as if all the courage had flown out of her.

"They split us," she said. "Just when we were ready to have a united front." She seemed to sway, and groped for the back of her chair.

"Herb didn't want to do it, I think," Willy said, while Arlène and he made Lisl sit down. "He didn't even believe in it himself. Someone had ordered him to do it."

"The fools," Arlène said. "It's worse than the Prussian Army. Obey, obey, obey. Even if it kills them."

Willy had yet to learn that while the most extraordinary changes are taking place people can go on eating, drinking, sleeping, as though nothing was happening. At the university both the N.A.S.T.U. and the Red Fighters had increased and, as Von Rhyn confided to Willy, they were provoking each other in the most shameless manner. Since Von Rhyn's order to eject and black-list any student found involved in a fight remained valid, outwardly classes, courses, seminars went on as usual. Toward the end of January, however, the N.A.S.T.U. demanded that the order be withdrawn. Professor Naumann and many others supported their motion, openly confessing their admiration for the intellectual storm troopers' "courage." Von Rhyn, backed by Paulus Hillden, remained firm.

The split of the Free Students' League was discussed widely by the press and Willy feared it might upset Melanie who, during all these weeks, insisted on having the *Frankfurter Zeitung,* all three editions.

He needn't have worried. One night, toward the end of January, Arlène and Willy were sitting in the living room, waiting for Theodor, when Nurse Brenner's call came through. Mother, through her, asked Willy to bring a small brocade-covered box up to the hospital. It contained old letters, and Melanie had been clamoring for it all morning. Nurse Brenner informed Willy she considered it her duty to tell him that Melanie hadn't been able to read for some weeks. Her eyes simply wouldn't function. Nurse Brenner couldn't imagine why she wanted the letters which she said were in the box. Tomorrow was "big-treatment" day, so Willy should bring the box toward evening.

The ambiguous hospital language left Willy extremely uneasy. Only after the phone had gone dead with a jarring click did Willy suspect Nurse Brenner had meant much more than she said. He went back into the living room and began rummaging through Melanie's sewing cabinet, spilling things on the floor.

"What happened, Will?" Arlène hurried toward him and put a hand on his arm. Willy told her. His hands were so unsteady he wouldn't have found the box if it had lain before him.

Arlène kissed his hair. "You mustn't let Theodor see what you know," she said.

Willy didn't answer. He had turned away to stare out into the dark, empty garden.

"She has suffered a great deal these last weeks," Arlène said softly. "The moment the morphine wears off, the pain comes back. . . . There's no brocade-covered box in the cabinet, Willy. We must search elsewhere."

Big Anna remembered the box: Mrs. Halder kept her family letters in it, and she had sometimes gone over them when she was alone. But Anna had no idea where it was, and why didn't Dr. Halder come home tonight?

"He might stay at the hospital, Anna," Arlène explained. Anna stared back, holding a pan in her enormous crinkly hand. Then she put down the pan and said in a rough voice: "Tell the doctor I won't leave him. No matter what happens." She turned, her enormous face twitching, and went back to polishing the pan.

As the night wore on, Arlène and Willy searched the entire apartment for the brocade box. It had become very quiet—the streetcars on Reuter Weg stopped running at two. Dr. Halder didn't come home. Twice they repeated their systematic investigation of each room.

It was almost morning when Arlène discovered it. Melanie had hidden the box in the laundry closet in the hall, under a heap of old hand-embroidered guest towels belonging to the Pallavant family. The box was very old and had no lock. It contained letters, turned dry and yellow, a few pressed flowers, a white silk evening glove which exuded a faint perfume of lavender, several fans, and some old photos of Melanie as a young girl.

285

They closed it without saying a word. It was Melanie's youth, her long-forgotten past locked away here, and perhaps she wanted to smell once more the lavender and touch the soft silk of the glove.

Arlène insisted Willy go to bed. She went to fetch a blanket for herself, and when she came back, Willy had fallen asleep. Arlène took the blanket and stretched out on the sofa in the living room. Before she dozed off, the apartment door opened. It was almost six and a sullen winter morning, pregnant with snow, threatened outside the window. Dr. Halder came into the living room and sat down next to her.

"She kept asking for the old box. I didn't even know she had one. She's unconscious now. We gave her a double dose."

"We found the box, Doctor," Arlène whispered. Theodor had aged ten years. His good square face seemed shrunken.

"Her mind is perfectly clear the moment the drug wears off," he said. "But she has seen too much of Hannah Goldschmidt. I couldn't tell her that Arthur thinks of putting Hannah in a sanatorium. Can you imagine, she planned to sell the house on Hoch Strasse, which is in her name, behind his back?"

The telephone rang, shockingly loud at this quiet hour. Dr. Halder and Arlène stared at each other. Then Theodor rushed into his studio, leaving the door open. Arlène heard him say: "I don't believe it," and "Are you sure?" before he hung up. He didn't move then. He stood there, his hand still on the receiver. The daylight had invaded his studio and played over the metal surfaces of the medical apparatus.

"It wasn't the hospital," Theodor said. "It was a friend from S. P. headquarters in Berlin. Hitler is going to see Hindenburg today. Von Papen is back. They say Hitler and he are going to form a government of National Concentration. And Hitler is going to be Chancellor of the Reich."

When Willy woke up at three o'clock the apartment was full of familiar noises—the running of water in Father's office, the opening and closing of doors, the low murmur of patients in the waiting room. Then he saw Arlène in the chair next to his bed. In a second he was wide awake.

"It has come, Will," Arlène said. "Hitler is going to be Reichs Chancellor. I phoned Ferdy—he's heard it, too, though it won't be official until five. Hugenberg, Von Papen, and the other old-timers are supposed to keep him in check. Goering will be Prussian Minister of the Interior."

For a second Willy remained motionless. He stared at the map over his bed with its familiar outlines of Europe's countries, its brownish-colored mountains, its fertile green plains. He waited for

286

the shock to overtake him but it didn't. He knew, then, that somewhere deep within himself he had almost waited for the inevitable to come to pass—had known that the fanatics and the farmers, the hopeless and embittered would rise one day. Hadn't he himself warned the meeting of those good-natured trade-union people? If someone had told him three months ago that the evil conjuror would rise to power, legitimately, as leader of the biggest party, he might have laughed. Yet his laugh would have been a lie. Ever since Hal's death, Willy had prepared himself for the worst.

"Ferdy thinks they won't last," Arlène said. "And Herb Simrock and his Communist students aren't afraid at all. Lisl, whom I phoned, too, told me Herb considers Hitler's advent a blessing. He's sure the Communists will take over within four weeks. And if the going gets tough, the K. P. is prepared to go underground."

There was a knock at the door. Big Anna entered with a cup of coffee and a buttered roll.

"Go up to the hospital now," Anna said. "That nurse just called. Said something about the box again."

She turned to Arlène. "Mrs. Halder wants you too. The doctor will be up later—many patients today." Anna's voice faltered, and for the first time Willy saw that she was an old, tired woman.

Nurse Brenner left Melanie's room when Arlène and Willy came in. The walls appeared whiter than ever, and the smell of antiseptic overpowered the sweetness of the flowers which stood in huge vases on the floor. An early, subdued evening made its way into the room.

"No light, children," Melanie whispered. Her voice sounded so faint that Willy and Arlène had to go very near the bed to understand her. Melanie's face was the color of old parchment, and it was out of shape. Only her eyes hadn't changed. Apparently she couldn't see very well: she just fingered the letters in the box. The photos, the pressed flowers, the glove had fallen on the bedspread. She held one blue note close to her eyes, then to her nose.

A faint hint of a smile drifted over her face.

"Still smelling of lilacs. Cousin Vera used strong scents. Will you read this to me, Willy?"

Slowly Willy read the short note. Cousin Vera, married to Gerhard Burckhardt, banker, of Basel, Switzerland, told Melanie of the birth of her child and invited her to stay at their house whenever she happened to pass through Basel. The town, she wrote, was old and friendly, very much like Frankfurt.

Melanie put back the flower, the fan, the silk glove. She started to say something, she even stretched out her arm to take back the letters, but suddenly fell back onto the pillow. The pain had overtaken her again. Willy went to the bed and took her hand. It was hot and rough, and it wasn't Melanie's hand—the shape of the fingers had changed.

He swallowed hard. He mustn't cry. He must play, act, pretend that he believed Melanie would be well soon.

Melanie opened her eyes. "I know what happened today. They have a radio next door . . ."

She stopped and put her hand to her throat. She seemed to collect all her strength, all her power, for her voice was perfectly clear when she spoke again, and in her eyes was a faint echo of the old Melanie who had gone and defied Lattau.

"I want you to go to Cousin Vera, Willy. Soon. Next week. You can study in Basel and later in Paris. Theodor won't leave, I know. Arlène, promise to make my son leave."

"I promise," Arlène said in a small voice. She stood behind Willy, who could no longer hold back his sobs.

"Take the box away," Melanie whispered. In vain she tried to lift the box. Her hands wouldn't obey her any more.

"Willy," Melanie said, "look at me. Promise to go away soon."

Her voice faded. Willy lifted his head. As through a veil, he saw into the enormousness of her dark eyes whose pupils were dilated. As so often before, they gave him a message he understood.

"Let me sleep now," Melanie said. Willy kissed her forehead, his eyes full of tears. Arlène walked him out, the brocade box under her arm. Melanie appeared almost contented in the dim light. Only her hands lying on the white cover seemed to belong to another person.

"I'll give her another injection right away," Nurse Brenner said outside. "You two go into the waiting room. Dr. Halder will be here shortly."

For a long time Willy and Arlène sat without speaking in the hospital waiting room with its impersonal cane chairs, its garish pictures suggesting leftovers from a cheap auction. Then they heard a commotion and went to the window.

It was a rhythmical noise, like the faraway roar of the surf. It came nearer and nearer, a hundred, a thousand feet stepping in the same beat. A thousand voices were singing—yes, it was the old Wandervogel melody Willy knew so well—but they had given it new words. The procession was visible now as it approached the hospital: endless ranks of uniformed youths bearing lighted torches, marching, drunk with success. They shouted of the coming glory of a new Reich, a new leader. They'd die for their leader, they sang, and in between they yelled: "Kill the Jews," and "Down with the Republic." Then, in youthful exuberance, they smashed the windows of the houses near the hospital.

288

To Willy looking out at the parade it seemed as if they had mobilized all of Frankfurt's young men. It was the hour of triumph for the storm troopers, and their marching was that of conquerors, unafraid and exultant.

When had he last seen such torches? At the Bergstrasse, when Hellmuth Handler's two patriotic groups had marched toward the fire to join and overrun the Wandervogel. Perhaps some of them were among the paraders, singing themselves hoarse, all united now, the youth movement and the tramps, the derelicts and the scarred fraternity brothers, the disinherited and the boys from the good families.

They finally passed by. The torches were still visible long after the raw voices, the stamping, the clatter of heavy boots had died away into the night.

Willy turned back to the waiting room. In the yellow light of a lonely bulb stood Theodor and Nurse Brenner.

"No, she didn't hear them," Theodor said. "Her heart stopped a while ago. God spared her this."

20. AFTER THE FUNERAL WILLY AND Arlène took Theodor to Mrs. Goldschmidt who had asked them to stay with her as long as they pleased. Right now Theodor couldn't face 66 Reuter Weg, with the patients streaming in despite the notice on the door. At Hannah's house they also were sure to avoid Cousin Hans Lange in his tailor-made storm trooper uniform and Aunt Helen's solicitous hackneyed consolations.

The sat in the large wood-paneled living room—Willy remembered when he had first sat there and admired the Goldschmidt family silver. Theodor obediently drank the sweet chocolate Hannah had prepared, and he answered Arthur's questions, although Willy knew Theodor was really still at the cemetery. Father, more than anyone, must have known how she had suffered, how the agonies had increased day by day, and that death was the only escape. Yet this didn't alter the fact that Father had to face a lonesome life, after all these years of being a part of two.

He bore it bravely, Willy thought. Perhaps he had seen death so often, perhaps it was simply will power, but after a while he began arguing with Arthur quite rationally.

To Willy's surprise, Hannah Goldschmidt, although genuinely grieved about Melanie, had lost all traces of her previous state of bereavement. She actually seemed to have undergone a profound transformation, as if she had won a fight but left all signs of it behind her. Arthur, by contrast, was irritable and, for the first time, his phlegmatic joviality was wearing thin.

While he listened to Theodor and Arthur debating what would happen now that President Hindenburg and Chancellor Hitler had signed a "decree for the defense of the nation," forbidding all political gatherings, reserving the government's right to suppress publications endangering public security, Willy began to understand what had happened to Hannah. She was no longer the half-crazed eccentric who foresaw evil in the brightest sunshine. Nobody would dream of sending her away to a neurologist for treatments. She simply had been proven right. She had done well

290

to smuggle out the jewelry for Robbi. Her lack of "common sense," of balance, had turned out to be a blessing, now that the king of the derelicts, the great swastika dervish, had become Chancellor. Arthur, the farsighted shrewd businessman, the sober, solid husband, worried about his wife's senseless fears, had been wrong.

Or had he? He was just explaining to Theodor that last night, at the meeting of the jewelers' club, all his friends had been in agreement.

"Things won't change too much," Arthur said, but there was an undertone as if he were pleading with Theodor to, please, back him up. "Our club has only a few Jewish members. We've met every Thursday for over twenty years. My friends know Frankfurt, they know what's being played in Germany. The conservative, experienced businessmen, Hugenberg, Von Neurath, and Von Papen will keep a leash on Hitler. Won't they?"

"I hope so," Theodor answered. "The *Red Flag* has been suppressed, and I'm afraid the same will happen to the *People's Voice*. I haven't been very active these last months. In any case I promised my wife to send Willy to her cousin Vera in Basel for at least one term at the university."

"Now, why should a young fellow like Willy . . ." Arthur began, but Hannah interrupted him.

"Melanie wanted it, Arthur. That's enough."

She turned to Theodor. "I think you should know what happened here."

Arthur made a motion to stop her, but Hannah ignored him. "Two days ago we received a letter from a real-estate firm. It contained an offer for our house. Someone is interested in acquiring it. The firm advised us to think it over very thoroughly. The buyer offered 15,000 marks for it. The real-estate firm of Erwin Duester & Co. was acting for Deputy Sprenger. He wants to live here."

"The house is worth over 100,000," Arthur Goldschmidt said angrily. "To offer 15,000 is plain impertinence. After all, business is business."

"I want to sell the house, Arthur," Hannah said, "and I want Dr. Halder to know it. I'm going to bargain with Erwin Duester, but I can't hold off Deputy Sprenger for long. Not now."

"My God," Willy said. "Erwin Duester! His brother Franz went to school with Robbi and me. If you want me to talk to him . . ."

"No," said Hannah. "Stay away fom the Duesters. I can manage alone—and it wouldn't do any good."

She rose and smiled at Arlène and Willy. She appeared more serene than Willy had ever seen her and she had summoned up an intrepid air of resoluteness that was very much like that of Melanie's years ago.

"When is your term at the university over, Willy?" she asked.

"In about four weeks," Arlène answered. "But I'm certain we could get our papers before that. The professors always start signing the college books earlier."

"Can't you take your father to cousin Vera too?" Hannah asked. "For a vacation? You deserve one, Theodor. The change might do you good."

Theodor shook his white head. "I can't leave," he said. "I'm an old man—nothing's going to happen to me. And my patients need me."

Never would Willy forget the gathering of Theodor's party friends at the house some days later in February. They met in Theodor's office while Arlène and Willy sat in the adjoining living room, talking to Ilona who had come to say good-by.

February of 1933 was gray, cold, and aggressively wet. Ilona, in high boots and a fur cap, looked more Russian than ever. Her registration at the Ecole des Beaux Arts had been accepted, her trunks were shipped to Paris: she was ready. Willy hadn't seen her for a long while. When he tried to apologize, Ilona cut him short.

"I know you were working hard for the Free Students. I even heard about your speech at the trade-union meeting. Willy, I went to the cemetery in Cronberg several times. I didn't have the heart to ask you to go with me."

She paused. From the next room floated the excited voices of Frankfurt's Social-Democratic deputies. Apparently they were arguing heatedly. Willy could make out whole phrases.

"Let 'em stew in their own juice," someone declared. "The Hitler government is weak. Feet of clay." There were shouts and another voice came through: "What about the broken-up meetings? What about the Rhineland?"

Then it subsided. Only a dull rumbling of male voices remained, like background music in a radio sketch.

"I want to see you two soon," Ilona went on. "In Paris. Yes, Willy, you, too, must show up. I have three uncles and innumerable cousins there."

"Mother and Father have already invited him," Arlène said. "We're all set for Switzerland, for one term at least. But we need the green students' books with the professors' signatures. Otherwise, Basel University won't give us credit for the previous terms."

"Well, hurry up," Ilona remarked. "I might as well tell you the rumor going around Toni's. Kurt Marland has furnished the N.A.S.T.U. with a list of all Free Students, past and present. You're among them, Will."

292

"I believe it," said Arlène quickly. She sounded worried. It showed only an instant, then her face relaxed and, smiling, she turned to Ilona.

"Look up Father in Paris, and give him my love. I so wanted to get home Christmas, but it will be Easter now—I hope. Do you have our Paris address?"

"Yes. And I have Robbi Goldschmidt's address too." Ilona took two glittering earrings out of her purse. "How do you like these?"

"Goodness," Arlène cried. "Real diamonds. Set in platinum. Ilona, what does it mean?"

"Hannah Goldschmidt gave them to me, to wear them on my trip to France. I'm playing mailman to Robbi. Of course many people still think Hannah's out of her mind putting her fortune into earrings worth more than 10,000 marks and sending them to Paris. I think she's smart. They're worth a lot anywhere. Will, I forgot to ask you, did you get your passport?"

"I got it all right," Willy said. He had caught a glance between Arlène and Ilona. "Dr. Hassler's interest in an autographed portrait of Camille Ronay finally did it. What's all this?"

"A good thing you have it!" Ilona said. "Things have changed. Your father's friend Puttkammer was thrown out. Hassler is the absolute boss. Yesterday Lisl Farner went there for her passport. She wants to visit friends in Holland. Hassler stalled her. She's afraid she won't get it."

"You knew about my being on Kurt's list, Arlène, didn't you?" Willy asked. "That's why I got invited to Paris all of a sudden."

"Yes," Arlène admitted. "I'm glad I thought of it. I don't care whether you're angry at me." She paused for a moment. Willy went over to her and put his hand on her head. He loved the touch of her hair. It was like silken fur, he had told her once, or, better, like something between raw silk and the cool touch of water on a hot day.

"I'm grateful to you, chérie," he said. "You were very clever. And after Hassler handed me the small brown booklet, it suddenly seemed very important." He turned to Ilona: "What can we do for Lisl?"

"Nothing," Ilona said calmly. "She knows she's on the black list. My father was on the black list too. Years ago. In 1917. He managed. Lisl will manage."

Ilona rose, put on her boots and her fur cap. Then she took Willy's hands.

"Yesterday I went out to Cronberg to say good-by to Mrs. Petersen. You haven't been there once. She has made Hal's room into a sort of shrine. All his drawings, even the childish ones made when he was ten or eleven, are hanging on the walls. In the center is a picture of your father, and another of your whole class. There is one sketch of you, alone, sitting near a river. You must have been fifteen or sixteen. Hal had written, 'Skinny Willy' underneath. Mrs. Petersen said she understood why you never came out. Melanie had written her for you, you know that, a short time after Hannsberg."

"I never knew," Willy said. "I didn't know Mother had written. I couldn't face Cronberg then. I'm a complete egotist, Ilona, when it comes to such things. I never considered what it meant to you, either. All I could think of was what it did to me."

"It's over, Will," Ilona said. "And forgiven." Tears stood in her eyes and she made no attempt to hide them. "I'll never forget Hal. He was my first love. But one has to go on living. If you have time, go out to Cronberg and say good-by. And get your books, and get out quick." She kissed Willy and Arlène and went out.

She was swallowed by the crowd of deputies leaving at the same time. Willy heard her voice, among the deeper ones of the men, talking to Anna. He should have seen her to the door. But he couldn't face the crowd out there, and Ilona's good-by had been final.

He took Arlène's hand. At this moment Theodor opened the door. He smiled at Arlène, who was sitting in Melanie's chair.

"It's good to see you children," he said. "Where's Ilona going?"

"To Paris," Arlène answered.

"Maybe she has more good sense than these old men here tonight." Theodor remarked, sitting down. "They argued that the Hitler government must succumb to its own weakness. They proved it with figures, with statistics. Our trade unions, they say, are still the strongest organization in Germany. I say the trade union won't do a thing. In a way, most of the visitors argued like my brother-in-law Herbert or like Arthur Goldschmidt."

"And what are you going to do?" Arlène asked.

"I told you. Take care of those who need me," Theodor said, looking over her head into the garden. "I can't forsake them now."

The next day Goering deposed every police president in Prussia who wasn't a member of the Nationalists or his own party. A few days later the S. A. men were made "Special Constables," a sort of auxiliary police force. They wore a white ribbon on their brown shirt sleeve and were supposed to keep order.

In Frankfurt, at least, there was no order to be kept. The town was quiet—too quiet, as if waiting for something. The new constables, with time on their hands, began to sell Hitler post cards in the restaurants and cafés. Yet the people of Frankfurt went about their business almost as before. Therese Braun's father even sold clothes to the men in brown uniform—they didn't mind buying at his store at all, and Mr. Braun, so Therese said, was confident that business in 1933 would be better than ever.

A few days after the Red Student Fighters had been dissolved, Arlène and Willy met Herb Simrock in the university. He was almost radiant.

"They know how weak they are," he declared as they stood in one of the dark corridors. "I guarantee you: they'll be finished in six to eight weeks. And then the K. P. will take over Germany. Just wait. We're organized for the illegal struggle. The others aren't."

It sounded theatrical to Willy. He forgot about it, particularly since Arlène and he began the tedious task of collecting the necessary papers. Basel University, Cousin Vera had written, demanded innumerable documents, copies of official records, of the matriculation, endorsements, et cetera. The Swiss were very punctilious.

Within a short span Willy realized that Arlène was much more successful than he in collecting the required official documents. It had become quite apparent when he entered the registrar's office. The old man who used to sit there had disappeared. The student in charge was a N.A.S.T.U. member. As Willy looked into his steady blue eyes, he knew. He was too well known. He'd never get the documents. Therefore he didn't inquire about his matriculation copy, asked the N.A.S.T.U. student a meaningless question, and left quickly.

What saved him was the slowness of the N.A.S.T.U. machine, its red tape and pedantry. Also, they couldn't move properly as long as Von Rhyn was president, and, miraculously, he still was.

Arlène's charm apparently was working on almost everybody. She managed to get all of Willy's papers, and the only thing they needed were the signatures in the green students' book: these Willy had to present himself.

Officially, the professors were ready to sign their names starting February 26, Arlène reported. Those of Pfeiffer-Belli, Hillden, Von Rhyn, and some others were no problem. The problem was Naumann and Schatter, the representatives of the Germanic seminar.

Hanns Naumann had refused his signature to several members of the Free Students' League—now dissolved—saying they hadn't attended class regularly. Even if he couldn't get these two signatures, Willy had decided to go ahead anyhow. They had to register in Basel during March.

This was the week when the first rumors filtered through Frankfurt. On their way home people were attacked by unknown assailants; patients stopped visiting their Jewish doctors in daylight, sneaking in after dark; a gathering of high Catholic dignitaries had been broken up by the new auxiliary police, and several of the

Fathers had been severely injured. And near the Rebstock neighborhood the stormtroopers had taken over some old warehouses—for "certain disciplinary measures," Anna reported, and the people living near by thought they had seen trucks unloading their strange cargo in the dead of night.

Early on the morning of the twenty-sixth, Ferdy Rohn phoned Willy. Obviously he was speaking from a telephone booth. His voice sounded tense and muffled. He was leaving town. He didn't know when he'd be back. Willy gave him Cousin Vera's address in Basel. Ferdy didn't like the idea of Willy's going to the university to get the signatures. He suggested a trip, for his health's sake. Willy didn't understand. Only weeks later did Willy know what people meant by advising "health trips." He said good-by, vaguely uncomfortable about what Ferdy really wanted.

The same morning Arlène and he went to the university, which impressed them as unusually silent. They were just on time for Hanns Naumann's lecture on medieval poetry, delivered in his lackadaisical, elegant manner and full of allusions to the new knightly heroes. Afterward Naumann chatted in French with Arlène while signing his name—she had first put Willy's book before him and then, discovering her error, had to ask him to sign again. There was a long waiting line behind her but Arlene was unruffled.

Hanns Naumann looked up, his bored matinee-idol face smiling. "I noticed your little trick, of course. But to me it doesn't matter. I'm sure you're going to have splendid spring days in Paris."

So he assumed she was leaving. Or did he know? They had told only a few friends about their plans. Probably Naumann was just bluffing.

Arlène dashed after Willy to the Schatter seminar. She shoved his book toward him. Willy opened it: he had all the needed signatures except Schatter's.

This time they failed. Professor Ferdinand Schatter, in croaking notes, refused to sign his name in Willy's book. After all, Willy had not attended the seminar regularly. Willy was almost glad he hadn't. This last seminar again proved to be a well of boredom, and at least he had avoided Friedelgunde Fischer, who was now staring at Arlène and Willy as if to pierce them with her eyes. All the time she kept consulting her wrist watch and showed signs of increasing nervousness.

"Chienne folle," Arlène couldn't help murmuring as they rushed past her.

They stood outside the seminar. "Let's go get Paulus Hillden and take him to Von Rhyn's office for lunch," Arlène suggested. "He must have finished by now. Hurry!"

296

They were rushing toward the philosophical seminar when Arlène stopped. Willy had heard it, too: it sounded like a whistle.

Quickly Willy glanced out of a window. A considerable number of big trucks were gathering in front of the university door. All were painted brown and they dislodged a stream of storm troopers, both in black and brown uniforms, all armed. At the same time Willy heard footsteps tramping up the stairs. He knew those steps—from the night when The Porcupine had been invaded.

"Quick. Let's get Paulus," he shouted to Arlène, who was already on her way. They ripped open the door to the philosophical seminar—it was a joint enterprise for the highly advanced graduate students, given by Hillden, Von Rhyn, and Walden-Arditi.

Dr. Walden-Arditi was still speaking: "Therefore the essential paradox of existence can only be bridged in a leap by the paradoxically heroic."

He turned toward Arlène and Willy. "Will you please wait until we have concluded?" he said sharply.

The few students looked dumfounded. Kurt von Rhyn had risen, and Willy tried to signal to him but Dr. Walden-Arditi interfered.

"Professor Hillden still owes me an answer to that," he said.

In the small anteroom behind the seminar stood three storm troopers, almost hidden by the long curtain. Willy pretended not to have seen them.

"Hurry, Paulus," Arlène cried. *"La canaille!"*

But before anyone could move, Dr. Walden-Arditi rushed toward the back of the seminar. He was ready to throw open the door to the anteroom when Paulus Hillden tripped him. He plunged to the floor, spilling his keys. The three storm troopers in the anteroom couldn't open the door from the inside and were forced to make a detour. Kurt von Rhyn, dragging Hillden after him, rushed out, followed by Willy and Arlène. Dr. Walden-Arditi had risen and attempted once more to stop them but Willy pushed him back with a vengeance. By now the three storm troopers were running into the seminar.

"After them, there," cried Dr. Walden-Arditi, pointing toward the long hallway. The three began to run after the group. At the same time Willy heard ominous steps approaching from all sides.

"Your office," Willy shouted. He had suddenly remembered something.

Von Rhyn threw open the office of the president of Frankfurt University and locked it just in time. A moment later the three troopers were trying to break in the solid oak door. Willy and Hillden pushed the heavy desk against it. They were out of breath.

Cautiously Von Rhyn peeped out the window.

"Sentries everywhere," he said. "They prepared it like a major military operation."

Hillden sank into a chair. "The barbarians have invaded Rome," he said. "And Arditi is with them."

"He's been shifting for a long time," Von Rhyn said, pushing a heavy armchair against the desk which protected the door. "He introduced the heroic into his existentialist double-talk quite some time ago."

For a moment the knocking at the door ceased, but from the street there rose a dull noise.

They looked out. A battle was going on. The uniformed troopers were trying to force a group of students into a truck. Willy recognized Herb Simrock and some others of the Red Fighters' group. The storm troopers used clubs and brass knuckles. Herbert was bleeding.

Von Rhyn made a move as though to walk down and put an end to this. His face was twitching. Then the telephone rang. It was so unexpected that at first nobody stirred. Somehow, Willy had expected the telephone to be disconnected.

Then Von Rhyn lifted the receiver. A look, first of incredulity, then of anger crossed his face. He covered the receiver.

"The N.A.S.T.U. has occupied the university. This is their leader, Mr. Henkel. They want us to surrender. I should depose you, Paulus, as of today. Your philosophy is not in accordance with their new principles. There has been a denunciation."

The knocks against the door set in again. This time much louder.

Willy didn't hear what Von Rhyn said. He only saw him throw the phone back on the receiver.

"The door!" Willy pointed to the wall where the desk had stood. "The staircase to the boiler room. Where we stored the costumes."

"God, yes," Von Rhyn said. "My alcoholic predecessor. Come on, Paulus."

The hammering at the door grew more violent. From the street came the sharp shocking sound of gunshots. The telephone was ringing again as they stumbled down the staircase into the boiler room. In a corner Willy recognized the backdrop and the costumes they had used for the cabaret. It seemed as if it had happened centuries ago.

"This is preposterous!" Paulus Hillden stopped. "To hide in a cellar. You're the president, Kurt. They won't dare."

Von Rhyn shrugged his shoulders. "I was attaché in Moscow in 1917. I know the game. The N.A.S.T.U. wouldn't have moved without permission from higher quarters. Goering is head of our police."

"And the Prussian police was once Social Democratic," Hillden

298

said as they went toward the south end of the cellar. Arlène had taken his arm.

Von Rhyn stopped. "The German police will always obey the strong man on top."

"Listen!" Willy cried out. They heard more shots, a regular criss-cross fire. Through one of the small, high windows they saw two pairs of boots, dragging between them a pair of legs, limp in civilian trousers.

"Here's the big furnace," Von Rhyn said. Almost hidden by a heap of coal they could distinguish the outlines of a tiny side door.

"Where does this lead to?" Hillden asked.

"We're in Bockenheim. It's the south end of the university annex. I'm sure it's not guarded." Von Rhyn hesitated. "The president of Frankfurt University sneaking through a furnace door with his most famous professor of philosophy. It would be funny if it weren't so grisly."

He put his hand on Hillden's shoulder. "Don't go back to your office before you hear from me. I expect they'll make Naumann president before long. Naumann knows he needs my records, so they'll treat me gently. When do you have to answer the Hudson University people in New York?"

"Within two weeks," Paulus said. They had forgotten Willy and Arlène. In the dusty light of the boiler room, between ashes and coal and rubbish, they said good-by to their lifework and to each other. Paulus Hillden, the idealist who had devoted his life to showing youth that it couldn't effect a better society if it threw overboard the traditions of the Western world, and Kurt von Rhyn, the diplomat, who had almost achieved the impossible, and made Frankfurt a peaceful, progressive center of free learning in Germany.

"Send a wire while they'll still let you," Von Rhyn said. "And tell the people in New York you'll come."

There came a rumbling noise overhead, the distinct sound of footsteps rushing to and fro, of furniture moved.

"They've broken into your office," Arlène said. She took a shovel and began moving the coal away from the exit. The others, as if to make up for the lost minutes, pushed the coal aside with their feet. Willy's trousers got blackened.

"Thank God it's not locked," Von Rhyn said, moving the rotting little door. From farther away came the explosion of another bullet.

"They're shooting into the university windows," reported Willy, who had slipped out first. "But it seems all right here."

The little lane in Bockenheim on which the cellar door opened seemed almost obscenely unperturbed. They went out, unnoticed.

Kurt von Rhyn hailed two taxis and pushed Hillden in the first.

"You kids take the second. Call me tomorrow morning."

He hurried after Paulus into the cab and it disappeared in the drab Bockenheim streets—obviously Von Rhyn had told the driver to take a detour.

Arlène and Willy jumped in the second one. They asked the driver to go through the deserted Miquel Allee and from there past the I. G. Farben to Reuter Weg. Outside of the university, Frankfurt seemed serene and undisturbed. Willy had taken Arlène's hand. Now that it was over, his heart began to beat fast. This was the end of Frankfurt University. Never could he go back to it. They had killed it as they had killed The Porcupine. He wondered if Pueschel and Duester were among the invaders.

"And all the time I hung on to our student books." Arlène almost giggled. "Without even being aware of it."

"It's idiotic," Willy said. "Escaping through a hidden door. It wouldn't be believed on the stage, Arlène."

"Relax, Will," Arlène said. "You must get hold of yourself. I'm going to start packing this afternoon."

Improbably enough the early afternoon at home was in no way different from the many he had known before, with patients wheezing up the stairs, and Anna opening and closing the door. The waiting room was full, the patients' voices, like the sound of running water, endlessly rumbling through the house. About three o'clock the night edition of the *Frankfurter Zeitung* appeared, without a word of the happenings at the university.

Arlène wasted no time. Walden-Arditi had seen them, she said, and Willy had been their target before. They'd better get busy fast. They dragged two of Theodor's big trunks down from the attic, packed them in a hurry, and had an express mover call for them. Big Anna knew of the vacation in Switzerland and approved.

"The doctor should take a vacation too," she declared.

Willy wasn't certain whether she accepted the "vacation" fiction or not. Arlène insisted on going to the station and buying the tickets herself. In the meantime Willy should hurry to the bank and dissolve his account. It didn't amount to more than a thousand marks but she wanted it in cash. She rushed Willy, and they were just on their way downstairs when Big Anna called after them.

"Telephone, Will. Hurry up."

Willy hesitated, then thinking it might be Von Rhyn, dashed up the stairs.

"This is Robbi Goldschmidt," said a voice which Willy immediately recognized as Franz Duester's. "I'm phoning from a booth. Are you alone?"

"Yes, I am," Willy answered, lowering his voice. The telephone was in the foyer but Franz had never been in his house.

300

"I have very little time," Franz stuttered. "Are you all right?"

"What do you want, Franz?" Willy said. "I'm very busy."

There was a pause. Then Duester, in a sheepish and unsteady tone, stumbled: "Take my advice, pal, You were once a member of that Socialist Youth group, and your dad is an S. P. deputy. Get those records before they are—taken away. Believe me, I'm still your old chum."

"What do you———"

"Don't ask questions. Files aren't safe these days. Someone might want them. Might be helpful if there are none. Get me? Wait."

There was a commotion, and then Willy heard Gerhard Pueschel's voice. It was even thicker than Duester's. Apparently they had been celebrating the conquest of the university.

"Hello, Will? Do what Franz says. I told him to put you wise. Call Franz if you need him. If something happens. It might, you know." He giggled, then coughed violently, and Franz took over again.

" 'By, Will. Must go back to the gang. We might see you soon. My number's in the book." He hung up.

Willy ran downstairs and told Arlène the strange message.

"They were warning you," Arlène said, baffled. "It's the second time. Of course they were drunk and sentimental—but thank God they were! We must get to S. P. headquarters."

They took a taxi. Willy collected his money from a stone-faced bank-teller while Arlène waited outside. The day was brisk and clear and the streets stretched out seemingly contented and peaceful. On a poster the opera house announced it was presenting *Die Walkuere* tonight. As Willy glanced at the few swastika flags fluttering over Opern Platz in the cold winter sun, the afternoon became glazed with a layer of unreality.

Around four they arrived at the headquarters of the Social-Democratic party, District Greater Frankfurt, a modern flat-roofed building that also contained the offices of the metal, the leather, and the chemical trade unions. The house was quietly busy. People here seemed to go about their business as usual. Of course some days ago Hitler had promised strictly "parliamentary procedure," and elections once again were set for March the fifth. But after this morning's events Willy felt shaky and he couldn't understand how the people here could be so self-assured.

The big boss wasn't in, the receptionist declared, but his assistant, Mr. Walter, would see them in a minute. The big boss, as Willy saw on the door, was Mr. Haas, and it was just as well that he couldn't receive them. Surely Mr. Haas had never forgiven him the rephrasing of the pamphlets years ago.

Mr. Walter, an elderly, friendly, fussy man, had the look of one who has always been assistant to someone else. He know Dr. Halder, he even knew of Willy. He started reminiscing about the early days when Arlène, quicker than Willy in sizing up people, broke in:

"We want to have a look at Willy's records, Mr. Walter. We have to get some facts straight. Also, Dr. Halder asked us to check on some dates for him."

Since Willy had ceased being a member, Dr. Walter explained, they had to search for it in the dead files and it might take some time. He called a girl, who disappeared in some darkish side room.

"We don't usually allow people to look up records," Mr. Walter declared, but Arlène answered with her most intriguing smile. "Well, surely Mr. Halder can look at his own and his father's file, can't he?"

The girl came back much faster than expected. Since Dr. Halder was a deputy, Mr. Walter admitted Willy had a certain right to look over the papers. Willy went through Theodor's file first. It was large, consisting of many folders. Here were the lectures on "Proper Nutrition" Theodor had given for the chemical, the railroad, and the leather workers; the pamphlets on "Health for the Low Income Bracket," written years ago; his old speeches, his appointments to different commissions, a lifetime of serving on boards, of taking on duties, of devotion and selflessness.

While Willy went through the sheets, many of them yellow with age, the girl brought in his own file. Arlène took it. It contained only the record of his having been a member of the S. Y. at the age of sixteen, and his speech at the trade-union meeting when he had acted as a representative of the Free Students.

"Did you hear what happened this morning?" Arlène asked Mr. Walter.

"No, I didn't." Mr. Walter looked up, baffled. "The *People's Voice* doesn't come out before four o'clock."

"The storm troopers laid siege to the university," Arlène said. "They beat up students, shot out windows, terrorized the professors."

Mr. Walter shrugged his shoulders. "Terrible. But to be expected. That S. A. riffraff has to have some outlet. The whole thing will collapse soon. We trade-union men aren't easily thrown off balance, you know."

"Wrong!" Willy said. He couldn't hold back any more. "Three times wrong. They're not afraid of anything. If I were you, I'd burn all these."

Willy pointed to the green steel cabinets solidly lining the walls.

His large gesture was copied from Mathilda, he knew, but he meant what he said, and by now he was trembling inside.

"It may help a little," he went on. "They haven't got all the names. They aren't yet properly organized. Throw all these papers in the furnace. Now."

"Burn our files? The membership cards? Why, Mr. Haas would never consent to that."

"Don't wait for Mr. Haas," Arlène said. "You know they searched the Liebknecht House some days ago."

"Those were the Communists," Mr. Walter explained. "Sure. They were bound to be searched. The *Observer* announced long ago they wouldn't tolerate Communists. Just riffraff fighting riffraff. They won't dare intrude here. After all, we have a police. Be kind enough to hand me back the folders. I'm responsible to Mr. Haas."

Willy rose quickly. He had taken both files, holding them under his arm, and dragged Arlène after him. "Good-by!"

Mr. Walter ran after them. "Why, you can't do that!"

But Willy and Arlène had swept past the secretaries, the desks, the anterooms furnished with steel furniture in the best ultra-modern fashion. They ran down the stairs, breathlessly. They didn't hear what Mr. Walter was shouting. When they reached the street they breathed deeply. The air was sharp and fresh under the immaculately blue sky. Arlène took Willy's arm.

"Take it easy, Will. We have lots to do."

Willy pressed her arm but he couldn't hide from her the throbbing restlessness that had grown within him.

They hailed another cab. "Main Station," Arlène told the driver as they got in. Then turning to Willy, she said: "We'll take the early train to Basel, at 7.15 A.M. I'll wire Cousin Vera." She looked out into Kaiser Strasse. "I only wish we could take your father along."

Unexpectedly they had an hour left before dinner. So instead of going home they went to Hoch Strasse to say good-by to Hannah Goldschmidt. They found her alone in the living room, sitting before a fire in the fireplace and playing solitaire. Hannah, in a completely matter-of-fact-tone, informed them of the sale of her house. She had had her way.

"Everything I feared came true," Hannah said almost triumphantly. "Sprenger was really after the house. If we hadn't sold now, he'd have forced us later."

She turned to Willy. "I'll visit Robbi soon. I haven't been in Paris for many years."

"Do you have a passport?" Willy asked.

Hannah smiled. "In the inflation your mother sold your antiques and I sold my best silver spoons to Erwin Duester. We got dollars for them. Erwin hasn't changed. I sold our house through him, and he got a passport for Arthur and me. There's a rumor they'll take away all passports from Jewish people. Until my visit to Robbi I'll look after your father, Willy. Perhaps he'll come along with me. Paris in spring is lovely."

"I can't leave Father," Willy said. It had jumped out of him. He turned away. He didn't want them to see his face.

Hannah Goldschmidt, not at all startled by his outburst, put her hand on his shoulder. When she spoke she sounded so much like Melanie that, instinctively, Willy loosened up, the way he always had relaxed when Melanie talked to him, showing him a way out where he hadn't seen one.

"It was Melanie's wish that you visit Cousin Vera. Your father and you promised her, before she died. You must go. Your father would be very unhappy if you stayed here."

She stroked Willy's hair. "I remember you, Will, when you were a small boy, quick and ready to laugh and nice to Robbi. You children were born into a bad time. I, too, shall go away soon. I must leave behind most of the things I treasure, but I don't mind, as long as Robbi is safe in Paris. Perhaps you and he will be back after two terms. Perhaps things will change for the better. Will you excuse me for a moment?"

She walked out quickly. She had lied to give him hope and Willy was deeply touched.

He looked at Arlène. The fire in the fireplace threw nervous tongues of light across the wooden panels. Without saying a word they began tossing the folders in, Willy's and Theodor's. Before the flames had eaten up the paper, Hannah returned, a small box in her hand.

"How do you like these?" she asked, holding up two exquisite rings, set with emeralds and diamonds.

When Arlène started to say something, Hannah raised her hand. "You'll accept my terms," she said. "The way Ilona did. You'll wear them tomorrow on your trip. They are inconspicuous. Only an expert can guess their real value. You'll visit Robbi soon, I expect, and then he'll have them appraised. One third is yours and Willy's. It's Mr. Sprenger's money, incidentally. The money of Frankfurt's future Gauleiter."

She kissed them both good-by. The fire had destroyed the papers; a few flakes were floating into the room. Willy would never forget Hannah Goldschmidt, standing in the middle of the room, her hair as white as Melanie's, smiling and almost contented now that her world had come to an end. A story suddenly occurred to him, the story of Cassandra as Professor Preiser had told it in Upper Tertia. Hannah had always foreseen the worst, trembled before dangers which people with common sense told her existed only in her imagination. Now she was Cassandra triumphant: the satisfaction that she had been right had given her back her balance, although she was on the verge of losing her house, her possessions, and the country she had thought was hers.

The last discussion with Father was the most painful. Theodor would not, under any circumstances, go on "a vacation." His place was here, he said simply, with all the others. In vain Arlène and Willy tried to persuade him that he was taking too much of a risk.

Theodor had opened a window and looked out into the peaceful Reuter Weg. No marching tonight. Everything was quiet. Even the streetcars' rattle seemed subdued. The only sound was the energetic rumble of the radio in some neighbor's house. It sounded louder than usual.

Perhaps he'd visit Willy around Easter, Theodor had ended the discussion. He would take them to the station the next morning, and he insisted that Willy go to bed earlier than usual—after all, he had to get up at six. Fortunately, the expressman had called for the trunks. And Big Anna would give them an especially nourishing breakfast.

As Willy lay there, the packed handbags waiting near the door, he found many more stringent arguments with which to persuade Father. But, as Hannah had foreseen, he would never neglect "his duty." Fervently Willy wished Arlène were here, right next to him, but then he reproached himself for his desire: he had no right to burden her with the pervading dark fear which had sprung up in him again, the old fear, dating back to Hannsberg and, perhaps, even much further.

He struggled to relax. The struggle made it worse, at first, but gradually a sublime tiredness stretched over him from the back of his head to his toes, and he was asleep.

Several times he woke up with a start. A cold moon fell through the slats of the blinds and illuminated a part of the big map of Europe over his bed. In between sleep and wakefulness the vision came back, the specter that had haunted him when he was ill in Hildesheim.

The familiar figures again stepped forward, in a perverted courtly dance. Professor Lattau, leading a group of boys toward a camp fire; no, it wasn't Lattau; it was Hellmuth Handler, in the trim uniform of a Reichswehr lieutenant. The boys held banners in their hands and blood trickled from the scars on their foreheads. They were marching around Willy, encircling him.

For one moment he was in the fortress of Hameln with the boys of the Black Reichswehr. Someone was bleeding—it was Hal, hold-

305

ing a wooden lamb, his mouth open for the cry of pain. But no sound came.

The fortress vanished. Willy was back in the forest. The procession was marching, only faster. It wasn't Lattau who led it, nor Hellmuth Handler. It was someone bigger: Lumber-Fritz, Haarmann, the werewolf, the murderer. Willy saw him clearly, muscle-padded and ruddy, his tongue licking his lips. He led the cortege, which had grown rapidly. A sun was shining, a brilliant stinging sun with rays thick as cannon shafts. There were the Black Reichswehr recruits and the unemployed from Old Town and the old Wandervogel, all carrying flags as red as the blood on their foreheads, and decorated with the sign of the new Messiah, the swastika.

Now it wasn't Haarmann any longer guiding the endless parade into the Forest of Shadows. It was Sarek, the rattrap vendor, looking like Hitler. He was swinging a baton, dancing like a dervish, fantastically dressed in shining armor while the boys wore tattered rags. Their faces were turned upward as if they didn't want to see where they were marching. The dervish was shouting incessantly. Willy could see his mouth open and close, open and close. But what he said Willy couldn't understand.

The landscape around them looked familiar. It was in a way like the Bergstrasse. Then fir trees began to rise darkly around a clearing—a friendly clearing where a brook sauntered through green grass.

And while the boys marched in, a big structure rose, similar to the cranes on the I. G. Farben building ground. The dervish conductor, swinging one of Sarek's rattraps as a baton, climbed up the structure with unearthly speed and pointed to the clearing's end.

Willy found himself among the marching boys, but Arlène was next to him, holding his hand, and they waited a long time for the prophet on the crane to conjure up the Beast. For Willy knew it was there.

The fir trees slid aside, as on a revolving stage, revealing a few derelict tenement houses, the cripples from Little Venice, isolated in the middle of the forest. They burst apart, like eggshells, when something gigantic rose within them. Willy didn't want to see it but he went closer, pushed by the thousands behind him. There sat Gunnivor, the dragon, his monstrous crocodile head as big as a house, and there was a smile on his face.

The crowd behind began pushing Willy faster. The dervish on the crane swang his rattrap baton, like a conductor leading an orchestra, and the boys rushed forward through the clearing while Gunnivor placidly opened his jaws. . . .

Sweat was trickling down Willy's sides as he sat up. He got up, took a towel, and dried himself. He raised the blinds, looked out

306

into Reuter Weg sleepily stretched out under a blanket of thin gray snow.

How often had he looked out into this street? He was wide awake now. He felt as though he had escaped a real danger, not a dream. He opened the window, and as the cold air struck against his face he saw them together, Haarmann and Hitler. They both belonged to an underworld, an underworld that had killed Hal and had driven him, Willy, out of his own world again and again.

No, better not worry about it now. How strange—he hadn't thought of Lattau for so long. Lattau had been the first, so to speak. The first to twist his life, to make it miserable. Then Mother had fought him off, Mother and Hal. They had protected him. Now they were dead and he had to fight alone. Haarmann was another: he had killed and destroyed and Willy hadn't been able to do anything against him. Haarmann had been one of the insane Dr. von Erb was writing about, a specter out of the bowels of a time Willy had been taught to accept as a civilized era. Haarmann had been washed to the surface, together with the derelicts, the kids on the road, the shiftless, and people like Mr. Sprenger, the epileptic plumber who was going to live in Hannah Goldschmidt's house. And the false prophet Hitler whom Arlène and he had once watched transform a crowd of drab and tired people into a band of happy, uncontrolled fanatics—he, too, had risen out of the depths.

Willy shivered, closed the window, and went back to bed. The moon had gone and the handbags near the door gave the impression of two misshapen dogs waiting to be taken out. It was four o'clock. He sat on the edge of the bed, his face in his hands. Sleep wouldn't come now and he had only two hours anyhow.

A longing for Melanie overcame him, a longing to go into the living room and find her sitting there, working quietly, and tell her everything. What would Mother say? She'd tell him that he was lucky because Arlène was with him.

Willy rose again and went through a bureau drawer without switching on the light. He found it: a picture of Melanie against the background of the summer garden outside the living room. He put it into the handbag though there was barely room for it. All at once he was seized by a foreboding he might never be able to come back to his room, his books, his pictures.

It was fifteen minutes past five when the telephone rang. It sounded so aggressive, piercing the small hours of the morning, that Willy jumped.

"The Reichstag is on fire!" It was Kurt von Rhyn speaking. "I know it sounds like third-rate melodrama, but it's true. I just had the news from Berlin. They arrested a madman of Dutch extraction who's supposed to have done it. A Communist, they say. It's a signal for them to start. We were lucky here. Hey, are you listening, Willy?"

"Yes," Willy managed to stutter. His voice sounded like someone else's. "Why were we lucky?"

"We were warned. They stormed the university too early. Paulus went to the country, isn't feeling well. Incidentally, he accepted the job with the Hudson University people. When is your train leaving?"

"Around seven," Willy answered. "What about you?"

"I still have a diplomatic passport," Von Rhyn said. "Don't worry about me."

"Cousin Vera Burckhardt lives at 12 St. Michel Strasse," Willy said. "Let us hear from you—and thanks. And my love to Paulus."

"It's cold here in my booth," Von Rhyn said. "I have more calls to make. Good-by, Willy. I shall see you and your charming girl friend soon."

As Willy hung up, Big Anna stood next to him.

"It's early, Willy boy," she said softly. "But I'll have breakfast ready in a minute."

If Theodor had heard the call he didn't mention it, neither to Willy nor to Arlène, who soon arrived. They ate silently while a hoarse voice told the German people over the radio that "our vigilance" had unearthed a gigantic plot of the Communist and their Jewish-capitalist helpers to overthrow the government, to poison food stores, and threaten the country's foundations. All documents would be published tomorrow. Goering's police, the voice soothed, would look after the people's security.

Theodor turned off the radio. He was pale and wan and ate hardly a thing. Outside, the morning looked icy but clear.

Big Anna didn't hide her tears as Willy and Arlène said good-by.

"I'll take good care of the doctor," she repeated over and over, and then she embraced Willy. The fleeting moment brought back long-forgotten years when he had been a small boy and Big Anna had carried him around in the kitchen, feeding him nourishing tidbits.

The taxi was waiting. Anna had telephoned a driver she knew. The man greeted Theodor and they threw in their baggage. They had enough time left, but the man drove with unusual speed and made several detours. None of them spoke a word. Near Hauptwache they got behind a big truck and the driver, cursing, had to slow down. It was the sort of truck butchers use to carry cattle to the market.

Through its open slates Willy then saw the men, sprawled on the dirty floor. Their clothes were muddy, they were covered with

308

blood, and they seemed unconscious. Two wore pajamas under their winter overcoats. As the truck stopped, three storm troopers dragged in another man. He couldn't walk. His face was ashen. He had dropped a suitcase which, falling through the loosely jointed floor planks, spilled its contents over Kaiser Strasse.

Theodor was hammering at the glass pane for the driver to stop but the man shook his head. The truck moved, with an uncontrolled, fast jerk, and the cab, skirting around, overtook the truck and raced toward the Main Station.

The driver moved back the glass pane. "No good, Doc. Nothing you can do. I've been up since three. Saw plenty of them. All going to the old warehouses in the Rebstock. The new emergency jails, as they call 'em. All brought in for questioning." He paused. "I haven't said a thing, Doc."

He slammed the glass pane shut, skidded around a corner, and came to a stop in front of the Main Station. Willy gave him a large tip.

"Going back, Doc?" the man asked.

Theodor nodded.

"I'll be waiting over there." He pointed to a little hotel. "I'll drive you back."

It was the Orient Express that was to take them to Basel. It stood there waiting, its engine puffing. Theodor carried Arlène's bags. They seemed too heavy for him, Willy thought. Newsboys were shouting "Reichstag burning! Thousands of arrests! Reichstag burning! Thousands of arrests!" They sounded quite cheerful about it. Arlène bought a *Frankfurter Zeitung* and followed Theodor along the train. They found two seats in a second-class compartment and threw their luggage in. There were only a few minutes left.

Theodor stood outside, looking up to them. When Arlène had thrown the paper on the seat, it had fallen open to a report from Hannsberg. The item told of the death of Dr. Ernst Tressler, former professor of economics, who had been found killed by unknown assailants. Willy looked away.

Arlène was holding Theodor's hand.

"You'll come and visit us soon," she said. "I want you to meet my father. You know you're invited to stay with him and Mother any time you want."

Theodor nodded. He turned to Willy. "If you need more of your books, let us know. Did I tell you that Mathilda called to say good-by? She was very angry at not finding you home."

"Father!" Willy started, but he stopped because he could never say aloud what he felt. He wanted to urge Theodor once more to follow them to Basel. But by now he knew: Theodor didn't care very much whether he went on living, now that Melanie was dead. His life had no meaning without her. He simply didn't care what happened to him, and Willy almost suspected him of secretly wishing for the worst.

As a whistle blew shrilly and the conductor could be heard urging the passengers aboard, he gripped Theodor's hands.

"We'll write you, Father, as soon as we're at Cousin Vera's."

"I'll pray for you to get there safe and sound," Theodor said.

He reached up and kissed Willy on the forehead while the train began to move slowly, throwing a big cloud of white steam up to the station's glass cupola. Theodor had taken off his hat. He waved at them. They waved back.

The platform was almost empty. Theodor stood alone there against the immense, dark station, his white hair shining like Greek marble under the sharp arc lights. On the other side, on Track 10, the local for Cronberg was leaving, puffing asthmatically, as it had done all these years. They outraced the local quickly, and soon Theodor was only a spot in the receding station's pattern. Willy kept looking back until he couldn't distinguish details any longer. He followed the course of the Cronberg local, which swerved off toward the Rebstock station.

Arlène had settled down in the empty second-class apartment, which was upholstered in tired-looking gaudy red plush.

"Look, Will, they raided the S. P. party office this morning," she said, scanning the paper. "Ransacked the files. Thank God we took Theodor's and yours."

Willy didn't answer. The Cronberg local was disappearing behind the first hills of the Taunus Mountains. For a while he stared after it. Then he turned to Arlène. If there were tears in his eyes he didn't care and Arlène didn't either.

She came over to his side and he took her hand. Together they looked out the window and watched the city slowly being engulfed by the mounting horizon. Would he ever see Frankfurt again? Or Cronberg? Or the round-shouldered Taunus Mountains and the forgotten fortress of Koenigstein? Would he ever return to Reuter Weg, the Main River, the Old Town? It didn't matter, Willy found himself thinking, it didn't matter—the Frankfurt where he was born and raised, the Frankfurt he loved, existed no longer.

310